The Couples

The Couples

Lauren Mackenzie

JOHN MURRAY

First published in Great Britain in 2023 by John Murray (Publishers)
An Hachette UK company

1

A CIP catalogue record for this title is available from the British Library

Hardback ISBN 9781399809436
Trade Paperback ISBN 9781399809443
eBook ISBN 9781399809467

Typeset in Sabon MT by Manipal Technologies Limited

Printed and bound in Great Britain by Clays Ltd, Elcograf S.p.A.

John Murray policy is to use papers that are natural, renewable and recyclable products and
made from wood grown in sustainable forests. The logging and manufacturing processes are
expected to conform to the environmental regulations of the country of origin.

John Murray (Publishers)
Carmelite House
50 Victoria Embankment
London EC4Y 0DZ

www.johnmurraypress.co.uk

For Brendan, Alex and Sam, with all my love

Love does not begin and end the way we seem to think it does. Love is a battle. Love is a war. Love is a growing up.

James Baldwin, *Nobody Knows My Name: More Notes of a Native Son*

We Are Like Children

Eva folded herself into the attic window seat, closed the curtains and pulled her knees tight to her chest. Outside, a thick, early-morning mist hovered. She was an astronaut in a space capsule, hovering, weightless. Vibrating.

She felt sick. She pulled the top sash down and leaned out into the soft, damp air. Yesterday she'd been able to see for miles in every direction – woods and mountains, stubbled fields and a wind farm. This morning there were no landmarks to navigate by. A dog barked. On the lawn below her window there was man in a black suit, feet bare, lying in a foetal curl.

Frank.

She was thinking she should go downstairs and check on him, was wondering if he could be dead, but then he rolled over on his back and threw his arms out wide, like some kind of crucifixion. It made her laugh. Even at his worst, he amused her. And last night, he'd been very amusing.

They'd spent weeks persuading Frank that his forty-eighth birthday needed celebrating and that a weekend away would be the best way to do it. There'd been nothing but bad news since the financial crash. Recovery seemed impossible, a complete collapse of society was imminent, and no one, not even the government, seemed to know what to do, only that the fault lay with them, the people. Eva wasn't sure how she managed such chaos, given that she'd spent most of the last seven years, since the twins were born, loading and unloading the washing machine.

Once Frank gave in, on the proviso that no children were invited – something no one objected to – finding overnight sitters for three sets of children almost scuppered them. Then came the search for somewhere far enough from Dublin to feel like they were *away away* but close enough to not waste precious time driving. They settled on Harwood House, a Georgian country estate in County Laois. The house's mild dereliction – whistling draughts and noisy plumbing, according to the reviews – ensured it was affordable.

It was just after three on a Saturday in September when they arrived, three couples in two cars. Harwood House was glorious; three storeys high, rising out of a thick, velvet lawn, chartreuse in the golden afternoon light, with granite steps spilling out from the panelled front door like the train of an evening dress. Eva climbed out of her tiny Fiat, stretched her legs, threw her shoulders back and filled her lungs. The scent of rotten oranges surprised her.

'What's that smell?'

Her husband was at the boot of the car, unloading the luggage. Bottles clinked. Shay stopped, sniffed, and shrugged. 'Countryside?'

Eva had lost sight of Conor and Beatrice on the motorway soon after they left, but now their silver BMW was parked off to the side of the gravel drive, the front seats empty, doors wide open. They were standing by the side of the house, pointing out details to each other, as if they were considering buying the place. In their thick woollens and green Hunter wellies, they looked like they already had.

The rear passenger doors of the BMW swung open. Frank and Lizzie emerged slowly from either side, clothes askew, shading their eyes against the low light. They came to a stop, side by side, and blinked.

'Jesus, wow,' said Lizzie.

'It's just us, yeah?' said Frank.

'No one else,' said Eva. 'Happy birthday.'

'Whoopee,' said Frank.

The front door, thick with layers of black paint juddered open. Davina Fitzsimons, their host, was around seventy, but wore her white hair loose and long. She had one arm opened wide in welcome, the other cocked with a lit cigarette. A black Labrador stood by her side and gave them the once-over. They all stood a little straighter.

'Welcome! Mi casa es su casa!' said Davina.

And so it was, through pre-dinner drinks in the panelled library where they were all on their best behaviour, through dinner – beef stroganoff and chocolate mousse – served by Davina herself, who smoked throughout and told them charming vignettes of the house's glory days. She'd been born in Harwood; she would die in Harwood. The latter was accompanied by a wink and a hacking cough.

In candlelight, the house's cracked plaster and torn curtains disappeared in the shadows and its former grandeur emerged. In response, the men's voices slowed and deepened, and the women's laughter sang. By the time the six set off walking to the village pub for some local colour and a post-dinner pint, they were all darling this and darling that.

It was Frank who purchased the ecstasy; half a dozen pills from a lad hanging out by the cigarette machine. Frank had been drinking non-stop since they arrived and had only become more himself than ever – effusive, genial and *loud*. Eva braced herself whenever he came too close; he was as likely to poke her as hug her. They were sat in a snug with red velour banquettes and amber bottle-glass screening them from the rest of the punters.

'Are you mad?' said Conor.

They all turned to look at the lad. He was young and wearing a Manchester City football jersey.

'I'd have questions about his choice of football team, but he seems sound,' said Frank. He washed a pill down with his pint, then offered the rest around, cupped in his palm. 'It's my birthday.' It was both statement of fact and a plea.

'Sure, if it's a bad trip we've a doctor on call,' said Shay, taking one.

'Get away out of that.' Conor took a full throaty swallow of his pint. 'Don't be relying on me.'

Even though herself and Shay had come of age in the nineties, five years after everyone else, Eva couldn't remember the last time they'd taken anything, and even then they'd never bought anything from someone they didn't know.

'Go on, Eva. I know you want to.' Frank had a way of looking at her that made her feel like she should apologise to Lizzie.

'I will if you will,' said Lizzie.

Shay whispered in Eva's ear. 'It won't be nearly as much fun without you.'

Eva didn't want to see the party divided so early. It had to be all or nothing and already nothing wasn't an option. She took one, split it in half with her nail and slipped the remainder to Lizzie.

'Clever woman,' said Lizzie.

Eva washed hers down with a sup of Merlot and felt her stomach recoil. Lizzie exhaled. 'I want you all to know I love you, should anything go . . . arseways.' Her eyes appeared to glisten. An actress, Lizzie could cry on demand. One had to be alert around her. Frank cocked his head, examining her with such cool scepticism they all laughed. Eva watched Beatrice and Conor exchange one of those side-eye/eyebrow/head-tilt conversations only couples can do. Beatrice tapped Frank's hand and he passed her a pill. The banquette sighed as Conor slumped in his seat.

'It was so much fun,' said Beatrice. 'Before children. We weren't afraid of anything then.'

'That's because we didn't have anything to lose,' said Conor. His laugh was thin; he was trying too hard.

'We still don't,' said Shay, laughing.

Frank turned to Conor and offered him a pill. 'You don't want to be the odd man out.'

'Don't I?' Conor dropped the pill into his shirt pocket. 'The coroner will need it for evidence.'

'Conor!' Lizzie squealed and soft-slapped him. They hate-flirted like teenagers.

Frank tipped his glass. 'Touché.'

When they left the pub, the wind was up and the road home shone in the moonlight. Beatrice strode ahead, her hair turned silver, the full skirt of her blue dress fluttering every which way. Lizzie hung off Shay's arm, claiming she was scared. She was also drunk, and her long velvet dress and platform sandals were a difficult combination. Eva, Conor and Frank brought up the rear, walking single file, turned in on themselves.

Eva heard a rustle and turned to see Frank disappear down a path into the estate's woods. With a finger to his lips, Conor grabbed her hand and pulled her in after. They found Frank in the foliage, his shining eyes giving him away. He dragged Eva and Conor into his hiding spot.

Out on the road, Beatrice was singing.

Eva's nostrils filled with the sharp rot of the damp ground and the malty heat of the men front and back of her. Her cheek brushed against Frank's whiskered chin. Conor's hand, hot and damp, remained tight around hers. She was twenty again, dancing in a crowd of bodies, touching and being touched. It was almost too much, and she was relieved when the others found them.

From her attic perch, Eva watched the rising sun creep across the lawn and felt dread. She wasn't going to survive the day without some sleep, but she couldn't lie down without spinning. The house shook beneath her as the heavy front door slammed closed. Beatrice jogged across the lawn, then circled back towards Frank, pausing briefly, presumably to check he was breathing, before running off again, her sleek blonde pony-tail bouncing with each step. Her resilience was miraculous.

Beatrice was almost the same age as Frank but looked twenty years younger. Eva had seen people walk into electricity poles turning to take a second look at her. No one ever disputed her beauty; no one ever suggested her eyes were too close together, or her hips a little wide. She had once, around a dinner table, insisted that it was difficult looking how she did; the attention wasn't always welcome or kind. Eva had flushed with embarrassment. She'd often caught herself staring at Beatrice instead of listening to her. When she was introduced to Conor and Beatrice at a party at Lizzie and Frank's, Eva couldn't believe they were a couple. Conor was unremarkable – average height, mild green eyes, mid-brown hair – neither ugly nor handsome. At first she'd assumed Beatrice married him for his medical degree. She wasn't judging her; sometimes she wished she'd married with as much practical foresight.

After seven years, Eva thought she knew Conor well enough, but last night alone with him she discovered he was like a pass-the-parcel game where the outline of the parcel gives no hint of the gift inside. She tried to recall what it was they talked about, but within the tangle of her thoughts only the most random notions came back to her; they loved lasagne with chips but were embarrassed to eat the combination in public; they cut labels off their clothing, finding the irritation of their skin unbearable. Conor pursued medicine because there was a lot to be said for making a difference one person at a time, the same reason Eva became a primary schoolteacher. He also had a way of breathing in and widening his eyes when she said something he liked, which seemed to be almost everything she said last night. She couldn't have been that scintillating – they were both too compromised – but even so, it was only when light spilled through the cracks in the shutters that they called it a night.

After climbing the stairs to her attic room, Eva found the door ajar and a man in her bed. At first she thought he was an intruder, but it was only Shay, deeply asleep, exactly where he was supposed to be.

*

6

Conor also found his wife in bed, exactly where she was supposed to be, her face washed clean of make-up and last night's dress hanging in the wardrobe. He climbed in beside her and fell asleep, soaking up her warmth. When he woke again, he was cold and alone. He thought he'd only dreamed her presence hours before. But her pyjamas were folded. Her runners missing. She would be back.

He brushed his teeth, showered, shaved, dressed, laced his shoes and combed his hair in complete denial of how ill he felt. A sign of the damage he'd done to himself. He laid their two suitcases side by side on the bed, folded everything and paired the dirty socks before packing them. When he came to fold Beatrice's blue dress he spotted a stain on the back – like an old bruise, perhaps grass and dirt. Had she fallen? If she had he didn't remember.

He was still holding the dress when Beatrice returned from her run. Her skin was blotchy from the cold morning air and a light sweat dotted her forehead. She seemed as surprised as him when she saw the stain.

'Oh. The dry-cleaner will get that out.' She took the dress off him, rolled it in a ball and tucked it in the corner of the bag. 'There is a smell in the hall. Like vomit.' She sat on the bed and unlaced her trainers.

'Really? Where?'

'I didn't look because then I would have to clean it up.'

'We should clean it up.'

'I won't stop you.' She made a sound, a slow rumble from deep in her belly. Conor grinned but as laughter engulfed her, he became nervous he hadn't got the joke after all.

'What? What is it?'

She stuttered, breathless. 'We. Are. Like children.' She rolled her leggings down and peeled off each leg. 'But we are not,' she said.

'No.' He was used to the little gap between Beatrice's German English and his own, like the air pocket in a window that could keep the heat in or out, but today it unnerved him.

7

'It's not funny?'

'I guess it depends how you look at it,' said Conor.

She laughed again and pecked his cheek before darting into the en suite. He collected her trail of damp Lycra and packed everything. Over the patter of the shower, he called out – 'Did you fall?' – but she didn't seem to hear him.

Frank would've remained unconscious for a while longer but for the dog's wet nose in his ear. He shoved him away and dragged himself to standing. Fallen leaves and large and small branches littered the lawn. A big wind must have passed over last night, but he had no idea when. He hitched his pants up and discovered a flaccid penis hanging out of his flies. He tucked himself back in and looked for his shoes. The only thing a cursory search unearthed was an empty vodka bottle.

He walked around the side of the house, his bare feet wincing on the sharp gravel, and came up against a bay window. Inside, the high walls of the room were lined with bookshelves, but the occasional tables were swamped with a wide array of empty glasses and liquor bottles. A Persian rug was rolled up and shoved to one side. The sofas and armchairs had been dragged into a tight circle around the black marble fireplace. Shoes and socks and a green velvet jacket lay scattered on the parquet floor.

It looked like a crime scene. Frank recognised nothing and was completely incapable of recalling his part in it. For all he knew a dead body was rolled up in the rug. His heart beat a little faster.

His friends' insistence on celebrating a birthday that was neither here nor there felt like a cruel comment on the fact that at forty-eight, he was neither here nor there. His film-making career, once so full of promise that Hollywood actually called, had been reduced to a story about attending the Oscars with his short film. The second he'd ever made. Almost twenty years later, the story had flipped inside out and become the saddest thing that ever happened to him. A low hum of anger had been running through him ever since. He had a wardrobe of rumpled Oxfam suits and four kids he couldn't afford. His ex was chasing him for fifteen thousand euro in child support that he didn't have. The only reason he agreed to the weekend away was because his friends offered to pay. His birthday gift. The absence of a cake at dinner confirmed that he was an excuse for a blowout and that was fine by him because he felt the exact same way. He started hard as soon as they arrived. Tequila. Lick. Sip. Suck. He made sure everyone partook. What he consumed after that was anybody's guess. He hoped they all felt as destroyed as he did.

When he tried the back door, the wood, swollen from centuries of rain, resisted. He slammed his shoulder into it until it swung open with a bang and hauled himself upstairs to the landing. Another few steps to what he was almost certain was his room. Peeking in, he saw Lizzie sat up in the giant four-poster bed in her pyjamas, blonde curls awry, her features blurred with last night's make-up.

'Where were you? I texted you! Why didn't you answer me?'

Frank had no idea what she was talking about. All he could think about was the getting of himself to the bed.

'Frank!'

A pillow came out of nowhere and slapped him in the face. It may have been full of feathers, but it felled him like a brick. He collapsed face down beside her.

'Where were you?' She thumped him in his side under the ribs. But apart from a small whoosh of air, there was only silence.

Eva floated on the threshold of consciousness as a hand moved slowly up her thigh. She sighed, aware she was neither awake nor asleep and the hand may not be real. The hand slid between her legs. She was wet, and there was no resistance at all. A warm naked body pressed up against her. She continued to feign sleep, feeling like a thief, as she imagined someone else along the length of her finding their way in.

Shay came quickly, planting a postscript of kisses up her spine.

Eva groaned. 'I can't tell whether I need to eat or throw up.'

'Stay right there.' Shay jumped out of bed and walked over to his bag, naked and graceful. Thanks to his landscape gardening work, he had more energy and exuberance than the five-year-olds she taught. He tipped his goodies onto the bed, Rennies, Solpadeine and Berocca, and divvied out two of each. 'You think Conor could do any better for you? I don't think so.'

Eva felt the air tighten between them. She made herself breathe. 'I think you've got us covered.'

Shay filled two glasses from the bathroom sink. 'I love the man, but jaysus he can be a bit . . .' He handed her the glass. 'Serious.'

'Serious?'

'Boring.'

She wasn't telling Shay that she'd come to think the opposite. 'Where d'you go? One minute everyone was in the library and then?'

'When I went to the jacks, I found Lizzie looking for Frank, crying. I took her back to her room, told her I'd look for him. She was pretty out of it.'

'Where was he?'

'No idea.'

'You didn't try finding him?'

'Don't think he wanted to be found.' Shay seemed to be more amused than was warranted. He was studying her, waiting for something from her. 'Did you have a good night with Conor?'

'Sure.'

'Sure?'

'We talked.'

'Talked? Or *talked*?'

He was too animated; like he knew something she didn't.

'Why didn't you come back to the library?'

'Didn't think I'd be welcome. I went to bed.' Shay lay down over her, pinning her down. 'So. What did you *talk* about?'

Eva felt again Conor's hands on her skin, his index finger rolling over her nipple. 'You know. Drunk talk. Shite talk. Lasagne.'

Shay laughed again. 'I should've come back and rescued you.'

Eva stopped herself from lying a second time. Everything would've been different had Shay returned. She rolled out from under him. 'It's almost eleven. We need to get going.' She wanted to be in her own home again, wanted her things around her, wanted to hold her daughters in her arms.

He slapped her naked rump as she passed by. Her arse stung. She couldn't tell if he meant to hurt her or not. He grinned at her. She loved him but today she couldn't stand him.

Eva found her way to the kitchen to settle the bill. Conor was already at the long pine table with Davina, sitting in a cloud of cigarette smoke. He gave Eva a smile. She felt her face contort and discovered she no longer knew how to smile. He pulled out a chair for her and she sat down, deciding it was better not to look at him at all. Davina painstakingly laid out the cost of the night in front of them. Three double rooms, six dinners and an embarrassing sum for the honour bar in the library. It was all possible, probable, but any thoughts of negotiation wilted before Davina and the cold, hard evidence of the empty liquor bottles lined up on the counter. Tequila. Vodka. Baileys Liqueur. And more wine bottles than she could count.

'I'm sorry if we got a bit too carried away last night. Lucky there's no neighbours.' Conor meant the last as a joke, but Davina, so charming last night, refused to engage.

Eva tried, 'Except for you? Hope we didn't disturb you?'

Davina glanced over the top of her reading glasses. 'When I have guests, I sleep in the groundsman's cottage. I hear nothing, see nothing. It's better for everyone that way. Cash or card?'

Shamed, they both handed over their credit cards.

'Split it down the middle, thank you,' said Conor. Eva prayed her card wouldn't be declined. Agreeing to split the bill was a mistake. Herself and Shay were as broke as Frank and Lizzie, but some bizarre need to keep up appearances prevented them from admitting it. She felt Conor looking at her and made the mistake of meeting his gaze. He quietly sucked in his breath and widened his green eyes, and Eva nearly choked.

Washed, dressed and almost sober, the six of them sidled out to the stable yard behind the house where Davina had made them move their cars. They walked in pairs – Frank and Lizzie, Conor and Beatrice, Shay and Eva – proper order restored and not a minute too soon.

Lizzie dropped back, pulling Eva with her, feigning an interest in a chestnut mare grazing in a field some distance away. Eva squeezed Lizzie's hand. 'Okay?'

'D'you know where Frank went last night?' Lizzie watched as Eva attempted to construct an answer and that was answer enough for her.

'But I did see him passed out on the front lawn this morning.' They glanced over at Frank, who happened to be watching Beatrice load her suitcase into the boot of the BMW. 'He could've been there all night,' offered Eva.

Beatrice turned around and smiled at the women as they approached. She looked like she'd had a full eight hours sleep and fruit for breakfast. Lizzie turned back to Eva. 'Can we get a ride back with you?' Eva would've let her ride on the roof if she wanted. Beatrice closed the boot without making a sound.

'What?' said Frank, as bewildered as if Lizzie had asked for a horse and carriage.

'Don't be slagging the car all the way back,' said Shay. He was bouncing on his toes. He always looked like he was ready to take off.

'I won't say a word.' Lizzie tried to squeeze her bag in beside Shay and Eva's in the boot of the Fiat. 'We should've brought our own car,' said Lizzie.

'We'd have had to push it from Naas,' said Frank.

Lizzie gave up on trying to squeeze her bag in and tried lying it flat on top, but the contents kept falling out.

'Okay, we don't bring you, but we can bring your luggage?' Beatrice reached for the tote. Lizzie slapped her hand away. Beatrice jumped back, emitting a tiny sound of surprise, somewhere between a laugh and a cry of pain.

'Here. Don't be stupid, just put it in the boot and let's go.' Frank grabbed the bag. Lizzie eyeballed him and held on. Frank swore, let go. Half the contents tumbled to the ground, dirty knickers, a razor, a dog-eared autobiography of Grace Kelly, and Frank's vomit-spattered suit jacket. Lizzie had imagined the oversized tote would look sweetly retro on their country retreat; now she saw it meant everything about them was on show.

Last night she'd been full of love for Frank, for their friends. She'd been besotted by everyone's beauty in the firelight, the grace of their lounging limbs, the timbre of their voices in the enormous rooms. She felt joy. She was joy. And then it was half three in the morning and she was stumbling in the yard, a ferocious wind whipping the ancient trees into a frenzy above her, calling and calling for Frank. He couldn't hear her or didn't want to. Once more he'd done as he pleased, sweet-talked her, asserted his birthday rights, expressed his insecurities, all before she'd had a chance to work out how she felt about his party games.

Tears ran down her face. She felt Frank's hand on her back, a pat or a stroke, she wasn't sure. There was no conviction in the gesture and that made it worse. Shay gathered their things off the ground and returned them to the bag. Frank dropped his head back and stared at the sky, looking for divine intervention.

Eva offered Lizzie tissues. 'We could all do with a nap.'

'And fluids,' said Conor.

It was Beatrice who darted forward and gave Lizzie the hug she clearly needed. 'It's okay. Everything is okay,' she said.

The hug felt so genuine, Lizzie remembered all the other times they'd hugged one another, telling whoever needed it at the time that everything would be okay. She pushed her away. For a moment, Beatrice grimaced like a hurt child. Lizzie couldn't afford to care.

The six of them stood in the gravel and dirt of the yard, among the rusted metal contraptions and detritus of a defunct farm and waited for someone else to do something.

'I want to go home. Now,' Frank wailed. 'Will someone please take me home? I don't give a flying fuck who.' Frank did look unwell. There was a green tint to his pallor and a sway in his standing.

'Lizzie, what do *you* want to do?' Conor's apparently benign question threatened to overwhelm her again. They'd been friends for almost as long she'd known Frank. He was always there for her when Frank let her down and always asked the same question, with the exact same emphasis on *you*, what do *you* want to do. And no matter how she'd answer, he'd help her.

'I want to go home.'

Conor placed his hand gently on Lizzie's back and nudged her forward, opened the passenger door of his car with the other, and eased her in. Frank fell into the seat beside her.

'We'll be home in super-fast time,' said Beatrice.

Trees formed lush green tunnels overhead as they drove home. Frank slept beside Lizzie, his head lolling back, his mouth slack. An acrid chemical smell surrounded him. She shifted over to the window side, pulled the armrest down between them and settled back into the coffee-coloured leather. Between the seats she could see the smooth line of Beatrice's slender, tanned arm, the cotton of her dress riding up her legs, her elegant, pointed knees. Lizzie pulled her own dress down. She wished she'd had time to iron it. Her black tights and sneakers looked childish and ill-considered.

In that moment, she felt all of her was ill-considered, her whole life ill-considered. Outside, the fields had disappeared and they were driving along a highway lined with industrial buildings and chain-link fences.

'Music okay?' asked Beatrice. She didn't wait for an answer; discordant jazz erupted from the speakers.

Frank rose from the dead. 'Please. No.'

Beatrice laughed and turned the music up. For an instant Lizzie loathed her; almost as much as she loathed jazz.

Frank pulled a beer coaster out of his back trouser pocket. The square edges had been nibbled to a circle by restless fingers, but you could still make out *McElhenny's Bar*. 'I know you're all going to give me hell, but I'm having trouble remembering anything from last night.'

'You're a fucking chancer, Frank Durkan,' said Lizzie.

He held up the coaster. 'I'll hazard a guess we had a few pints in McElhenny's fine establishment?'

'Unbelievable,' said Lizzie.

The car jolted as Conor guffawed, Beatrice only a breath behind him. Then Lizzie cracked. Tears fell again. No one was sure if she was laughing crying or crying laughing. Soon everything went quiet and stayed quiet.

2

My Sweet Boy

After dropping Lizzie and Frank off at their house, Conor let down all the car windows and revelled in the rush of fresh air. He felt like he'd shucked off a backpack full of stones after a day-long hike.

'Poor Lizzie,' said Conor.

'She is always crying. Hormones.' Beatrice wasn't necessarily wrong, but she was blunt. 'She told me she was in perimenopause. It is completely normal.'

'Well sure, but Frank can be a selfish prick,' said Conor.

'Frank is Frank. He has always been frank.' She giggled at her own joke.

Conor didn't know what reply he'd expected, but laughter wasn't it.

Conor had grown up in Crumlin, on a cul-de-sac of two-storey pebble-dash Corporation houses. He was an only child, but it didn't matter; he spent most of his time next door with the six Farrelly kids. When he pulled up outside his parents' house and saw Mrs Farrelly waving frantically from her living room window he knew it couldn't be good news. He told Beatrice to go on without him.

Mrs Farrelly hovered inside her porch. 'Conor. How are you?'

Conor's head pounded and he felt so dehydrated his eyes stung. 'Grand, thanks. All good?'

'Molly's been wandering. Did ya know?' She kept her voice low.

Conor's father had made a few jokes about his seventy-four-year-old mother being faster than you'd think. Conor hadn't been paying attention.

'Last week she was down the park, looking for you to come in for your tea, and she was so upset 'cause she couldn't find you—'

'Yep. Okay. Don't you worry, Mrs F.' He made his excuses and jumped over the little brick wall between the houses. Molly was standing on the doorstep, holding six-year-old Fiach behind her, preventing Beatrice from coming in.

'Fiach has to come home with us now,' said Beatrice. 'Thank you for minding him, Molly.'

Molly called over her shoulder. 'Dermot! There's someone at the door.' She was not letting go of Fiach.

'It's only us,' called Beatrice.

'Hi Mam,' said Conor.

Molly gave him a cursory glance; her eyes were glued on Beatrice.

Conor's father hurried down the hall. 'Our boy's all grown, Moll.' Dermot squeezed Conor's upper arm, as if demonstrating that he was real, and made of muscle and bone. Conor tried not to wince. Dermot's grip had always been firm; he believed a man's grip reflected his moral character. 'Look again, love.'

Molly scanned the length of Conor before settling on his face. He tried to smile in the most normal way he knew. She gathered herself up and stroked Conor's cheek. 'Are ye coming in or what? I'll put the kettle on.' She shuffled down the hall. Fiach dashed out and stood on the step behind Conor. Dermot handed over Fiach's backpack and gave them the nod to go.

Once the three of them were back in the car, all belted up, Beatrice turned to Conor. 'No more sleepovers, it's too much for Dermot.' She glanced back at Fiach, propped up like a little prince in his booster seat. 'Anything could've happened.'

'I don't want to stay at Nanny's any more,' said Fiach.

Conor could feel Beatrice looking at him, but he didn't take his eyes off the road. The storm had blown the last of the leaves off the trees on Clogher Road. The whole area was stripped of colour and would remain so until spring. He felt dread rising, tailgating him. They mounted the bridge over the canal and descended into redbrick land. Nearly home.

3

I Choose You

After Harwood House, 44 Oscar Square was a Monopoly piece. A roof, four windows, with a door in the middle. Lizzie called their home the Tardis, but it was more like an economy seat on a long-haul flight; no matter how small you made yourself you were always going to be too big. When they first moved to the area, it was full of students and old people whose children had grown up and moved away, leaving them hanging about at their front gates desperate for a chat. And then they began to die one by one and for a while there were more skips than cars on the street. Doors were painted in muted colours, blue-black, green-grey, and the tiny concrete front yards were replaced with purple slate and screens of bamboo. Soon after, the streets filled with people pushing high-tech baby buggies in the same muted colours.

The leaves from last night's storm blocked the drains. A small lake lapped at their front gate. It happened every year and every year Frank swore he'd contact the council to clear the drains before it was too late. They had no choice but to trudge through the water, the wet seeping into their shoes. Frank was thinking of a nice hot cup of tea, the sofa and the football when he was assaulted three steps beyond his front door by two small bodies – Georgia and Jimmy, nine and six – clamouring for sweets that had been promised and promptly forgotten about.

A third child, fifteen-year-old Maya, stood at the end of the hall, scowling. 'If you ever leave me alone with them again I will take them up into the mountains and lose them for ever.'

Jimmy froze.

'She doesn't mean it, sweetheart,' Lizzie told him.

'I do,' said Maya. Frank knew she was serious. There were no half measures with Maya. She was his stepdaughter, his judge and his jury. He adored her.

Maya looked Frank over. 'The state of you.'

Frank wished he knew how to be the kind of man that didn't disappoint Maya.

'Paula called; she said you were ignoring her,' said Maya.

'Yep,' said Frank. Lizzie gave him a look. 'I'll go see her tomorrow.'

Jimmy climbed onto his feet. They shuffled and squelched down the hall and into the kitchen. Frank ransacked the cupboards for Solpadeine and poured a glass of water. Together they watched the fizzing water clear. Frank's phone beeped. The text was from Beatrice – *How is your heart? Bx.*

Frank stared at the text as if an explanation was going to emerge from the spaces between the words. Lizzie came in and put the kettle on. A quick swipe and the text was deleted.

'I'm hungry,' said Jimmy.

'Let's go to the chipper?' Frank needed salt.

Jimmy squealed with pleasure. Frank waited for a hint of approval from Lizzie, but she didn't turn around. He could tell from the rigidity of her back that she was set against him. He needed more information before he could undo whatever it was he had done.

While Frank waited in the chipper for their order, he phoned Shay. Through the plate glass window, he could see their crappy Nissan parked on the double yellows. Jimmy was strapped into his booster seat in the back, looking straight ahead, his arms tightly crossed, furious at not being allowed to come inside.

Shay finally answered. 'Hey, Frank?'

'What the hell happened last night?'

'You tell me?' said Shay.

'I don't know, that's why I'm asking.'

Shay chuckled as if this might be a joke and he was hedging his bets.

'I'm okay up to the pub?' Frank's headache wasn't helped by his efforts to remember. 'Were we in the library or was that before dinner?'

'Before *and* after.'

'Did something happen with Bea?' asked Frank.

'Oh, man,' said Shay. He sounded like he was choking.

Jimmy glared at Frank through the chipper's window, an angry furrow between his brows. Frank made a funny face. Jimmy didn't blink. They didn't have long. He could hear Shay over the phone, working hard to calm himself down. He liked Shay a lot. They'd played on the same five-a-side team for a few years until Frank's knee gave out. Shay was the better player by far, yet he always took Frank's advice. Frank was tired and hungry. He needed Shay to stop laughing and help him out.

Despite Shay running through the events of the night step by step, Frank still couldn't remember anything after they left the pub. And as much as he wished it was all an elaborate prank of Shay's, he knew it was possible. He knew he was perfectly capable, and the most likely, to challenge everyone to party games. Somehow, according to Shay, a game of Truth or Dare led to a proposal to swap partners for the rest of the night, no obligation, no expectations.

All the women needed to do was text the man of their choice.

Shay confessed he thought at first they were messing; everyone was laughing as they made up rules – one night only, no hickeys, no secrets, and *no* falling in love – but when he came back from taking a piss, Frank, Beatrice and Lizzie had disappeared.

Frank scrolled back through his phone and saw a text from Beatrice at 2.36 a.m. – *I am going to the stables for a ride.*

And Lizzie's, one minute later – *I choose you.* x

4

An Unusual Turn for a Sunday

Eva startled. She'd been eavesdropping on Shay's call with Frank while watching but not watching her twin daughters in the bath. The water was up to their necks and lapping over the sides and the tap was still running. 'Goodness me. That's . . . why didn't you say?'

Ella and Kate whispered to each other and then looked up, smiling like angels. It was completely possible she'd turned the tap off and they'd turned it back on again when she wasn't looking. She rolled up her sleeve and reached in for the plug. Water rolled over the sides, swamping the floor.

'Hope you've left some hot water for me.' Shay was at the door.

'All right, all right. Time's up.' Eva coaxed Kate and Ella out and into towels. Shay stripped and climbed into the bath.

'Daddy!' The girls made a big show of covering their eyes.

'Mam's gone. She said to say goodbye,' Eva told Shay. 'She wanted to beat the traffic.' Her mother stayed the weekend to mind the twins. Shay seemed genuinely disappointed. He loved Eunice. Eunice once took food off Eva's plate and gave it to Shay when he asked for seconds. He submerged his face in the water. When he came up again, he shook his head like a dog. 'I hope nobody peed,' he said.

There was silence.

'It's good for the skin,' said Eva.

Eva sat between Kate and Ella, reading them a story as she had every night since they were two. The girls' room was tidy, their drawers full of washed and folded clothes, their toys lined up on the windowsill, their books back on the shelves. All Eunice's work. The heady combination of the golden light of the night lamp and the soapy, warm scent of the girls made Eva hyper-aware of the chemicals leaching from her. She needed to get out before she poisoned her babies.

The house was in complete darkness when she pulled the girls' door closed. She called for Shay, turning the lights on as she went, her hands out in front to keep herself from careering into their endless clutter. They threw nothing away. Shay was in the kitchen, in tracksuit bottoms, eating the girls' left-over pasta. She stood behind him, leaning against the kitchen counter, and watched their reflections in the glass doors that opened onto the courtyard.

'So, what did Frank have to say for himself? Did he tell you what happened with Bea?'

'She got off with him.'

Eva thought of teenage bonfires where a tap on the shoulder led directly to people wearing the faces off each other. After a litre of cider, it didn't matter who. There was a time, in the library of Harwood House, when they had all been sitting close to each other, legs over legs, heads on laps, while feet were massaged and hair stroked. She had felt young again: that sense of endless possibility, of many selves left to explore.

'I thought you said he couldn't remember anything?' she asked Shay.

'Yeah, I believe him, but she did text him.'

'She did?' A text was evidence. 'That's mad. Honestly, I thought we were having a laugh,' said Eva. 'I didn't know anyone was going to *play*.'

'What? But you chose Conor?' Shay turned around to see her. He was smiling but she could see the tension spiralled in his back.

'I didn't *choose* anyone.'

Shay laughed. Stopped, laughed again.

'Check my phone.' She offered it to him, but he didn't take it. He took his time finishing the pasta, wiped his finger around the plate, sucked his finger clean.

'I was wondering why no one texted me.'

Eva exhaled. But then, the question came to her: why wouldn't her friends want to spend time with her husband? Either way, she didn't want to know. She had stepped through the looking glass, and everything had shifted.

'Oh God,' said Eva. 'There's six kids between us. It was so reckless.'

'Good craic all the same.' He opened the fridge and disappeared behind the door. 'Is there anything nice to eat?'

Eva was beginning to feel like Shay understood something she hadn't. It was usually the other way around. 'What would you have done? If Bea or Lizzie texted you?'

'Hmm?' Shay shut the fridge door and shrugged at her, slowly and deliberately. 'Which one?'

She shoved him, but he was braced and ready for her. He pulled her into his arms and kissed her so hard she tasted blood. They shuffled towards the bedroom as one, clothes peeling open, trying, and failing, to be quiet. The coat stand in the hall fell over and they froze but there was no sound from the girls and they were able to consume each other without interruption. It was an unusual turn for them, for a Sunday night, but the weekend had left a space between them that needed to be filled.

Eva lay on her back, awake. Shay slept on his side, his bent knees digging into her thighs. A crack of blue beside the window blind announced morning wasn't far away. In the quiet, before he went to sleep, Shay had told her it would've been okay if she'd texted Conor. He trusted her not to do anything. She'd laughed.

In a few hours, she needed to get the girls ready for school, she needed to think about Halloween decorations for the classroom, decide what to do about five-year-old Eliza Bourke's refusal to sit down in class, work out whether she could make time to do a supermarket shop. She didn't have the space to think about Conor. She would not think about Conor.

5

I'm Not Cross

Early Monday morning, the streetlights gold against a lilac sky, Conor took Jaro for his walk along the canal. Jaro was a rescue dog, probably a Jack Russell, no one was sure. For once, Jaro ignored the sleeping swans as he bolted down the road, barking at a woman who appeared to be walking a small horse on a lead. She looked familiar. Conor felt his heart quicken but, when he reached her, he saw she was a stranger, the horse was a Great Dane, and both were politely ignoring Jaro's yapping.

Conor snatched Jaro up into his arms. The woman smiled and walked on. He set the dog down and glanced back at the woman. She looked like Eva: long, straight dark hair, parted in the middle, very fair skin, and a dancer's straight, slender neck. Her pale-blue coat glowed. Eva had told him a story when they were in the library, about being bullied in school. Her uniform and PE kit were stolen from the changing rooms after basketball practice, and she'd had to walk home in her school coat with nothing but her underwear beneath. How quickly she'd forgotten the cruelty and relished her secret. When Eva told stories, you could never be sure where she'd turn. He smiled again, imagining her walking home in her coat. Spending the early hours with Eva had been like meeting someone in the pub and choosing to walk them home, no matter how far, just so you could keep talking. They'd done nothing he'd call unfaithful, yet he knew he didn't want to tell Beatrice the details. Beatrice had asked no questions about his weekend, and he was relieved. Last night she'd been focused on Fiach, trying to explain what Alzheimer's was doing to his nanny. Another conversation Conor didn't want to be part of.

Conor and Beatrice's home was a two-storey over-basement Georgian terrace on Grantham Street; the renovation cost nearly as much as the house and the repayments continued to be a strain every month. And now the house was only worth half what they'd spent on it. Beatrice phrased it as an investment in their long-term future; ironic, considering the three storeys would torture arthritic knees and aging pelvic floors. From the street he could choose to ascend granite steps and enter by the grand front door or descend steps to enter via the basement. They conducted most of their living in the basement kitchen. If they forgot something from the top-floor bedrooms, he took it upon himself to take the stairs two at a time. It was a tip passed on by a cardiologist when he was on rotation; these runs up and down the stairs were the only cardio exercise he managed.

He put Jaro down in the kitchen. The dog scuttled across the wooden floor and jumped up on Fiach. 'No Jaro! Bad dog!' Fiach pushed Jaro away and climbed up on a stool at the kitchen island out of reach. Conor had hoped getting a dog would help Fiach's confidence, allow him to forget himself in some rough-and-tumble play, but Fiach only liked Jaro when he slept on his bed and he could snuggle against him. Conor had been a nervous child too and he wanted Fiach to find his way out of it.

'He's not a bad dog, Fi, he's saying hello. Like dogs do.'

'I don't like what dogs do then.'

Conor poured kibble into Jaro's bowl. Jaro instantly sat up straight, waiting for the signal. 'Okay,' said Conor and Jaro got stuck in. 'Good boy.' Conor loved Jaro.

Beatrice passed over freshly squeezed orange juice. 'He'll grow out of it,' she said as she glanced at Conor. He knew she meant both boy and dog. She was in her Lycra, ponytail up, waiting for him so she could go for her run.

'Good morning.' She kissed him on the cheek as she passed. He followed her around the kitchen.

'I think it might be time to look for a nursing home for Molly.'

Beatrice didn't pause. 'I have a list of homes.' She made it sound as if it was a truth known for some time and she'd been patiently waiting for him to catch up. He imagined that was exactly what she'd been doing.

The house sighed as the door closed after her. Conor felt irritated. Sometimes Beatrice would seem to forget there were people involved in these things. And feelings. But, as she often said, they were a complementary couple: she was the doer and he was the thinker. It had always been that way.

They met at the afters of a wedding. Or at the after afters, as they'd put it when people asked. Conor was of the age when there were five or six weddings a year, and he hadn't the energy or inclination left to mingle with strangers. He'd left just before midnight. When he reached the taxi queue on Dame Street, it was depressingly long. He was weighing up waiting or walking when Beatrice joined the queue behind him. He recognised her. On the dance floor she'd stood out; unlike the other single women, who were dancing in a circle, she seemed happy dancing by herself. When they reached the top of the queue half an hour later, he'd learned that she worked in hotel management, the wedding had been so well organised that she took notes, she laughed as she admitted this. She lived on the southside and would usually walk home but tonight her shoes were new and they were killing her. She preferred to be called Bea, couldn't get used to how the Irish mispronounced her name. A taxi pulled up and he opened the door for her. 'Maybe we could, if you would like, get a coffee, this week, or whenever? Or a drink?' She mumbled something he couldn't catch and climbed into the back seat, not a word of thanks for his letting her jump the queue ahead of him. She was out of his league, and he felt a fool for hoping otherwise. Deflated, he was about to close the door when she popped her head out. 'Aren't you coming?' she asked.

'But we're going in different directions?' She gave him a look that went right through him. And that was it.

Drinking coffee in Beatrice's bedsit at 2 a.m. after they'd kissed but before they'd slept together, he'd been surprised to hear how lonely she was after two years in Dublin. She'd followed an Irish man home from Hamburg, but they'd split up after she told him she wanted children but didn't want to have anything to do with the Catholic Church. They'd been sitting on her bed in the corner, backs against the wall, her legs across his lap. He knew he'd fallen for her when his first thought was how he would tell his parents he wasn't baptising his imaginary children. She wanted to stay in Ireland.

'But it's hard, I try to make friends, everyone is friendly, they say let's go for a pint or to the movies and then they forget to call me back. I think, people, Irish people think I don't need anyone.' He had nothing to counter with because he had thought the same and perhaps still did.

'Daddy,' said Fiach, 'Aisling says we need to be kind to bees because they pollinate the fruit and if we don't have any bees, there won't be any fruit. But how can we be kind if they're gonna sting us?' It took the full question for Conor to remember Aisling was his son's teacher. He still hadn't got over the fact that his son's teachers looked like they were still in school themselves. And the school's policy of using first names only made it worse.

'They won't sting you if you leave them alone.'

'But we're supposed to mind them.'

'I think Aisling means, leave them alone to do whatever they want to do?'

Conor poured himself a coffee and served up the porridge Beatrice had left for them.

'Why are you cross?' Fiach stared at him.

'What? I'm not cross.'

'Your eyes are squeezed.'

Conor took a deep breath, let it out, and rearranged his expression for his son.

'I'm not cross, Fi, but we need to stop talking and eat up, we gotta hit the road—'

'Like a toad!' Fiach returned to his porridge, reassured.

'And remember Fi, bees don't *want* to sting you, because if they sting you they die.' Fiach examined this new information, every tiny adjustment of what he understood playing out over his face until he nodded.

Conor scraped his uneaten porridge into the bin. He was going to buy a doughnut on his way into work.

6

The Best Night of Her Life

Frank fumbled for the glass of water on the bedside table. The soft rumble of the news was on the radio alarm clock. Enough to wake them up but not loud enough to ruin their day. They were the only people they knew who didn't worry about a run on the banks. They had no money in them. He turned over for another bit of sleep only to get a foot in his groin; Jimmy was starfished in the middle of their bed. He rolled Jimmy out of the way and discovered the other side of the bed was empty. Lizzie was gone, the alarm clock was reading eight twenty-five and they were going to be late for school.

'Lizzie!'

Last night Lizzie was in passive-aggressive mode; all super-efficient mothering of children, lots of please and thank-yous and one-word answers for him. She slipped up to bed without telling him. When he came up the lights were out, and she appeared to be asleep. He wrapped himself around her, kissed the back of her neck. 'I'm asleep,' she told him. A short while later, he heard her sniff. She was crying. He considered telling her everything, or the everything that was nothing; he couldn't remember going off with Beatrice, let alone suggesting anything in the first place. What was worse, having the opportunity to have sexual relations with a woman who looked like Jessica Lange in *Postman,* and not taking it up, or having sexual relations and forgetting about having done so? One was foolish, the other tragic. His penis swelled with his efforts to remember. Somewhere between deciding if he should ignore Lizzie's protests and hold her, he fell asleep.

Lizzie walked into the bedroom carrying clothes for Jimmy.

'I don't want to go to school.' Jimmy said this every day, and every day he was ignored. Lizzie wrestled his pyjamas off and his clothes on, all while he remained in a stubborn curl. She dumped him on Frank. 'You have to take him today.'

'Ah Lizbet, please?' Frank knew he was completely incapable of looking Beatrice or Conor in the eye. Not until he had more details. 'My hangover's still raging.'

'I've got things to do. And call Paula, she's driving me demented.'

'I told you not to answer.'

'Today, Frank. Today.'

Lizzie was fully dressed. She stood as tall as her five foot three inches would allow her.

'Where are you going?'

'I'm going to see my agent. I want to get back to work.'

She sounded rehearsed. Frank had a lot of catching up to do.

'What're you saying?'

'I need to be acting again. I'm not myself without it.'

'What's brought this on?'

'You mean what took me so long? Are you really asking?'

He smiled but he didn't dare answer. All he could think of was a job he had next week, a commercial for a non-dairy spread. And there was also a possibility of a show shooting in Belfast next month. Who would mind the kids if she went off to auditions? He needed to be careful.

Jimmy climbed into his lap, held onto his face. 'Daddy, Daddy, we can stay home. I don't care.' Frank tossed him off. 'Get your shoes, Jimbo. Now.' Jimmy slunk out of the room. Frank ran his fingers through his hair and stood up to face Lizzie. 'Yes. Yes! You *should* be working. A talent like yours.'

Lizzie exhaled. Her eyes were puffy after last night's crying.

He walked towards her with his arms wide, but she side-stepped him. 'Don't be angry with me, please,' Frank begged.

'Nothing happened, okay? I was off my face. I love *you*. I'm mad about you.'

'How do you know nothing happened if you can't remember?'

'I'd remember if I'd betrayed you.'

'You held Eva's face and stuck your tongue in her mouth. She had to push you off. Then you kissed Shay.'

This was news to Frank. 'Shay?'

'You embarrassed me in front of our friends.' She was about to cry again.

'Sounds like I embarrassed myself more,' said Frank. 'I don't know what you're doing with me. I'm miserable, Lizbet. I was looking for total erasure. Anything to silence the demons. You know how it is.'

'Your demons only seem to want to show you a good time.'

Georgia and Jimmy's voices floated up from downstairs; they were squabbling, their voices melding like a high-pitched chorus. Slapping and pinching was only seconds away. Lizzie cocked an ear trying to work out how long they had.

'Ah come on. That's not fair. What about you, Liz?' Frank felt his teeth grind as he tried to smile.

'What?'

'You were all over Conor and Shay, doing that touchy-feely actress thing that you do when you're drunk. I'm not saying they were complaining. It was that kind of night. We were all in. *All* in. That I remember.' Lizzie was the youngest of five and you could see that in her; she trusted that everyone adored her.

Lizzie was clearly struggling to think of a retort.

'And what was Shay doing in our room?'

Her eyes widened; he could almost hear her internal panic. 'Shay told you?'

'He said you were upset, *and* I found a long brown hair in the bed.'

Lizzie slumped for a moment and then pulled herself erect. 'When I couldn't find you, I texted him. We had a ball. One of the best nights of my life.' She narrowed her eyes, let out a tiny sigh. 'You know he hasn't a mark on his skin, not even a freckle—'

'That's 'cause he's a child.'

Lizzie cackled.

He reached for her again, but she turned away. 'You're late for school, and don't forget Paula. I promised you'd go see her today.' He listened to her footsteps as she walked away.

Washington Street Primary was a home-made kind of school; a mix of Victorian redbrick buildings, Portakabins and wooden sheds where they stored odds and ends, like angel wings for the Christmas play that hadn't been used since the multi-denominational school had become more culturally sensitive. With kids, it was a ten-minute walk down to South Circular Road, but there was no time for that. He threw them on his bike, Jimmy in the child seat on the back and Georgia on the crossbar. They arrived as the last line of children was snaking into the classroom. Georgia scarpered without a goodbye; she hated being late. Frank lifted Jimmy off the bike but when he tried to put him on his feet Jimmy collapsed in a heap.

Frank was thinking he would wait him out when, out of the corner of his eye, he saw a familiar silver BMW pull up. He wasn't sure which of the Twomeys he'd prefer it to be. 'Not today, kid.' He dragged Jimmy up. He burst into life, wriggling, and screaming like a feral cat. Frank carried him under his arm into the classroom and handed him, still kicking, over to his teacher. Frank didn't know who he pitied most, Jimmy or Aisling. She urged him to leave; better to not drag things out. Back in the hall, he came face to face with Conor walking Fiach in. Frank was ready with the sorry can't stop, got to do something important when Conor spoke.

'Enjoy yourself? I hope so, because Christ, I can't tell you how shattered I was yesterday. Still am.' Conor grimaced. 'How's Lizzie? Is she okay?'

Frank bristled. He thought Conor dull when he first met him, but as time went on he learned that Conor's mild manner hid a sharp intelligence and a forensic memory. His powers of observation gave him an edge that made Frank wary but were very amusing when directed at someone else. Did he enjoy himself? To answer, Frank needed to be sure he understood what Conor was asking. From the classroom they heard Jimmy give vent to a final despairing roar.

'He's still at it?' asked Conor.

Frank nodded.

'Desperate.'

They'd had many chats about their boys and how one needed to be more obliging and one less so.

Fiach tugged on Conor. 'Daa-ddy!'

Conor let himself be pulled away. 'Back in a sec.' They disappeared into the classroom.

In the yard, Frank swung a leg over his bike and rode away. Was Lizzie okay? Frank was overfamiliar with the guilt he felt when he thought of Lizzie. He called it guilt, but it was more complicated than that, a little stone in his heart: hard, smooth, sometimes painful, but as much a part of him as the metal that shored up his once-fractured wrist. He had not, for one minute, believed that her time with Shay was one of the best nights of her life. He was almost certain nothing of significance had happened between them but he also knew everyone had the potential to step outside themselves for a moment. Especially Lizzie. He asked it of actors every day. It was a source of constant frustration in his work, script notes from above claiming a character would never say or do something. It was those liminal spaces that interested him most. Lizzie was hurt and it was never intended. They used to be the kind of couple that took risks, scoffed at rules, leaned into the dark. And now they were middle-aged, monogamous and mortgaged. The only thing they'd avoided was marriage but they were as good as, just fools for denying themselves the wedding party and the presents.

33

He was halfway down the street before it came to him like a slap – if Shay had told him all the important details about Saturday night, then he had nothing to worry about because, according to Shay, everyone agreed.

7

A Figment of Her Imagination

Eva's day always started with untangling her junior infants from their coats and their backpacks and helping them to hang everything up; one of those life skills that adults took for granted but five-year-olds found physically and emotionally taxing. Through the window of her classroom's Portakabin, she witnessed Conor's late arrival. She'd waved but even though he seemed to be looking straight at her, Conor didn't wave back. She felt bereft.

When she was fifteen, living in Leitrim with her sister and her parents, she'd spent the best part of a year convinced only she was real, and everyone else was a figment of her imagination. Her interactions with people, her friends, her teachers, her family, were all narrated by a voice in her head. *Don't be an idiot. This is boring. She's behind you! You're too late. He's gone.* When Conor saw her but didn't see her she questioned if anything that had passed between them was real.

At lunch, everyone asked after her weekend away. It was a tonic, she told them, the house was beautiful, surrounded by ancient woods, the leaves had turned, they'd sat around a log fire in the book-lined library. All in all, Eva made it sound like a genteel and relaxing weekend. It was only when Margaret, the school's principal, asked for the details, needing a weekend away herself, that Eva felt herself flushing. Who knows what Davina saw and heard? Who knows what she might tell Margaret over a full Irish? She lied: the plumbing spent the night complaining loudly and the breakfast wasn't good, eggs like mattress foam. Margaret's disappointment was alleviated by an avalanche of helpful suggestions regarding other country houses to visit. Eva retreated and watched them all as if looking at a screen.

8

If Jack's Fine, I'm Fine

Before he and Lizzie had kids of their own, when they were just *going out*, Lizzie's star was on the rise. With her agent's support, she flew to LA to audition for a pilot season. Frank couldn't go, he had a music video to shoot. On the last day, after too much of everything, he had a one-night stand with Paula Gleeson, an actress. He had no reason to believe anyone would find out about Paula, and no desire to see her again, but then they discovered she was pregnant. After several meetings tucked up in a pub's snug, crying and bargaining, Paula decided she would go through with the pregnancy alone and promised to keep his name out of it. In return, Frank promised to help if he could, but he wasn't ready for fatherhood. A couple of months later he was in the dentist's waiting room flicking through an abandoned tabloid when he read that Paula had announced her pregnancy, naming him, Oscar-nominated film director, as the father. She was dressed in grey satin, her modest belly enhanced by the sheen. *THE ROLE OF HER LIFE!*

The dental nurse assumed Frank's state of panic was brought on by fear. She ignored his protests and led him straight to the dentist's chair. There was a needle sinking into his gums before he fully understood that it was too late, there was nothing he could do to mitigate the damage to Lizzie. When his phone started ringing, he was dribbling out of one side of his mouth from the anaesthetic and unable to form a word. He tried and tried to reach Lizzie, but her friends ran interference and he never got to say anything more than *I love you* and *I'm sorry.* Lizzie found her revenge in Max Gannon, a friend of Conor's.

Six months after Frank and Paula's son was born, Lizzie gave birth to Maya and found herself on her own. Life was very messy for a while and her career, so full of promise, wasted away from neglect.

Jack lived an entirely different life in Rathgar with Paula and Tommy, his stepfather. He was in boarding school and Frank only saw him three or four times a year. The sole purpose of these visits, it seemed to Frank, was to give the boy the opportunity to sneer at him. The only subjects that interested Jack were what kind of pizza they'd get for dinner and what time would he drop him home.

Frank had never understood the fashion for potted plants shaped like lollipops. He was examining Paula's lavender lollipops when she opened the door. Her long auburn hair fell in smooth waves like she'd just walked out of a salon, but her brown eyes were bloodshot. She kissed him on both cheeks. An affectation of hers that he always failed to remember in time, and they bumped noses as usual.

'Your lavender's dead,' said Frank.

'It was waiting for you.'

Paula wasn't interested in listening to his half-hearted excuses about how busy he was. 'They're kicking Jack out today; you've got to stop them.' She ushered him into the living room. He was taken aback by the mess – dirty plates and glasses covering the top of the marble coffee table, a stain on the pale carpet. Paula caught him scanning the room. 'I had to let the cleaner go. Tommy's in a bit of a . . . he's bankrupt. We're bankrupt.'

'Oh Paula. I'm sorry.'

She sighed. A smile hovered and disappeared. 'It's going to be all right. He's gone to India. He's got some investments to liquidate. Should be enough to start again.'

'India?'

'Things are a little more relaxed there. Anyway, I didn't tell you anything.' She pulled the curtains over, plunging the room into twilight. 'It's not so bad in the dark. If you can't pay the school fees, and you still can't, right?' He shook his head, and she barrelled on, 'Then you're going to have to persuade them to keep him until Tommy does his thing. They'll make allowances for ex-pupils like yourself, I'm sure.'

Frank hadn't had anything to do with the school since his last day toilet-papering the tree in the courtyard.

'I can't have him here, Frank. I can't afford to feed him.' She said this in such a matter-of-fact way that he understood things must be worse than she was saying. 'Don't look at me like that. I've enough to get by. And if Jack's fine, I'm very very fine.' The school's last missive had outlined plans to deliver Jack home this evening. Frank tried to persuade her to come with him; better to present a united front, besides he was on his bike and would have to go home to get the car. She'd already been to the school several times, burned her bridges. Handing him her keys, she suggested he take her car for the optics. It was a cream Audi convertible. Frank couldn't say no.

Paula waved goodbye to him from the shadows of her front door. He sat back in the cream leather of the Audi and adjusted the driver's seat. Frank was fond of Paula. She may have been the only person left in the world who had such confidence in him. 'Frank,' she'd said once, 'you're a genius, you could make a person do almost anything.' He thought, yes, that was true.

As he drove in a clean arc out of the drive, two empty wine bottles rolled out from under the passenger seat and clanked together.

9

Only Messing

Beatrice put an ear to Molly and Dermot's front door. She could hear a faint ringing inside. She had a key, but she didn't like to let herself in if Molly and Dermot were home. When she opened the door and called out, there was no answer, only the hum of the fridge and a blind tapping against an open window. Dermot's phone had been left on the kitchen counter. She moved slowly through the house, calling out as she went, and was relieved to find it empty. She'd imagined Molly and Dermot dead in their bed, poisoned by carbon monoxide or worse, some dark pact. If something terrible had happened, she would've laid it squarely at Conor's feet. He was too slow to act, too passive. Always waiting for someone else. It was the same passivity that caused him to say nothing in Harwood. To fall in with the crowd. To not even try to stop her. She could feel Frank's grasping hands; the banality of them and the surprise of her own desire. It was not something she needed to know. But even worse, she had discovered, was Conor's complete lack of curiosity about what had transpired between herself and Frank, leaving her unable to ask him anything about what he did that night.

When she was very small, her grandmother minded her while her parents worked shifts, her mother a nurse, her father in the port. After her baba died, there were many days she'd let herself in after school, feed herself, do her homework and go to bed, all without talking to another person.

One winter's day when she was ten, she walked home from school, her boots squeaking in fresh snow. It was evening and the streetlights bounced light off the snow making the whole

40

world glow. She was at her front door pulling the key out of her pocket when she heard a man walk up behind her. An ordinary-looking man with a moustache. He smiled and told her she had nice legs. She remembers glancing down at her thick green woollen tights, a ladder stretching over her right knee, unable to understand what he meant. He wrapped his arms around himself, shivered, and asked if he please could come inside. She grinned at him; even now she could feel the imprint of that grin on her face. How fixed it was. How hard she was working at what she should say or do. A neighbour hurried by, scarf up over her chin, head down against the flurries. They both watched the woman stop and stare at them. The man took one more look at Beatrice, gave her a little bow in farewell and retreated. When she couldn't see nor hear him any more, when the street had returned to its soft, glowing silence, she went inside, locked the door behind her and turned on the television. She never told anyone about the man; she didn't have the words back then. This situation with Frank felt the same; Conor's silence confused her so much she couldn't figure out how to put it in to words.

Beatrice switched on all the lights and added the television for company while she cleaned. They'd once hired a cleaning service to help ease Dermot's load, but Dermot called a halt to it. Molly could never remember the women and variously feared they were burglars, Dermot's mistress, or, the strangest of all, her own mother. Dermot said he'd prefer scrubbing the floors with a toothbrush to having to calm Molly down. Beatrice didn't mind cleaning for them, making lunch. It was only a few hours a week and she had the time. She had too much time. She hadn't worked since she'd found out she was pregnant with Fiach. After three late miscarriages and two rounds of IVF she wasn't going to take any chances. But by the time Fiach started school, the hospitality industry had collapsed, she knew no one and couldn't get an interview. Bringing Fiach to and from school and working on the parents association gave her days a welcome structure, filled with friends and neighbours to talk to. On days like today, when Conor dropped Fiach in to school, her mornings felt a little wrong-footed.

She was upstairs making the bed when she heard voices in the hall. *No. No. No.* She came to the top of the stairs in time to see Dermot trying to get Molly's coat off her. Molly was having none of it. He yanked down hard on the coat until both her arms were pulled behind her and he could drag it off. Once freed, Molly whipped around and slapped him. He raised a clenched fist and shook it in front of Molly's face.

'Dermot.'

He spun around, a fury on his face until he saw her looking down. His shoulders rounded, and his gaze dropped to the floor.

'She wanted to go out. Wouldn't let up. Then didn't want to walk back.' He was shouting. 'What is that godawful noise?' Beatrice hurried downstairs and slipped past him to turn the television off. She returned to kiss him hello; his cheeks were icy. They must've been out for some time.

'How are you, love?' said Dermot.

'Nearly finished. Only the vacuuming left—'

'You're very good but I can do that. Sit down, let me put the kettle on.'

'I've made you a soup. Parsnip and apple.'

'Parsnip and apple. Hmm.' He didn't seem convinced.

Beatrice drank the tea, didn't eat the soup. Molly sat beside them, slurping her soup. 'What's this again?' she asked, several times over. 'It's delicious.' Dermot talked about Fiach and the weekend; he was good as gold, no complaints, and she didn't believe a word. They talked about the best way to eat Mikados. The price of milk. Their chats had the soothing repetitions of a lullaby. She often heard herself saying, ah sure, and it'll do me, and I'm only after. It was an unintentional mimicry that could linger for hours after she'd been with Dermot and hugely amused Conor. Dermot never commented on her accent or her syntax; his accommodation of her difference made her love him even more. When she accompanied them on a walk, he always included her in the chats with his friends and neighbours.

'It is time for Molly to go to a home,' said Beatrice. She held her breath. Afraid again. Please do not be angry with me.

'I'm going nowhere,' said Molly. 'Tell her, Dermot.'

'She's grand where she is.' Dermot stood up and cleared the table, tipping the remainder of his tea down the sink. Even Molly could feel the shift in the air. She moved to the far side of the room and busied herself lining up her collection of porcelain figurines on the mantelpiece.

'It must be very hard for you.'

He whipped around to look at Beatrice, his face crinkled with distrust. 'What you saw, I was only messing. Wasn't I, Moll?'

Molly turned at her name and smiled at Dermot.

'What does Conor say?' said Dermot. 'Does he think I can't look after her?'

'He thinks you're tired and he worries about you. So do I.'

'Tell him I'm fine. Thanks for the cleaning. It's a big help.' He checked the time. 'It's nearly quarter past. You don't want to leave Fiach waiting.'

It was only five past one. 'I'm sorry, Dermot, but don't be mad. It is only for you I say this.'

'You said what you think, love, don't be sorry. But you're wrong.'

Beatrice gathered up her bag and coat and left the house. She berated herself for not having considered her strategy first. She used to be good at anticipating her guests' needs and steering them in a direction that was of mutual benefit.

When she drove away from Dermot's she was grateful she had the school to go to.

43

10

Exposure

Lizzie's agent thought she was both too young and too old. She was past her use-by date for anything romantic and not old enough for grandmother or annoying neighbour. She was no longer slim enough to make sandwiches for the family in bread commercials, not chubby enough to be funny in a beer commercial. Her agent never said any of this out loud; instead, Cara was absolutely thrilled and delighted to have an actor as talented as Lizzie on her books again. Together they scanned the current call-outs for anything suitable, and it was through that humiliating exercise that Lizzie learned how far she'd fallen into the chasm of the in-between. And of her past collaborators who might have thrown her a rope, they'd either moved to London for work, given up the business or had babies. Cara had insisted there were great opportunities in independent theatre or student films that would give her much-needed exposure. Unpaid, of course.

Lizzie walked out of the agent's offices and into a moody wind dragging litter along the quays and whipping her hair back and forth. She darted into a cafe and almost cried with relief when the door closed behind her. Music was playing and bright yellow chrysanthemums in glass jars adorned each table. She ordered a latte and a slice of carrot cake without checking to see if she had enough money. But no matter how many times she counted the spare coins from the bottom of her bag, she didn't have enough for cake *and* a bus home and, if she walked, she'd be too late to pick up Jimmy from school.

The cashier, a pixie-haired girl with perfect skin and a nose ring, leaned on the counter, propped her head on her hands and yawned.

Lizzie needed money; without an income she had no options. She needed Frank to believe she could leave, otherwise he'd keep walking all over her. She didn't doubt his love but there were many women like Beatrice, beautiful and uncertain. A killer combo. How she got herself into this position, she didn't know, but she understood she hadn't spent nearly long enough thinking about things like career and income while rearing children. Before Maya came along, she took a martyr's pride in living the life of an artist, living on toast, sustained by praise, turning down the soap operas and the commercials. She thought she was going places. But a child couldn't eat praise. If Frank was hit by a bus tomorrow, God forbid, she'd have to forge her own life with the children. She would need to be determined and selfless. She would need to work day and night to feed and educate them. Art would be irrelevant. On the bright side, there'd be no room for second thoughts, and no time to hate Frank. The real problem, as always, was that she loved him.

'I'm fifteen cents short,' said Lizzie.

The cashier shrugged into her hands, losing her neck entirely.

Lizzie eyed the tip jar and considered taking back some of what she'd left in there over the years but then her throat tightened, the tears came, and the girl stared. Lizzie abandoned everything, knocking over a table in her hurry to leave. Her impulse was to make right and apologise profusely but she wrestled it down and kept walking. Then she heard a muttered curse. Keep going, Liz, keep going, but her body had already turned back. Pixie-haired bitch was on her knees picking up shards of glass from a puddle of chrysanthemums. She sat back on her haunches and stared at Lizzie with contempt.

Lizzie knocked over another jar of flowers and ran out the door.

11

Ladybird, Ladybird, Fly Away Home

Beatrice reached the school five minutes early. Across the road, a huddle of parents gathered at the gates, Lizzie among them. Beatrice called and waved. Lizzie turned towards her, but her expression was unreadable. Beatrice couldn't help glancing behind her in case Lizzie was staring at someone else but no, Lizzie's frown was just for her. When the lights changed, Beatrice strode over, wearing a sunny smile. She ducked into each side of Lizzie's face and kissed her.

'How are you?'

'Fine,' said Lizzie. Lizzie's face was unusually mobile and reactive; sometimes it was hard to know if she was pleased to see you or simply mirroring you. Today, she was giving nothing away. Beatrice felt the ground shift beneath her.

'Are you mad at me?' It burst out of Beatrice's mouth, with an undeniably desperate edge.

Lizzie blinked.

The black iron gate opened and banged against the opposite wall. The queue surged through the gap, sweeping Beatrice and Lizzie into the playground. Children spilled out of the classrooms. The teachers held on to arms, shoulders, sometimes a slip of jumper, trying to prevent mayhem. It wasn't hard to find Jimmy and Fiach; they were the only two standing behind Aisling, their heads close, examining something in Jimmy's cupped hands.

'It's a ladybird,' Fiach announced. 'Did you know boy ladybirds are still called ladybirds?'

'Interesting,' said Beatrice. 'I didn't know that.'

'Aisling said there are no manbirds. Which is stupid,' said Jimmy.

'It wouldn't be manbirds, anyway, it would be gentleman-birds.' Fiach and Jimmy cracked up. When they looked back the ladybird was gone. They sighed.

'Let's go, Jimmy,' said Lizzie, grabbing his hand.

'Ladybirdladybirdflyawayhomeyourhouseisonfireyourchildrenaregone,' sang Fiach without taking a breath. 'Can Jimmy come to our house?'

'Yes!' said Jimmy. 'Please.'

Lizzie didn't hesitate. 'I'm sorry, no, we've a lot to do today.'

'I want to go to Fiach's. Now.' Jimmy was working up to a scene. 'Please. Please. *Please.*'

'Please?' asked Beatrice. 'We can talk.' Beatrice didn't wait for another objection. She walked out of the yard, the two boys scampering at her heels. Lizzie had no choice but to follow.

Beatrice fed the boys orange quarters and water and made fruit tea for herself and Lizzie. She directed Lizzie to the sofa, but Lizzie chose to remain perched on a stool at the kitchen island. 'Can't stay long,' said Lizzie, again. They talked about the tea, the boys' homework, owning a dog – Jaro was being adorable – but not one word was said about the weekend. She decided to let Lizzie lead in this; all she could do was create the opportunity. But after exactly half an hour, Lizzie jumped down off the stool and announced she needed to pick up Georgia from soccer practice.

In minutes, Beatrice was on the top of the steps watching them walk down the street. She felt a wave of vertigo.

'Lizzie!'

Lizzie stopped.

'Are you coming Saturday?' Beatrice could see Lizzie was trying to think of another excuse, but she wasn't going to let her. They'd been having pizza nights once a month since their youngest were babies and no one could go anywhere. To back out now would require serious illness or suggest irreconcilable differences.

'Six o'clock. Okay, bye.' Beatrice stepped back inside and shut the door. The effort of not saying anything left her drained.

She jumped when the doorbell rang. Lizzie was back.

'What exactly happened between you and Frank? Don't lie to me, I'll know.' Lizzie sounded tough, but her eyes were already tearing up. She was squeezing the railing so tightly her hand turned white. 'I'm warning you I've had a shite day.'

Beatrice wanted to say nothing happened, that they should put it all behind them, but could see that wasn't going to work. 'We kissed.'

Lizzie nodded. 'Properly? With tongues?'

'Yes. That was all.'

'Did he touch you?'

'Yes.'

'Then that wasn't all. I told you, everything, I want to know everything.'

Though she was taller than Lizzie, Beatrice was feeling small and that made her defensive. 'Does it matter?'

'Of course it matters! Where did he touch you?'

Beatrice felt his hand between her legs, the heat of it. She ran her hands down her breasts and sides. She saw Jimmy on the street, watching them, squinting with curiosity. She let her hands fall back by her sides.

'That's it, Lizzie. Through my clothes. It was nothing. Like teenagers.'

'No sex?' asked Lizzie.

'He was so drunk.'

'That's all that stopped you?'

Tiny needles of Lizzie's spit landed on her face. 'I thought you agreed.'

Lizzie's face folded and tears fell. 'I texted him straight away. *I choose you.*'

Beatrice wasn't going to argue, but she had texted Frank and he had come to her without hesitation. 'I didn't know that.'

'Why? When you have Conor. You have everything! Everything.' Lizzie gestured at Beatrice's house, at the tree-lined street, and even the blue sky as if she had some claim to the sun too.

'I'm sorry Lizzie, I am. I didn't think. I never meant to hurt you. I would never want to hurt you. If I'd known—'

'Don't go near him again, no matter what he says, okay, promise me? I will ruin you.'

The threat was ridiculous and sad. 'Okay. Yes,' said Beatrice. 'Of course.' And she meant it.

Lizzie took Jimmy by the hand and hurried away. Jimmy glanced back at Beatrice. She waved at him. He waved back.

12

Does He Play Football?

Despite a long sweeping drive through an avenue of giant beech trees, Jack's boarding school was an infinitely underwhelming seventies concrete block in a mossy swamp of asphalt. Large windows ensured the classrooms were saunas in summer and walk-in freezers in winter. The absence of comfort was a cornerstone of Kilbradden School's educational policy. Frank's father, his honour Judge Robert Durkan, believed childhood hardship had made him the man he was. There was no arguing with him.

In the school's entrance foyer the quiet was unnerving until he saw that it was class time and he'd better find shelter before the bell rang and boys flooded the halls. There was a lone boy sitting on the bench outside the principal's office, a large suitcase beside him. He was all bony right angles like a praying mantis. It was Jack, and he'd grown again. He jumped up and, in two loping strides, towered over Frank.

'What're you doing here? Is Mum okay? She's not answering her phone.' Despite his height, Jack was still a boy and he was scared. 'They want to send me home. They made me pack *everything*.'

'She's fine. There's been a problem with the bank about the fees. I'm going to see what I can do.'

'You?'

'Yes.'

'Fuck.'

Frank pretended he didn't hear anything. He knocked once and opened the door to the principal's office. The secretary didn't care who he was. He still had to wait. Frank wandered down the corridor to the school's display cases jammed with trophies of running and jumping brass boys. He scanned the shelves until he found a lump of artfully charred wood with an engraved plaque on the side. *Battle of the Bands* 1979. Behind the trophy was a photo of Frank eating a microphone, sweaty hair striped across his face, skinny black legs askew. The little bolt of joy surprised him.

'Look, Jack. It's your old man.'

Jack, back on the bench, head in his hands, didn't bother looking up.

'Did I show you already?'

'Every time.'

Frank wanted to remind him that he was here to help address his stepfather's failure. 'Where's your trophy? There isn't one? I didn't think so.' Frank smiled as if he was joking.

Jack moved his head very slowly back and forth.

The secretary called him. 'Mr Durkan?' Frank stood to attention.

Back on the road, with music blaring and the top down thanks to Jack's insider knowledge of the Audi, Frank launched into a bitter rant. He had nothing good to say about the school, never had anything good to say about the school, wished he'd intervened years ago when Paula told him they'd be sending Jack there. He apologised to Jack for letting him down. Jack said nothing, his eyes on the brown stubbled fields flying past them.

'Now you can go to school with your Dublin friends.'

Frank listened to the silence, waiting for a dismissive comment, but when Jack eventually turned to him his eyes were shining with unshed tears.

'Can I come live with you and Lizzie?'

Jack had disparaged everything about the way Frank and Lizzie lived. Frank worked hard to still his panic. 'Ah Jack, yeah but, um, it's not a good time right now.'

'What d'you mean? Jack's voice cracked. 'You're not splitting up are you?'

Frank quickly reassured him it was only the usual: work, money, and Jimmy was still a pain. 'A full-time job,' said Frank.

Jack sighed. 'I can't go home. I can't. Please, Dad?'

When Paula opened the door to Frank and Jack, her eyes roved from Jack to his suitcase, and then to Frank.

'Welcome home, love.'

Jack politely endured her embrace and then thundered up the stairs two at a time with his suitcase.

'It was worth a shot,' said Paula. She walked very carefully back to the sofa she'd got up from. Frank suspected she'd had a few. He perched uncomfortably on the arm of the sofa.

'I've good news and bad news.'

'I love this game,' said Paula.

'I've called St Pat's, Maya's school. It's as good as any, it's free and they have a place for him.'

'Well, that's a help.' She pulled herself up and took a big breath, 'I'm going to have to get my act together now, aren't I? Do the mother thing. Make him lunch. Take him to football.' She frowned. 'Does he still play football?

Frank was trying to remember when a violent padum-padum came down the stairs. Jack passed the doorway wearing his winter parka and a backpack and wheeling his suitcase.

'Where's he going?' asked Paula.

'That's the bad news.'

'Jack. Get in here. Now,' said Paula. Jack appeared in the doorway, not daring to cross the threshold. 'Where are you going?' she asked.

Jack made eyes at Frank. Help.

'You're taking him?' asked Paula.

'No. No. I'm not *taking* him.'

Paula returned to Jack. 'Is that it? You're going to Frank's?'

Finally, Jack nodded.

'Whose idea was that?'

Jack turned to Frank for help again. Frank stared back, pleading with him to speak up. But Jack stared at the floor as if he could drill down and escape through the basement.

'It was mine,' said Frank. With surprising speed, Paula slapped him hard across the face. Frank started to defend himself but stopped when he saw she was about to cry.

'Fine. If that's what he wants. It's well past your turn,' said Paula.

'I'm sorry, Mum,' Jack whispered and wheeled his bag out of the house.

Frank leaned in close to Paula, his voice bright, as if they were talking about a sleepover. 'Let's see how it goes,' he said. 'It's not like we have anything to offer him, and Jimmy drives him mad. You'll see, he'll be back in no time.'

'Give me my car keys and get out of my sight,' said Paula.

Frank didn't have enough cash for a taxi, so they walked home, wheeling the bike, carrying the luggage. Every bump in the footpath sent Jack and his ungainly suitcase spiralling into walls or into Frank's legs. Apart from the odd *oomph*, neither spoke. Frank felt terrible. He feared he'd exacerbated Paula's distress, perhaps removed the only incentive she had to pull herself together, but Jack had to come first.

When they arrived home an hour later, Lizzie met them in the hall. The luggage surprised her, but she said nothing as she wrapped Jack in a generous hug. Jack returned the hug in the same spirit; he loved Lizzie.

'So, what's up, Jack the Beanstalk?' asked Lizzie, as the boy towered over her. Once more, Jack turned to Frank for help. Frank was so exhausted by the journey home that he'd forgotten to work out what he was going to say to Lizzie.

Frank and Lizzie made up a temporary bed for Georgia on the floor of Maya's room and put Jack in with Jimmy. Maya retreated to the far corner of her bed and scribbled furiously in a notepad.

'Who are you writing to? Child protection?' asked Frank.

Maya gave Frank a withering look. 'Rules for Georgia.' Frank glimpsed a few – no talking was one of them. Georgia didn't stand a chance. Jimmy, the only one thrilled by the upheaval, took Jack by the hand. 'You can have the top bunk. It's the best. Or the bottom? What do you want?'

Jack shrugged, his head hanging, hiding behind his long black fringe.

'I want to sleep in my room with the boys,' said Georgia.

'There's no space,' said Frank.

'There is, same as here, on the floor.'

'It's a boys' room now,' said Jimmy.

Georgia hit him.

Lizzie dragged Frank down to his office slash shed at the bottom of the backyard, the only place they wouldn't be overheard. The night was cold. The grass crisp with frost.

'How could you do this to me?' asked Lizzie.

Frank was taken aback by her fury. 'It was an emergency. And you love Jack.'

'Course I do but we're bursting at the seams. We're not managing as it is.'

'Jack's a big lad, he'll be a great help.' Frank beamed, pleased with his own quick thinking. 'And he needs a mother.'

'He's got one,' said Lizzie. 'And two fathers. An excess of parents.'

'Paula's a total disaster right now and Tommy's in India. Jack's miserable. And scared.' Frank wrapped his arms around Lizzie. 'You're really good with kids. He needs you.'

'You should've asked me first.'

'Would you have said no?'

'You take me for granted.' In the dark, her eyes sparkled. It was hard to tell these days what tears he needed to pay attention to. 'I saw Bea.'

'Ah-huh?' Frank's voice went a little higher than usual. 'Did she tell you what . . . happened?' Lizzie stood very still, assessing him. He was afraid of her at times, especially when he couldn't tell what she might say or do.

'It was humiliating.'

'I can imagine. Wait. Humiliating for you? Or me?'

Lizzie gave him a look that made him feel like dirt.

'Both of us. Okay, I get it. Look. I'll do whatever you want me to do to make it right. Tell me what to do?' She seemed to consider this, but then, he imagined, realised there was nothing he could do to make it right. 'I love you. I'm mad about you. You're the best thing that ever happened to me.' He meant every word.

'Oh shut up, Frank.'

He slipped his hands around her waist. She flinched and held him at arm's-length. 'Your hands are freezing.'

13

Vegas

Eva and Lizzie had the best bench in the playground, with a clear view of their four young children but far enough away to be forgotten. The leaves on the trees had turned and the golden backdrop cast the children in a nostalgic light. Completely misleading; the three youngest were hungry and cranky, Georgia was sulking on the bench, the monkey bars were rusty, and the swings had no seats.

'Is that what Frank says happened?' asked Eva.

'He says he still can't remember.'

Frank was clever.

'What about you and Conor?' asked Lizzie.

Eva felt herself go very still. 'What about us?'

'Did you get up to anything?'

'Lizzie. What happens in Vegas stays in Vegas.'

Lizzie spun towards her. 'No. Just no.'

Eva couldn't risk lying to Lizzie. She always caught her out. When she was four months pregnant with the twins, Lizzie was the only person who ignored her sunny insistence that she was thrilled to be having twins and asked how she was, really. At the time, Lizzie was just another of one of the school mothers. 'I don't want to be rude,' she had said, 'but to be honest, sweetheart, you look like you're about to have a complete meltdown.' At that, Eva did melt down and confessed that she'd never been more scared in her life. The whole situation was ridiculous. Two babies at the same time? How was she supposed to keep them alive? Eva didn't recall what Lizzie said to reassure her, but she trusted her completely. Lizzie's Georgia was a wild, happy toddler, eight-year-old Maya was a chatty delight and Lizzie revelled in them. She promised to help Eva keep them all alive. It wasn't long after that Lizzie fell pregnant again with Jimmy and heartburn and haemorrhoids cemented the friendship. By the time Beatrice was pregnant with Fiach six months later, they had their own mother and baby group on call.

Eva glanced over at the kids. Jimmy was trying to pull Ella and Kate off the top of the monkey bars. 'That's not going to end well.'

Lizzie stood up and roared at Jimmy. He froze. She sat back down and turned to Eva. 'So, Conor?'

Eva put her arm around Lizzie and rested against her, shoulder to shoulder. 'Don't know why I didn't text *you*,' said Eva. 'You sexy thing.' She'd once heard a conspiracy theory that centred on the whole happy-family construction, where the overlords would direct your attention to what wholegrains your family was eating, what words you used with your children, the quality of the sexual communication with your spouse, so that you wouldn't notice what rights they were stripping away, what monies they were siphoning from your pay packet into theirs; you'd be too anxiety-ridden and insecure to march out of the house and protest.

'You think I don't know what you're doing?' Lizzie laughed, then she went quiet and watched the kids. 'You're lucky. You don't have to worry about Shay. He's not going anywhere. He told me he didn't know what love was until he met you.'

Eva rolled her eyes. 'You can't believe everything Shay says.'

The first time Eva saw Shay, it was at a rave on an eco-farm in Leitrim where he was working. He was twenty-two, she was a year older. With or without drugs, he bounced around like Tigger, smiling, always happy. He had brown curly hair that turned blond in the sun and when he danced he was sometimes mistaken for Michael Hutchence. In photos from back then, she can see how totally lost in each other they were. They were always touching, holding hands, thighs side by side, shoulders and heads leaning into each other. For a while they even dressed alike, partly because they wore each other's clothes, picking them off the floor of their shared bedroom. They lived with invisible electric tendrils between them. Shay had a way of finding her skin under her clothes, a couple of fingers under a jumper to her bony hip. A thumb up a sleeve to rub her inner wrist. Conor's touch was as electric as Shay's had once been. She hadn't realised how much she'd forgotten.

Eva turned back to Lizzie, suddenly desperate to know what passed between herself and Shay. 'What about you and Shay?'

'Oh Jesus,' said Lizzie. 'We didn't do anything, we didn't even kiss. He listened to me rant and gave me a back rub. It calmed me down so I could sleep.'

Why couldn't Shay tell her that?

'He's gorgeous,' said Lizzie. 'And he knows how to listen. That's priceless. But I swear to you, I wouldn't go there.' She took Eva's hands in hers. 'The thing is. I might've told Frank we did things.' Her hands shook with tension. 'But it was a complete lie. I wanted to hurt him.' Lizzie looked so earnest that Eva couldn't bear it. She stopped herself laughing; everything felt too fragile.

'It's okay. I understand,' said Eva. 'Did it work?'

Lizzie wouldn't look at her. 'You'd tell me, wouldn't you, should I be worried about Bea?'

Eva had seen nothing to suggest Frank was in love with Beatrice, nor she with him. This is what she told Lizzie and Lizzie seemed reassured.

Family Man

It was as if Jimmy had been replaced with a changeling. He'd stayed in his bed all night, for the first time since he was able to climb out of it. When Frank went to get him up for school, he was half-dressed, sitting on Jack trying to wake him up. Frank suggested Jack come with them to drop Jimmy off at school and then they could go straight on to check out Maya's school. Jimmy didn't give Jack a chance to say no.

Breakfast was overwhelming. Jimmy babbled constantly, demanding Jack's attention. Georgia and Maya were locked in a verbal spat that Frank failed to de-escalate no matter what he tried. Lizzie ignored his pathetic calls to come down and help. Frank shouted. Porridge was thrown. As they raced into the school, late again, Jack told him it was like being in a sitcom. 'Like where some single person inherits a bunch of orphans, and nobody knows what they're doing.' Frank had laughed but then felt the sting of offence. Jimmy waved goodbye before skipping into his classroom by himself. Frank declared a miracle, crediting Jack's positive influence. Jack stuttered and grinned, trying not to show how pleased he was.

Beatrice was at the school gate, chatting to other mothers. When she saw them, she smiled. Frank felt relief wash through him. He'd feared that whatever passed between them in Harwood had been so traumatic that his mind had decided to protect him by erasing all memory of it. She was wearing wide trousers and a long, unbuttoned coat, giving the impression that she was gliding on wheels as she came over to them. When she leaned in to kiss Frank hello, her blouse gaped, exposing a shiny, green bra strap on golden skin. He was unable to look away. Beatrice placed her hand lightly on his shoulder and pivoted him back around so she could see Jack properly.

'Jack?' she asked.

'Yes.' Jack stuck out his hand like an over-eager Boy Scout, then, realising his error, tried to withdraw, but Beatrice didn't give him a chance. She shook his hand and complimented his good looks.

'Maya's confirmation? Was that when I last saw you? When you were only a boy?' asked Beatrice.

Jack blushed. She glanced at Frank, but he was as paralysed as Jack.

'Well. Let's not leave it so long next time,' said Beatrice.

Frank and Jack watched as she glided away.

'Who was that?'

'Beatrice.'

'She's hot and you're seriously embarrassing.'

'Me?' Frank laughed as he held his hand out, mocking Jack's Boy Scout handshake.

'Who is she anyway?' asked Jack.

'She's married to Conor.'

Jack threw him a strange look.

'You know Conor, Maya's godfather?'

'The confirmation?'

'Yes. She's a friend of Lizzie's too,' said Frank. 'I mean she's my friend too, of course. We're all friends. Her son and Jimmy are in the same class. They're friends too.' Frank hadn't felt so tongue-tied in years. Fortunately, Jack was no longer listening.

St Pat's was small and had only admitted girls in the last ten years. The asphalt yard was covered with grey-uniformed teenage boys playing five-a-side football, white shirts untucked, trousers torn. As they walked across the yard, boys stopped and stared. The girls, by choice or order, huddled along the side of the buildings in small groups, heads bowed over phones, looking like they were plotting revolution. Jack looked among them for Maya, but the girls turned like meerkats and stared him down.

Frank enthused about the facilities. Look at that. A bike shed. A basketball hoop. When they entered the school, he remarked on the warmth and the pleasant smell. Was that lemon?

'It's floor polish,' said Jack. 'Is there no way I can go back to Kilbradden? All my friends are there.'

'You'll make new friends.'

Jack gave a sad shake of the head, then turned back.

'Where are you going?'

'Anywhere but here.'

'You haven't a choice, Jack.'

The boy reached the exit. Frank fought every urge to let him go. 'I promise I will feed you and house you, that's my job as your dad. In return, you go to school. If you want to take a punt on going it alone, that's up to you. Are you coming to meet the principal or not?' Frank immediately regretted his tone – it wasn't the boy's choice to change school – but to his surprise, Jack turned back.

Jack stood on a stool in the kitchen while Frank pinned up the hem of his new school trousers. Maya arrived home and made herself a cup of tea. Frank grunted a hello, but it was a while before Maya spoke.

'Jack?'

He peered through his fringe. Smiled.

'Don't talk to me at school. Okay?'

Before Frank could scold her, Jack spat, 'You're such a bitch.'

Maya shrugged. 'And please, don't tell anyone we're related.'

'That's enough, Maya.' Frank might as well have been invisible as the two squared off.

'Or what? We're not related anyway—'

'Thank God.' Maya took her tea upstairs.

Frank finished pinning and tried to think of something to say to Jack to make it okay, but he'd gone blank. The doorbell rang.

It was Max, Maya's father, standing on the path, in a blue suit, white shirt, no tie, clearly straight from work. He never came inside.

'Didn't know you were coming tonight.'

'There's a lot you don't know, Frank,' said Max, grinning.

Frank might have bantered with Max but tonight he was exhausted. He yelled up the stairs for Maya.

'Happy birthday,' said Max.

'Thanks.'

'Sorry we had to leave your party early. Kids, you know.'

'Kids,' said Max. As if he had any idea what it was really like.

It was Max's fiftieth a few weeks ago. Frank and Lizzie had adorned themselves in their finery, met up with Conor and Beatrice for a few cocktails to warm up before going in fashionably late and discovering they were completely out of sync with the gathering, most of whom were still sipping champagne and nibbling canapés. They perched on stools at the free bar, entertaining themselves with impressions of Max's consultant friends, mostly men, who seemed to be obsessed with wine cellars and bicycles; men who had no idea how boring they had become because no one ever dared challenge them. After a polite hour when it was clear there wasn't going to be any dancing, they all slipped out without saying goodbye. On the walk home, Lizzie became maudlin. Max used to be the wildest of them all. She made them all promise to rage against the dying of the light. It was in that moment, Frank realised, the weekend in Harwood House was born.

'Pity,' said Max. 'It *was* a brilliant party. But that's it. It's all over for us now.'

'Not quite.' Frank was not giving up the last two years of his *youth*.

'Nothing left on the to-do list, nothing left to long for,' said Max.

That was easy to say when you were at the top of your field, in line to become master of the National Maternity Hospital. Still, Frank knew what Max was getting at; maybe age was more of a leveller than he imagined. Frank wasn't done with longing, though. He longed for Beatrice; she'd been gliding through his thoughts all day. She hadn't texted again.

'We'll always have golf,' said Frank.

Max frowned. 'Sure.' He didn't catch Frank's sarcasm. 'Lizzie here?'

'No.' Frank hadn't seen nor heard from her since he'd brought her a cup of tea that morning. He prayed she hadn't run away.

'Tell her I forgot to bring a cheque for Barcelona, but I'll transfer it with the child support at the end of the month.'

Frank was about to ask Max what he was talking about when Maya came to the door in track pants, Ugg boots and a serious layer of make-up under a curtain of long straight hair. She slunk down the steps and got into the car. Frank felt a moment's relief; Maya may not have stopped to farewell him but neither did she greet her father. The exchange over, the men went their separate ways.

At a quarter past five, Frank finally made it out to his shed office for the first time that day. He had a list of commercial producers and TV executives to email suggesting a coffee. If there was any work out there, he wanted to be sure his name came to mind. There was a kerfuffle at the door. Jimmy called out in a loud whisper, 'Daddy?' The door handle rattled. He heard Georgia saying 'nononono.'

'Don't come in unless you're bleeding to death.'

The noise stopped and after some feverish whispering, he heard little feet pattering away. Lizzie's absence was worrying him but then he remembered it was Wednesday. Lizzie taught a kids' drama class in the community centre on Wednesday and Thursday nights, for pocket money and sanity, she'd say. He drafted an email, working the tone to sound enthusiastic, optimistic, and focused.

The minute Frank stepped inside the back door he was accosted by Georgia. 'Jimmy's crying.'

He found Jimmy in the bathroom, holding reams of bloody toilet paper to his knee, tracks of dried tears on his face. 'Jack pushed him off the top bunk,' said Georgia.

'He shouldn't have done that.'

'Then he told me to shut the *eff* up,' said Jimmy.

'You should've come to me,' said Frank.

'I did!' Jimmy's hiccups started again. His bottom lip trembled.

'I'm sorry, Jimmy. Does it still hurt?'

Jimmy nodded.

'It's okay to cry if it hurts.' Frank pulled him onto his lap.

'I'm too big to cry.'

'Never too big for a cry. I sometimes feel like having a big cry myself.' Frank was annoyed at himself for running Jimmy off when he was hurt, furious at Jack for causing the fall, pissed off at Maya for being a bitch, and worried about Lizzie. He was regretting everything.

'I'm hungry and I want Mummy.'

'Me too,' said Frank, 'let's go get chips.'

'Again!' Jimmy jumped off his lap. 'I'll tell Jack.'

Frank hoped Jack could appreciate Jimmy's capacity for forgiveness.

When Lizzie finally came home, long after the chips were eaten, the wrappers binned, she was very quiet. She had visited Paula after her class. Paula was so drunk she fell asleep mid-sentence.

'The place was a tip. I did what I could to tidy up.'

'You're a good woman.'

'Jack can't go home to that.'

Frank felt an enormous sense of relief. 'To be honest,' he said, 'I like having all my brood under one roof.'

Lizzie made a noise. She wasn't impressed. 'Did you cook?'

Frank put a plate of left-over chips in front of her. 'We saved them for you,' he lied. 'Will I warm them?'

Lizzie picked out the crispy bits and ate them. 'We need bunk beds for Maya's room. There's some on DoneDeal. Fifty euro but they're in Meath. We can tie them on the roof of the car.'

They'd be okay. Lizzie had it all worked out. He pulled her into his arms, and this time she didn't resist. 'It's going to be all right,' said Frank.

15

A One Time Only

Beatrice arrived in the cafe five minutes early. She stood in the middle of the room waiting for the table she had in mind, the one in the corner with a clear view of the entrance. Two girls dawdled there, coffees long finished. She ordered an espresso and was forced to settle for the second-best table; in the corner but angled so she would have to turn her head to see the door. She didn't see him until he was standing right beside her, red-faced and shiny with sweat. One pants leg was rolled up, exposing a Christmas novelty sock. He leaned over to kiss her on both cheeks. His sweaty cheek slid over hers and she cringed, but then she felt a flutter of lips on the skin below her earlobe and an unsettling tug down low. She pulled back. No. No. No. This was not why she asked him for coffee. All she wanted was a debrief so they could ensure they were on the same page moving forward. Frank was still smiling at her. She told him to sit while she ordered him a coffee. When she came back, he'd ignored her table and was lounging in a nearby armchair. The high colour in his face had eased and he seemed more than pleased with her serving him coffee. She didn't like that.

'Lizzie and I talked.' She had his attention.

'Do you want to know what we talked about?' said Beatrice.

'Pizza on Saturday?'

'Okay yes, that too.' He was watching her too closely, still smiling. Beatrice found herself shifting in her seat. 'She wanted to know exactly what we did.'

Frank went very still. 'Did you tell her?'

'Yes.' She watched him consider this. He seemed to decide it was of no importance.

'Well. Okay.'

He looked so comfortable with himself. 'Does it happen often?' she asked.

'Once a year. Birthdays are good for a blowjob.'

'Is nothing serious for you?'

'Is that a serious question?'

'Yes,' said Beatrice.

'Everything is serious, and nothing is serious. Except death and that is a given. So not worth taking that seriously.' He was smiling, daring her to react.

She wanted to slap him. 'I thought you were having a heart attack. You thought you were too. You went blue, Frank. I was scared.'

For the first time, he let his real feelings show. He seemed bewildered. Seemed to have no memory of the moment they had both feared he was dying.

'I shouted for someone to help us, but the wind was so loud. I wanted to run to get help, but you wouldn't let go of my hand.'

'Jesus.' She had frightened him.

'But then you stood up and laughed.'

Frank let out a little snort.

'It wasn't funny,' said Beatrice. She watched him glance around the room before he came back to her.

'I'm sorry, Bea. I honestly don't remember anything.' He put a hand on her knee. 'I didn't mean to scare you. We could try it again, see what happens, it might jog my memory?' He winked.

She wanted to laugh but if she did she might never stop. 'Frank, you are so bad. You had your chance. It was a one time only.'

Frank sighed long and slow as if she'd told him his puppy had died.

'I promised Lizzie,' said Beatrice.

'That's a pity.' He drained his coffee and stood up. 'Thanks for the coffee.' She fought the temptation to turn her head and watch him leave. But he was watching her. She could see his reflection in the cafe's windows, looking back.

16

The Tradesman's Entrance

It had been a perfect Saturday for Conor and Beatrice: dry and bright with crunchy piles of autumn leaves for Fiach to stomp through as they made their way to the market. They dawdled home with a shopping bag full of tissue-wrapped treasures – olives, cheese, spicy almonds, chocolates and strawberries – for tonight's gathering.

As Beatrice dressed, she worried over the question of where to eat, the kitchen or the upstairs dining room. When Conor offered advice and was quickly rebuffed, he questioned why she'd asked him. He was still distracted by the weekend; if she'd asked, he might have said no to pizza night, not yet. But to do so would suggest he had made some mistake, that things were not okay. He sprawled on their bed, waiting for Beatrice to finish in the en suite, and now he didn't want to get up. She wandered around their bedroom picking out an item of clothing at a time and putting it on. He liked the way her back arched and her stomach rounded when she did up her bra, and how she'd lift and arrange her breasts in the cups. She pulled on tight jeans and a floaty cerise-pink top before sitting down to do her make-up. Between the two sash windows at the front of the house was a small glass table with a drawer and slender brass legs. They'd found it in an antique shop in Porto; shipping it home had cost more than the table itself. Several bottles of creams and perfumes and oils stood either side of a three-way mirror. Beatrice wasn't planning to get old. He didn't dare say it out loud, but Beatrice chased a perfection of body and mind in a way that precluded the achievement of it. She'd ask him if he would still love her if she were fat and wrinkled with bags under the eyes. He'd say yes, always. And she'd accuse him of lying. She'd say I know you better than you know me. That was possible, as he often thought he didn't know her at all.

'Stop watching me.' She addressed this to the mirror. He saw himself diminished by perspective, looking pale and grey on their pale and grey linen.

'Tell me again why we're having everyone over?' he asked.

'Because it's our turn?' She smiled at him, before turning back to her mirror.

'Are we going to talk about the weekend?' asked Conor.

'Do you want to? Wait, do you mean with everybody or just us?' She frowned, considering the weight of his question.

'Either or both?'

'With everyone? No. No way. You know what they'd say. They were drunk and crazy.'

'You weren't?'

Beatrice shrugged. 'A little crazy, maybe. But I spat out the pill when no one was looking. Nobody knew what was in it, that was the really crazy part.'

No wonder she'd been so *normal* on Sunday.

'I like my sleep more.' She padded over to him in bare feet. 'What do you want to know?'

He pulled her down onto the bed, and over him. She propped herself on her arms, her hair falling free against his neck, and kissed him. 'We don't have very long,' she said. He pulled off her top. Unhooked her bra. Helped her wiggle out of her jeans, her underwear. He looked her over as if to be sure it was his Beatrice underneath. She took him in, responding the same as she always had. He waited for her to come before letting himself go. 'I love you.'

She whispered in his ear, 'du bist mein Ein und Alles,' and he believed her.

Beatrice washed again, touched up her make-up, tidied her hair. 'Did you talk to your father?'

He didn't want to believe her when she told him about Dermot being rough with his mam, but knew it would be more surprising if Dermot never lost his temper. He made some calls, but his mother was way down in the queue for under-funded and over-subscribed respite care.

'It is your mother, Conor. You must do better for her. And for your father.'

'Tell me, when would I have had the chance to talk to him?' He had given his family his Saturday, his only day off this week, as tomorrow would be spent writing up reports and referrals.

'Oh Conor! You have to make the chance.'

Conor hauled himself off the bed and into the en suite. The air in the bathroom was sticky with steam and lemon soap.

'Don't walk away,' said Beatrice.

He rehearsed a few sharp retorts in his head but discarded them as excuses or outright lies. He prepared to shave at the sink, clearing the mirror, lathering his cheeks with foam. But she was right, as usual.

'I'll go over tomorrow. If we can get someone to mind Fi will you come with me?' There was no answer. He stuck his head out the door and found he was alone.

Eva chose a simple navy chiffon dress. Black suede ankle boots. She was thinking about tights and whether she could get away without them – were her legs too pale, was it too cold – when Shay came in with the girls dressed in coats and ready to go. It was too late.

'Have you got the wine?' she asked.

'What's the point? They never open the wine we bring anyway.'

This was true. 'It doesn't matter, we can't arrive empty-handed. Get two.'

He returned to the kitchen. The twins sidled up close to her and stroked her through the dress.

'You look nice, Mummy.' Ella rubbed her cheek against the fabric.

'You're so beautiful,' added Kate. Their two little faces smiled up at her.

'You're both so beautiful, I think I'm going blind.' Eva closed her eyes and patted their faces, pinching noses and chins. 'Oh, what a nose! What charming chinny chins!' They squirmed away from her tickling fingers, squealing in delight.

Shay returned with two bottles clinking in a plastic bag and ushered them out of the house. The girls skipped ahead, fearless in the dark and frosty night. Eva took Shay's hand. His hand was large and dry, calloused from his work. Conor's had been surprisingly soft.

'D'you think Frank's going to behave himself tonight?' asked Shay.

'We should agree a signal so we can make a quick escape if he doesn't.' Eva was only half-joking.

Shay sighed. 'That would be the mature thing to do . . .'

'You'd better behave yourself,' said Eva.

'You've nothing to worry about. No one wants me, not even my wife. But I'll be keeping an eye on you.'

Eva felt her heart jump. He was grinning as usual. She murmured consolations. He squeezed her hand.

Lizzie and Frank arrived outside Conor and Beatrice's with Georgia and Jimmy in tow. Maya wasn't interested and Jack had plans, or so he said. Frank was happy to let him be, but Lizzie argued Jack should be under the same house rules as Maya. Answering 'out' to the question of 'where are you going' wasn't good enough. It was only a matter of time before Maya demanded the same freedoms and then what would they do? Frank was reluctant to cross the boy, he had enough crap going on. He needs to let loose, he said. She argued he was being sexist. Now at the steps to Conor and Beatrice's, Frank went up to the front door and Lizzie went down the steps to the basement. 'Frank!' she called, 'they'll be in the kitchen.'

Frank pressed the front doorbell. 'That's the tradesman's entrance.'

'You're ridiculous,' said Lizzie. Jimmy and Georgia slid past her and banged on the basement door. 'Great,' said Lizzie, 'now they won't know which door to answer.'

Beatrice came to the hall door. Lizzie could see she was taken aback to find Frank on his own on the step. Beatrice greeted him as usual – a kiss on each cheek – before she saw Lizzie looking up from below. Her relief bubbled over.

'There is everybody! You want to come up or I come down?' she asked.

The basement door screeched open. The children tumbled over Fiach like puppies to get inside. Lizzie went to follow them but feared leaving Beatrice and Frank alone. Watching Frank and Beatrice side by side at the front door, she saw that they were as unlikely a pair as Marlene Dietrich and Charlie Chaplin. Frank's second-hand blue suit was rumpled and baggy. He hadn't shaved in a few days, rarely combed his hair. God love him. In her heels, Beatrice towered over him, contained and unassailable as a politician in a greeting line.

Frank stepped inside the grand hall. Beatrice closed the front door after him and glided down the basement steps to hug Lizzie. She smelled of lemon. Jo Malone probably.

'Are we okay?' asked Beatrice.

'Almost,' said Lizzie, as she handed over a plastic bag of crisps, ice cream and minerals for the kids.

Beatrice glanced at the bag but didn't thank her for it. 'You didn't need to bring anything. I have food for the children.'

Lizzie had seen her offerings disappear many times before, probably into the bin. She used to pretend she didn't care but it was rude. Beatrice wasn't going to get away with it any more. 'The children picked out everything themselves. They'll be expecting ice cream. If you want, we can make sure Fiach doesn't have any.' Lizzie smiled, knowing that no one, not even Beatrice, would torture a child like that.

'Of course,' said Beatrice. 'Come in.' She led Lizzie into the basement, past a guest bedroom, a bathroom, and a playroom, outlining the agenda for the evening. Children would eat first, then they would watch a movie in the playroom – *Asterix at the Olympic Games*, Fiach's current favourite – while the adults ate. She announced that nobody wanted a late night. Lizzie asked herself who the nobody was since she hadn't been asked her opinion.

Every time she emerged from the dark corridor into the open living and kitchen extension at the back of the house, Lizzie felt envy. Upstairs the high-ceilinged rooms were bright, with tall sash windows, honey-coloured boards and deep Persian rugs, but down here the basement was bright and modern with large white tiles, and a wall of black folding glass doors to the garden. Extra height in the ceiling had been gained by digging down. The oversized scale always made Lizzie feel like a child. It was a cold house, she told herself. Children could slip and hurt themselves on the tiles; everything that hit those tiles shattered into a million pieces.

They'd made the mistake of being the first to arrive. Lizzie watched Beatrice disappear into the pantry with the bag of treats. Frank, at the kitchen island, was pontificating to Conor on the wine they'd brought with them and how leaving it to breathe was a good idea, decanting it even better. Lizzie didn't know how much he'd paid for it but suspected it was a lot more than the eight-euro Lidl wine they usually drank. Conor, always polite, smiled and nodded but, when he saw Lizzie, he immediately pivoted to welcome her, leaving Frank stuttering in mid-sentence. He'd opened a bottle of Pinot Grigio specially for her, one she'd enjoyed the last time she was here.

The basement doorbell rang. Unlike Frank, Shay and Eva didn't have notions. As they greeted each other, everyone and everything sounded as usual, the hugs and the kisses, the quick catch-up on the week, their slow, quiet split into men and women. She used to think it was because they all were so happily partnered, they had no interest in flirting with the opposite sex, but tonight it looked like a smokescreen. She drank some more. It wasn't long before the sharp cold wine and Conor's sweet attendance soothed the tensions in her and let her hope that maybe everything was as before.

Conor was having a hard time keeping up with the wine. He'd only have one cork pulled before they clamoured for another bottle. There was one slice of pizza left in the middle of the table – the spinach and goat's cheese. He'd give it another minute and, if no one else took it, he'd eat it. He excused himself to fetch more wine from the garage at the back of the garden. Looking back on his home, he was struck by how unfamiliar it looked – like a dollhouse with the windows lit up. He could see everyone around the kitchen table, caught in a pool of light from the pendant lamp. His usual sense of pride at his house, his friends, his wife, made him feel uneasy. It was a bit like crying at a department store Christmas ad while knowing that an advertising agency had worked very hard to make sure you did.

When he walked back inside, he was hit by a wall of noise – the same argument about the housing market, their falling property values – there was always some new piece of information to be outraged over. He was glad he'd missed it. He was acutely aware of how lucky he was, they all were, when families were being evicted. What did it matter what their houses were worth if they didn't need to sell them? Unless things got worse. And sure, they'd all be ruined then.

'A girl could die of thirst around here.' Eva joined him at the kitchen island with her empty glass.

'Not on my watch.' He filled her glass. 'How's Eliza doing?'

Eva waited for more information.

'The little girl who can't sit still?'

Eva had no memory of telling him about Eliza Bourke. She attempted to bring him up to date but didn't know where to start. 'I'm sorry, I don't remember telling you about her?'

He raised an eyebrow. She put her glass to her lips and took too large a swallow. Wine spilled down her front.

'Oh hell.' Dark drops stained her dress. Conor ripped off a paper towel and handed it to her. He watched as she made a cursory pass over her breasts with the towel. She was overwhelmed by a memory of lying back in his arms. She glanced over her shoulder to see what Shay was doing. He was totally focused on whatever Frank was saying. She turned back to Conor and said, 'I remember very little.' She couldn't tell whether he believed her, but he seemed to accept that she wasn't going to talk about it.

'Do you have any idea how much teenage boys eat? Just wait. I'd start putting some tins of beans aside now, Bea.' Lizzie was laughing but Conor could feel the tension in her. 'We start with a breakfast buffet – half a box of cereal with a pint of milk, a fry, then it's a two-sandwich lunch with all the fruit in the bowl, an after-school meal that looks a lot like dinner and then another dinner eaten with the rest of us. And somewhere in between he snacks on whatever's left in the fridge.' Lizzie had been talking about Jack ever since she'd sat down at the table.

'It only looks like a lot when Maya lives on yoghurt and crackers,' said Frank.

'Is he overweight?' asked Beatrice.

Lizzie shook her head. 'Tall and skinny. Hollow legs. I asked Frank to make up the difference by eating less, save us some money, but he's a pig.'

'True.' Frank picked up the last slice of spinach and goat's cheese pizza. Conor resented his every bite.

'Where did you put him, where's he sleeping?' asked Eva.

'With Jimmy,' said Lizzie. 'We moved Georgia into Maya's room. She's being a complete bitch about it. Nobody should have to live with an unhappy teenage girl.'

'What other kind of teenage girl is there?' asked Eva.

'Watch it. That's my goddaughter you're slagging off,' said Conor.

Eva turned to Lizzie. 'Am I wrong?' Lizzie shook her head.

'Jimmy likes having him around,' said Frank. 'When Jack takes him to school, Jimmy walks himself inside.'

75

'That's an improvement,' said Conor.

'Do you think Paula will pull herself together?' asked Beatrice.

This, Frank and Lizzie seemed to agree on. If she did pull herself together, it wouldn't be anytime soon.

'That's shite,' said Shay.

'If we can help?' said Beatrice. Conor had no idea what she had in mind.

'If you've fifteen thousand to spare, we could send him back to school.' Lizzie spoke without thinking but was taken aback when Frank said, 'Yeah, honestly that'd be a great help.'

Conor blanched.

Beatrice turned to Conor. 'I guess we could look into some kind of arrangement, couldn't we?'

Conor found himself nodding, while thinking *absolutely no way*. They'd never see it again.

For a moment, Lizzie looked thrilled.

Frank placed both hands flat on the table in front of him. He spoke slowly, his South Dublin accent coming to the fore, the vowels slowed right down. 'You don't think I can afford to feed my own children?'

Beatrice muttered apologies. She swore she knew what it was to be poor, swings and carousels, there was no need for embarrassment among any of them. What are friends for? Conor longed for Beatrice to stop; he was fed up with how everyone tried to placate Frank when he was in a mood.

'It's swings and roundabouts,' he corrected Beatrice.

She stopped. 'Same thing.'

'Seriously, it was a joke but thanks for your concern,' said Frank, 'we'll be fine, we've decided to get rid of Maya instead.' Lizzie shrieked. 'That's a joke too, by the way,' said Frank. He smiled at the others one by one, willing them to laugh. When Frank reached Conor, the two men held each other's gaze, a mere second, and Conor did not smile.

'How is it anyway, that you two have kids with other people who are the exact same age?' asked Shay. Eva choked on a laugh, grateful to Shay for his perfectly timed distraction. He had a way of getting straight to the point.

'It was so long ago,' said Frank, 'I can't—'

'Fifteen years and nine months,' said Lizzie.

'—remember.'

'Not this again. Maybe we should get you tested for Alzheimer's,' said Lizzie. She looked around the table, wearing a big smile, but no one would catch her eye. She settled on Shay. 'I was in LA. Frank was here. He slept around and impregnated Paula—'

'One night,' said Frank. 'One woman. One night.'

Lizzie ignored him. 'We broke up and I slept around. Max, Maya's dad, was a friend of Conor's. Maya's six months younger than Jack.' Lizzie held up her glass. 'Any more of this delicious white?' Conor poured her a generous glass.

'Ah come on people, things were different back then.' Lizzie needed Beatrice on side. 'We all slept around, didn't we?'

'A little,' said Beatrice, with a smile that implied there was more than a little.

'I didn't,' said Eva. 'Shay was the first man I slept with. Had intercourse with if we're going to be technical.'

'Yep.' Shay grinned, nodded. 'I taught her everything she knows.'

'Fuck off,' said Eva, giving him a dig.

'Seriously?' said Frank, leaning in. Lizzie's gaze flitted around the table; she seemed to be regretting the turn of the conversation.

'I kissed a lot of dogs first,' said Eva. 'There wasn't much else to do in Drumshanbo on a Saturday night.'

She was smiling, there was no embarrassment. Conor would never have considered Eva prudish, and she wasn't a devout Catholic as far as he knew. It irked him to realise that, like Frank, he was intrigued.

'Most teenage boys, the ones I knew, who also ate too much, were far too interested in each other to be of any interest to anyone else.' Eva was talking to Conor. 'I had no interest in competing for anyone's attention.'

It was only then Conor noticed Shay watching him.

Beatrice was upstairs, peeing in the en suite off her bedroom. There'd been too many nights when either Frank or Shay pissed on the downstairs toilet seat, too lazy or unable to lift the seat up. She wiped herself, then checked her make-up in the mirror. Her teeth were stained with wine. She brushed them again and decided that was enough for the night.

On her way back to the kitchen, she looked in on the children in the playroom. Georgia and the boys were watching *Ninja Turtles* on the television, and the twins were in the corner playing with Lego. A tray of strawberries had been mauled, a few mashed into the carpet. She wasn't bothered. The carpet had been specifically chosen for a playroom and was designed for this kind of thing. She fetched a damp cloth from the kitchen. The conversation around the table had moved on from sex. Shay was talking about his birthday next month and asking where they would go to celebrate. She held her breath, listening. The ensuing silence made her laugh.

When she returned to the playroom, she ran straight into Frank, who'd been checking on the children, or so he said. She suspected he had been looking for her. She shuffled past him to wipe up the strawberry pulp, hoping he would continue on, but when she looked behind her he was lounging in the doorway watching her. A draught blew across her lower back. Her blouse had ridden up, her jeans had slid down and she knew she was showing a builder's crack. She stood up quickly, dragging her jeans up at the same time. Too quickly. The blood rushed from her head, and she swayed. Frank reached a hand out to steady her.

'All right?' He was standing very close, his hand hot on her forearm.

'Dizzy. But okay now.' She shook him off.

'Mama, can we have ice cream, please?' said Fiach.

'We don't have any ice cream.'

'My mum brought some,' said Georgia. 'Chocolate Chip and Raspberry Ripple.' Fiach and the twins echoed Georgia. 'Chocolate Chip and Raspberry Ripple!'

'I'll have a look.' Beatrice sighed; she'd been hoping the children would forget the ice cream.

'And crisps!' said Jimmy.

Frank followed her down the hall. She turned around to confront him and caught him looking at her backside. His eyes met hers. He had no shame.

'It's ludicrous, isn't it?' said Frank.

'What?'

'This pretence.'

'I am not pretending.' They spoke softly, aware of children behind them and spouses ahead. He seemed to be studying her. She tried to keep her expression neutral.

'Did I say you were?'

Beatrice became flustered. 'No . . .'

He had propped himself against the wall, feet crossed at the ankles, like some eighties musician in a back-alley photo shoot.

'Conor thinks it was a panic attack,' said Beatrice.

'What?'

'That it wasn't your heart.' By Frank's expression, Beatrice knew she'd hit a bullseye.

An image returned to Frank: Beatrice backed up against a stone wall. His phone on the ground, ringing. Lizzie's face, smiling at him from the screen. Beatrice rough-handling him. The look of dismay on her face at his limp penis. And the pain in his chest.

'What did you tell him?' he asked.

'Everything. We tell each other everything.' Another lie. But she wasn't going to let this man think he had the better of her Conor.

'Ice cream,' said Beatrice as she walked away.

'You should wear a belt with those jeans, you haven't enough of an arse to hold them up,' said Frank. 'A great arse but you know. Tell Conor I think he's a lucky man.'

Beatrice made sure he heard her laugh before she opened the door and walked into the kitchen. She felt Conor's eyes on her as she took the ice cream out of the freezer in the pantry and lined up five small bowls and spoons. Lizzie joined her at the island. 'I'll give you a hand.' They heard the flush of a toilet and then Frank emerged from the hallway.

'I hope you lifted the seat, Frank,' said Beatrice. Lizzie snickered.

'You'd only be complaining we didn't put it down again,' said Frank.

She handed two of the bowls to Lizzie. 'Could you bring these out to the kids?'

Once Jimmy decided he wanted to go home, that was it. He'd climb on laps, under the table, pick fights, whinge and cry until no one could bear it any more. Tonight though, as soon as he wandered in and declared his want, Lizzie stood up and launched into her thanks and goodbyes. Eva felt they had to leave too; she didn't want to risk appearing to take sides, although no one was suggesting there was anything to take sides over.

In the hall upstairs, they hugged each other goodbye, their farewells much warmer, thanks to the wine, than the arrivals. Frank managed to lean in and slap Conor on the back in a hug. Conor slapped him back. Eva watched Shay give Lizzie an extra-special squeeze and heard him quietly ask if she was okay. Lizzie whispered in his ear. Eva caught Frank watching her watching them. He tilted his head as if questioning was *she* okay? She smiled in return. He shook, laughing without making a sound.

Beatrice pulled open the heavy old door. The night blew in, a sharp, frosty edge to it. 'Thank you for coming.' Beatrice was looking at Lizzie when she said this. 'My friends, I love you for coming.' There was a chorus of why wouldn't we?

Eva shouted a final goodnight as she bounded down the steps after the twins. Georgia raced past her to join the girls.

'Wait,' yelled Eva, while knowing nobody would. Frank threw Jimmy over his shoulder to carry him home. Lizzie and Shay brought up the rear. Eva paused at the corner of Heytesbury Street. Conor and Beatrice were standing side by side on their front steps, arms around each other's waists, waving. With the Georgian arch behind them, they looked uncannily like an American family's Christmas card – wholesome, prosperous, united. Beatrice retreated inside but Conor waited on the step, his eyes on Eva. Then the others caught up and turned the corner, taking her with them.

Jack wasn't home or answering his phone when Lizzie and Frank returned. Lizzie made Frank wait up for him. It was past two in the morning when Frank heard the scratching of Jack's keys at the door. He opened the door and Jack fell inside. Frank, drunk himself – he'd opened a bottle of whiskey when he returned – was amused. Jack worked hard to appear sober, spoke clearly and precisely. The boy was wearing a jacket Frank didn't recognise. When Frank admired it, Jack seemed as surprised by it as he was. They surmised that he must have picked up someone else's jacket by mistake.

'Yes. That's it,' Jack said, as he climbed the stairs, hand on the rail. 'That must be it, yes,' he repeated all the way to Jimmy's room.

17

The Boiler's Banjaxed and the Insurance is Up

Shay carried a chainsaw, a pair of garden shears and a rake down the side passage of Mrs Daly's cottage to her back garden. It was tight; he had to inch sideways like a crab, the rake bashing into his shins with each step. He could feel Mrs Daly right behind him.

'You sure I can't help you, Shay?'

'You'd only send me off balance. There's an art to my madness.'

'Looks like a lazy man's load to me.'

Although ninety, she had the high-pitched laugh of a young girl. Mrs Daly's garden – a square of lawn front and back, bordered with narrow flower beds – wasn't his most demanding job, but it was a regular gig and Mrs Daly bought him Penguin bars for his tea breaks. He'd taken the morning off his big job on an apartment development in Dundrum, to clear up a fallen tree. 'It looks so bare,' said Mrs Daly after he'd finished. The ancient apple tree might have been as gnarly as Mrs Daly's hands, but the blossom in spring turned her garden a delicious pink. 'Funny how you don't see something until it's not there any more,' said Mrs Daly.

It was almost lunchtime when Shay arrived at the site and found it deserted and the gates locked. He scanned the street but there was no sign of any contractors' vans. He had the strangest feeling of having the day wrong. He hoped there hadn't been an accident forcing them to shut the site down. He called McDonagh, the builder, only to have the phone ring out. He then called Mark, a labourer he'd been lunching with.

When Mark answered, he sounded groggy. He'd been up late, drinking his sorrows away. 'McDonagh's gone under. They came yesterday evening, kicked us off site. Locked the fucking gates. Donal left his drill on site, and the bastards wouldn't let him back for it. McDonagh totally lost it, drove his digger out, should've seen him, drove straight at 'em, unfortunately they jumped out of the way.'

Fuck.

'We should've known,' said Mark.

How could they have known? McDonagh had been in the business for years, always had several jobs on the go; one of the few to keep going since the Crash. Shay had assumed that meant he was decent.

The apartment block was aimed at young professionals, yellow brick with glass balconies and slate-grey windows. It was the biggest job he'd ever tendered for, and he'd expected it to lead to more, believed that things were back on track. When the contract was agreed, himself and Eva splurged on a babysitter and headed straight to the pub. McDonagh persuaded Shay he could avoid some taxes if it was a fixed-price contract and included materials. Eva wasn't happy with the arrangement but Shay trusted McDonagh.

His hands were shaking when he rang the nursery to cancel the order and discovered his order had been delivered in full yesterday. Was there something wrong? Shay peered through the chain-link fence and glimpsed a few plants stacked right at the back. High timber hoarding surrounded the site. On the gates was a sign warning that APOCA Security were patrolling the site and trespassers would be arrested. He tried McDonagh again. The phone went directly to answer machine.

He scanned the street, then scrambled up the gates and dropped over the other side. The plants had been dumped in a heap as if tipped straight off the delivery truck. The escaping digger's tracks had cleaved a trough through the stack, obliterating most of the plants and breaking the trees. Rain in the night had turned the soil to mud. All that could be salvaged were a couple of festucas and an ornamental wedding-cake tree. At the gates, as he tried to work out how to carry the plants over the top, he saw a man pass by, guiding a child on a scooter, watching him. It was only a matter of time before someone decided he was a thief as well as a trespasser. He dropped the plants over the fence, watched them smash on the pavement and roll into the gutter, spewing out muddy compost along the way. He threw himself over after them.

Shay thundered down the motorway in his truck, his head full of various iterations of a fuck you McDonagh speech. He hunched over the wheel, flying up behind cars and trucks, pulling out and overtaking, snapping back in lane again. He couldn't afford to stay on the motorway in this mood, he'd kill someone, probably himself. He forced his back against the seat and eased off the accelerator. The abrupt adjustment in speed and the accompanying inertia sickened him.

He stopped by Mrs Daly's and offered her the wedding-cake tree. It was only a foot high now, the trunk splintered, one thin branch left. He told her everything. She was furious on his behalf.

He was emptying a bucket of water around the newly planted tree stump when she came out with a cup of tea for him. 'You've had a bit of a shock haven't you love?' She took him by the hand and brought him inside, sat him down at her little kitchen table. Shay suddenly felt utterly exhausted. Mrs Daly put a sandwich in front of him. Jam and butter. Cut into triangles. His mother, over twenty-five years dead from cancer, used to do the same. The ache of missing her felt as strong as ever. Mrs Daly searched in her cupboards and pulled out a bottle of her Christmas brandy and gave him a dash in his tea. For the shock. He objected that he still had to drive home, but she wasn't taking no for an answer. He heard himself laughing, asking for another jam sandwich, in no hurry to face Eva.

*

84

Eva was in the kitchen helping the girls with their sums when he arrived home.

'You're early?' she said as she leaned over Kate's shoulder. A three was backwards. 'Are you happy with that one, chicken?' Kate stole a look at Ella's homework, then scribbled her three out so hard she nearly went through the paper. Eva put on the kettle. At first she only glanced at him as she put out cups, but his silence made her turn around and give him a proper looking-over. 'And very clean?'

He wiped his damp palms on his jeans and took a breath. 'McDonagh's gone under. Everyone's off site.'

Eva swore. The girls turned in their chairs, unsure what they'd heard. Eva tapped the table to get them back to work. 'What about what he owes you?' Shay told her that it was very unlikely he'd get any compensation for his labour so far, four weeks gone, or for the plants and materials. Eva did her thing, mouth opening and closing, the hint of words moving across her lips but without a making a sound. It was a teacher thing, consider your response before you react. He hated it.

'Well. Next time.'

'Next time, what?'

'You'll do things differently.'

'Finished!' Ella slapped her copybook closed and slid out of her chair. Eva stuck out a cautioning hand. 'That was quick. Should we have a look over, see if we remembered everything?'

'I did already, and I did,' said Ella.

'You won't be able to change anything if you make a mistake. Ask Daddy.'

'I didn't make a mistake,' said Shay, his anger rising.

'Finished.' Kate was off her chair and out the door, Ella racing behind her, annoyed at being pipped.

Eva closed the kitchen door and turned to Shay. 'I asked you not to use our credit card.' She tidied the girls' homework away, putting everything back in their school bags, her movements sharp and fast.

'I would've lost the gig.'

'Doesn't that tell you something?' She was smiling, head tilted, eyes wide, mocking him. 'It wasn't the time to gamble.'

'The job was almost complete. Half the apartments were sold!'

'And yet, here we are.'

Her smile seemed drawn on, like a clown's. If only she'd broken down in tears, then he could've comforted her and assured her he'd make things right. 'You're supposed to be on *my* side.'

'We're on your side, for better or worse. D'you ever think about that?'

Every day, he wanted to tell her, ever since he'd seen the way Conor was looking at her across the table. 'You're not being fair.'

'Shay. It's two months to Christmas. The boiler's banjaxed and the insurance is up in January.'

'I know. I'll make it right.'

She closed her eyes and shook her head slowly.

'What? Say it. Go on. You don't believe I can?'

'No.'

'Ask Conor for a loan, then,' said Shay. 'I'm sure he'd be happy to help.'

'What're you saying?'

'Nothing.' He felt small and furious, like a scolded child unable to understand what they'd done wrong.

'You're being ridiculous.' She closed the door behind her as she left.

'Fuck you,' he said to the closed door.

Eva shouted back. 'We heard that.'

18

Letting the Light Blow

Frank couldn't help thinking of 16mm film when he watched her moving through the empty rooms, her skin gold against the grainy, dark background, the only light coming from the windows, bright white and blowing away the detail of all around them. She didn't seem real; even the feel of her, silky and hard, her buttocks and thighs firm from running, was like an expensive silicone prop. When they lay on their sides on the rough carpeted floor, a corrugation of aging skin would form between her breasts. He adored the tiny folds, the perfect imperfection.

In the beginning there'd been furniture, a bed, a bedspread, but since the house had been put up for sale everything had been cleared out. They lay on the carpet only long enough to get their breath back, then they'd wash and dress and return to their real lives.

19

Beatrice Twomey

It was only a week or two after pizza night when Frank stopped Beatrice outside the school gates. She had dropped Fiach off and was walking back home. It was cold, the ground covered in slippery, rotting leaves, the sky heavy with rain. Conor had left very early that morning to attend a conference in Cork. She hadn't been able to go for a run and it was all she was thinking about. Frank was on his way into town to meet a producer about a new television drama for RTE. They were near the turn-off to her street when the skies opened. They ran to hers, jumped up the steps and hunkered under the shallow portico while she searched for her keys. With their backs to the door, the rain was kept off their faces, their bodies, but it was hitting their shoes with such force, like tiny explosions. They watched a man run across the road, paper bags of groceries clutched to his chest.

'Don't mind me,' said Frank, 'I'll wait here until it eases and continue on my way. Go in, dry yourself.' Beatrice was reluctant to invite him into the empty house. She told herself off for being rude, opened the door wide and stepped inside. Her sweater was soaked; she dragged her arms out of it and pulled it over her head. When she opened her eyes, Frank was inside the hall and standing very close to her.

'Are you cold?' he asked.

She was shivering; the hair on her arms was standing on end. Water ran down her face. Her green skirt clung to her thighs.

When he brought his lips to hers, they were startlingly warm. How she'd been lying to herself. How long she'd been waiting for his hot, still hand between her legs. She stumbled back against the stairs and was forced to sit. He took hold of her hips, her buttocks, pushing her wet skirt up to her waist, and sank his face between her legs. She jolted away from his hunger, fearing being irrevocably consumed. With his head in her hands, she could hold him at a remove, could feel each element, spiky, unshaven face, viscous lips, his tongue moving like a muscle against her, both part of him and not of him. She took him in and held him, heavy and hot against her skin, rising to meet him again and again. The hall filled with the slaps of their skin and their raw and ragged sound. For a time, she didn't have a name; Beatrycze Koslowski and Beatrice Twomey were somewhere else, waiting.

After Frank lifted himself off her, she was only two steps from the top of the stairs. The thundering rain had eased. Gutters dripped. Frank lay zigzagged, halfway up the stairs, breathing heavily, his naked rump peeking out from under his shirt like a half-dressed child. Through the fanlight above the front door, she watched her neighbour picking oranges out of a river racing along the kerb.

'Bea?' said Frank.

She smiled.

He left, still in time for his meeting.

Beatrice showered and dressed. She felt as if she was starting the day anew, the sex as fleeting as a waking dream. They would need to do it again.

20

No Place for Love

A place came up in a private care home in Rathmines, ten minutes away. Conor knew the home to be a good one, had referred patients there himself. He and Beatrice talked about how they would approach Dermot but when they suggested a sit-down chat after Sunday dinner, he knew what was coming. It was Dermot who asked Mrs Farrelly to take Molly for a walk so they wouldn't be interrupted.

'Sure look, I know', said Dermot once the dishes were done and they'd sat down again. 'Your mother deserves the very best. Better than I can—' Dermot's voice shook. 'It's time to take the bull by the horns. It is what it is.' He focused on Conor, unable to look Beatrice in the eye. He swallowed several times as if he was going to speak again. Conor kept taking a breath as if he too was about to say something. But he didn't.

Beatrice took Dermot's hand in hers and that undid him.

'I love her. I tried my best,' said Dermot.

'Ah sure, we know,' she said, unconsciously mimicking him.

Dermot glanced up at her. 'Do you now?'

'Ah sure, I do.'

Conor laughed. Dermot wiped his eyes and smiled.

For Molly's first day in St Agatha's, she sang *I want to go home, please take me home*, to anyone who came in range. She grabbed at arms, sleeves, skirts. *Please I want to go home. Ho-ome.* A nurse gave Molly a doll she nursed in the crook of her arm, and it calmed her. In the second week, Molly stopped talking. Beatrice tried to comfort Conor, but Conor was abrupt. He had expected the disruption to Molly to cause a significant decline, his only concern was that he hadn't pre-pared Dermot well enough. Dermot said little, other than *it is what it is*. When either of them showed any hint of regret, Beatrice would repeat that Molly needed twenty-four-hour supervision and it was only a matter of time before one of them died, either Dermot from exhaustion or Molly from an accident. Neither Conor nor Dermot appreciated her saying it out loud, but she swore she'd say it again and again until they heard her.

Dermot visited Molly in the home every day, morning and evening. After a month, she stopped asking him to bring her home. One could say Molly was happy; she'd forgotten what went before and lived in the now.

They would sell Molly and Dermot's house to free up cash to pay for the nursing home and buy a small apartment for Dermot. As much as Conor wanted to pay for his mother's care himself, they couldn't manage the exorbitant monthly cost of the home and their own mortgage. Dermot maintained he wouldn't have let him anyway. He fretted about the housing market and whether his house would sell at all, fretted about where he could afford to buy, fretted that it would be too far from his old friends and neighbours. And what would they do when the money ran out? What do they do then?

It was Beatrice's suggestion that Dermot move into their guest room in the basement. It was the right thing to do for many rea-sons, not least because of Dermot's unequivocal delight when it was put to him. Privately, Conor was less sure about what it would take to live with his father, but Beatrice was more con-fident about multigenerational living. She'd shared a bed with her baba until she was five. For months after she died, Beatrice had talked to her when she went to bed, unable to believe she'd gone so far away she couldn't hear her.

There were many good reasons for inviting Dermot to live with them, but Beatrice had also convinced herself that Dermot's presence would provide a buffer against any further incursions of Frank's. She underestimated her own desire.

Frank was a different animal to Conor. He knew what he wanted and kept after her. What Beatrice had also failed to foresee was that moving Dermot into their home left the Crumlin house empty until it sold. When she met Frank there, she told herself she'd already transgressed, what difference did it make now.

At home Beatrice was even more attentive to Conor. She would reach for him as he passed, or rest on his shoulder as they watched television. They made love more than ever; she seemed to be permanently aroused. Conor would've needed to look very closely to notice anything wrong. Uncharacteristic tardiness and forgotten arrangements were attributed to the adjustments needed after his father moved in and the work she was putting into selling the house. Fiach was thrilled to have his grandfather around and badgered Beatrice to let Dermot walk him to school and back. Conor remarked on her happiness.

She wasn't lying when she told Conor she *was* happy. Frank scared and exhilarated her. Preparing the house for sale and managing an affair kept her focused and busy. She had no time to ask herself what she was doing; she was only thinking about when she could be doing it again. They had only one rule. This was no place for love.

21

Nobody Makes It Out Alive

Sunday was a soft day, as her mother would say. Eva had been lying awake since 4 a.m. waiting for her family to wake up. Shay snored beside her, mocking her as he took up too much of the bed lying flat on his back, arms and legs wide. She was trapped in that space where she needed more sleep, but knew it wasn't going to come, yet wasn't awake enough to get up and do anything useful with the extra hours. Instead, she was *thinking*. Thinking at 4 a.m. was a dangerous activity.

As soon as the shops opened, she left Shay and the girls in their bed cuddling and went to the bakery to buy something nice for breakfast. The plane trees along South Circular Road were stripped of leaves, stark and black against the white sky; it was colder than she'd expected. After buying a Vienna loaf and four croissants, she found herself on the corner of Conor and Beatrice's street. She had to stop and think about what she was going to say. 'Just passing' was an easily disputed lie; she was at least three blocks out of her way. While Lizzie and herself often dropped in on each other – passing by was reason enough – neither of them just dropped in on Beatrice.

Dermot answered the door. Eva had forgotten about him. She held out her hand. Everything felt uncomfortably formal and a very bad idea.

'Hello, I'm Eva Brennan, Bea's friend. You must be Conor's father?'

'Dermot. Pleased to meet you.' His hand was big and warm, his grip painfully firm as he pulled her inside.

Beatrice was making coffee. She was sweaty and pink, back from a run. On seeing Eva, she startled. 'Eva?' She gave her hair and clothing a quick pull to order. 'Was I, were we supposed to, did I forget something?'

'Relax,' said Eva, 'I was nearby, and I wanted to run something by you. About the school.' Beatrice was happy to offer her opinion on anything but insisted she needed to shower first. She made Eva a coffee before she went, espresso no sugar. Her white kitchen was spotless; nothing on the surfaces, bar a bowl of oranges. The only decoration was a multicoloured sunburst clock on the wall. Eva thought she would go mad if she had to live like this. She glanced at Dermot, who was sitting on the sofa with the newspapers and his tea.

'How's your wife settling into the nursing home?' she asked.

It was the right question. Eva was sat at the kitchen island a quarter of an hour before Conor's name came up. He was out on call. An elderly patient of his had fainted. She remarked it was very good of Conor to go out on a Sunday.

'A shoemaker's children often go barefoot,' said Dermot.

Eva didn't know whether to laugh or console him but then Dermot sucked in his breath and widened his eyes. Like father, like son.

Shay texted with a plaintive – *We're hungry?*

'I better go, my family are waiting for their breakfast.' She waved the bakery bag about as if proof was needed. 'Please tell Bea I'll catch her during the week.'

Eva bounded back up the basement stairs, thinking how charming Dermot was, and ran straight into Conor at the top. He stumbled, lost his balance and almost went down. He had to tell her to stop apologising, he'd never been known for his grace. And no, she wouldn't be the first to laugh at him.

'Sorry for laughing.'

'It's only going to get worse,' he said. 'Be prepared.'

'We'll get you a Zimmer frame.' Behind Conor, a low winter sun broke out of the clouds. She shaded her eyes with her hand but couldn't see his expression.

'Not for a while I hope.' He seemed in no hurry to move on.

'Don't you think middle age feels a bit like a holding cell? After you get the career sorted, the partner, the house, the kids, then what? You're waiting for old age. And sure, nobody comes out of that alive.' Eva regretted her admission, despite the truth of it. Or because of it. She felt flustered. Was this what she believed?

Conor tilted his head and waited for her to elaborate.

'Obviously that's a very conventional way of looking at things,' she added, 'I mean no one put a gun to my head but here I am.' She wanted to stress how much she loved her family, but feared she'd already been so morose that any declarations of love would ring false.

'Have you considered buying a sports car?' asked Conor. He had a little frown between his brows.

She laughed hard. Conor laughed at her laughter. The phone pinged, and she dropped it. It was Shay again – *where r u?*

'Gotta go, tell Bea I'm sorry I couldn't wait any longer.' She stepped away, but Conor reached out and gently held her upper arm.

'Everything passes.'

Everything stopped. She felt as if he had been rummaging around in her thoughts, as if he had seen her childish crush.

'And if it doesn't, there's pills for that.'

It took a moment for Eva to find the lost thread of their conversation. Sports car. Age. She laughed again, embarrassed. 'Don't mind me. I'm not often this maudlin. I try to keep that to the middle of the night.'

'You're not sleeping well?'

'Yes and no.'

'You can call me anytime.' His voice had changed, slowed. He'd gone into GP mode and that wasn't what she wanted from him.

'Thanks, but any more seriousness and I will self-implode. Entrails everywhere. Blood spatter. You don't want to know.'

'Sports car it is then.'

She walked away with a bounce in her step, trying to hold back little giggles bubbling up inside her. At the corner, when she snuck a look back, he was still at his gate, waving her off. Her phone pinged again. She thought it would be Shay, but it was Beatrice – *Sorry! I hope it wasn't urgent. Call me. B X*

Eva could no longer remember what she'd pretended she wanted to talk to her about.

22

Jelly Tots

Every day Conor challenged himself to get through his morning appointments by his lunch break at 1 p.m. and, except for the odd snow day when people bailed, he always failed. Appointments rolled over every fifteen minutes. He was supposed to take ten minutes face to face, leaving five minutes to make notes, tidy the surgery, relieve himself if need be. But the worst secrets were often revealed in the last moments, sometimes when the patient was halfway out the door. He was haunted by a patient who'd drowned himself, leaving a wife and three children. Everyone, including himself, asked how did no one see it coming? By extension that meant any one of his unhappy patients could do the same. The secretary would ring to hurry him up and he would ignore her.

His conversation with Eva occupied him for days after. He was concerned for her; but couldn't decide whether it was depression or a valid response to the world they were living in. And then there was the burden of feeling like one couldn't complain when many had it so much worse. The party's over, everyone said. They'd learned that if you didn't pay attention, keep your head down, someone would turn up and take away everything that mattered to you. And sometimes, they came, even when you were paying attention. *Nobody gets out alive.* He laughed even though it wasn't funny.

Dermot called to ask Conor to drop in on his mother on the way home from work. The day had been long, and Conor was bone tired, but his father insisted. There'd been an accident and Molly had burned herself, would he look at it?

97

At night the nursing home looked like a large, comfortable family home, the two-storey block of private rooms extending discreetly out the back. Conor rang the doorbell and a young Polish nurse let him in. He greeted her in Polish – *Dobry wieczór* – and asked her name. He always enjoyed the look of surprise. She was Lena. When he said Molly's name, she asked him to wait in the foyer.

A parade of wheelchairs and walkers and shuffling slippers passed by. Staff were cleaning up after tea and putting residents to bed; a bad time to visit. He was in the way. He worried a packet of Jelly Tots in his pocket. In the early, befuddled days of Molly's arrival in the home, Dermot would feed the sweets to her one by one, to keep her attention on him, and keep her in her seat. Conor had stopped on the way to buy some, concerned he'd have nothing to keep his mother with him.

Geraldine, the home's manager, greeted him. She was in her fifties, friendly and efficient, and wearing a plastic apron. Molly was absolutely fine, there was no need for concern, she told him. Conor bristled; he didn't like to be told how he felt. Earlier that afternoon, she explained, Molly had knocked a cup of tea onto her lap and scalded her thighs. They'd dressed the area and given her Panadol. She didn't seem to be in pain. Everything Geraldine relayed was reasonable. The accident, he presumed, was unavoidable, the treatment appropriate. Molly was in her room. Geraldine would accompany him should he want to examine her. He couldn't believe she'd need to ask.

'Yes,' he said, 'I do.'

His mother was lying on top of her bed dressed in night-gown and slippers, watching television. The news was on. Her hands were folding and refolding a section of her nightgown.

'Conor's here, Molly. Your son, Conor?' announced Geraldine.

There was always a moment of uncertainty before she recognised him and smiled. He kissed her on the cheek, felt a whisker jab him. She smelled different. Washing powder or soap or both. It was disconcerting. Almost a month had passed since he'd last visited. There was always an excuse, but he knew he was avoiding her. It was irrational, but he couldn't help feeling anxious every time she turned a blank face to him. The day would come when he'd have no meaning for her at all.

'How are you, Mam? I heard you had an accident?'

'No? I don't think so. Did I?'

'Can I have a look?'

'What?' She pulled away from him.

'I want to look at your leg, you spilled a cup of tea?' She looked so confused, he questioned whether he'd been told the truth. But then she gently patted her thigh.

'It's awful sore.'

Conor pulled up the edge of her nightgown. She slapped his hands away.

'Get away out of that.'

'Just a look, Mam.'

'No.' Molly stared at him, holding her gown down. Geraldine stepped around Conor, leaned in close to Molly and spoke to her. While Molly's eyes were on her, Geraldine reached down and gently raised the nightgown. There was a large dressing over Molly's upper right thigh, no sign of scalded skin around the edges. He was struck by how youthful his mother's pale, slender legs seemed, almost like a child's, there was so little muscle.

'I'm sure it'll heal fine.' He stepped away from the bed.

Geraldine straightened Molly's gown, pulled a throw up over her legs. Molly smiled at her like Fiach would when he was being tucked in. 'I'll leave you to chat.' She slipped out the door before he could tell her he wasn't staying.

He sat down in the chair beside Molly; he'd spend a few minutes with her watching the news, something she'd done every evening for as long as he could remember. He commented on the uselessness of the Minister for Health, and the athletes he believed were abusing steroids. Occasionally Molly made a companionable sound, and he was lulled into the sense that he and his mother were watching the news together. After ten minutes, he announced it was time to go home, get some dinner. When he leaned over to kiss her goodbye, she grabbed his hand, brought it to her lips and kissed it.

'Love ya.'

A jolt went through him. Her eyes went back to the television. He kissed her on the forehead.

'Love you too, Mam.'

Conor drove home, lights pixelating in front of him, thinking again, he must get his eyes tested. At home, he kissed his wife and child, reassured his father that Molly was going to be fine, ate a reheated stir-fry, and took himself to bed, all the while remembering the tenderness of his mam's kiss. You have to keep busy, he told himself, or your heart would break. When he undressed, he found the Jelly Tots in his trouser pocket. He laid them on top of the dresser for next time.

23

When the Parachute Fails

Shay's birthday fell on a school day. A present and dinner out was all they'd usually do. But as simple as that sounded, Eva hadn't been able to decide what to buy Shay or where to eat. Every present that came to mind she'd already given him. A watch, a book, a fleece. He was a man of modest habits, and he never asked for anything. It didn't help that this year they were broke. She could save some money by inviting their friends around instead of eating out, but she couldn't do it again – the looking but not looking at Conor, feeling his eyes on her. She couldn't do it to Shay again, not on his birthday.

She decided to buy him a warm hat and scarf, but days were passing by, and she hadn't gone into town. Finding the time wasn't a problem. Since the girls were born her whole life had been about finding time where there was none. Lately small pockets of time had been opening up; a game could occupy them for an hour, or they'd go to someone's birthday party on a Saturday afternoon. She'd sit at the kitchen table with a coffee and look out at the garden. Their single-storey cottage was in an L-shape and their living happened around the crook of the L. Shay called his garden the orphanage. Some people had him make over their gardens as often as they made over their living rooms. Grasses would be out and bamboo in. He'd bring the rejects home, all shapes and sizes, and squeeze them into the beds. She'd watch the light play on the swaying grasses. The nodding flowers. The fat bees at work. Then she'd check her watch and discover it was time to pick up the girls.

At first, these interludes, as unplanned as they were, must've been necessary; a reflexive absence, like falling ill on holiday. She'd confided in Lizzie one afternoon that she was a little concerned by how easily she could disappear into herself, a place where there didn't seem to be a lot going on. Lizzie assured her it sounded a lot like meditation, something she had never managed. Eva wasn't wholly convinced. She was once a bright young thing from a hard-working family. These afternoons felt like an abdication. Even so, Lizzie was right, there was an element of coming to, shedding the frantic busyness of the twins' babyhood, the impossible to-do lists, the noise, external and internal, and just being. Here. Now. Awake.

It seemed she had the time, but not the inclination.

Shay, usually so grateful, amazed to be remembered each year, fell into a strange silence when he opened his birthday card. Yesterday, completely empty-handed, Eva had gone online and splashed out on a tandem skydive for him. There was no time to wait for a fancy gift card in the post, so she made do with printing out the order form. Unfortunately, that also meant the price was in full view.

'There's no refund,' she told him. 'You have to do it.'

'Hell yes. I've always wanted to skydive,' he said. 'But I thought we were broke?'

'So broke it's not going to make any difference.'

'Are you going to jump out of the sky, Daddy?' said Ella. The girls had both drawn a figure with very big boots falling through the sky on their birthday cards.

'I'll jump out of an aeroplane.'

'I don't want you to,' said Kate. Shay pulled her in close beside him.

'Me neither,' said Ella. She climbed over Eva to get to the other side of him.

'It's perfectly safe, lots of people do it, all the time,' said Eva. 'They say it's not like falling, but like flying.' Neither child seemed convinced Shay had the right equipment to fly.

The morning went downhill from there.

Eva helped her class cut out paper snowflakes and stuck them on the windows with Sellotape. Snow had begun to fall outside, and the children gathered at the windows, mesmerised. All except Eliza Bourke, who was walking in a figure of eight around the tables.

Eva was cleaning up for the day when Lizzie, Jimmy and the twins arrived in with a blast of cold air. The snow had stopped falling but the melt was freezing again, and the playground had turned into an ice rink.

'Why didn't you remind me it was Shay's birthday? Are we going out?'

'I didn't get a chance to organise anything,' said Eva. 'I bought him a skydive online.'

'Like jumping out of a plane kind of thing?' Lizzie made a face.

'Attached to someone who is attached to a parachute.' Eva felt judged, like she was being careless with her husband.

'Did you hear about the man who bought his wife an anniversary present of a skydive and then cut the ropes?' Lizzie had a fascination with true crime stories. She claimed it was common sense to find out what people were capable of.

'No! What a way to go.'

'She survived. Every bone broken, that kind of thing. He was done for attempted murder.'

Eva wondered if she knew what she herself was capable of. If Shay died, insurance would clear the mortgage and give her a payout of one hundred grand. There was a strange, twisted comfort in the thought.

Margaret texted, would Eva come up to her office for a chat.

'Will you mind the girls for a few minutes while I see what Margaret wants?'

Lizzie looked around; she'd need to find them first.

*

Margaret asked Eva how she was, how were the girls, how was Shay? Eva, perched on a broken office chair opposite, was sitting a foot lower than Margaret. The curtains were open, and the afternoon sun was shining in Eva's eyes. Margaret had never acknowledged the broken chair nor shown any inclination to close the curtains. A child, sitting in the chair, would experience Margaret as a giant on a throne with a golden halo.

Eva started to answer her questions, but it became clear that what Margaret wanted to talk about was something else entirely. Orla, the vice-principal, would be going on maternity leave at Christmas and Margaret doubted that she'd be back. Third children ruined lives. Buying a new car because you couldn't fit three car seats in the back of a sedan was only the beginning. In other company, Eva might have made a joke about having some children to spare in case you broke one. Margaret wanted her to cover for Orla during her maternity leave. She would then mentor Eva to formally apply for the permanent position when it was advertised. There was an allowance for the extra hours to cover the maternity leave and a raise if she was successful. Margaret urged her to consider the offer; she needed Eva's intelligence and calm beside her.

Eva walked home in the dusky afternoon carrying the girls' backpacks, one over each shoulder, while they skated in little bursts down the icy footpath. She was giddy with the news. She deserved it. The next step, principal. It was why she'd spent two years of weekends studying for a postgraduate diploma in educational psychology. Back then, before the twins were born, she'd believed the diploma was about being the best teacher she could be. But now it was her salary that was keeping them fed and it wasn't enough. This job was a gift, and she wanted to celebrate.

They arrived home to find the house was colder inside than out. Shay must have been gone for some time or he would've intervened. The boiler still needed replacing, but they needed a pay cheque first. She told the girls to keep their coats on and went to adjust the pressure. After a second or two, she heard the click-whoosh of the heating coming back on. She was warming some soup when Shay called.

'Pickmeup? I'm on Walkinstown Road, near the SuperValu. In the truck.'

He was slurring. She guessed he'd been a having a birthday drink. Shay often met up with a mate after a job, to have a few pints, but he'd usually bring the truck home first.

'I've put soup on for the girls. Can you wait?' There was a long silence. 'The house is freezing; the boiler went off again. Shay?'

'Be quick.' He hung up.

After driving all the way down Walkinstown Rd, she hadn't spotted him. They circled the roundabout and drove back. The girls squealed when they spotted the truck on a side street, up on the footpath. She pulled up behind, honked the horn several times, but nothing stirred in the cabin. Having to get out of the car and into the excruciating cold only fuelled her anger. By the time she had walked up beside the truck, she had run most of her speech through her head. She didn't care that it was his birthday. He couldn't afford to drink himself unconscious. Life wasn't about him any more.

Shay was in the driver's seat slumped over to one side sleeping it off. The door was locked. She rapped hard on the window. He lifted his head slowly, as if it were full of lead. She'd made a mistake. Despite the recognisable dent in the side of the truck, she didn't know this man. Half his face was purple-black, hair streaked across, glued in place by dried blood. His left eye protruded like a split plum, his cheek was scraped and swollen, and his bottom lip, split in two, stuck out in a monstrous sulk. In his hand, he held a wrench. A sound erupted from her throat. She ran around the truck, skidded on the ice, and slammed down on her hands and knees. She pulled herself up and threw open the driver's door.

'Shay, oh my God, what happened?' He dropped the wrench and grabbed her hand. It was the hand of a dead man, so cold. His t-shirt was bloody and ripped, baring his chest. She couldn't see a fleece or a coat in the cabin, so she took off her coat and laid it over his chest. 'What do I do, tell me what to do? Will I call an ambulance?'

'No! I'mkay.' His mouth struggled to shape words.

'What happened? Who did this?'

Shay shook his head, made a guttural sound that could've been a laugh. 'Juth bring me home. Pleath.'

'The girls are in the car; I can't let them see you like this.'

He checked his reflection in the rear-view mirror. Then reached over and retrieved a packet of wet wipes from the glovebox. His hands seemed to be unhurt, so that would suggest the beating was all one way. It took most of the packet to clear the blood off his face. He turned from the mirror to look at her.

'You need to go to A and E.'

'No gars.' He sat himself up straight as if to convince her.

'No guards? Why?'

He opened his door and slid out onto the street, dragging himself upright by the door handle. 'I wannagome.'

'Wait.'

Eva ran to the girls, told them Daddy was hurt and they weren't to worry, it looked much worse than it was. When Shay eased into the Fiat's front seat, they stared, shocked into silence. He turned around and growled. They screamed and grabbed each other.

'Don't be silly,' said Eva. 'Put your belts back on.'

The girls did as they were told. Eva leaned over Shay and put his belt on for him. His whole body was shaking. As she drove home, carefully avoiding bumps and potholes, Eva debated whether she should turn around and take him to Tallaght Hospital; she feared concussion or broken bones. She couldn't imagine anything Shay was involved in that would justify risking his health. The heating was pushed as far as it would go but he was still so cold she could feel it emanating from him. In the mirror, she saw the girls were holding hands. They hadn't made a sound.

She flipped the indicator on. 'I'm taking you to St James's.' They were stopped at lights on the canal, three blocks from home; a left turn would take them to the hospital.

Shay grabbed the wheel to prevent her from turning. 'Call Conor.' The lights changed.

Eva drove straight on.

She ran a hot bath for Shay, helped him undress and get in. His body was mottled with bruises from a stray boot, fist, grip. It was ten minutes before he stopped shivering. She trickled water over his face to clean off the rest of the blood. The bath turned pink. The girls fetched his slippers. Eva gave him Solpadeine and warm, sweet tea, and put him to bed.

Conor came straight from work, bringing with him the right balance of serious professional concern and friendly reassurance. He gave Shay a complete going-over. Checked his ribs, his vision, his jaw. Put steri-strips on his split lip. He advised X-rays of Shay's eye socket and skull but admitted he didn't believe they were fractured. Several times he asked Shay whether he remembered everything, could he have been knocked unconscious? Shay assured him he felt every blow.

'Who did this? Tell us, Shay, please?' asked Eva. 'You're scaring me.'

'And me,' said Conor.

'Mucdonna's lazz.'

'McDonagh? Jesus, what did you do?' said Eva.

Shay peered through the slit in his swollen eyelids.

'I mean what happened?'

'They thor I wath wobbing the plath.'

Eva saw the girls peeking in the bedroom door. 'Go to your room. NOW!' The girls scarpered. Eva heard the bedroom door shut behind them.

'What the hell were you doing?'

*

Conor ushered Eva out of the room, into the kitchen, and made her sit. 'You've had a shock. Take a few deep breaths.' He saw an opened bottle of red wine on the counter and poured her a large glass.

Eva took a gulp. 'I thought you were supposed to give sweet tea for shock.'

'If you were an old lady who'd been mugged, maybe.' He rubbed her back. 'Stay here, drink that, let me talk to him.' He left, shutting the door on her too. The dining table was swamped with the girls' backpacks and homework they hadn't had a chance to start. Breakfast dishes were still in the sink, soup bowls were lined up on the counter. Shay's birthday cards were pinned to the fridge with magnets; the falling booted man. Was it possible to manifest catastrophe?

Snow fell softly on the garden. The kitchen light washed over the plants, heavy with snow, sending shadows onto the back wall. Everything was made strange. On the table, Shay's phone pinged. A message from McDonagh. – *There's more were that came from now fuck off.*

She stared at the text, still finding it hard to believe Shay, her gentle Shay, had tried to confront McDonagh. He had said nothing since the day the site closed. And she hadn't asked. Some days it felt like they only communicated in instructions. We need milk. Put on a wash. Who's getting the girls? Yesterday they had no secrets. Eva staggered outside and threw up.

Conor found Eva cradling a second glass of wine.

'So. Why won't he go to the guards?'

'He broke into McDonagh's yard in Tallaght, where he stores tools and equipment, looking for compensation, if not cash, then tools or materials.'

Eva let out a long, hopeless sigh. 'So stupid.'

Conor raised an eyebrow and laughed. Eva felt a wave of wellbeing flood over her followed by an exhaustion so deep she was certain that even if she tried, she wouldn't be able to stand up.

'I don't think he needs to go to hospital,' said Conor, 'he'd only spend the night on a chair in A and E. But I'll hang on for a bit longer to keep an eye on him. Is that okay?'

'Sure.'

Conor picked up her glass and took a good sup of her wine.

'I'm so rude, let me get you one,' said Eva. The bottle was empty. She was already up, opening cupboards searching for another.

'I would but I need to be sober. In case.'

She sat down again with another bottle for herself but when she tried to twist the bottle opener, a sharp pain in her wrist made her cry out.

'I fell on the ice.'

He took her hand and felt her bones, putting gentle pressure along the length of her arm There was no pain, only when she turned her wrist.

'I think it's a sprain.'

She cried. Conor kept her hand in his.

Shay was no longer able to talk when they checked on him; the swelling made it impossible to form words. They propped him up on pillows and gave him more painkillers and a bag of frozen sweetcorn for his face. He held on to Eva's shirt and made some sounds. He might have said – 'I'm sorry. I love you.'

'You're an eejit,' said Eva. 'And I'm still raging.'

It took her a long time to settle the girls. They were in Kate's bed, in each other's arms, tears snaking down their cheeks. It was a fine line between explaining how upset she was about their daddy being hurt and assuring them that he was fine, that everything was fine. She stayed by their side stroking their hair until they both fell asleep. When she emerged, Shay too was asleep, his face even less recognisable, the contusions growing, colours shifting and deepening. She removed the defrosted sweetcorn, took his cold hand, and tucked it under the covers.

In the kitchen, Conor had made himself a coffee and was on his phone, saying goodnight to Fiach.

'Shay's asleep,' said Eva as she sat down.

'I'll wake him in an hour and if he's still good, I'll go.'

'You know when he told me about the contract McDonagh offered him I thought it was obvious he was being scammed but he was so confident and excited I felt so mean doubting him.'

'He wanted to make things right, get some money back for you.'

'For us? That's ridiculous. I would never have asked him to do this. He would know that. He was only pleasing himself because his pride was wounded.' Eva felt a cold streak fly through her. Conor, as always, seemed unshockable. 'No site's going to hire him now. McDonagh will make sure his name is mud.'

'He's not going to be doing anything for a while.'

'No.' Eva added the cost of his time off work to the credit card debt. 'D'you ever feel that marriage sometimes feels more like a small business, bookkeeping, managing the staff, training them up, maintaining the shopfront?'

Conor laughed. 'Except you can't sack the staff for wasting resources.'

'You can. It's called divorce.'

He raised an eyebrow.

She panicked. 'I don't mean literally or here and now. I love Shay. When I found him, I thought he was dead.' Her voice stretched thin, the air gone from her. She was right back in the cold looking at his bloody face. Conor breathed out through his lips as if he'd been right there with her, had seen what she'd seen. She found herself mirroring him. A slow breath in and out. 'I'm an awful bitch. He's hurt and I'm giving out.'

'You were frightened.'

She took another slow breath in and out. 'Yes. But we're going to be fine. Everything's going to be fine.'

'If it's any consolation,' said Conor, 'Bea goes headfirst into fights too.'

'Bea?' She pulled a third chair out and put her feet up.

'I know. Not with us obviously, but if someone crosses her or someone she loves she goes for them. Tradesmen ripping you off, bad drivers, rude people. I don't think she really appreciates that I'm the one who'd get punched first.'

'You would. That's true.' Eva thought herself and Shay were well matched; they would both run at the first sign of trouble. How scared Shay must've been.

'Obviously, I'd prefer they hit me than her but if we could avoid it, all the better.'

Eva laughed. He glanced at her sideways, suddenly vulnerable. She sat up, put her feet on the ground. 'Are you cold? I think the boiler's gone again. It's been playing up.'

'No, I'm fine. Don't you hate winter,' said Conor. 'The dark? The freezing cold. I'm a summer person.'

'Yes! But for the midges.'

'What's the point of midges?'

'I hate people who wear socks with sandals.'

Conor grimaced. 'Note to self: no more socks with sandals.'

Eva laughed and hoped he was joking.

'I don't have time for people who hate the smell of curry chips and will not allow them in the car or the house,' said Conor.

Eva chuckled.

Conor smiled. 'I was thinking, I could get some on the way home, but I'd have to eat them on the street.'

Eva stood up, flustered. It was after ten, and none of them had eaten, not even the girls. 'There's some soup—'

'Hey. Hey. Were you not listening? I *love* curry chips. I should be thanking you for the opportunity to have some.'

Eva giggled again, and feared she sounded a bit unhinged. She needed to eat, or sleep, and she wasn't sure what should come first.

*

They woke Shay. He mumbled something almost coherent. Conor was happy to leave him sleep. In the hall, as he pulled on his coat, he made her promise to call him if anything changed in the night; he kept his phone by his bed.

'Wish him a happy birthday from me and Bea. We'll take him out when he's feeling better.'

They reached the door together. She hugged him goodbye. 'Thank you.'

'Are you sure you don't want some chips?' said Conor, his face close to hers, his hands still around her. She couldn't move with the uncertainty.

'I should sleep.'

He withdrew. Eva stood back against the wall to give him room to open the door and close it behind him. The wall was cold against her back, but her front, from her breasts to her belly to her thighs, could still feel the heat of his embrace. And now the loss of it. She was starving and she hadn't had a chance to tell him her good news. Everyone was sound asleep. No one would know she'd gone anywhere. She grabbed her coat and threw open the door. The cold air made her gasp. At the far end of the street, she saw two shiny red taillights turning left. Of course, he had the car with him. She stood there for a moment, lost, before retreating inside and hanging her coat back up. When she turned, she was startled to find Shay behind her, swaying.

'Conor's gone?' he asked.

'Yep.' Her heart pounded, as if caught out.

'I need a piss,' he said. Eva shuffled him to the toilet. While he relieved himself, she looked in on the girls. They were sleeping, their breath soft and steady. She helped Shay back to bed. She was afraid to sleep with him, afraid of inadvertently hurting him, but he wouldn't let her go. Nestled lightly against the familiar heft of his back, she felt him fall into sleep. He moaned and twitched. She couldn't imagine him not being here in this bed with her. With her fingers twisted in the hem of his t-shirt, she held on tight.

24

Monsters Drawn in Blue Biro

The only room in Dermot and Molly's house that Beatrice and Frank hadn't fucked in was Conor's childhood bedroom. That was where Beatrice found him at 10.45 a.m. on a Thursday. She was late. Fiach had spent the morning complaining of a sore tummy. It had taken her a long time to persuade him he was fine and would regret missing school.

Frank sat cross-legged on the floor of the empty room in a sea of blue plaid carpet, the duvet under and over him like some mountain monk. He was on his phone, his face lit up under the hood. Beatrice stood on the threshold watching him, surprised he hadn't heard her arrive. She traced a line drawn across the inside of the door frame – *Conor. August 1965. 5 ½ years*. It was one of many lines inching up the frame.

'What're you doing in here?' asked Beatrice.

Frank threw the duvet off his shoulders and stood up. He was naked, his penis rudely pointing straight at her. He opened his arms wide, calling her to him.

'Not in here.' She turned away but with two long strides he was behind her, his arms at her waist, spinning her around to face him. She laughed.

'I don't like this room.'

'It's just a room.'

She opened her mouth to explain but he silenced her with his. She couldn't pull away even if she wanted to. His determined grasp was why she was here. His lack of hesitation, his lack of manners, was why she was here. He was all want and she was all forgetting. She was skin and heat and nothing else mattered.

They rooted blindly at each other like baby mammals, only falling away when exhausted but never satiated. Lying on her back, breathless and separate from him on the duvet, she remained uneasy in the room and uneasy with his insistence on being in here.

On the wall behind her, under the window, there were tiny, illicit drawings in blue biro. 'This has nothing to do with Conor, does it?' she asked.

'What, me fucking you? No. I like the man.'

She wasn't convinced this was true. 'You like to beat him.'

'I do,' said Frank.

He lowered his voice like some B-grade villain and let the words roll in the back of his throat. 'Fucking you is about fucking you. In short, all about me.'

'Oh Frank.' She was amused but she didn't like to let him see it.

He rolled onto his side to see her. 'What about you?'

'Same.'

He laughed. This wasn't the first time they'd had this conversation. What is this exactly? What are we doing? There didn't seem to be an answer to that either.

After the rainy morning when Frank had taken refuge in Beatrice's hall, he'd walked to his meeting, his head high, strutting. A huge weight had gone from him. In the weeks since Harwood he'd been haunted by what may or may not have happened, what was started and not finished, what joys he may have missed in his addled state. In his meeting about the television series, he held the floor, referenced Tarkovsky and Ephron, Bigelow and Meadows. He dropped names without dropping actual names. He charmed and amused while never letting them see how desperately he needed to get the job. He'd reached the bottom of their overdraft, which was deep, and Christmas was coming.

The call letting him know he had the gig came the same evening, as he was about to eat with the family. He took his four kids in: Jack, fully acclimatised, sitting at the table between Georgia and Maya making them laugh, his darling Lizzie trying to get Jimmy to stop whinging, and, for a moment, he wanted to beat his chest. The world had been righted, and not a minute too soon. Lizzie was puzzled by how pleased he was, given that he had dismissed the job as selling out. A detective series? Shot like a western in the hills of Wicklow? He was annoyed by her questions. This was money, good money, and might lead to a regular gig if the series renewed. Wasn't that what she wanted, could she not stop nagging him? The gig was only a gig; what he felt was relief more than anything. His joy came from having had Beatrice in his arms and knowing, absolutely, that she wanted him.

Lizzie plagued Frank to let her audition. There was a wisecracking Madame, a part that could've been written for her; a woman in full bloom, both fierce and loving. Getting Lizzie an audition was easy for him, as the director, to arrange but the complications of having her around all day were unpredictable. He couldn't risk it. He suggested to the producers that if they changed the age of the Madame to a much younger woman, almost an equal to her working girls, they could increase the potential for conflict and muddy the moral choices. The producers hailed Frank as a genius. When he told Lizzie, Frank feigned outrage. He blamed the scriptwriters chasing ratings. The scriptwriters, a middle-aged married couple, accused Frank of dismissing older women.

Frank cast the talented Marlie Thomas as the Madame. She was twenty-eight, all long limbs and dry wit. It surprised him that he could appreciate Marlie and her honey-coloured hair, but not actively desire her. He presumed it was because his hands were already full of Beatrice. When he was filming on location or night shoots and couldn't see Beatrice, he was thrown by how frustrated he was. His block of episodes was in post next week, and he'd had no confirmation of further episodes in the new year. The uncertainty was worrying but knowing he would soon have more time to see Beatrice helped.

In the local pub after wrap on a Friday evening, tucked into a corner, he told Marlie about his almost Oscar, about attending the Academy Awards in a monkey suit, about CAA signing him, meetings in Miramax, Fox Searchlight and Paramount, about how everyone wanted to work with him. He didn't tell her that nothing of value came of it, and that the agent dumped him six months later. For Frank and his peers, those early successes, when the whole world was still theirs, were painful to recall, to have peaked and not know that was the peak, to have not relished it because you were too busy looking over the next mountain. It was a conversation that often happened in the early hours, brought about by drink and thankfully buried by drink.

The youngsters, the actors and the crew, didn't know anything about his nomination. To them he was another jobbing middle-aged television director to be tolerated, much like their dads. Thanks to ambitious Marlie and her gossiping skills, soon everyone under thirty-five knew that Frank Durkan once wrote *and* directed a short that *almost* won an Oscar but was too modest to tell anyone. The actors smiled more readily when he arrived on set, crew listened more attentively to his instructions. His hope was that the elevated goodwill would make its way upstairs to the producers. This job made him feel validated and a complete failure for needing the validation.

He made the mistake of asking Beatrice what she would think of him if she'd never seen him before. 'If I walked into a party and you saw me across a crowded room, say?'

She was lying on his chest, still astride him, his penis curling inside her. Their chests slippery with sweat.

'Why?'

'Just tell me.'

'I would think nothing.' Her breath was slow and easy, rising up and down with his. Her hair smelled of citrus.

'Okay,' said Frank. 'I'll go first. I would think she's not Irish – your height, your cheekbones. I would think, she's beautiful like every other beautiful woman.'

At this, Beatrice lifted her head and looked him, trying to ascertain the intention behind his words.

'But then there's the way you look at a person. Direct and shameless. That intrigues me. I think you're fed up with people looking at you and you're trying to deflect their attention by staring at them until they leave you alone.' She sat up again, still looking at him, direct and shameless. She could've been a Bond girl. 'I have no idea what's going on in your head right now,' he said. 'I don't know whether you are about to kiss me or kill me.'

She smiled. 'I think you are funny.'

Funny, Frank knew, was all that was left for men who had gone to seed.

'What do you mean funny? Funny how?' He waited but she didn't respond. There were always these moments with Beatrice. It wasn't that she didn't get his references, she often didn't know there was any reference to get.

'Okay. I would see a middle-aged man. I would know you were Irish because Irish men don't take good care of themselves.' She pressed her hand down on the soft mound of his belly with an affection that surprised him. 'You're hairy, like a peasant, but dark, so you may be some Spanish sailor.' Frank was stung. He was dark and hairy, true, but he had been told he had other, more attractive attributes. Beautiful eyes, for one.

'That's very German of you.'

'You think that where I'm from is me.'

'Isn't it?'

'I was born in Germany but my parents were Polish. We spoke Polish at home, our neighbours were Polish but when we went back to Poland to visit we were Germans. And now I also have a passport that says I am Irish.'

Frank was embarrassed. He knew so little about her and nothing about her childhood.

'Are you Irish in the same way that a man in Cork or Donegal is Irish?'

He laughed. She had a point. 'Tell me everything about you. I want to know,' he said.

She smiled at him like a child who thinks they're being tricked. 'I think you're only saying that to be polite.'

It struck Frank that Beatrice must be lonely. And a second, more difficult thought; she wasn't here for his hairy belly.

'No. I do want to know.'

'I'll tell you why I don't want sex in this room.' She climbed off him and picked up her clothes.

'Because it was Conor's?'

'Yes, but see here,' she pointed to the tidemarks of growth on the door frame. 'This is Conor when he was seven, eleven, fourteen.' She bent down to another line, about three feet off the floor. 'This is Fiach when he was four and then last June on his sixth birthday. On the wall over there, under the window, are some drawings that Fiach did when he was staying over.'

Frank crawled over to see monsters in blue biro on the yellow paint. They had round bellies, short stick legs and huge, many-fingered hands.

'You can pretend I'm a stranger, a foreigner, who walked into a room, and fancies you, but it's not true. You've eaten at my table with my husband and my child.'

Frank sat back on the floor and wrapped the duvet around him.

'You chose this room,' said Beatrice.

'It's just a room. You brought up your husband and child.'

'But don't you see, that's what I'm saying. They were already in here.'

'Ah come on. You think I don't have baggage too?'

'Baggage?'

'Family, responsibilities.'

'I know what baggage is. But you don't carry yours with you. You are careless, without care, like a man who is single.'

Frank stood up, letting the duvet fall to the ground, and snatched up his clothes. That was bullshit. His family took up every other minute of his fucking day. 'The only difference between you and me, Bea, is that you think you're letting yourself down when the truth is, you're here because you need to be. You're lonely. And that's okay.'

She looked stung.

'It's really okay, Bea. And I do want to know more. I'd like to know everything about you.'

She stopped for a moment, considering him. He reached out to pull her close, but instead, she grabbed the duvet, shook it out and left the room to return it neatly folded, to an understair cupboard.

Beatrice was in a hurry to leave. She knew she could've insisted on moving rooms, but she had been afraid of revealing too much to Frank. He'd seen through her regardless. She had wanted to fold herself back into his arms and tell him everything. He wouldn't judge her; more likely he would relish the details of her transgressions. Unlike Conor, Frank had no ambition to be good.

When she arrived at the school Dermot was at the gates waiting to collect Fiach. Dermot seemed small and doddery these days, the collars of his shirts were loose, and his slacks flapped around his legs. His frailty was underlined by the dirty snow and ice surrounding him. November had been the coldest on record. There'd been so many falls on the ice that some hospitals had run out of orthopaedic metal. It felt like the country would never warm up again.

'Thought you were meeting the real estate people? I could've saved my legs,' said Dermot. They both knew he was joking; picking up Fiach was the highlight of his day. He offered his cheek for her to kiss. It was a strange thing to do, but, like a child, she obliged.

'They cancelled. I sent you a text.'

'No, you didn't.' Dermot checked his phone. 'So, you did. I bought you a present.' He held up a small brown paper bag. 'It's a hook for my dressing gown.'

'There's a hook in the bathroom.'

'Yes, that's where I hang it when I have a shower but then I put it on to walk back to the bedroom.'

She was about to remind him that there was no one to see him in the basement if he walked from the bathroom to bedroom in a towel, but then understood it was the cold he was feeling. He pulled the hook out of the bag, as if showing it off. It was Victorian pastiche, brass.

'Is there something wrong with it?' he asked.

'No. No.'

The bell rang. Dermot was off like a shot to get to Fiach before her. Beatrice saw Lizzie coming down the street, waving. Smiling.

'Hey darling, how are you?' asked Lizzie, kissing her on both cheeks. 'We have to talk about Christmas, are we going out, are you doing New Year's? They say it's going to be a white Christmas.' Lizzie was bouncing up and down, banging her hands, her cheeks flushed pink like a child in a vintage Christmas card. Lizzie's obliviousness set Beatrice's teeth grinding. Get your house in order. What she wanted was for Lizzie to take charge and demand an immediate end to the affair, because it didn't look like Frank or herself were able to do anything about ending it anytime soon. While she'd never imagined herself having an affair with anyone, and certainly never with Frank, she now wondered how she'd lived without being in one.

'I don't know. Will Shay be well enough?'

'Oh, what a nightmare. Poor Shay. He looks like a truck hit him.' Lizzie looked like she might cry. 'We have to do something for his birthday.'

'We sent a hamper,' said Beatrice.

'Oh, we could have all gone in on it?'

Beatrice imagined that if they had, they would still be waiting for Frank and Lizzie to pay their share. 'Sorry, sorry. I must hurry, I promised Fi we'd go somewhere today.'

'*Somewhere?*' said Lizzie, recognising the brush-off.

'Yes, the movies. In Rathmines.' Beatrice checked her watch, then hurried over to Fiach and made a fuss of doing up his coat and pulling up his hood. Fiach was telling his grandfather about his day and wasn't impressed by her coming between them. Fiach took Dermot's hand, leaving Beatrice to walk behind them. She could feel Lizzie's eyes on them but didn't dare look back.

Before she could stop him, Dermot had screwed holes in the oak doors and put up his hook. 'That's not going anywhere,' he announced. He tugged on the hook, already holding his frayed, grey dressing gown, to demonstrate. Beatrice said 'nice,' walked into the kitchen and made a lot of noise preparing food for the three of them. Dermot's quiet insistence on putting the hook up annoyed her. The single brass hook in a house of chrome annoyed her. She knew Conor would wait until his father died before he'd let her replace the hook. He wouldn't want to annoy his dad. And that annoyed her. Her teeth were clenched. She stopped and made herself do some deep breathing. She'd caught herself checking for exits when she entered rooms, something she hadn't done for years. A juice cleanse, some yoga and meditation would ground her. Frank was getting under her skin, but she didn't know how to cleanse herself of him.

25

The Golden Boys

Every year Lizzie prayed for a proper white Christmas with snowdrifts and log fires, hot whiskeys and snowmen. This year the snow had been so heavy the schools had to close a week early. All over the neighbourhood, snowball-fighting gangs had formed. Every twenty minutes a child ran into the house, leaving the door open, a puddle of melting ice behind them, looking for a bump to be kissed better or a pair of dry socks. Lizzie wasn't complaining; everything was magical, and the kids were deliriously happy.

And every year Lizzie swore next year she'd do things differently. She'd wrap the presents way before Christmas Eve, she'd tell herself there was nothing wrong with frozen vegetables and Christmas pudding from the supermarket. Yet every year she would be up until 3 a.m. chopping, stuffing, wrapping, putting stockings out, collecting the carrots left out for the reindeer, then falling into bed exhausted only to be woken a minute later by small, overexcited people to spend the day half-crazed with sleep deprivation and liable to put the turkey in the hot press instead of the oven. This Christmas was looking no different but for one lovely thing – Jack and Maya. They took on the 6 a.m. shift, wrangled Jimmy and Georgia into their outdoor clothes, made an igloo, and then peeled potatoes.

It was a true Christmas miracle, thought Lizzie, as she sat up in bed with her cup of tea. She'd no idea who influenced who and she didn't care; this was the best gift ever. And she told them so.

Santa brought Jimmy two nerf guns as long as he was tall, one for him and one for an opponent. Georgia had asked for a science set and a rope ladder. They didn't know that she intended to use the ladder as an escape out her first-floor bedroom window. From what? they asked. Georgia glanced at Maya but said nothing more. Frank tied the ladder to the swing set, a compromise prompting the only tantrum of the day. 'That's a ladder to nowhere!' cried Georgia.

Since Frank had been working, Lizzie bought half a dozen bottles of prosecco, an M&S Christmas pudding with brandy butter, and Belgian chocolates. Several glasses in, she counted her blessings. The turkey was browning. Frank was doing a fine job of curating Christmas cooking music and flirting with her. Georgia and Jimmy were in the living room watching a movie while gorging themselves on chocolate. And Frank, dear Frank, had gifted her a cream cashmere scarf. It was the most luxurious thing she'd ever owned, let alone worn against her skin. She'd admired Beatrice's pale-blue scarf weeks before. Christmas in a four-star hotel was still her ideal – but this Christmas Day came a close second.

Jack returned earlier than expected after visiting his mother. His stepfather had remained in India, something to do with visas. He was starving. Paula had bought croissants for his Christmas breakfast, only one each, as she was joining her friends for lunch. Jack assured Lizzie Paula was fine, in good form and sober. He called everyone into the kitchen for presents. Georgia and Jimmy lined up on either side of him.

'I'll have one of those. Please.' Jack pointed to Lizzie's prosecco.

Lizzie hadn't yet had to consider when they would allow the children to drink with them. 'Why not?' she said, as she poured Jack a glass. 'It's the one day of the year anything goes, bar violence and stealing other people's toys.' She eyed Georgia.

'I lent it!'

'You mean borrowed, eejit,' said Maya. 'I'd like to try a prosecco too.'

'First time?' teased Frank.

'Yes,' said Maya.

Jack coughed. Maya, sitting next to him, gave him a jab in the ribs.

'What was that for?' said Jack, all innocence.

'I've never had a prosecco,' said Maya.

'I didn't say you had,' said Jack.

Lizzie was struck by Jack's confidence, how charming he could be. It was Dublin's southside, the private schools and big houses, that gave them their swagger. Maya had her own moments of entitlement; her father brought her to fancy restaurants and sailing club lunches, but thanks to where they lived she had retained her own brand of awkward, urban scepticism. Frank was the king of swagger, regardless of his relative poverty in adult life. Lizzie grew up on a farm with her four brothers and all of them understood nothing was certain until the crop was in and even then a tractor could break down, a field could flood. Yet as often as things went against you they could also go for you. Frank was happy to live as if there would always be plenty but in practice, it meant they simply used up their plenty sooner than expected. Lizzie worked hard to hold on to her optimism.

Jimmy aimed his Oliver Twist face, hands cupped under his chin, at Jack. 'Present please. Pretty please.'

Lizzie had no idea where Jimmy had learned how to beg like this and hoped it would soon pass. Jack handed his presents around. One each. The wrapping was abominable. No folded corners, Sellotape used like string. At first they laughed, then the excessive tape made Jimmy cry. Scissors were brought out. For Frank, there were top-of-the-range headphones. For Lizzie, a gold bracelet, heavy with exquisite charms. For Maya, an iPhone 4. And iPads for Georgia and Jimmy, who jumped up and down, hugged Jack and shouted out their good fortune.

Lizzie, Frank and Maya shared glances as they tried to figure out how to react. No one seemed to be breathing. Lizzie leaned forward and placed her hand on Jack's. She slid the bracelet across the table. 'It's gorgeous, sweetheart, but I can't take this, it's too much.'

'Oh, it's not real gold,' said Jack. 'I wish.' He pushed the bracelet back to her.

Lizzie examined the bracelet again. It was the best fake gold she'd ever seen.

'It's from eBay,' said Jack. 'Second-hand. But don't worry, I checked everything works and the iPads and iPhone are unlocked.' He spoke without hesitation.

'But even second-hand, a 4 is over two hundred euro,' said Maya. She turned the phone over and over, as if looking for compromising scratches. There were none.

'I'm an excellent negotiator. Anyway, Mum says it's rude to ask the cost of a gift. Happy Christmas, from me.' This was delivered without a smile.

'Oh Jack. You didn't need to buy us anything. You're family.' Lizzie tried to embrace him, but he ducked down to his back-pack and pulled out a bottle of champagne. Moët.

'This is it. I promise.'

Frank came over and gave Jack a one-armed, back-slapping hug. 'Thank you.' Jack hugged him back, then gestured towards Lizzie and Maya, expecting the same. Maya turned away.

'It's too much,' said Lizzie.

Later, Frank admitted to Lizzie that he didn't think it was worth the drama of taking the iPads off the kids, but he had tried to persuade Jack to take back the headphones. Jack refused again, said he felt he owed them. Lizzie felt awful – the boy already had their love; he didn't need to pay for it.

Maya retreated to her room for the afternoon. She had claimed the bottom of the new second-hand bunk beds and spent most of her time hidden behind home-made curtains. Lizzie wasn't going to stand for it. Not today. It was time to watch *It's a Wonderful Life*. 'It's a family tradition. You can't say no. What's that?' She picked the iPhone out of Maya's bin.

'I don't want it.'

'You can't throw it away.'

'I can't give it back.'

'He could sell it on and get some of his money back.'

'Mum. Seriously?'

Lizzie plonked herself down on the bed beside Maya. 'Tell me what's going on.' Georgia strolled into the room and jumped up on the bed. 'Not now Georgia, I'm talking to Maya.'

'I won't say anything. I'll just sit here,' said Georgia.

'There's more crisps in the cupboard under the sink,' said Lizzie. Georgia disappeared.

'You're such a bad mother,' said Maya.

'Excuse me, you turned out perfect, so I can't be that bad at it.' Maya tried not to grin. 'Spill?' said Lizzie.

'Jack has no money. Paula drained his savings account months ago.'

Lizzie didn't know what to say. She was shocked that Paula could do that to her son, but was more fearful about the state she must be in.

'I had to lend him a tenner last week.'

'Could Paula have bought the gifts?'

'Then why would she take money from his account?'

'Where did the stuff come from then?'

Maya gave her a look that said – you know the answer, please don't make me say it out loud. 'Seriously, Mum? They're STO-len? It's all stolen.'

Lizzie felt faint.

Lizzie didn't get Frank on his own until they went to bed.

'Maybe he had another account somewhere?' he said. 'Maybe Paula had done it before, and he'd wised up?' Frank was clutching. He was as reluctant to believe the goods were stolen as Lizzie was.

'Maya thinks it could be a thousand euro worth of stuff.'

Frank didn't look surprised. 'I'll talk to him.'

'When?'

'Let him have his Christmas. This morning was hard for him. Paula was drunk when he got there. She passed out while watching *Elf*. That's why he came home so early.'

Lizzie felt her eyes well up. 'The poor kid.'

'I called her this evening. She made some excuse about antihistamines making her sleepy. I'll go round with Jack tomorrow after Mum and Dad's.'

Frank climbed into bed and pulled back the covers for her. 'Come on, I'm wrecked.'

'I love it when you talk dirty.' She slipped in beside him and he pulled her close.

'I like you in an apron,' he said.

'Get away out of that.' Lizzie felt herself sinking into sleep in his arms. She too was exhausted. 'Where or who could he have stolen them from?'

Frank made a noise. Could've been 'I don't know' or 'not now'; either way Lizzie didn't have the energy to ask again.

Tradition demanded Lizzie and Frank spend Stephen's Day with Frank's parents. Rosemary and the Judge, also known as Robert, had never been interested in spending Christmas Day with over-excited grandchildren. Of Lizzie's brothers, the two who hadn't emigrated had conceded to their wives' families and they never spent Christmas together. Her parents, frail dotes, were passed around every year. Next year would be Lizzie's turn again.

Lizzie enjoyed visiting Frank's parents far more than he did. Rosemary and Robert were charming conversationalists and generous hosts. In their house, Lizzie's coat was hung up for her and her glass was never empty. They lived on a Victorian square in Dun Laoghaire, three storeys, large sash windows, gardens to the front and back. The house was well past its best – there was a stink of damp in the basement and the white woodwork had turned yellow. When Frank stepped through the front door, he shrank into something akin to the fifteen-year-old self he'd once described to her. Sullen, hunched, with a fine, sarcastic commentary on proceedings; that's if you could decipher the mumbling.

They had pears poached in wine for dessert. The children, including Maya and Jack, were offered jelly and ice cream.

'I like a good fruit fork. We should get some fruit forks?' Frank waved his tiny silver implement at Lizzie.

Rosemary, a small, thin woman, continually in movement, ignored her son. She was also intermittently deaf. Kept her sane, she once confided to Lizzie. Frank would throw out comments like confetti in the hope something would land. Lizzie scolded him; Rosemary's steely constitution might be enough to withstand his childish snipes, but she was sure Frank's bloody-minded determination to get a reaction was corrosive in and of itself. Frank believed his mother had no feelings for him one way or another. He had heard her many times extolling the benefits of boarding school to anyone who'd listen. Frank, being an only child, needed the company of other children. His sense of self, she'd opine, was unfortunately too robust. As far as Lizzie could tell, Frank was like his father, Judge Robert Durkan, demanding, absolute, and never not in charge. Father and son also had the same dark eyes, essential to their powers of persuasion.

The kids endured another lottery round of presents. Always hit and miss in Robert and Rosemary's. This year's seventies-inspired minidress wasn't on Georgia's list, but Maya loved her pearl earrings. Jimmy would enjoy his books when she read them to him. Jack was never going to wear the blazer they bought him, unless someone died before he grew out of it. His attendance at the Stephen's Day lunch had occurred no more than a handful of times over the years. This year, Jack's newly acquired height and his fresh, flirtatious charm had transformed him into the star of the day. Robert guffawed. Rosemary giggled. Frank basked in Jack's reflected light, as if Jack was an expression of his true self, a self they had failed to appreciate first time round. Maya, on the other hand, seemed to have taken over Frank's role as sulky fifteen-year-old; not a stretch for her. But today was different – instead of her ire being directed at the world and everything in it, she directed it at Jack. Everything he did was met with a sneer.

No matter the gales or the lashing rain or today's bitter cold, after Stephen's Day lunch the family walked Dun Laoghaire's mile-long pier to the very end and back. Robert and Rosemary stayed back to clean up. They didn't enjoy the crowds on the pier. Lizzie knew they meant them. She usually spent the walk yelling, her heart in constant palpitations, as the children zig-zagged to the edges, where the dark-green sea was waiting to swallow them up. *Come away from the water. Too close. Too CLOSE!* Today was even worse, the paving stones slippery with pockets of ice. Jack took charge and kept himself between Georgia and Jimmy and the sea, expertly herding them. Maya dawdled, scowling under her hoodie.

On the walk back, hand in hand with Frank, Lizzie asked when was he going to confront Jack.

'It's too late to say anything.'

'But you said—'

'You ask him if you want. But what's he going to say? Yes, I stole everything, rifled through some handbags? Shoplifted? He's gonna say no, and what're you gonna do then? Water-board him?'

Frank did have a point.

'Besides, you've been wearing that bracelet all day.'

Lizzie didn't want to give the bracelet back. It was warm and heavy on her wrist. It was lush. She wanted to be able to wear it without guilt. She could already appreciate how useful the iPads were to keep the young ones quiet. She hoped Maya was wrong. But if Maya was right it would be much worse to do nothing. Was it her problem, though? Really? Could she even be considered Jack's stepmother when she had spent so little time with him? Jack was Frank's responsibility. It wasn't for her to intervene.

Jack ran in circles around them, chasing the children away from the sea. It had turned into a game where they'd inch closer and closer to the edge, prompting Jack to chase them away. Even Maya had begun to smile.

26

The Tree

Two weeks before Christmas, Beatrice found a grubby old duvet in her hall. She would never have mistaken it for one of hers – it was polyester and pilled. She picked up the duvet, intending to dump it out the back until she could find out who it belonged to. It had an odour, musty and something else. She sniffed again and her knees went from under her. If she hadn't been able to grab the banisters, she might've tumbled down the stairs. It was her own lemon soap. As she willed her heart to stop pounding, she listened carefully to the chatter of Fiach and Dermot in the kitchen. Nothing seemed to be amiss.

'Hello. I'm home.' The effort to keep her voice steady made the words sound ridiculous. Fiach flew up the stairs and wrapped himself around her legs.

'Mummy!'

She pulled his little round head close and held it to her belly.

'We're putting up the Christmas tree. I put the star on the top. Granda lifted me up. Daddy made it when he was a little boy. Come see.'

He took her hand and led her down the stairs.

Dermot was on a ladder, finishing the tree off with strands of coloured tinsel. He briefly turned around and greeted her. 'Hello, love.'

He knew nothing.

The tree had been delivered that morning. Dermot had taken the bus to his old house to look for his Christmas decorations, stored in the attic and forgotten in the move. He was look-ing for the thingamajig they used to pull the attic ladder down when he found the duvet in the under-stair cupboard. It was the only thing on the shelves, he told her. An odd thing to have been left behind. He didn't know what to do with the duvet, so he carried it home on the bus along with the decorations.

Her relief was such that she didn't mind that he'd decorated the tree without her. She didn't mind the faded cardboard decorations from Conor's childhood. The scrappy tinsel. The yellow cardboard star. Conor would enjoy seeing them. Dermot had saved Molly's favourites for a small artificial tree he'd bought for her room.

'She probably won't recognise any of it.' Dermot's eyes were welling; it happened often when he spoke of Molly, but she'd never seen him cry.

'She will like it, I'm sure.'

They were going to bring Molly home for Christmas Day. Every morning Dermot came to the kitchen with thoughts on how to make it go as smoothly as possible, to keep her calm and happy. That's why he wanted the Christmas tree to look the same as it used to in theirs. Beatrice allowed that Molly's happiness, and by extension Dermot's, was more important than any traditions she'd established. Who was she to ask anything of this family when she was treating them so carelessly?

She stepped back, fearing Dermot would smell her shame.

The tree stood crooked, the star on top leant to the left, the whole effect balanced by an excess of decorations on the lower quadrant of the right side, all that was in Fiach's reach.

She clapped. 'It is the best tree I have ever seen.'

On Stephen's Day, Frank texted. He had a couple of hours, early evening, could she get away? She didn't reply. She was still suffering waves of the sickening shame that she had felt in the hall, holding the rancid duvet. Fiach complained about her being overly affectionate. Too much grabbing, he said. She watched Conor with his father, watched him sit with his addled mother, play with his son, watched his tenderness and care. His silly jokes – she'd had to assure him she was smiling inside – made her feel like crying. It wasn't that she had woken up and discovered how much she loved him, she loved him much the same as before. Conor and Fiach, her home, Dermot, their morning porridge, were more important to her now than her parents' house ever was. This was the fabric of her life. She was terrified of losing it.

27

The Snowman

It was in that lull between Christmas and New Year, those dark, nothing days, that Conor kissed Eva.

It had been a quiet, strained Christmas. They did everything to ensure Molly would be comfortable and happy but on the day itself, it was like having a stranger to lunch. Dermot called it a success but then Stephen's Day, for the most part, he spent alone in his room. He was grand, he told Conor, just resting.

For the last few years Conor and Beatrice had hosted a New Year's Eve party with a caterer, DJ and fireworks. Beatrice's hotel experience meant she was good at parties, the organisation and setting the scene. This year she'd been slow getting started and then Dermot's move and the house sale had taken over her spare time. They had a few invitations to New Year parties, but Dermot had no interest in going, and they weren't going to leave him on his own. For once, she let Conor decide. He cancelled everything. He'd never liked New Year's Eve. There was way too much expectation; as if everyone was going to be sprinkled with magic dust, the sins of the past year wiped away, their flaws revised, in time for the incoming year to change everything. The clinic enjoyed an upsweep in appointments of people wanting their health assessed before they began a new exercise regime. He liked best the middle-aged women who came in looking for diet pills. It was honest and self-aware in the way the new gym members weren't.

Conor was out walking Jaro, who was sniffing every tree, bin, corner, when they passed a little restaurant on Montague Lane. A crowd of revellers spilled out over the footpath, smoking.

The women sparkled in sequinned clothes, the cloud of smoke and fog bringing a sultry otherworldliness. They were totally unaware of anyone else, laughing and gesticulating. He picked up Jaro, fearing a stiletto going through him, and stepped out onto the road to avoid them.

'Conor!' Eva came flying out of the group. As she hugged him, he saw a flick of her finger as a half-smoked cigarette fell to the ground. Her lids were sleepy, her mascara smudged.

'Didn't know you smoked.'

'Only on Wednesdays.' Lurching forward, she leant in close to Jaro and rubbed his little head. 'Who's a good boooooy? Huh? Huh?' Jaro wriggled in Conor's arms; he was always nervous around drunk people. And she seemed to be very drunk.

'It's Orla's leaving do. Maternity leave. Her last day at school was meant to be the last day of term but then the snow and you know the rest. Come in, have a drink. We might need you. I swear she looks like she's about to burst. I don't think I'm up to delivering any babies.'

'Hot water and towels.'

She giggled. 'Come in, join us. Aisling's here. And Martin. Fifth class? You know most of them.'

He gestured with Jaro, knowing he wouldn't be let in, thankful he had an excuse. There was no way anyone could catch up with a group of drunk teachers.

'I'll put him in my handbag. It's big. Holds everything. Stay here, I'll go get it.' She turned to go inside. He took her arm.

'Eva, no. It's not Jaro's kind of scene.'

She stood in front of him, suddenly deflated. 'No. you're right. I think I need to go home.'

'Will I walk with you?'

She returned with her bag and her coat and let him hold her bag while she put her coat on. He buttoned her up to the top and pulled up the collar. She watched him. Her shining eyes were all he could see among the wool and the hair.

'How's Shay?' he asked.

'He's fine. You can't help yourself, can you?'

He stopped, no idea what she meant.

'Looking after people.'

He apologised as a reflex and then felt embarrassed. It was true, obvious even. In the clinic his inclinations were totally appropriate, but outside the clinic it was different. He'd been caught out before. Not everyone wanted or needed a hand up onto the bus.

She hooked her arm in his. 'It's okay. I like it.'

It was a twenty-minute walk to Eva's house. She kept her arm in his, sharing his warmth, until they were startled by violent crashes around them, and they'd pull even closer. The big freeze had lifted, and the world was thawing around them. Everything dripped. Blocks of ice slid off roofs, bringing gutters down with them. Halfway down Eva's street, Jaro selected a parking meter. They both stopped to watch him – his careful sniffing, his fine three-legged balancing, the spray of urine and the shake of his little tush. Conor turned to Eva meaning to say his farewell and found her face was very close to his. And then her lips. Warm, dry. Her tongue moving across his mouth. He could taste alcohol and cigarettes. It was so strange, he didn't like the taste of cigarettes, but he was unable to move away from the feel of her lips on his, her tongue and his tongue rolling over each other. She stepped forward and her whole weight leaned against his, her breasts apparent through their heavy coats. They kissed as if they might go on for ever. He felt her sliding down, her legs giving way, and grabbed her before she sat on the ground.

'My legs've gone to jelly.' Eva stepped away from him, looking at her legs, as if they might appear as they felt. 'Sorry,' she said, 'I haven't kissed anyone but Shay in twenty years.'

'I've never made anyone collapse before.'

She smiled and turned away. He watched her walk past the next three houses and turn in to hers, carefully closing the black iron gate behind her. At the door, with her key in the lock, she glanced back briefly, a serious expression on her face, before she went inside. Conor hadn't moved. He wasn't sure what had happened or what he was supposed to do. When Fiach tasted his first ice cream as a toddler, he'd buried his face in it as if he could inhale it. That's what kissing Eva had felt like. He was uncomfortably aroused in his jeans. He rearranged himself, and then, with a little tug on Jaro's lead, turned back for home.

The house was quiet, Fiach and Dermot long gone to bed. Beatrice was in the living room, in front of a fire, watching a movie and drinking wine. The lights were low, the curtains pulled. She sat with her knees tucked up on the sofa, holding on to a pillow. He took her glass out of her hands. He needed to get rid of any trace of Eva's cigarette.

'Will I get you one?' asked Beatrice.

'No, I'll just drink yours.'

From behind the sofa, he could see her breasts loose under her linen t-shirt. He put the glass down on the table and leaned over her, his lips lightly brushing her neck. She sighed and turned her face to kiss him.

2.27 a.m. and Conor was still awake. The room was as dark as it could be, cocooned by heavy velvet curtains. There was no sound from Beatrice, asleep beside him. He told himself the kiss with Eva was only a kiss. These things happen. She was drunk. He was happily married. He wasn't looking for anyone else. He felt no need of anyone else.

What Conor remembered of Harwood was the ease that came over him when he was alone with Eva. For much of the evening before, despite the drink, his imposter syndrome had left him feeling that everything that came out of his mouth was a lie of some kind. He was intimidated by the oily gentry looking down on him from the walls, the shelves of leather-covered books and the stiff, lumpy furniture. The air felt thick with ancient layers of human skin cells. Yet the others had looked perfectly at home. They moved differently, lounged differently, luxuriating in the environment. Frank, birthday boy and the centre of their attention, inhabited the space as if he had stepped down from one of the paintings on the wall. But when it was Eva and himself in the library, he forgot where he was.

His desire hadn't been sated by having sex with his wife; instead, it had been stoked; the whole time he caressed his wife, he was tasting Eva's mouth on his.

The next morning, Conor left Beatrice and Fiach at the swimming pool and went to the nursing home with Dermot. Dermot greeted the staff by name and many of the residents greeted him back. They found Molly in the sunroom, sitting in an armchair with a small table in front of her, colouring an A4 printout of a farmyard. Her hair was parted to the wrong side and her curls brushed out. She looked thinner – hollowed face, bony hands – but that could have been an illusion, swamped as she was in an oversized cardigan that Conor didn't recognise. She tilted her face for Dermot's kiss. Tolerated Conor's. Keeping a bright chatter all the while. He wasn't sure she knew who he was. They pulled up chairs to sit on either side of her. She was colouring with the kind of focus she used to apply to the crossword. So far she'd done the animals – a purple cow, red dog, green duck.

Dermot talked about the weather, mild, cloudy; how Fiach and he were building a Lego castle, a gift from Santa; Beatrice's cooking – her apple tart was good but not as good as Molly's. 'It's all about the butter,' said Molly. Dermot winked at Conor. Conor wasn't sure if he was indicating that was a conciliatory lie or warning him not to pass his opinion on to Bea. Dermot tried to include Conor in the conversation by talking about all the things they were going to do together. Conor smiled and nodded, but they'd been running through the list for some time and done nothing, no match in Croker, no fish and chips at the Bull Wall, no walk up to the Hellfire Club. Conor apologised. He was tired, end-of-year exhaustion and all that.

'Jaysus, I'm not complaining. Don't worry about it.'

Dermot pulled out the Jelly Tots. Molly stopped what she was doing while he tore open the bag with his teeth. He fed her the Jelly Tots one by one. Molly named each colour as they came out of the bag. Red. Yellow. Green. Dermot offered the bag to him. Conor didn't think his mam cared one bit where her Jelly Tots came from, but he took the bag and held one out. Molly opened her mouth wide. Her front teeth were gone. Conor was so surprised he dropped the sweet. He picked it off the floor and put it on the table, intending to throw it out. Molly picked it up and ate it.

'Orange,' said Molly.

'Where are your teeth, Ma?'

Molly grinned, her mouth open, her tongue poking through the gap. 'Don't know.'

'She kept losing her bridge. It's in her drawer, for special occasions, but better out so she doesn't swallow it.'

Two months in the nursing home and his mother had been reduced to a caricature of old-womanhood, one wart short of a fairy tale. Conor stood abruptly, and announced he was going to the toilet. After, as he washed his hands, he told himself she wouldn't know if he was there or not. He found a nurse to let him out; the nursing home had passcode locks on every entrance to prevent escapes. There was a bench in the gardens, where he sat and prepared a lie for his father.

Tiny brown birds skittered across the gravel, pecking at something he couldn't see. Conor checked his phone, moving carefully to not frighten them away. There was an email from Harwood House advertising a special dinner, bed and breakfast deal, almost half the price they'd paid in September. Business must be difficult. He was getting cold, so he stood, stamping his feet and scattering the birds into the woolly, grey sky.

After twenty minutes, Dermot came to the door, brightly farewelling the nurse who let him out. After the door closed behind him, Dermot looked to the heavens and crossed himself. Conor gave him a smile, very broad, and very fake.

'I had to take a call, a patient. Sorry.'

'Guessed as much. Let's go. This place makes me itchy.'

Conor was coasting along the motorway when Beatrice called and asked them to buy milk on the way home. He asked if Dermot needed anything for himself. He drove on for a bit before he'd became aware that Dermot hadn't said anything.

'Da?'

His father was crying. 'She's happy, isn't she? Doesn't she seem happy to you?' he asked.

'She seems very settled.'

'She's not asking to leave at any rate.'

Dermot stayed in the car while Conor ran into SuperValu and picked up the milk. When he sat in again, he saw that Dermot had something white in his hands.

'What's that?'

'You don't recognise it?'

It was a piece of white card shaped as an eight with cotton-wool balls stuck on. A ribbon was tied around the narrowing. There seemed to be only one eye. A snowman.

'You made it.'

Conor studied it. He did remember it, perhaps not the making of it, but seeing it on their Christmas tree.

'I went up to her room for her laundry. I found it in the bin with all the other decorations from the tree. This was the only one still in one piece. They said she did it some time on Christmas night. Stripped the tree, tore all the decorations into pieces.'

Molly had been so quiet and docile during her visit to them on Christmas Day that Conor suspected the home had sedated her.

'If you ask me, she wasn't fooled by it,' said Dermot. 'Not one bit of it.'

'It was grand.'

'We dumped her back here and washed our hands of her.'

'Da. She doesn't remember enough to know what she's missing.'

'Bullshit. She picked out the snowman when I showed her the decorations. She said your name. It breaks my heart to see you not talking to her. Rarely visiting her. She adored you.' Dermot turned face-on to Conor, his face tight with anger.

'But I . . .' Conor tried to think of the right answer, one that wouldn't upset his father any further. 'You're right. I could do better.'

Dermot wiped his face with his hanky and returned to staring at the road ahead.

When they arrived home, Fiach was sitting on the floor, two feet away from the TV.

'I'm hungry,' he told them. 'I didn't even have lunch.'

Conor found Beatrice lying on their bed texting. She jumped when she heard him, and quickly put her phone face down on the cover.

'How's Molly?'

'Fine. It's after three, Fiach says he hasn't eaten?'

Beatrice seemed genuinely surprised that it was so late. She picked up her phone to head downstairs.

'Who were you texting?' asked Conor.

She frowned. 'Nobody.'

Beatrice buttered toast for Fiach, who was sitting at the island, legs swinging. Conor leaned over Fiach and gave him a hug. The boy ignored him.

'I'm SO hungry,' he growled.

'Where's Dad gone?' asked Conor.

'To his room for a lie-down,' said Beatrice. 'I'll bring him a cup of tea when I've fed Fi.'

'He thinks I've been neglecting Ma.'

Beatrice cut Fiach's toast into triangles and slid the plate across to him, then put the kettle on for tea.

'Do you?' asked Conor. It irritated him that he needed to ask for a response.

'You don't visit her.'

'I do. I could be another chair in the room as far as she's concerned.'

Beatrice shot a warning glance in Fiach's direction. 'Not for her, but for Dermot. She is his wife. After so many years together, they are like one person. You neglect her, you neglect him.' She stirred Dermot's tea, milk and two sugars, and headed off with it.

Conor took a few deep breaths and forced himself to focus on Fiach, munching toast and swinging his legs at the island. 'Better now?' He ruffled his hair. Fiach rewarded him with a smile full of soggy toast.

28

A Good Laugh

While everyone else relished the kids returning to school, Eva woke on the first day back feeling anxious. At little break, when Eva was asked how her Christmas was, she said it was quiet; they were in Leitrim, same as every year, spending precious time with her parents. Her childhood home was a tidy seventies bungalow, with a stone fireplace in the living room and rows of school photos of herself and her younger sister, Grace, along the hall. Twenty years ago, Grace left for San Francisco as soon as she finished school, and now, living without a Green Card, she refused to risk losing her home for a holiday, a slight stoically borne by their parents. While Eunice and Sean were mild and gentle people, Grace had been born with an energy that turned the bungalow into a cage where she bounced from wall to wall. Eva, the *good* daughter, had longed for Grace to disappear, to leave their permanently bewildered parents alone, but, now she had, Eva couldn't believe she'd been so blind. Grace had also been the root of laughter, the instigator of adventures, the voice of truth. Eva had sided with her parents and lost.

This Christmas, her precious little girls and her sweet, bouncy husband felt so wrong in that house that she'd wanted to run after Grace, a child in each hand, and never look back. She wanted to save her girls from the grey seeping out of the walls, from her parents' half-smiles and slow nods, from their good, plain food. She kept coming across her parents staring out the window at the birds feeding in the garden, *passing time*, when they had so little *time* left. Eva packed her family up and they left first thing St Stephen's morning, claiming they needed time and daylight for the icy roads.

In the days after, Eva asked herself if that was why she had kissed Conor. Even at home, the walls around her were too close and she felt like she was bouncing from one unyielding surface to another. Something had to give.

On her first day as acting vice-principal, Eva went over the jobs list for the year with Margaret. It wasn't only exhaustingly long; it was also financially impossible. December's heating bill drained their meagre funds. If another cold snap came, they would have to send everyone home. The school was scrambling to maintain basic standards of care. It was no longer about teaching tools, sports equipment, a new assembly hall; it was about leaking roofs and toilet paper. The parents held fetes at Christmas and spring, a massive amount of work that only ever brought in a couple of thousand euro. Every school was in the same boat. With a painful clarity, Eva understood her job as vice-principal was going to be about learning how to say no, even to the tiny things like coloured pencils or Blu-Tack. Susannah, of sixth class, snuck her a joint she had left over from a night out. She thought she looked stressed.

After school, Eva cornered Lizzie and suggested a trip to the park with the kids. Lizzie wasn't keen to smoke. Georgia had caught her and Frank before and asked what the funny smell was. She didn't think she'd get away with it again.

Across the yard they saw Dermot pick up Fiach.

'You think everything's okay there?' asked Eva. She hadn't talked to Beatrice since a call on Christmas Day.

'I think she's avoiding me,' said Lizzie. 'Did she say anything to you?'

'No?'

'I missed their party all the same.'

They both understood the reasoning – too much disruption for Dermot – and worked hard to be sympathetic, but Conor and Beatrice's New Year's Eve party had been brilliant. Eva and Shay, Frank and Lizzie had forced the expansion of the

event to include them staying until dawn, when they would finish the exquisite canapés, the carpaccio and the cheese. No one
was allowed to leave until the sun was fully up.

'It wasn't like she had to do anything much, a few phone
calls to book the caterer, the DJ. Get her hair done. I mean we
would've done all that for her.' Lizzie smirked.

Eva laughed. 'You're such a bitch. Come on. Let's go to the
park. Please? I need a good laugh.'

Lizzie appeased her with an invitation to dinner the weekend
after next and urged her to bring the joint home and share it
with Shay. He could do with a laugh too, she said.

Eva came home to dirty breakfast bowls on the table and the
saucepans from last night's dinner still waiting to be washed up.
Shay was out, he'd texted to say he was at Mrs Daly's. Why he
couldn't have done the washing up before he left, she didn't know.
It wasn't as if he was swamped with work. He was still fragile after
McDonagh, and she wanted to be kind, but everything needled.
Eva left the girls at the kitchen table doing their homework, with a
warning to stay put until it was done. When they complained, she
roared at them and then apologised as she often did. 'Mummy's in
a bad mood. Better leave me alone for a bit.'

Eva went out to the back lane and lit up her joint. If only
she'd put on her coat; fetching it now would alert the girls.
Night had fallen and she couldn't remember if she'd seen the
sun that day. Winter had little to say for itself. Sometimes even
her thoughts felt frostbitten.

Many years ago, before children, herself and Shay had taken
backpacks and travelled around the Greek islands. The heat
of the sun left them slow and in a permanent state of content-
ment, as relaxed as babies on the edge of sleep. Thanks to the
joint, a similar feeling of benign wellbeing was creeping up on
her and warming her from within. When she came back in, the
girls had finished their homework but were waiting at the table,
scared into submission. She giggled. 'What good girls you are.'

'Can we watch TV now, please?'

'Yes! Off you go.'

If they were surprised by the change in her they didn't show it. Dinner needed to be cooked but instead she made cookies. She sat with the girls while the cookies were in the oven and giggled all the way through *SpongeBob*. Every now and then she caught one of the girls sneaking a look at her.

'It's not that funny.'

'It is for me.'

She ran a bath for the girls. When they were in it she'd make something decent for dinner, then put the girls to bed, give out to Shay, and go to bed herself. What a waste of a joint. She turned off the taps, locked the bathroom door, stripped off and lowered herself in. She slipped and slid under the water. Hauling herself back up, sent a wave over the side. She laughed and laughed again. The door rattled as the girls tried to open it.

'Mummy? Why are you laughing?'

She worked hard to sound sober. 'I was thinking about something Lizzie said today.' Remembering Lizzie made her laugh again. She dropped under the water to hide her laughter. Bubbles burst the surface.

'Mummy, are you in the bath?'

'Are you in *our* bath?'

'I was a very dirty girl,' she said. 'Five minutes, then it's yours. Go grab a cookie.'

They scuttled away. She lay back and let her limbs float in the water. She texted Conor.

– *Happy New Year. We missed your party. Stared at the walls instead.*

His reply was almost instant.

We climbed Lugnaquilla.

– *Ok u win.*

The girls squealed at the sound of the front door opening. Shay was home. Any minute now, he would be at the bathroom door, wanting to know what's for dinner. Then he'd see that she was stoned, and he'd complain about her not waiting for him to share the joint, or the bath. Or both. She climbed out, dried herself and wrapped the towel around her. Once upon a time she would have opened the door and pulled him inside.

He knocked. 'Hi. Want me to get dinner on?'

'Wash up. I'll be a minute.'

She listened to him walk on. Her phone pinged.

– *Not my idea. I was dragged up. I would have given anything to stare at the walls with you.*

Eva was startled. She wasn't prepared for what he was implying, if he was implying anything. She couldn't afford to not reply because that was another kind of answer. He was too quick.

– *You and Sha you know what I mena.*

She sent a laughing emoji, then deleted all the texts.

When she walked into the kitchen, Shay was at the sink, starting on the dishes. She stood up against him and wrapped her arms around him, her head resting on his back.

'Hello.'

'Hello.'

He turned around and sniffed the air around her. Then peered into her eyes. 'You're stoned.'

Instead of outrage, or even faux outrage, he was happy for her. Thought she needed to let off a bit of steam. If she wanted to get back in the bath, he'd do dinner.

'What're you saying?'

'Nothing.'

'Bullshit.'

'Chill.'

'I am! I'm stoned, remember.'

'And I'm happy for you, remember?'

'Fuck you.'

29

What Do You Mean Unable?

Early in January, Frank was asked to do another block of episodes. Starting Monday, same fee. An hour after he'd said yes, another of the directors rang him. Barry Fowler had been playing hardball for more money; he begged Frank to join the fight and hold out with him. Barry had only signed the first contract based on the producers' promise that there would be more for the second season. Frank understood he was the producers' second choice and suspected that if he joined the fight the producers would only move on to the third choice. There once was a time his pride would've had him stand with Barry, but they'd already spent everything he'd earned from his first block. He took the gig. As he told Barry, he was sorry, but these were difficult times.

On his first day of prep, everyone in the office was giddy or hungover. The day before nominations had been announced for the Irish TV awards and several had been out celebrating. Frank caught himself thinking his episodes, eligible next year, might stand a chance of being nominated. He'd return to the tailor who'd made his tuxedo for the Oscars. He liked the circularity of the gesture.

Paula had been texting him for days and he hadn't replied. Today she called him, and he sent her straight to voicemail. He didn't want to ruin his good mood. Shortly after, Lizzie called him. Paula had called her and asked her to ask him to call her. 'She sounded upset Frank, wouldn't tell me what's going on. Did you go see her after Christmas?'

He hadn't. 'I can't do anything, I'm in work.'

'It's only prep. Call her.' She hung up.

He didn't. An hour later an unknown number came up on his phone. It was the Gardai. Paula had been arrested for dangerous driving, driving over the limit and criminal damage. Would he pick her up and take responsibility for her? Otherwise, they'd keep her in a cell until she sobered up. Frank thanked them, made his excuses to the producers, and drove over to Santry Garda Station. He caught himself speeding down the motorway and forced himself to slow down; the worst had already happened.

Santry Garda Station was a functional blur of concrete blocks, asphalt, and rows of parked cars. Inside was worse, fluorescent lights and walls scarred with the scratched initials of resistance. He feared for Paula. The guard at the front desk, young and perky, had asked what his relationship to the offender was. He hadn't known how to answer. She was an ex-girlfriend but that was so long ago and in hindsight felt like a gross exaggeration of whatever it was they'd had between them. 'Friends?' suggested the guard. Frank nodded. But *friend* only made him feel like a total arse. If he'd been a true friend to her he wouldn't have left her calls unanswered. But this was the paradox; if he'd felt nothing for her then he would've been more immune to her desperation.

He heard her voice before he saw her. She sounded upbeat, flirty, babbling something about sexy uniforms, but when he saw her he couldn't hide his dismay. Her eyes were blackened from mascara and tears, her nose was swollen, blue-tinged, her hair lank. The front of her t-shirt was covered in blood, and she was wearing a training jacket and sweatpants. He recognised the Kilbradden school crest – Jack's.

'I've had a whoopsie.' Her face twisted as she tried to hide a sob. He pulled her into his chest and held her as a guard watched.

'Her car's impounded at the airport. She's after clearing several bollards.' Frank winced at the thought of damage to the Audi. She hiccoughed against him.

149

'Ms Gleeson will have to pay costs before she can retrieve the car.'

He kept his arm around her as they walked back to the car. Under the bulky clothes, he could feel bony edges. There was a smell of urine, long since dried.

'Where were you going?

'Mumbai. After Tommy. He's taken up with his interpreter and is going to stay in India. He found what he's always wanted, a woman who hangs on his every word.'

'I'm so sorry, Paula.' Frank questioned whether he'd ever truly liked Tommy; even if he once had, he hated him now.

'Don't be. I'm going to strangle him. And then throw her on the funeral pyre.'

He helped Paula into the car, put her seatbelt on and told her to wait, he had to make a call. He sat on the boot of the car and rang Lizzie. She was shocked, adamant they couldn't leave Paula on her own. He had to bring her home and stay with her. Frank wanted to bring her to theirs, wanted to hand her over to Lizzie. 'You're so good at this kind of thing.'

'Minding drunks?' said Lizzie.

'And distressed women.'

'But the kids, Frank?'

Frank decided he'd pick up Jack and they'd bring Paula back to hers. Jack would know his way around the house, and around Paula. When Frank arrived home, he left Paula in the car and went inside for Jack. Jack ambled down the stairs, oblivious. Lizzie hadn't told him anything.

'Your mum's had an accident – she's okay – a bit shook up.'

Panic washed over Jack's face. 'Where is she?'

'In the car.'

Jack pushed past him and ran out the door. Paula saw him coming and stepped out of the car with her arms open wide. He stuttered to a stop. Paula swayed in front of him. Frank knew what Jack was seeing – the blood, the urine stain, the mascara. Paula's arms fell to her sides.

'Jackjack?'

Jack spun around and went back inside. Frank was caught. He'd made a huge mistake calling on Jack, confronting him with the state of his mother. He wanted to go after him but now Paula was crying. Frank bundled her into the car, murmuring words of comfort as he sat back behind the wheel. Don't mind him, he'll come round, everything will be better tomorrow.

A text pinged. It was Lizzie – *I've got Jack. Take her home. I'll call you.*

'I need a fucking drink,' said Paula.

He bought her a bottle of white wine; encouraging sobriety was a job for another day. She scoffed as she read the label. 'You never did have any class, Frank Durkan.' He suggested she take a bath and go to bed. She opened the wine and drank until she lay back on the sofa and passed out. Around the sofa, she'd created a bower bird's nest of comforts, hand cream, crackers, a candle jar doubling as an ashtray, several boxes of cigarettes with only one or two left, empty bottles of a wine no fancier than what he'd bought, a few coins, a rosary, lipstick, coffee plunger, Solpadeine and Rennies. The house was bone cold; the heating must've been off for days. He pulled a blanket off the floor. The whiff of urine unleashed was overwhelming. He threw it out the back door. Upstairs he found a clean blanket and brought it down to cover her. He'd once sneered at gas log fires but when he flicked the switch and the flames appeared, it felt like a miracle.

His phone rang. The production manager was wondering if he was going to be back in time for the casting.

No, he told the production manager, he was sorry, but he wouldn't be making it back in today. Family crisis.

He couldn't find any bin bags so made do with some filing boxes from the basement, dumping the files on the floor. Fuck Tommy. He went through the living room and the kitchen, throwing everything that was dirty or soiled or broken into the boxes until every surface was clear. He left the boxes outside the back door beside an impressive pile of empty bottles. Paula snored all the way through.

He texted Lizzie – *Paula's asleep. I've cleaned up. Dya think I can come home?*

No.

– *I'm starving.*

Order in. When she's sober, talk to her. She needs help. Do it for Jack.

– *OK.*

Xxx.

Frank ordered pizza. While he waited, he texted Beatrice. They hadn't seen each other for over a month, not since she freaked out over the duvet and then Christmas itself made it impossible. He studied Paula and decided she was likely to be out for another few hours. He considered what he could do to persuade Beatrice to come out. He texted her – *Meet you for a drink? I need to see you.* On Beatrice's phone the text would come up as Amy Walsh, a mother from the school's parents association. On his phone, she was Dave, an old mate from soccer. He'd told Lizzie Dave wanted to buddy up to improve his fitness. Lizzie, maddeningly, was excited by the idea that Frank wanted to work out. Not for his appearance but for his health. He hadn't believed her. Frank had to buy a tracksuit and trainers to keep up the ruse. Sometimes when they met in the morning, Beatrice would also be in her running gear. The moments before they were naked in Dermot and Molly's house felt surreal, as if Frank had walked into an alternative, Stepford version of his life.

His phone pinged. Beatrice.

– *I am unable to work with you any more. Sorry Dave!*

Frank had to take a moment to collect himself before he could reply as Amy – *What do you mean unable?* She didn't answer and he couldn't wait any longer. – *Like never?* He stared at the phone, holding his breath, waiting for more.

– *Yes. Sorry.*

He called her, knowing she could choose to ignore him.

She answered – 'Hi Amy, wait, I will find somewhere quiet.' He listened to her walking upstairs, opening and shutting a door.

'Please don't call me any more.' She couldn't have sounded more matter-of-fact.

'Did something happen?'

'Lizzie invited us to dinner.'

Frank didn't know about the invitation, would've put the kibosh on it if he had. He was getting too many weird vibes off Conor, but was never sure if it was his own guilt manifested.

'Don't mind Lizzie, she doesn't know anything.'

'We must stop, Frank.'

'You can't. I think I'm in lo—'

She hung up on him. Frank flopped down into the armchair. It was wet. He leapt up. Fuck. He felt ill; he couldn't tell if it was due to Beatrice's news or the fetid air. He wrestled a window open. Maybe it was both.

'You're a fool, Frank.' Paula was awake and watching him.

'It's not what you think,' said Frank. She laughed so hard at the cliché that Frank laughed with her. There was no bullshitting Paula. 'The heart wants what the heart wants.'

'I want another drink, but I'd guess you're gonna be telling me it's bad for me and I should give up.'

'I was going to suggest you go stay with someone,' said Frank.

'There isn't anyone. I have no one left,' said Paula. 'Look at me.' She pulled herself upright. Her bloody t-shirt had fallen off her shoulder, her clavicle stuck out, her bra sagged, but her breasts, enhanced, looked like two puddings on a platter. 'I didn't do this to myself.'

Frank wasn't sure what she was getting at. 'No?'

'You think I had no idea Tommy was unfaithful? I told myself I was the problem. I told myself I was being paranoid. He never had time to call, or he'd have to stay a few days longer. Once it was a month. They went to Bali, Frank. Bali. It was me who really wanted to go there. They went to the hotel I chose! If you love someone and they hurt you, and believe me Frank, this hurts. If a person you love can do this to you, it's either your fault or they never loved you in the first place. She was his interpreter on his last five trips.' She found the bottle of wine and drained the last glass. She swore. 'You should go home right now and beat Lizzie up, give her a black eye, break a rib. It's much the same, but at least she'd know what to call it and please God she'd have the sense to kick you out.'

Frank, already upset by Beatrice's rejection, was having trouble keeping his temper under control; what he was doing with Beatrice was hurting no one because no one was going to find out. Paula's drinking was the problem here. It was more than enough to drive Tommy away.

'It's not like it's the first time, is it?' said Paula.

'Why don't you go take a shower, sober up. You stink.'

'Why don't you go to hell?' Paula pulled her coat back on. She found one shoe, put it on and hobbled around looking for the other.

'What're you doing?'

'I'm going to the shops,' said Paula.

'I'm going home, I'll drop you off on the way.'

'Seriously?'

'No. Fuck off.'

Frank heard her cackling behind him as he walked out of there. He passed the pizza delivery driver on the road. What a waste. The streetlights refracted in the rain, and nothing looked as it should.

Frank told Lizzie that Paula had sobered up after a nap and seemed okay, that she'd told him to go home. He'd call around again tomorrow. Lizzie sent him up to Jack. The poor kid was in bits, she said. Frank found Jimmy sitting in the hall playing a game on his iPad. The swoosh and pings were like darts. Frank leaned over and turned the sound off.

'What're you doing out here, Jimbo?'

'Jack said he needed space.'

'He's inside?'

Jimmy nodded, never pausing in his game.

Jack was lying on his stomach on the top bunk, headphones on, face to the wall. 'Want to talk?' Jack didn't move. Frank patted his leg to get his attention. Jack pulled one side of the headphones away but didn't turn around.

'Paula's okay. She had a sleep. I thought you'd want to know.'

Jack grunted.

'She was upset because she'd had some news about Tommy.'

Frank waited. Jack's whole body, laid out in front of him at eye level, was tense. He didn't seem to be breathing.

'Did you know he's got himself a girlfriend?'

Still nothing.

'That's why your mum was so devastated.' As Frank was saying this he had a moment's panic; what if Paula told Jack about Beatrice? He couldn't predict what Jack would do with the information. 'Are you okay?'

'I'm fine,' said Jack.

'You've always got a home here. I promise.'

Jack gave him a little nod, then pulled up his headphones.

Jack and Maya spent most of the evening in the living room lying on the floor by the fire, talking. Frank was grateful Jack had someone he could talk to.

By the time Frank fell into his own bed, every inch of him exhausted, he had resolved to accept Beatrice's decision. He had no regrets. No damage was done. Maybe in the future they'd manage the odd encounter. He slid his arm around Lizzie. She snuggled her rump against his lap and sighed in her sleep.

The longer he lay in bed, the more awake he felt. Paula had got her nails into him. There was no comparison between her situation and his, nor between the past and now. When he cheated on Lizzie with her, that was back before children, back when they were still working out if they wanted to be together. That wasn't real. He'd worked hard to make it up to Lizzie. It had taken him months to persuade her to speak to him and, even then, he suspected that it was only because she was over-whelmed by being a single mother. Maya had been plagued with a cough that wouldn't go away. All winter, her first and her second, Lizzie would be up in the middle of the night hold-ing Maya upright until her little body stopped convulsing and she fell asleep on Lizzie's shoulders. The GP thought it might be asthma but suggested they wait it out; at three years old, these things often disappeared. Lizzie was fading away herself. Frank didn't think she'd last another two years like this. He'd stay over, when he was between jobs, and take care of her, leav-ing her free to mind Maya. Frank made tea and toast and eggs and washed Babygros. The rest of the time he worked on com-mercials, flirted with the hair and make-up department, going home with one or two of them after a night in the pub. Lizzie knew some of the women, and would encourage or discourage according to whether she liked them or not. Gemma was too meek – he'd walk all over her; Laura – too bossy; Anne – he could do much better. Lizzie was his Goldilocks, just right. He had worked so hard to appear sensitive, patient, stable, until the day he turned up drunk and vulnerable. He'd been scolded on set, in front of a full crew and half the cast, over a mis-take he'd made. He wanted to walk. Lizzie talked him down; it helped that she knew how sets worked. Happens to everyone, she said; tomorrow he'd gain more friends for being human. Then she kissed him better. Next morning at work, she was proved right.

Lizzie and Maya moved into his one-bedroom hall-floor flat on South Circular Road. The bedroom was to the front of the house, with tall sash windows. Double doors led to their living room and another tall window overlooked the back garden. In the return was a kitchen and a mouldy bathroom. Maya cried every night. They tried moving her cot into the living room, but she'd cry until Lizzie brought her into bed with them.

The love Frank felt for Maya confused and often overwhelmed him. She could scream all night but then, as he'd fall into a deep sleep, she would literally walk right over him – their mattress was on the floor – her little hands would pat his face, and he'd forgive her anything. For over a year, he tried to bring Jack into his and Lizzie's life with overnights on the weekend, but two toddlers in the flat was more than exhausting. Maya resented the interloper and Jack cried for his mother. Frank felt like the babysitter. He gave up, believing he'd left it too late for either of them to bond.

It was almost 3 a.m. when Frank's heart pounded in his chest. Should Paula tell Jack about Beatrice on purpose or by accident, there was absolutely no reason for Jack to be loyal to him.

30

Trespass

Eva and Shay left the house not speaking to each other. She'd complained about him not bothering to change his clothes. He was wearing jeans, a t-shirt, and a fleece. The only difference, she told him, between the clothes he worked in and the clothes he was wearing was that these were clean. It's Frank and Lizzie, he said. They don't give a shit what I wear. What was her problem? And while they were at it, what or who was she dressing up for? She was also wearing jeans, but she had on a flowered satin bomber jacket she'd bought years ago and never worn, chunky gold bangles, high-heeled boots, and full make-up. She felt like making an effort, she said, it would be nice if he'd do the same for her sometimes. He seemed hurt and she was unable to muster the energy to make it right. These days he sought her opinion on everything from whether to do the washing – did she think it was going to rain – to what should he cook for dinner. She could see he was trying but not in a way that would make her life significantly easier. If she said anything, she only made things worse. It was safer to keep some distance between them.

The girls felt the space around them expanding and filled it accordingly. They were less inclined these days to huddle together talking in their special code. Instead they egged each other on to more and more outrageousness. This morning, a Saturday, Eva was working at the kitchen table while Shay was out. She was supposed to be writing a proposal for a parent/school engagement scheme, in truth a search for free classroom assistants, but instead she drew a picture of the garden in front of her. She was fully absorbed, making her way through every one of the girls' coloured pencils. By the time she stopped and listened, some time had passed, and the girls were too quiet.

They were in her bedroom playing dress-up. The wardrobe doors were open, as were the drawers. All the surfaces in the room were piled high with every item of clothing Eva owned. Her make-up was scattered across the floor, lipstick ground into the carpet, mascara spiralled up a wall. Kate was naked under Eva's favourite floral tea dress, her nipples visible through the gaping sleeves. Ella's hips jutted with the effort of balancing in heels. Their lips were red. Their hair, long and dark like hers, was tangled as if they'd emerged from a vigorous sexual encounter. Eva saw herself in her daughters' dress-up, a nightmarish exaggeration of femininity, flippant with flowers and bright colours but also teetering, vulnerable and exposed. The girls took her initial shocked silence as an appreciation of their efforts. They tottered towards her, smiles wide, hips swinging left right left. She yelled and they ran, tripping out of the shoes and stripping off as they went.

There was a mirror on the inside of the wardrobe door. She rarely looked at herself, only checked to ensure her clothes weren't inside out or mismatched. Almost everything she wore was navy, everything went together, and she never had to waste time thinking about clothes. Now she looked at herself without pulling anything in or up. Her posture drooped. Her belly was round. She had no belt in her jeans and they slumped under her buttocks. Her face was without expression, but her lips had thinned and implied a disapproving mood. There was a middle-aged woman in front of her, one she wasn't confident her twenty-year-old self would recognise. A woman her twenty-year-old self might have ignored.

As she folded and tidied, Eva discovered things she hadn't seen for years. She tried on jeans that were once too tight and discovered they fitted. The bomber jacket was on the floor of the wardrobe with sale tags attached. It must've been there for some time; she couldn't remember buying it. It was black satin with brightly coloured flowers popping like the oriental textiles in the Chester Beatty. She put on her red, high-heeled boots, last worn when she was pregnant, abandoned once her twin belly threatened to upend her. The woman in the mirror reminded her of someone she'd known years ago. Someone who knew exactly what they looked like in tight jeans, who knew anything could happen and was open to it.

It was a mistake. Old friends didn't necessarily embrace change; change made everyone nervous and instigated a search for the reasons why. Their friendships appeared to depend on them all remaining the same as they were when they first met. Lizzie and Frank were so struck by her appearance that they made strange noises as they openly scanned the length of her. Frank's embrace knocked the breath out of her. She wasn't two feet down the hall before Lizzie slapped her bottom. It was far more attention than Eva was comfortable with.

When they reached the kitchen she caught a glimpse of Conor standing in the corner, but feared looking too directly at him. They hadn't seen each other since she'd kissed him. Frank handed her a drink, and she took a gulp without knowing what it was. It was cold, probably gin. When she looked up again, Conor was looking at her, smiling. Did he think she'd dressed for him?

The small kitchen was painted sunflower yellow and the pine table with six chairs took up most of the space. An old fan oven rattled away as it heated the room to sauna levels. It seemed everyone else had something to do, setting the table, moving vegetables from oven to bowl to table, and yet Conor was this hot still centre pulling on her from the other side of the room. His khaki shirt, his close-cut hair and four- or five-day-old beard made him look like some kind of Hollywood movie architect. To greet him with a hug as she had greeted everyone else would've required moving furniture. She offered him a discreet wave using only her fingers. He did the same. Everything slowed down.

'Excuse me.' Lizzie nudged Eva out of the way to put a casserole of Moroccan tajine on the table. 'Hope you like chickpeas. It was supposed to be lamb, but I would've had to sell the family silver. And we didn't have any.' While Lizzie was always apologising for the size of her kitchen, her house, her food, Eva liked eating at her table. They were sat so close that they could participate in the one conversation. Under the table limbs and feet bounced off each other. Sorry. Sorry. Was that you? After a few glasses of wine, they let their limbs rest where they wanted to. Prior to Harwood, Eva would've insisted it was relaxed and affectionate, like siblings, but now it felt as if every touch on her ankle and thighs was intentional, and, more confusingly, erotic. And it could've been any one of them.

Lizzie tried to separate the couples as she sat them at the table. Conor, following instructions, sat opposite Eva. Shay would've sat opposite Beatrice but that would have left Lizzie and Frank together. When Frank, impatient, sat opposite Beatrice, Lizzie made a point of sitting herself across from Shay. The women ended up on one side of the table facing the men on the other. Lizzie gave up.

Beatrice turned in her chair. 'You must wear colour more often,' she told Eva. 'You look fantastic. Much younger. Like someone else.'

'Who did I look like before?' asked Eva.

'You know what I mean. Like a mother. And a schoolteacher.'

'Well. Well. Okay. Oops.'

Beatrice laughed, more than was justified by the joke. And as Beatrice talked she kept laughing. She laughed to punctuate her stories regardless of whether they were funny – Fiach – or tragic – Molly. Across the table, Eva could see Frank listening in. Occasionally he'd interject but Beatrice hardly acknowledged him; her whole body was spiralled towards Eva. Frank switched his attention to Conor beside him, but Conor was involved in Shay's conversation with Lizzie.

Beatrice was saying something to Eva about her father-in-law's house, and how much money they lost holding out for a better offer. 'Oh well,' said Beatrice. She waited for Eva to respond but Eva's attention was on Shay. Shay was telling Lizzie how angry Eva was with him about McDonagh's bankruptcy. Eva mumbled an excuse at Beatrice and cut across –

'You couldn't do anything about McDonagh going bankrupt, but you could've protected yourself, us, from the fallout.'

'How? With my crystal ball?' said Shay.

Eva told the whole table about Shay's landscape contract with McDonagh, or, to be precise, McDonagh's abuse of Shay's naivety and their credit card. Frank, having learned the necessity of watertight contracts himself, was scornful. 'No one can be trusted. The world's a snakepit.' Beatrice responded with a tiny, instinctive nod.

'You have to trust people,' said Lizzie. 'What kind of world would it be if there was no trust?'

'I wouldn't trust me,' said Frank. 'If I was hungry, bored, pissed off, I could change my mind about any one of you at any time.'

'That's true,' said Lizzie.

Eva guffawed. Shay's expression remained fixed in a half-smile like he didn't want to be seen to be angry, but still the anger was radiating off him. She had broken the rules; complaints about spouses were for quiet corners and whispered conversations. Who were they all pretending to be okay for? Half of marriages failed without anyone knowing anything was wrong. Eva could hardly breathe with the desire to blow everything up.

'I'm with Lizzie . . .' Conor paused for effect. 'I think.' He made a point of laughing but sounded scared. 'Most people can be trusted.'

'Contracts remove the option of betraying anyone's trust,' said Frank.

'I *had* a contract,' said Shay.

Eva couldn't leave it there. 'It cost us, Shay, that's what I'm saying. Your nature literally cost us, and now I must be the main breadwinner and everything else. It's impossible.'

Shay's chin dropped. 'You make it sound like I do nothing.' He tried to feign fake outrage, but everyone knew it was real.

'Nobody ever died of a dirty house,' said Lizzie. Beatrice and Conor exchanged anxious glances, the *is it time to leave* look. Shay leaned across Beatrice, so close Eva smelled his garlic breath as he ranted. He was the *victim* of McDonagh, and she was completely wrong to blame him. *And* he'd tried to make it right.

'By stealing from him and getting yourself beaten up?' Eva turned to the others, cupped her hand over her eye socket. 'His eye was out to here. The girls had nightmares. When I first saw you, I thought you were dead.'

'I'm sorry about that but I was jumped by three men,' said Shay.

'You were trespassing. You broke the law.'

Beatrice put a hand on Eva's arm. 'That must've been very frightening.'

'It was,' said Eva. 'And now we can't join the compensation claim or McDonagh will report him for breaking and entering.'

As one they looked at Shay. He was running his finger over a coin-sized gouge in the table.

Conor's empty glass chimed as he placed it down.

Frank stood up, his chair falling backwards with a thump, and bellowed, 'The fault, unforgiveable as it is, lies with me.'

There was a bewildered silence.

'We have run out of wine,' said Frank. 'Drunk enough to fight, not drunk enough to love. It's a disaster.'

'A goddamn catastrophe!' said Lizzie, beaming at Frank, relieved by his intervention. 'Unforgiveable!'

Shay sat back in his chair, spent. Eva let out a long slow breath. Beatrice patted her arm again. There. There. Lizzie gave Shay's hand a squeeze. Yes, comfort him please, thought Eva, it's beyond me.

'I am going to make it up to you lovely people.' Frank climbed up on his chair and brought down a dusty bottle of Jägermeister from the top of the kitchen press – the liquor of choice at 2 a.m. in the nineties when none of them knew what real hangovers felt like. There was a general groan – Jäger-meister tasted like cough syrup – but when Frank handed out shot glasses no one refused.

As one, they drank the liquor until they were completely plas-tered. Their dirty plates from dinner and dessert were stacked high on the counters around them. The empty bottles filled all the space between. The air was thick with their shouting and gesticu-lating. Lizzie was dancing. Shay was watching Eva. She stood up to go to the toilet, to escape his gaze, but she misjudged her step around the table, turned her ankle and went down. She tried to get up but quickly went down again. She was drunk and useless and laughing so much she feared wetting herself. Someone pulled her upright. It was Conor, his hands on her elbows, his solid chest against her back. He pivoted Eva back into her chair.

'Time to go,' said Shay.

'No, no,' said Eva, 'we haven't finished the Jägermeister, master.'

'We have,' said Frank.

Conor asked if she was hurt. She wanted to say yes she was hurt; she wanted him to pull her boot off, slide her sock down and take her ankle in his hands.

'She's fine. I'll get the girls,' said Shay.

Everyone waited for Eva to answer. 'I'm fine,' she said.

The twins were sleeping with Georgia and Jimmy on a giant bed made of cushions on the living room floor. They didn't wake when Shay put their shoes and coats on. Conor and Beatrice led the way home, silhouetted by streetlights and the sparkle of South Circular Road after a light rain. Shay walked beside Eva, carrying Ella, holding sleepwalking Kate by the hand.

'I'm sorry,' she said. She gently bumped shoulders with him. 'I am so drunk.'

'If you want me to do more in the house, you have to tell me. I can't read your mind.' He didn't look at her.

'Fair enough.' She waited for more but that seemed to be the only complaint he was going to make. He shifted Ella from one shoulder to the other and kept walking. Up ahead, Beatrice and Conor were laughing at something they didn't want to share. Usually they'd pause at the corner of Eva and Shay's street to say goodbye before they turned off, but tonight Conor and Beatrice kept walking. Shay turned the corner, but Eva paused. Beatrice glanced over her shoulder and, without missing a step, slipped her left arm into the crook of Conor's elbow and waved goodbye with the back of the other.

31

You Could Just Believe Me?

Frank had been waiting outside Tamara's office for over ten minutes. The corridors were empty; everyone else was in the canteen having lunch. They were three scenes behind after a disastrous morning's shoot with Marlie, resulting in her breaking down in tears. She'd been struggling for weeks. Frank concluded that she didn't have enough sexual experience to understand the storyline, let alone act it, and he was weighing up how to encourage her to do some research. Assuming it was a scolding he was about to get from the line producer, he had a speech ready about how he was well aware of the issues, it wasn't his fault they were behind and, if they'd let him get on with it, he was confident he'd able to make up the lost scenes this afternoon. By the time he was called in and saw the two executive producers, Maher and Gleeson, squeezed into the line producer's office, he was agitated. This was interference.

'Hi Tamara, gentlemen,' said Frank. 'I've had some thoughts about how to deal with the issues that came up this morning. Great that you're here, I'd appreciate your opinions.' He smiled. Tamara didn't. She glanced at the two executives.

Maher spoke first. 'Tamara filled us in when we arrived but to be frank, Frank' – at this, he grinned. It wasn't the first time he'd made this joke, but Frank smiled anyway – 'the situation this morning has only exacerbated an already difficult decision.'

'I would suggest,' interjected Gleeson, 'it's made a difficult decision easier.'

'I'm afraid lads, you're going to have to come at me a little straighter?' Frank had no idea what was going on, only that it wasn't going well for him.

Tamara leaned forward. He was uncomfortably aware that there was absolutely no trace of the warmth that normally accompanied their chats. Tamara had a great sense of humour and a raunchy cackle and Frank enjoyed making her laugh.

'A complaint of sexual harassment has been made against you.'

'What?' Frank hadn't tried it on with anyone on the show and was sure he hadn't touched anyone in any way that could be misconstrued. He left too much silence and found himself filling it while he thought some more. 'I, uh . . . have to be honest, this is a surprise. That's awful. For the person. But I can't think of, I mean, I sincerely apologise if I've inadvertently made someone uncomfortable.' Frank made eye contact with each of them but no one was letting him off the hook.

'If?' said Tamara.

'Tell me who it is, and I'll make it up to them.' Frank leaned forward. He meant it.

'There's more than one complainant,' said Tamara.

'It's a misunderstanding.'

'If it was only one maybe, but it reads a lot like a concerted effort.'

Frank's chest was getting tight. He could feel a rage building that he suspected wouldn't help him but there it was.

'This is bullshit. I haven't done anything.'

The two men looked away. Tamara rolled her eyes to the ceiling.

'Hey, here's a radical suggestion,' said Frank. 'You could just believe me?'

The three of them looked away.

The Equity rep threatened a cast walkout if Frank didn't leave immediately. Frank was overwhelmed by an internal battle. Stand up, fight, you've done nothing wrong. If no one will tell him who and what, how is he to defend himself? He considered talking to hair and make-up, they knew everything. Bruce, the only other director prepping, claimed to be completely surprised by the news but wasn't keen on speaking for him. Frank slowly arrived at the conclusion that the louder he fought, the broader the stain on his reputation. On set, it would be him against the complainants, and he hadn't been around long enough to have any traction. He was an easy target. Tamara already had a director lined up to cover the rest of Frank's block. Barry Fowler. His better option, as Maher and Gleeson had argued, was to leave quietly. They were sorry, they appreciated his work, his talent, and when things calmed down they'd give him a call. They promised.

Maher waited at the door to escort him out of the building. Thankfully many of the cast and crew were still at lunch so it wasn't as much of a public spectacle as Maher might have wanted. Frank had seen Maher at many a wrap party, cornering the latest beautiful teenage up-and-coming actor. Male and female. At first the actors loved being singled out for attention but then they discovered there was no way to get out from under that attention and keep Maher on side. It was a power play Maher was known for, and not a behaviour Frank had ever indulged in.

At the exit, Frank stopped. 'The stories I've heard about you would make a cracking front page. You should be more careful.'

Maher paled.

Frank consoled himself with a few whiskeys in the pub while he tried to work out what to do. When he arrived home drunk, he tried to lie, but Lizzie knew he never drank during a shoot. She sent the kids out of the kitchen and shut the door.

'We've got five minutes at best, spit it out Frank, you're scaring me.'

'I've been fired.'

'What? The bastards!'

Frank felt himself swell with love. He could depend on Lizzie to take his side without question. 'Someone accused me of sexually harassing them.'

Lizzie had gone still; he couldn't tell what she was thinking. 'Who?' she asked, but he had no idea. 'They've got to tell you who. How are you supposed to defend yourself?'

'But I didn't do anything.'

'Are you sure? You can be a bit handsy and that look you give—'

'Handsy? What look?' asked Frank, panicked.

'Like you're undressing someone.'

Frank knew the look she was referring to. 'Well, I'm not and I didn't.'

Jimmy stuck his head around the door. 'Mummy?'

'Out.' Jimmy knew there was no arguing with that tone of voice and shut the door behind him. Safely behind the door he shouted, 'We're hungry.'

'I know you didn't do anything intentionally,' said Lizzie. 'That's why you have to find out who made the complaint so you can talk to them. It could be crew but it's probably an actress.'

'I don't mess with the actors. How could you say that?'

'No, but like any good director you get up close and into their heads. That's how it works. It's not right but it's intimate. It's how you pulled me. All you directors do it. Male directors. It's funny isn't it? You need to build trust quickly and the first route you take is sexual. It's like a little love affair for six weeks. And then it's over.'

'This is not helpful.' Frank knew what she was talking about but also knew that approach was so far from how he worked on the series. If they completed the schedule, that was a good day. He needed to work a lot harder to win people over these days; hardly anyone was flirting back.

'Fuck,' said Frank. 'I sound like a sleaze.'

'Did you call the Directors Guild?' asked Lizzie.

'Yeah. They're looking into it. But to be honest, they weren't happy with me undercutting Barry Fowler.'

'Could he have had something to do with this?'

'Like how?'

'You know, feeding the gripes, urging people to speak up, take up arms against you.'

Frank suddenly saw it all laid out in front of him. He'd provided the kindling. Barry lit the flame and toasted marshmallows. Lizzie sat in Frank's lap, wrapped her arms around him and held him until the children knocked again. By the time dinner was eaten and they were clearing up, Frank had sunk into a benign resignation. This would pass; he needed patience. He put his arm around Lizzie's shoulder as she stood over the sink and leaned in, meaning to whisper his gratitude in her ear. He could see down her blouse, her full bosom dusted with tiny freckles. There'd been other breasts he'd snuck a look at. Actresses he had put his arm around in the exact same way to discuss a scene, or praise, or encourage. Oh God, that was it. He'd been all over Marlie that morning trying to reel her back in, trying to prevent her imploding. His arm around her, praising her. But the more he tried, the harder she'd pulled away. He'd assumed she was sulking. He thanked God he hadn't got around to suggesting she watch some porn to widen her horizons.

Frank did the rounds, hitting a lot of ad agencies, reasoning that their paths were unlikely to cross with the television crowd. Some people were happy to meet him, assured him they'd put him on their lists, but then he'd hear nothing. Only one of them, Josephine McIllwain, a friend since college, bothered to call him back and ask about 'this harassment thing she's been hearing?' Ireland was a small place. But even Josephine wasn't prepared to breach the gap and hire him. Not for six months at least.

Lizzie waited a polite two weeks before she came to him with the bills. Apart from the everyday – mortgage, electricity, food – that his last pay cheque would cover, there was the final payment of a thousand euro for Jack and Maya's transition-year school trip to Barcelona. They'd lose the thousand they'd already paid if they didn't make the final payment. 'Five hundred would be better than nothing. Maya has to go.'

'We can't pay for one and not the other,' said Frank. 'Hang on, why aren't we asking Max to cover Maya?'

Lizzie looked at him like he was an idiot. 'Because he already paid for Maya's trip in full. We used it to pay the deposit for both kids.'

Frank swore.

'What about teaching?' asked Lizzie.

Frank cringed at the idea.

'Frank. Cop on to yourself. Everyone teaches.'

'And what about you, you could get a job?' asked Frank.

'I'm trying.' Lizzie had fallen out with her agent after ringing her too often.

'I don't mean acting. Or the drama classes. I mean a real job.'

Lizzie gave him her most withering look. 'If you'd auditioned me for the show. Any role. I would've done anything.'

Frank would not go there. 'Don't look at me like it's all my fault.'

She continued to look at him that way.

'You used to call yourself a feminist.'

'I still do. I'm raising children, it's a full-time job.'

They ended up in the same place as they always did in the money argument; she wanted him to go to his father and ask for a loan. 'What's the point of having a safety net if you never use it?' Frank no longer bothered to respond.

Paula sold the Audi after the accident. There was no reason to keep it since she'd been banned from driving for two years. Frank tried to persuade her to use the money for rehab, but she swore that she had her drinking under control. She only drank on the weekends and if there was something on during the week. That might've been fine, but Paula's weekend began on Thursday and ended in the early hours of Monday.

'Aren't you proud of me?' she asked.

He prevaricated, hoping this was a joke. It was Friday, five minutes after five, and she'd opened the first bottle of wine.

'How's Jack? He doesn't answer my texts.' asked Paula. Jack hadn't contacted her since Christmas. Frank had seen him with Maya, their two heads huddled together over his phone, mocking Paula's texts. When Paula didn't get an answer from him she often replied with a long line of crying emojis.

'It's Jack I wanted to talk about.'

Paula heard him out but wasn't too sympathetic to his request for her to share the cost of rearing him. She had done it for fifteen years and hadn't asked for a cent from Frank. It was his turn.

'I haven't got it. I wouldn't ask if I did,' said Frank.

'Well, then. If Jack needs money for his trip to Spain then he can come and ask for it himself.'

'You can't bribe kids, they won't thank you for it,' said Frank.

Paula gave him a look so scornful it burned. 'That's the deal.'

Frank told himself it was a good thing that Paula was back to her stubborn, fighting self. Paula kissed him on each cheek and sent him on his way.

When Frank called on Beatrice one day after school, almost six weeks after Lizzie's dinner party, she didn't seem pleased to see him. He held a small green jumper in his hands.

'Fiach left this behind in our house, I was passing.'

She glanced at the jumper. 'It's not Fiach's.'

'You sure?'

'Yes, I'm sure.' She continued to hold the door only partially open, as if he was some kind of salesman; you want to be polite but you're not buying. He could hear the bells and whistles of cartoons from downstairs.

'Fiach's here?'

She nodded.

'Dermot?'

She shook her head. 'He's with Molly.'

'Let me in.'

'I've nothing to say, Frank.'

'Please, I need to ask you something.' He nudged the door. She held on to it. 'It's really important.' She stepped aside to let him in, and he closed the door behind him.

'Frank,' she chided, 'you take too many liberties.' She was wearing bubblegum-pink cigarette trousers. She'd kicked her heels off somewhere and stood before him in bare feet.

'I'm sorry.'

Beatrice frowned. Her voice was soft. 'Something is wrong?'

Frank was relieved by her attention; he didn't enjoy feeling like she couldn't wait to be rid of him. He'd felt much the same when she came to dinner. Iced.

'I lost my job. Someone accused me of sexual harassment.'

She expelled a long breath. 'That is not good. Will there be police involved?'

'Nope. Looks like I got away with it.' He saw Beatrice reassess him. 'A joke. I was joking. I didn't do anything. Okay?'

'Okay. I am sorry for you.'

A fine gold chain lay around her neck, curling over her clavicle. 'I miss you,' said Frank. 'Everything has fallen apart since you dumped me.'

'No. It has stayed together.'

'Do you miss me?'

He took her hesitation as evidence that she did and moved a step closer. The old house creaked under them. Fiach's giggle drifted up from the basement. He leaned over Beatrice. She arched her body up to meet his, opened her mouth to him. They fell against the wall, their kiss unbroken. He held her hands up, one in each of his, as he buried his face in her neck and kissed, into her breasts and kissed. He became aware of the noise she was making. A deep, rolling sigh. He pushed his hand down into her trousers and found her wet. Everything dissolved around him, the accusation, Tamara's disdain, the debt, the floor they were standing on. And then she peeled him off her, stepped back and opened the front door. He started to ask if they could meet again, but she pushed him out the door. He descended the steps in two strides and continued down the street. Restored. Only good had come from his encounters with Beatrice. He needed her back in his life.

Beatrice looked at herself in the hall mirror. There was no sign of the riot she felt inside. The green jumper lay on the hall table. As she picked it up, she heard a little voice –
   'Why do you have Jimmy's jumper, Mummy?'
   Fiach stood halfway up the stairs. His right foot on the next step up, his hand on the rail, suspended. She could no longer hear the cartoons. How long he'd been there, she had no idea.

Jack and Maya bypassed Frank and asked their grandfather for the money. The Judge paid the remaining fees and added some spending money. If anyone had considered discussing this with him first, and Lizzie had that chance, Frank would've outlawed such a move, which was exactly why they didn't. Once he might've admired their cop-on but this time it was hard to see it as anything other than a total undermining of his paternal authority. Maya refused to let him give out. She could've gone to Max, could've told him Frank and Lizzie stole from her trip fund. She told him he should be pleased they were going to Barcelona.
   As the week went on, he spent most of his days in his shed, texting Beatrice and not getting an answer. He was one tap from sending her a crying emoji. Lizzie accused Frank of sulking over the kids. Told him to grow up. He didn't have the strength to counter her accusation. He felt impotent. His career was dead, or very soon would be if he was out of the industry for six months or more. His kids were old enough to scorn him. Beatrice was able to resist him. Even Lizzie was tiring of him.

32

The Kiss

Eva stood on stony Bray beach, battered by an icy wind, watching Ella and Kate throw stones into the waves. They inched closer and closer to the water and then let the waves chase them back. Shay had gone in search of chips. The sky was blue with a few white clouds floating by. Seagulls arced overhead. She felt the perfection of the scene, as if it were a painting, but an over-familiar one, the kind you'd find in the dining room of a seaside B & B. She saw herself in the foreground, black coat, shoulders hunched against the crisp sea air, arms crossed, her wild hair flying.

There was a rot in her, creeping up from her toes, that she was barely keeping at bay. Her nerves sparked, like a limb trying to come back to life. Conor occupied her thoughts, leaving her permanently conflicted. She felt guilty for thinking of him when he was so clearly a fantasy, and a sad one at that, and simultaneous resentment towards anyone who came between her and her fantasy.

Shay was working again; she'd slipped him the quote from the previous tender for the school's maintenance contract, allowing him to best it. Margaret, who was delighted to save some money, remarked on the coincidence. Eva had never cheated before and for days fought an urge to confess. Shay still wasn't earning much, but the pressure had eased, and they seemed to have put the McDonagh saga behind them. The girls were a delight and, when they weren't, they were only behaving as children should. New lime-green leaf buds had appeared on the trees, blossom carpeted the ground and the gentle sun made everything shine. Yet sleep eluded her.

Eva had built this life for herself; had sought it out, endured the hard graft, negotiated, compromised and hung in there. It was the kind of life she imagined her younger self would've been happy to know was coming. Now she was here in the thick of it she didn't know what she was supposed to do next. Older female colleagues had joined book clubs and taken up crafts or sea swimming. They talked of having earned the time to please themselves, now their children were in college, and were adamant no one was allowed to encroach on that time. Martin, the sole man in the staffroom, never joined in these conversations. He had small children *and* cycled for hours in the mountains and didn't seem conflicted about the two.

Eva watched the waves rise and roll. The girls. Where were they? She heard a shout behind her and turned to see them running towards Shay and his bags of hot chips.

They walked the narrow cliff path around Bray Head. It was crowded with people and dogs out for the Sunday walk. Waves, regular and relentless, pounded the rocks hundreds of metres below. Every time Eva had to step closer to the edge of the cliff to let someone pass, she could feel the vastness of the space between herself and the sea. What was it like to fall from such a height, to have time to experience the falling, to forget the landing that is coming and simply let go?

That night, after Eva and Shay put two tired girls to bed, they declared the day a wholehearted success, promised to do it more often and went to bed early themselves.

'Are you happy?'

Shay pulled her close. 'Very.'

'There's nothing more you want?' asked Eva.

'Like what?'

'Like of life?'

'No. I don't think so. You and the girls. That's all I need. And a good night out. I wouldn't mind a night out. Why are you asking? Are you not happy?'

'Yes . . . but no. I want more.' She hadn't expected to say it out loud, but it had been running through her head all day. I want more. I want MORE.

'Of what?'

'Just more.'

'Money?'

'It would help, but that's not it.'

'Sex? I can help you with that.'

She laughed. 'The opposite, I think. Something like faith. Not God, or Buddhism or anything else. But faith. A direction. Like having a job that means something.'

'Teaching is meaningful.'

'Is it? I teach a curriculum designed by the state. I teach them to be polite and clean up after themselves. I teach them to wash their hands after they pee.'

'Essential.'

She went quiet. There seemed to be little point in trying to explain further.

'When you work out what you want, let me know and I'll do what I can.' He turned over to sleep and within seconds she heard him snore.

She wanted something to hold on to, something to hold on to with both hands. If the girls had been washed out to sea, she would've gone straight in after them. Her love for the girls was so primal she often wanted to eat them; chew their toes, one by one, take a mouthful of belly. But if it was the other way round, if she had fallen off the cliff path, and out of their lives, would things change that much for them? Would they even remember all the days she spent feeding, washing, herding, scolding, praising, cuddling them? She had no doubt anyone could do that for them. This ambivalence was unbearable; she didn't feel attached to her life, yet she had no other life to go to.

On Tuesday morning, Eva prepared her class for a trip to the zoo on the Friday. Last week they'd made animal masks out of paper plates. Lions were a clear favourite, elephants second. She projected slides of animals they might see on their day out and asked what they knew about them.

'Elephants have a long memory,' said Blessing.

'And tusks. People saw them off. *Grchgrchgrch*.' Michael used the side of his hand to saw off Ruth's arm resting on the table beside him. She seemed to like it.

'Tigers rip you apart with teeth and claws.' Oisín took bites out of the air.

'Then you shoot them,' said Michael. He held his hand out, thumb cocked, and shot Eliza Bourke. *Pow*. Eliza, who'd been lightly bouncing between the tables, startled. *Pow. Pow*.

'No guns allowed, Michael.' Ruby liked rules and liked to see them kept.

'It's only my hand. Idiot,' said Michael.

'Michael.' Eva needed to move them on. 'Any other animals we can think of?'

Eliza hooted and scratched her armpit like a monkey. Someone yelled gorilla. The kids giggled. Oisín growled. Michael shot him. *Pow. Pow*. Naveen squeaked. A chicken clucked. A piglet oinked. The room filled with squealing, roaring, chattering animals, roaming wild.

She clapped her hands. 'People. People. Quiet please. It's time to sit back down and put our listening hats on.' She clapped again, so hard her hands stung.

The children returned to their seats, all except Eliza, who remained a happy, gibbering monkey. 'Eliza. You too.' Eliza screeched and babbled in response. 'Eliza. Please sit down so we can continue.' Eliza rolled from side to side, between the tables, swinging her arms low. Michael raised his hand, index finger out straight, thumb cocked.

Eva shouted. 'Michael!'

The boy startled and dropped his hand. Eliza screeched and scurried away.

'Eliza. Sit. SIT! Eliza Bourke, you are spoiling things for the rest of us. I'm going to sit down now and so are you.' Eva sat down behind her desk. Eliza kept wandering in and out of the tables. Rolling her shoulders. Swinging her arms. Scratching and hooting. The children watched Eliza to see what she was going to do, snuck glances back at Eva. Ruby plucked uselessly at Eliza as she passed, trying to get her to sit. 'Sit, sit,' she whispered. Eliza swung around the room again and came to a stop in front of Eva. Eva pointed to her seat.

'Good girl.'

Eliza raised her right arm as if to grab a branch, curled the left into her armpit and scratched.

'Sit.'

Eliza flared her nostrils and opened her mouth.

'Don't you—'

She screeched in Eva's face. Eva reared back, slamming her head against the shelf of the whiteboard behind her. Landing on her back on the floor. Her head reverberating with the blow.

The class giggled.

Eva felt her eyes fill with tears. Eliza stood over her, astonished by her own power. Eva sat up, wiped away her tears, but more and more kept falling. She searched her bag for a tissue but there was none.

'Sit, Eliza.'

Eliza sat.

Eva went to the toilet and tore off a handful of toilet paper to wipe her face, blow her nose. But the tears weren't stopping. She texted for help. The lie came easily; the guards called, her mother had an accident and she needed to go to her immediately. It was Susannah of sixth class who answered her text and offered to amalgamate her class with Eva's; the sixth class loved looking after the little ones. She warned Eva to drive carefully, and hoped her mother was okay. The superstitious fear that she may have invited an accident on her mother by lying about such things brought her to tears again. Now she needed to see her mother, needed to be sure she *was* okay.

It wasn't until she started the car that she thought of Ella and Kate. She texted Lizzie to pick them up after school, mentioned an emergency. Then she drove out of the school.

Eva found herself on the motorway, speeding towards Leitrim as if still acting out her grotesque lie, the Fiat rattling with the effort. Rain was lashing so hard the windscreen wipers were failing to keep on top of it. Her Fiat wobbled under the wash from overtaking cars, but she feared slowing down too much and being ploughed into from behind. She'd stop off in Mullingar, halfway between Dublin and Drumshanbo. Eva needed a toasted sandwich and a cup of tea. Her feet tingled. She lifted a hand off the steering wheel and watched it tremble. A large hotel appeared off to the left. Eva swerved. Horns blew. She ignored them, same as she ignored her ringing phone.

The hotel restaurant was crowded with white, cloth-covered tables, largely empty. A bearded man, wearing a scarlet waistcoat, waved a menu at her. She withdrew to the dark of the bar and the plush, plum-coloured leather banquettes. There were menus on the table and a French version of a ham and cheese toastie with relish and salad. Ten euro. There'd better be chips on the side. As she relayed her order to the barman, her phone rang again. The barman kindly brought her attention to the phone, but Eva continued to ignore it. It was Shay. Until Eva worked out what to say to him she had no intention of picking up.

When the sandwich arrived, she found she wasn't hungry any more. She drank the tea and then, since she hadn't decided where she was going or what she was going to do there, she ordered a glass of Cabernet Sauvignon. She drank until her heart slowed and her body melted into the seat.

She didn't *have* to do anything. She could pretend she didn't know anything. She could forget.

*

Yesterday had been unusually warm for March. After school, Eva persuaded Lizzie and Beatrice to bring the children back to hers, to sit in the garden in the sun and drink wine. She wanted to make the most of the sun, she said. After the week-end, she was restless and didn't want to be alone. Shay was doing a job for a mate and wouldn't be back until late. The children disappeared, and they had the garden to themselves. The women stretched their pale legs out in the sun and idly debated whether a degree or two of global warming was going to improve their summers or give them more rain. Eva believed Shay when he argued any change, either way, would be a disaster for the natural order of things. One needed to be careful what one wished for.

Eva was on her way to fetch a second bottle of wine when she heard a fierce scream from deep inside the house. Ella came running, holding her neck, crying. She threw herself at Eva, buried her face in her lap. 'Fiach bit me!'

Eva gently tugged Ella's hand away. Under Ella's ear was a circle of tiny red teeth marks. Beatrice was already on her way inside, shouting for Fiach. Unlike other mothers, Beatrice never fussed about the details or the circumstances. What was wrong, was wrong. Eva loved that about her. She rubbed Ella's back and murmured soft nothings until she stopped crying.

'Was he hungry?' asked Lizzie.

Eva tried not to laugh in front of Ella. They were a bit drunk.

'I'm serious. It's nearly seven and we haven't fed them.'

'Stop.'

Beatrice marched Fiach out and planted him in front of Ella. Despite looking like he too could cry, he stood tall. A brave little soldier. Fiach could be too good at times.

'I'm sorry. I didn't mean to hurt you,' Fiach told Ella.

Ella peeked out from under her hair. 'But you bit me! Really hard.'

Jimmy and Kate watched from the kitchen doorway. 'He did. We saw him,' said Kate.

'He bit with his teeth,' said Jimmy.

Fiach hung his head.

It took a while but, as soon as Ella accepted the apology, Beatrice announced they were going home. Lizzie decided she and Jimmy ought to go too, get some food. The girls, tired and hungry, cried. Eva fed them and cleaned up.

When she was getting the girls ready for bed, Eva asked how Fiach came to bite Ella. Were they fighting? The girls didn't want to talk about it. Eva worked on Kate; she was hopeless at keeping secrets.

'It was a game,' Kate admitted. 'That mummies and daddies do. Playing sexy.'

'Like kissing?' asked Eva.

'Kind of,' said Kate.

Ella announced that she would demonstrate. She ran at Kate and squashed her against the wall with her own body, held her hands up so she couldn't move, then rubbed her face into Kate's neck like she was eating her. Eva recognised the move.

'Okay, right. Well, mummies and daddies sometimes do funny things when they're playing but they don't hurt each other. They don't bite. No biting allowed anywhere at any time.'

'But it wasn't mummies and daddies.'

Ella shushed Kate. But it was too late.

'What do you mean?' asked Eva.

More people had landed in the bar. A family of four, almost identical, dark hair, sallow skin, were eating burgers. American, she decided. Their sportswear may have been casual, but it looked brand new, same as their white teeth and shiny hair. They wouldn't be out of place in a catalogue.

A man in a grey business suit slid by her, dropped his briefcase on the bar and sat on a stool. She watched him order a whiskey and a glass of white. He took out his phone, scrolled rapidly through messages. When it rang, he startled and dropped it. The caller ID was the face of a boy, maybe thirteen, in a Meath GAA jersey. He spoke softly to him. Eva decided he must be a good father, attentive and gentle. Her attention was drawn to a woman at the door, clutching a tiny bag to her chest. She was in heels and a purple trouser suit. Gorgeous but for her brittle blonde hair, sitting like a bike helmet on her head. She walked slowly over to the businessman, arriving at his side before he was aware she was there. He immediately cut off the call and put the phone in his pocket. Eva didn't hear a goodbye of any kind. The blonde perched herself on the stool next to him and took the white wine he offered.

Eva drank enough glasses of wine that the bearded waiter joked that she might've been better off buying a bottle. So, she ordered one. When asked if she was a guest in the hotel, she said yes, she was, and off he went. She nibbled the sandwich. It was cold. The chips were cold, but she needed to line her stomach or else the party would be over too soon. Her mother texted to ask what was going on, why did Shay think she'd had an accident? Where was she? Was she coming to Leitrim? She was worried about her.

Eva stood up. She needed to pee urgently. It was difficult to slide out of the banquette, would be for anyone, but the Americans watching her seemed to think she was putting on some kind of show. She walked in the direction the bearded waiter pointed her in. The bathroom was empty. Eva bounced off the sides of the cubicle as she sat down. She was lucky most of the urine went into the bowl. Her tights were a bit damp, but they'd dry.

On her return she found a young man at her table. To be fair, her bottle and her glass were empty. Her plate had been cleared away.

'I'm sorry, were you sitting here?' he asked.

'Yes.'

'The bottle was empty. I thought whoever was here had finished and gone.' He stood, ready to go. Eva felt herself sway. 'Are you okay?' he said.

She plonked down onto the edge of the banquette. 'I need to go to bed.'

He watched her, not saying a word. She couldn't take her eyes off his. Sea green. Black lashes. He seemed to be genuinely concerned for her.

'Can I help you?'

'I'm going to sit here for a moment.'

'Please. Go ahead.'

The businessman and the blonde were still at the bar, their heads close, talking. He sat with his legs wide open, bringing his thigh up against hers.

'They're having sex and they shouldn't be.'

'How do you know?' said the young man. 'I mean I agree, totally, they look like they've done it before but how do you know they shouldn't be?'

Eva hadn't meant to speak out loud. 'He has a family somewhere. A boy.'

'He might be separated or divorced or widowed? Maybe he's been lonely and now he's falling in love again?'

'I know because he's lying to the woman and to the boy.'

Eva pulled herself to standing. Searched for her handbag. Found it over her shoulder. Checked the exits. Picked one and walked. She found herself in the beer garden. When she turned to go back, Mr Green Eyes was right behind her. 'I'm sure it's better out here when it's sunny,' he said. 'But beggars can't be choosers, can they?'

Did she hear him right? Say nothing.

'I'm going to the reception desk myself. I thought you knew the way.'

'Oh,' she said.

'Let's give it another go.'

She followed him to the desk, as he'd probably meant her to, then copied everything he did. One double, one night, yes to breakfast. He headed to the lift with his bag. An O'Neill's gym bag. Classy. When she reached the lifts, he was inside one, keeping the doors open for her.

'Thank you.'

She entered and turned to face the doors. He was hers if she wanted, she thought.

They emerged on the same floor, but Mr Green Eyes went left, and she went right. Eva stopped. She couldn't remember the room number and the little white card she was holding was blank.

'It was 212. That's down this way. I'm not stalking you by the way, I couldn't help overhearing.' Mr Green Eyes had come back.

'Thank you. I think I've got it now.'

Eva found 212, but the lock didn't work. When she tapped her card, the red light stayed red. She was tapping away when she saw there was a slit down the side. Ah yes. But then it slipped out of her hand and fell onto the royal-blue carpet. It was a long way down and impossible to pick up without falling over. She almost had it when a hand swept in and picked it up.

'These doors are tricky.' Mr Green Eyes swiped the card and held the door open. She felt a hand under her elbow, gently pulling her inside.

'Thank you.'

In the centre of the room was a king-size bed. She let herself fall into a cloud of white. Mr Green Eyes was doing something to her shoes, then he had his hands on her legs.

'What are you doing?'

'I'm going to cover you up and then I'm going to leave you to sleep.' He lifted her legs onto the bed and pulled the throw up to her shoulders, leaning in as he did so. Those green eyes were something else.

'I might let you stay for a bit if you wanted to. You seem to know what you're doing.'

She heard him laugh. 'My mother used to drink.'

She wasn't sure what he meant; was she like his mother because she was drunk? Or because she was the same age? She heard the door click behind him as he left.

The ceiling was white.

The room was warm.

The bed was soft.

The girls would like this bed. It would be good for jumping on.

Not only mummies and daddies, said Kate, mummies and friends. Like Fiach's mummy and Jimmy's daddy.

Eva would've done anything to have unheard that.

Boom. Boom. Boom. Cluster bombs ricocheted around her skull. Her mouth felt like it was inside out. Waves of nausea rushed through her. Boom. Boom. The carpet was scattered with tiny bottles from the minibar. A knocking fist.

'Eva! Open up. It's me.'

She slid to the end of the bed and dragged herself to standing. She moved slowly, opened the door. Shay.

He took her in, yesterday's clothes, smudged mascara, eyes the colour of a blood orange. 'Christ, Eva. What's going on, you okay?'

She tried to answer but fell into his arms instead.

'I've been so worried. Lizzie rang me, wanted to find out how your mum was. I rang your mum, and she didn't know what I was talking about. Then Margaret called, she said you'd taken off after lunch. She said you'd been crying. Wanted to know what she could do to help. She thought your mother must be in a very bad way. And then you didn't answer your phone.' He opened a window. The cool air was a blessing. 'You scared me.'

'How did you find me?' asked Eva.

'Conor.'

'Conor?' For a briefest moment, Eva was certain there'd been some telepathy between herself and Conor. It didn't surprise her.

'You texted him. He said you were upset, and I should go get you.'

186

Her stomach twisted again. She ran to the bathroom and threw up for a second and third time. She washed her face and tried to clean up the pools of mascara under her eyes.

'Where are the girls?'

'At school. Lizzie took them in. What happened?'

'Nothing. The kids were playing up. Out of control. I lost it with Eliza, she was screeching in my face, then I cried and I couldn't stop. I'm so tired, Shay. So tired.'

Shay put her shoes on. Brushed her hair. He picked up her phone, dead, and put it in her bag. They were on the motorway ten minutes later.

'Why'd you text Conor?' asked Shay.

'I don't know. Maybe I couldn't get through to you?'

'You didn't call me. Not once.'

Eva couldn't remember enough to even attempt a lie.

Shay called the school, told Margaret that Eva's mother had been lucky, but was badly bruised and shaken up. She would need Eva's help for the rest of the week. Eva plugged in her phone and went to bed. She lay there vibrating until she fell into a deep sleep. The girls danced in the periphery of her vision, laid kisses on her cheeks. Patted her. She slept again.

Eva woke in the night when her family were asleep. She tip-toed through the dark to the kitchen and found her phone still plugged in. She had decided that since Shay didn't mention anything about Conor's being upset, she couldn't have told Conor anything about Beatrice and Frank. Her heart jumped as her phone came back to life.

Eva saw that Conor had called her at 3.59 a.m. and the call lasted thirty-five minutes.

In the garden, moonlight fell like glass.

A child murmured in her sleep.

When the knock came at the door, she knew it would be one of them. She was afraid but she wasn't sorry.

187

33

Home

Conor drove Fiach to school on Wednesday morning. It had been so long since Dermot had taken over the school run that Fiach thought Daddy dropping him was a special treat and was giddy with the joy of it. There was something about the cocoon of his backseat booster that caused Fiach to chatter non-stop, slipping seamlessly from how he got the scab on his knee to monsters under the bed.

'What do you do if you see something that scares you?'

'Stand up big and tell them to go away.'

In the mirror, Conor watched his son sit up high in his throne, his little fist pumping, his face contorted as he shouted at the empty space in front of him, 'Go away. Leave me alone!'

'I think you scared me then.'

Fiach trilled like a happy little bird.

'What about when you see something you don't understand?'

'I ask a question.'

Crowds of kids and parents milled around the pedestrian lights and the gates in front of the school. He slowed but kept driving.

'Daddy! You missed the school!' Fiach peered around in his seat as if keeping sight of the school would keep it close.

'I wanted to talk to you for a little bit longer.' Conor passed the mosque, turned left at Sally's Bridge. Up and over. Heading home to Crumlin.

'We'll be late.'

'No, we won't. I promise.'

'I don't want to miss news, Daddy.'

*

Last night, when Eva's first text came through, Conor had woken instantly. He left the bedroom, not wanting to disturb Beatrice. There wasn't anything strange about the text other than the time it was sent – 03:57.

Hello

Conor waited in case it was a mistake. Then the text appeared.

Weve Ben taken for a ride.

– *Are you okay?*

Rules are for fols.

– *What's happened?*

Ive ben drunking

– *Where are you?*

Mullingar. lol

– *Is Shay with you?* He walked down to the kitchen using the light of the phone. Poured himself a glass of water, his eyes on the phone the whole time.

I arna way

ran

He dialled her. The phone rang longer than it should. Then he heard her voice. Crying. 'Where are you?' he asked.

'A hotel. Mullingar. They never stopped.'

'Are you safe?'

'I'm sorry, Conor.' She was crying again. 'I'm so sorry. I didn't know—'

'Eva. What's going on? What are you sorry about?'

'I'm going to tell you something and it's going to change everything. Okay?'

Conor felt a tremor run through him. He sat on the sofa. His bare feet like ice, unable to feel the soft rug beneath. This call, this hour, the state of her, no good could come of it. Was it wiser to let it wait until tomorrow, and should she sober up and change her mind, accept not knowing what she might have wanted to say? Was it more mature to listen now? To hear her lay it out for him. The things that needed to be said. The things distorting a person, sickening a person.

189

'I love you, remember this,' said Eva.

Conor let out a sigh. This was something he already knew, and it didn't scare him. Eva's love was full of potential. Something he could choose to pursue or not, like those life dreams about volunteering in the third world or learning how to sail. Never practical but unwise to ignore. 'It's okay, we can talk about this in the morning. I think you should drink some water and go to sleep now. I want you to take care of yourself. Okay?'

A bird was singing, heralding a sun that had yet to show itself in the pale sky.

'Fiach saw them kiss.'

Conor's hand dropped, the phone falling to the sofa. He knew this was true.

Conor drove around the green in front of his childhood home. The *For Sale* sign was gone. Their front lawn was thick with dandelions. White laminate sheets of varying sizes were stacked on the driveway. His mother's kitchen presses. Her blue Formica countertop, wiped clean again and again, lay on the grass waiting to be dumped.

Conor once stood at that counter asking his mother why she was crying and how she'd say no she wasn't; how helpless he felt knowing something was wrong but being refused an explanation. He couldn't ask Fiach anything about what he saw between Frank and Beatrice. He couldn't let him see anything was wrong because he had no way to explain it. He would bring Fiach to school and he would go to work. He'd do his best to keep to his schedule. For lunch he'd have a bacon roll and an americano at his desk and research setting up a website for the clinic. In this way he would move forward.

Conor was reversing out of the school car park when Frank appeared in his rear-view mirror flying past on his bike. No helmet. Long black coat flying. Conor swung the car around and followed him onto the main road. Frank stood up on his pedals to gather some speed. Conor accelerated. Frank glanced over his shoulder and saw him.

Frank spinning cartwheels in the air.

Frank laid out on the mortuary slab, skull caved in, limbs degloved.

Two inches away from clipping Frank's rear wheel, Conor pulled hard right and overtook him; the force of his displaced air unbalanced Frank. In the rear-view mirror, Conor watched as Frank's bike wobbled uncontrollably before throwing Frank into the gutter. He came to a stop and waited until Frank staggered upright. Then he drove away.

Conor diagnosed an eight-year-old's tonsillitis, listened to the cough of a forty-three-year-old smoker, took his bloods, signed a sick note for a call centre worker, no questions asked, took a biopsy from a mole, reviewed a woman's antidepressants. Filled forms, made notes, wrote prescriptions, made referrals. Sympathised with the clinic nurse about her cancer-riddled cat. Conor hated cats but he wasn't going to let her in on that. At lunchtime he had no interest in his bacon roll and could only watch the clock. He was unable to articulate to anyone else, let alone himself, what was happening to him. This same inarticulacy meant he was unable to imagine what he might say or do when he arrived home to his wife, his child, his father. He was holding his breath. An angry rash had erupted in his inner elbow, lumpy and red. He'd scratched recklessly, enjoying the relief of the itch and the aftermath of burn. He diagnosed a stress-induced eruption.

It was 6.10 p.m., and he was packing up to go home when a young boy came in with his mother. Ross had found himself on the wrong side of a rugby tackle in an after-school training session. He was ginger-haired, fifteen and ripe with cystic acne. His mother tried to leave space for the boy to speak for himself, but Conor couldn't bear the silence. Ross held his arm tight to his chest. Conor gently pulled the arm out straight and the mother flinched.

Apart from one sharp intake of breath, the boy didn't make a sound as he examined him. If there was a fracture, it was minor. A few weeks in a cast and he could be back in the game. The mother was anxious that her son be able for a special Cup match in two months. Conor was in the process of warning that until he saw an X-ray he couldn't be sure of anything, when Ross announced he was finished with rugby. He hated it. He was good but not good enough. The mother, who, it seemed, had already bought the ticket, the shirt, the future, tried to shush him. He'd been admitted to the Junior Cup team only to sit on the bench. To be the spare.

Conor had been that boy. Good enough to be on the school hurling team but not good enough to play. The private humiliation – as a loyal team player he was constantly cheering enthusiastically from the sidelines – only ended when he topped the school in the Leaving Certificate.

Here he was again. Benched.

In the car, creeping along in traffic, Conor said the words out loud again and again. Remember Fiach? Remember our little boy who's known nothing but love? How could you do this to him? How could you walk away? It's over. The boy stays with me.

BITCH.

A driver pulled up alongside and was openly staring at him. Conor was screaming at the windscreen, at the red light that refused to change, at the cyclists waiting, crowding the car.

Frank's skull smashing on the concrete kerb. The entitled prick. Conor knew them only too well. Medicine was full of them, selfish, amoral scumbags who assumed the world belonged to them.

FUCKING SCUM.

He couldn't go home, couldn't let Fiach see him like this. Couldn't worry his father as he wrapped his hands around Beatrice's neck and cut off her oxygen supply. Shattered her hyoid. He drove on down South Circular Road, turned at Dolphin's Barn and headed back to the nursing home.

Molly was in a wheelchair queue of people waiting to be taken somewhere. As he wheeled her out of the queue and down the hall, she grumbled with surprise but, when he checked, she was smiling. He pushed her into her room. Her bed was turned down, waiting for her.

'It's too early for bed, right Mam? Will I see what's on the telly?' He turned on the TV, flicked past a cooking programme, football, and found the news. Pulling up a chair beside hers, he sat and watched a grey-suited pundit talk into a microphone. A new government had been elected and there was some expectation that things were going to change. He didn't believe it.

'Who's that?' said Molly.

'Don't know.'

'Wouldn't trust him far as I could throw him. Thinks he's God's gift. Look at his eyes. Come-to-bed eyes, they are.' She turned to see if he agreed. 'Oh,' she said.

Conor was crying.

'Oh dear. Oh dear. You tell me who upset you and I swear I'll put this right through them.' She made a fist. This had been his mother's response to any slight against him, major or minor, and it always made him laugh. His phone pinged with a text. Beatrice – *are you working late, will we wait for you for dinner?*

'Bea's had an affair.' He gulped back a sob as he said this.

'Dirty hoor.' Molly took his hand in hers and patted it. Conor couldn't tell whether she knew who he was talking about or not. This might have always been her answer to infidelity.

'Good riddance,' she said.

All the air flew out of him, as if his mother had socked him in the stomach. This was why he couldn't tell anyone. He didn't want to be told he must leave or be told he must stay and make it work. Either way he would lose.

He bent to kiss her as he left. She swatted him away.

Conor waited in the car outside his house until the lights went off inside and everyone was in bed. He didn't need an audience. His phone pinged. Beatrice.

Is something wrong? Why won't you come in?

She was at their bedroom window, staring down at him.

Beatrice had received a text from Frank at 9.32 a.m. that morning.

Your husband nearly ran me off the road. Everything all right?

She'd answered without thinking. – *He was worried about a patient. U ok?*

That's what Conor had told her this morning. He was woken in the middle of the night by a patient of his, their age, possible heart attack. He stayed on the phone with him until the paramedics arrived. She told Frank that Conor was sleep-deprived and not paying attention.

She walked on to a meeting with a solicitor in the spring sunshine, feeling like she'd forgotten something, but she'd checked her phone, her wallet, her keys. Dermot confirmed she hadn't left anything on that shouldn't be on. This sense of something wrong was familiar but hadn't happened since she stopped seeing Frank in January.

In the afternoon, when Beatrice arrived at the school to pick up Fiach, Lizzie told her Eva's mum had been in an accident yesterday and Eva had raced home to Leitrim. Beatrice hoped it wasn't serious. Lizzie told her Shay said her mum was fine but still Eva hadn't replied to any of her texts. At the gates, as they kissed cheeks, Lizzie mentioned that it was time they met up for dinner. It was Shay and Eva's turn but maybe it wasn't the right time to suggest it.

'No. I don't think so.'

'I would host but the teens have exams. It doesn't mean they're studying but I don't want to give them any excuses, you know?' Lizzie waited for Beatrice to offer.

Beatrice knew how the night would go because it would be the same as all the other nights. She didn't want to see Frank. She hated him *and* couldn't resist him. She loved Lizzie but couldn't help thinking Lizzie was a fool to have settled for Frank, a man who would cheat on her so readily. She liked Eva but her ambivalence frustrated her. She wanted the job. She didn't want the job. And Shay, well he was sweet, but he was useless. She was tired of them all and more significantly she no longer liked herself when she was around them. She was the adulterer, she'd betrayed their friendship, and she'd lied. She wanted to start all over again somewhere else. She'd done it before, she could do it again.

She promised Lizzie she'd talk to Conor about a date for dinner and get back to her.

Beatrice watched the lights in the car go off, but Conor didn't get out. His patient must've died. Perhaps he was sitting there blaming himself. After she was sure Fiach was asleep, she would go down to him.

34

The Child

It'd been a long time since Dermot had shared a bed with a small boy. They were hot little animals and the tossing and turning meant he didn't sleep. It wasn't Fiach's fault. All night he listened to Conor moving about the house, on the stairs, in the kitchen, pacing in the living room above, every creaking step.

It was the heavy footsteps he'd heard first from his little cave in the basement, frantically moving from room to room. Dermot feared something was wrong; perhaps the boy was sick. He waited, not imagining he would be much help, but then he heard the strange, whispered shouting, all force but no air, and the broken-up begging of Beatrice. He sat up quickly and climbed the stairs in his pyjamas. No time for a dressing gown or slippers. Beatrice was saying, please don't, please don't. Dermot's heart raced with anxiety, fearing something was wrong with the boy. When he reached the top of the stairs he saw the doors open, Conor holding a gym bag, clothing spilling over the sides, Beatrice pulling on him. At first Dermot thought Beatrice was trying to stop Conor from leaving. Fiach came to his bedroom door blinking in his yellow rocket pyjamas. Dermot found his breath.

'The child.' They both turned to Dermot, then saw Fiach. The boy was swaying, unsure whether he was asleep or awake.

'Mummy?'

Beatrice immediately turned to Fiach, but Conor grabbed her wrist so hard she spun back against him, wincing with pain. He kept his body between her and Fiach.

'Conor!' said Dermot.

Conor held on to Beatrice's shoulders and pointed her at the stairs. 'Go now.'

'Muuuummmmy?'

Beatrice pushed against Conor, her eyes swinging between Dermot and Fiach, wanting Dermot to help, wanting to hold Fiach, her face long with distress.

Fiach wailed. 'Mummydaddystopfightingstop.'

Dermot stepped around them and lifted Fiach up into his arms. 'Cop on to yourselves for Christ's sake.'

Conor let go of Beatrice and took a step back, more out of habit than intent. He obeyed his father, but he wasn't surrendering. Beatrice breathed in and out. She tried to smile at Fiach, but Fiach wouldn't look at her.

'It's okay,' said Beatrice, 'better if I go for now.' She rubbed Fiach's back, the top of his head. 'I'm sorry we woke you. I'll see you in the morning. Mummy loves you.' She turned to Conor. 'And Daddy.'

They listened to her close the front door quietly behind her. Conor still had her gym bag in his hand. He put it down. 'She can collect it tomorrow.'

He went into his bedroom and shut the door.

Fiach trembled in Dermot's arms.

'Want to sleep in my bed?'

He felt a little nod against his shoulder, and they made their way carefully downstairs.

35

We Have All Day

With every step, every little bump Conor's chest ached; ached when he showered, brushed teeth, dressed. The pain made it difficult to breathe. His hands shook. His vision was blurry. He had been awake for twenty-nine hours; he was late for work, and he couldn't find his car keys. He was racing around upending everything when he saw Dermot had them.

'I'm not letting you go anywhere, son. Nobody would be safe with you.'

'I'm fine, Da. Give me the keys.'

Dermot handed him a cup of tea. 'Take that and shut up. I already rang the clinic and said you were vomiting all night.'

'For fuck's sake.' There was no undoing Dermot's lie without exposing himself to his colleagues. He sat and drank his tea. Fiach, who had been quietly sitting on a stool at the kitchen island, was watching him closely. Conor tried to smile for him. 'Good morning.'

'Where's Mummy?'

'She's staying at a friend's, a sleepover,' said Conor.

'Why were you so mean? You made her cry.'

Conor should have known Fiach would dive straight in with the questions. That's how they reared him. Conor appealed to Dermot. *Please help me.*

'It was grown-up business,' said Dermot. 'I'm sure he'll say sorry when he sees your mam.'

As a child, Conor had been confused by his parents' arguments; how he never saw them apologise as they made him do. And how confusing it was when one day, like magic, they would be talking again.

'It's time to go,' said Dermot. 'Get your school bag, Fi.'

Conor opened his arms for a hug and Fiach ran straight in. 'Go on, little man, get your bag.' Fiach hurried away.

'I'll be straight back,' Dermot told Conor. 'Don't you do anything rash. Don't do anything. You're in no state.'

'Did you know about Frank?'

'Frank? Your friend? The loud one? Is that what this is about?' Dermot turned away from him. Whatever he was thinking, he didn't want Conor to guess. When he turned back, his eyes were glassy. 'Believe me son, I didn't know anything. I can see you're angry, anyone would be, but what happened last night can't happen again. You were a disgrace.'

Conor reeled. 'Bea has an affair and I'm the disgrace?'

Dermot took his time. 'She shouldn't have done that. But you manhandled her. In front of the boy.'

Conor couldn't maintain his defiance. Shame cut through him like a knife.

Fiach returned with his school bag, his attention swinging from one to the other. Dermot took his hand and walked him out the door.

Conor was alone in the house in a way he'd never been before. The house felt like it belonged to someone else. It was quiet but for his phone, vibrating all morning with calls and texts, all unanswered. All Bea, bar one from Eva last night and one from Shay this morning. Shay had left an emotional voice message. Bea was with them, she hadn't told him anything, he said, but she was very upset. He offered to listen, no judgement, no sides. Of their friends, Shay was probably the only one Conor felt could genuinely offer that, but Conor wasn't ready to tell anyone anything. Beatrice was the only person he wanted to talk to. The Beatrice of before who loved him and knew when he was overreacting or under-reacting. The Beatrice who would know what to do. The Beatrice he trusted was gone for ever. She might as well be dead.

*

Beatrice rang the doorbell nine minutes after he texted her. He had packed a proper suitcase for her but hadn't decided if he'd invite her in or send her on her way. All he did know was that he hoped she was suffering as he was.

She stood before him in last night's clothes. Her hair was lank, her face pale. He'd left her suitcase by the door. She ignored it. 'Please can I come in?'

He walked down the hall, leaving her to follow. 'We have all day,' he told her. 'To talk or whatever. Dad's not going to come back until I text him. Would you like—' He stopped himself from offering her a drink.

'A coffee, yes.' She was halfway to the kitchen to get it herself, as she'd done thousands of times before, but then she stopped, and he saw that she was questioning if she should. Had he decided the rules had changed or had she? Either way, he relished her uncertainty.

'I'm not going to make it for you,' he said.

She fetched a cup and turned on the Gaggia, glancing back at him the whole time. She made coffee in the exact same order every day. The same small china cup placed on its saucer, the single espresso button hit twice, instead of the double espresso. It was stronger this way, she insisted. Then she'd stand at the kitchen island, rest her left hand on it, and down the coffee in two mouthfuls. When she was done she would put the cup and saucer in the dishwasher. Today was no different except the breakfast dishes were still waiting to go in the dishwasher. She rinsed a bowl.

'Don't. Leave them.'

She stepped back. 'How was Fi?'

Conor shrugged. 'He was okay. He's at school. We need to agree on what to tell him.'

'About what?'

'About you fucking Frank.'

She took the hit, collected herself again. 'You want to tell him? That's what you want?'

'I don't want to tell him anything. But he's going to notice his mammy doesn't live here any more.'

'You don't mean that.' She remained standing behind the island, looking down on him. Her finger traced a silver streak that ran through the marble worktop.

'So, Frank's not about to leave Lizzie, set up house with you?'

'No.'

'It's not a love story then?'

'I love you.'

'Bullshit.' He felt mocked.

'I never stopped loving you.'

Conor didn't like her looking down on him. He rose from the sofa and paced. 'Frank. Frank fucking Durkan. That's what I don't get. He's a wanker who thinks he's better than everyone else. Was he exceptional in bed? Help me out here? I want to understand.'

'Conor—'

He had inadvertently moved closer to her. He forced himself to laugh. 'Cause it wasn't his looks.'

Beatrice held on to the cold, marble island, as if it were a raft keeping her afloat. 'I will tell you. Is that what you want?'

He wanted to know why, because if he could know why then they might find their way back together. But if finding out why meant he had to know the how, a reconciliation would be impossible. That was Bea, turning it right back on him. He had no doubt she would tell him everything if he asked.

'Of course I don't want to know.'

She slid down behind the island and sat on the floor. He sank into the sofa and listened to her crying. He could see her legs and arms stretched out before her like a broken puppet.

'How did you find out?'

Conor hadn't considered this question. 'You can't guess?'

'Not Dermot?'

'Jesus, no.' Conor felt his whole body constrict. Would his father have told him if he had suspected anything? Maybe not.

'Who knows, Bea?'

'I thought no one. We'd stopped. It was over. Finished. Was it Eva who told you?'

Conor laughed. 'I might never have known. What bad luck.'

Jaro wandered in from the garden and padded over to Beatrice. She reached out and pulled him into her lap.

'How long? When did it start?'

'Harwood.'

Relief washed through him. His mind had been reeling back through the years wondering if he'd been blind to their attraction.

From behind the kitchen island, out of sight, she said, 'You should've said no.'

'What?'

'In Harwood House. If you'd said no, I wouldn't've gone with him.'

Conor took a minute to understand what she was saying. He couldn't recall the question.

'I would never have gone with him,' said Beatrice.

'If I had said no? What're you talking about? You never asked me?'

'Frank's game.'

'Truth or Dare?' He was having trouble catching his breath. 'Did you text him?'

She was silent. He wanted to smash something. Upturn tables, punch walls. All he had within reach was a cushion on the sofa. It bounced off the bookshelves, knocking a vase onto the tiles. Pieces flew across the floor and into every corner.

Beatrice jumped up, keeping the island between them.

'This is my fault?' shouted Conor. 'Is that what you're saying? Oh my God. It was a drunken dare. A game. Only you were stupid enough to follow through. Only you. I'd say Frank couldn't believe his luck. You don't get to blame me. I *loved* you.' As he said the word, love, he wanted to pull her into his arms, hold her close, and whisper, *I love you*. He wouldn't survive this ambivalence.

When she finally spoke, she sounded like a child. 'But Eva chose you?'

'Eva didn't *choose* anyone.'

'But you and her were together?'

'I stayed in the library. She stayed in the library. I thought you'd gone to bed.'

'Oh. I —' Beatrice's hands fluttered around her face, picking at her skin. 'I try so hard. I try to do the right thing. I didn't know. I didn't know. Why didn't you say anything?'

Conor laughed. 'You did what you wanted. You always do.'

Her eyes focused on him. There was a hardness there that he'd only seen her turn on strangers.

'I never see you!' she shouted. 'And even when you're here your mind is somewhere else. With someone else. You are always looking after other people.'

'It's my fucking job.'

'And I am your wife.'

He was going to lose his temper again. 'I can't. I just can't— You need to go now.' He tried to usher her to the door without touching her.

'What about Fi?'

'He stays here, in his own home, with me.' Conor was almost on top of her, forcing her to walk backwards, away from him.

'But when you're not here? When you're at work?' She stumbled.

'Dad'll mind him.'

'Please Conor, please. He's a baby. Don't punish him.'

'Me?' All Conor wanted was for Fiach to have what he had yesterday. Two parents. A happy home. The thought that it couldn't have been that happy a home if Bea was having an affair flashed through his mind.

'I am his mother. He needs me. Please?'

She placed her hand on his chest. It burned. He pushed her away. 'You turned your back on him when you— Jesus Christ! Frank?'

Beatrice recoiled. 'This is not you, Conor. You are not cruel. You are good and kind.'

If it was ever true, it was only a useless vanity. 'We can talk about Fiach tomorrow, whenever, but he's not going anywhere.'

She was awash with snot and tears as she left, and he couldn't have cared less.

36

Everything's Fine

Beatrice texted Frank as soon as she left Conor.

Call me.

Frank felt a rush of joy when he read the text. He needed Beatrice. She was his superpower.

– See you at school?

No. Call now.

In the safety of his shed, he called her.

'He knows,' she said. Frank wasn't a worrier, hadn't wasted any time preparing for this moment. He had never been caught before – apart from the large accident of Paula's pregnancy – so he had no response ready. He waited for her to tell him what she wanted him to do. But all he could hear was her breathing, shallow and fast. 'What are you going to do?' he asked.

Beatrice wailed; so loud Frank feared Lizzie could hear it from the house. It wasn't simply the decibels, but the scale of her distress blasting from the phone. It took everything he had to not hang up, shut the shed door behind him and go back to doing the school run. He ached for her, would never have wished it on her, but he had to put his own family first. He had a part in Beatrice's distress but in his mind they remained adults, responsible, independent individuals. He believed that, like a virus, havoc could be quarantined. The havoc must not reach his household.

At school pick-up on Thursday, Lizzie saw Beatrice and Dermot standing outside the children's classroom. They were talking intensely; heads close, whispering. Fiach emerged with Jimmy but, when he spotted his mother, he yelped and ran at her. She lifted him high and let him wrap himself around her. Dermot steered the two of them over to a quiet corner. Fiach remained glued to Beatrice. Lizzie watched as Beatrice got down on her haunches, held Fiach's face in her hands, kissed him goodbye and hurried away. Something was very wrong.

Lizzie ran after her. 'Bea!' she called. 'BEA!'

Beatrice kept walking, head down, as if she didn't hear anything. She was fast; Lizzie didn't have a hope of catching up. By the time Lizzie reached the school gates, she'd disappeared. Lizzie stared down the empty street as if Bea might come back. Dermot and Fiach walked up behind her. Fiach was sniffing back tears.

'Fiach, sweetheart, what's wrong?' She glanced at Dermot. 'Is everything okay?'

Dermot didn't stop moving. 'We're grand, thanks, bye, bye, bye.'

Lizzie heard a distant child yelling, 'MUMMY!' Hers. Jimmy was jumping up and down at the classroom door with the teacher, waiting to be handed over. She had to turn back.

On the way home, dawdling behind Jimmy and Georgia, Lizzie rang Eva and described in detail what happened. 'She looked so upset. Destroyed,' said Lizzie.

'She stayed in ours last night,' said Eva. 'They had an argument.'

Lizzie grilled Eva but she said she didn't know what was behind the fight. Only that it was serious. Despite their long history of shared indiscretions with or without wine, Lizzie had no faith that Eva was going to tell her anything more. And the only reason for that, in Lizzie's experience, was because it somehow concerned Eva or herself.

'Hang on, does this mean you're not in Leitrim?'

At this, Eva gave a long explanation about being deputy vice-principal, exhaustion and needing an excuse to stay home. No, her mother didn't have an accident and yes everything was fine. Everything was clearly not fine.

Lizzie texted Beatrice. *U ok? if theres anything I can do let me know. xxxxxxxx*

She texted Conor by copy and pasting her message to Beatrice. *U ok? if theres anything I can do let me know. xxxxxxxx*

Conor replied almost immediately – *No. Everything's fine. x.*

Lizzie fed Georgia and Jimmy crackers and milk while shamelessly interrogating Jimmy about Fiach. Did he say anything about his mummy and daddy? Or about something happening last night? Jimmy talked about the classroom guinea pig who slept *all* day. How Chloe Griffin's new haircut felt like a brush. He didn't remember Fiach in the class; maybe he wasn't there. 'He was,' prompted Georgia, 'I saw him in the playground. He was all by himself.'

Lizzie brought two cups of tea out to the shed. She had a notion that Frank might know more about what was going on. Outside the door, she hesitated. If he did, then the implications were difficult to countenance. She put that thought to one side. With her hands full, she kicked the foot of the door to let him know she was there. The clatter made her sound more violent than she felt. He was slow to come to the door and, when he did, he took the tea, said cheers and was about to shut it on her.

'Wait!' she cried. She had her own cup of tea in her hand.

'Were you coming in?'

'I wanted to talk to you.'

The shed, a three-by-three-metre space, was filled with bicycles, footballs, super-soakers, and new year resolutions, like a Pilates ball and a mini-trampoline. Shelves threatened to topple at any moment. The desk, placed under the window, was the only tidy space, with his phone, laptop and pen. Suspiciously tidy for a man who was supposed to be writing a screenplay, but Lizzie decided to save that for another day.

'Well . . .' Lizzie paused for effect. 'Something has happened between Bea and Conor. She spent the night in the Brennans'. You should've seen her at school, she was so upset,

207

she couldn't talk to me.' She was watching him, waiting for his tell – the sigh with a roll of the eyes, a 'not this again' slump, a studied patience – while he'd try to convince her she was being paranoid.

Frank sat himself back down at the desk, took a long sip of his tea. 'Just what I needed,' he said.

'You're not surprised?'

'At Bea and Conor? What am I supposed to be surprised about? That they had a fight? Or that Bea was upset?' His lack of curiosity worried her.

'Aren't you curious?'

'I feel sorry for them,' said Frank.

'Well, yeah, of course,' said Lizzie.

'What does Eva say?'

'She said she didn't know anything. I don't believe her. I would've thought they seemed good, that they were getting on, wouldn't you?' Of all of them, Beatrice and Conor had always seemed the most content, the most agreeable, even after Harwood.

Frank pulled Lizzie onto his lap and looked out the window. 'Lots of people are good at surface. Conor and Bea are particularly good at it.'

Lizzie felt the warmth of him around her, felt his affection for her. She tried to see what he was looking at through the window, but it was clouded with spiderwebs and criss-crossed with ivy.

'You need to give that a clean,' she said. 'It'd make a big difference to the light in here.'

'But then people would be able to see in.' Frank double-tapped her bum, encouraging her off him. 'Right so. I've a scene to finish before I can call it a day. I'm looking for funding and the deadline's next week.'

As she was closing the door behind her, she stuck her head back inside. 'You said you'd do dinner tonight.'

Frank looked up; his phone was in his hand. He lowered the phone to his lap as if hoping she hadn't seen it. He smiled.

It was a careful smile. Not quite full, and not quite staying in place.

'What? Dinner, yeah sure.'

'You're a good man, Frank Durkan.'

'I try.'

'It's why I'm still here.' Frank nodded his head slowly.

She closed the door and made her way back down the garden path. She'd been with him long enough to understand some things are better left unsaid. Some things are better not examined too closely. With time, things right themselves. She felt ill, so she went inside and became someone else. Someone who hunted tigers with the children.

37

The Great South Wall

Beatrice walked fast, past the Grand Canal Dock, turned onto the bridge and continued through Ringsend and Irishtown. She saw nothing and no one. Her head was full of voices, her own and others, damning and fearful. What had she done? What was she to do? She couldn't live without Fiach. They'd have to sell the house, buy two places. The mortgage was impossible; negative equity meant that even if they could manage to buy two houses or apartments, there would be nothing left. She could cope with being poor again, but she didn't want that for Fiach. She kept walking, past the kite surfers on Sandymount Strand, past the water treatment plant, past the scrappy little beach scattered with rubbish and on to the Great South Wall, a breaker between the Irish Sea and Dublin harbour. She kept walking over the uneven granite blocks, waves pounding on one side, a calm deep blue on the other. An easterly wind cut through her. When she reached the squat red lighthouse at the end of the seawall, she was cold to the bone.

Beatrice checked her phone. There was a message. She knew what she wanted it to be – Conor texting her to come home. But it was Frank asking if he should talk to Conor. Obviously he didn't *want* to, but would if she thought it might help.

She rang him. 'What would you say?'

'What?'

She turned away from the wind, only to have her hair flying around her face. 'What would you say to Conor?'

'Where are you? It's hard to hear you.'

She shouted into the phone. 'What would you say to Conor?'

'I don't know. What do you want me to say?'

'I thought you had an idea?'

'What? I can't hear you.'

'Forget it.'

He kept talking. She thought he mentioned counselling. The wind dropped for a moment, and she heard him clearly.

'Did Conor kick you out or did you leave him?'

'He was so angry. So crazy. I left. He scared me and Fiach, he . . .' She sobbed. There was another silence before she heard, 'What?' She hung up; she couldn't do it any more. A few moments later a text came through from Frank.

Did he hit you?

– No!

What do you want me to do?

Beatrice put the phone away. She had been hoping he had a solution despite knowing there was none, none that involved him. Magical thinking. In the schoolyard Dermot had promised he'd do what he could to persuade Conor to let her come home, but he didn't want to know any details. She was certain that once Dermot knew what she had done, he would turn against her. Her guts rolled over again, sickening her.

She had to find the way back by herself.

Gulls tore through the air around her, cawing and diving into the sea beyond the wall, decimating a school of fish. In Majorca, last summer, Fiach had been afraid of the gulls. They were everywhere, the beach, the port, the plazas, and in his dreams. They'd reassured him as best they could but then a gull swooped in and plucked a churro right out of his hand. He was inconsolable, told them they were liars. He climbed into their bed in the middle of the night, stealing their sleep with his hot, sweaty restlessness.

They were staying in an old stone villa on a hill overlooking the port. There were dark-green shutters on the windows and fans on the ceilings. At night, they slept with the windows open, and the shutters closed. Breezes passed over them all night, like a caress.

On their last morning she felt a puff of air on her face and turned towards it seeking more. Shards of light reached into the room, bounced off white walls and white bedsheets, burned a stripe across her calf. She had tentatively opened her eyes. Fiach was on his hands and knees blowing on their faces, trying to wake them up. He'd shifted from her to Conor but seemed to be having no effect on him. She closed her eyes again, pretending to sleep, and he soon came back to her.

'Mummymummymummy?' he whispered.

She kept up the pretence of sleep.

He licked her cheek. The surprise of the hot, sticky roughness of his tongue made her squeal. Fiach, collapsing into giggles, fell onto Conor, waking him. Conor groaned and turned away, as if to sleep some more. Fiach leaned down and licked him too. Conor flipped over and pounced, tickling Fiach into a gasping helplessness until he couldn't breathe. They fell back, lying side by side. Fiach pulled the white sheet up over their heads. He filled his cheeks and puffed to make the sheet dance above.

'We're in the clouds,' said Fiach.

'Flying,' said Beatrice.

'I think I'm going to fart,' said Conor.

'Daddy, no!' Fiach pulled the sheet down. It was too hot in there. 'Lick me,' said Fiach.

'Yuck,' said Conor.

Beatrice licked his left cheek. 'Mmm, salty.'

Fiach writhed, unsure whether he liked it. 'Daddy?'

'Mind if I put some jam on first?'

'Okay.' Fiach was open to anything, but Beatrice feared where this was going.

'No! Don't. Not in the bed, please.'

Conor leaned in and licked him from his jaw to his hairline. Fiach chortled.

'You do it, Mummy. Now. And Daddy, do it at the same time.'

Conor raised his eyebrow in a little questioning look to Beatrice. As if to ask, is this okay, not weird? She counted, one, two, three, and stuck out her tongue.

They licked Fiach's cheeks until he could take no more.

Conor made coffee and brought it in on a tray with bread and honey. Beatrice announced that as it was their last day, crumbs in the bed no longer mattered. Fiach ran his little trains over the hills and valleys of their bodies while she read a novel and Conor played sudoku on his iPad.

From the Great South Wall, Beatrice could see the three of them on the bed, floating in sunshine, each of them alone with their thoughts and their pleasures, but content together. Back in Dublin, straight into a grey, wet week, the morning was lost among all the other lazy holiday mornings. Now that she knew that morning in Majorca may have been the last of its kind, she replayed every exquisite detail. It was happiness, abundant and beautiful, it was a peony in full bloom.

She walked back to Portobello and let herself into the house. Dermot and Fiach were playing with his zoo set on the living room floor. Fiach launched himself at her.

'Mama! Are you home now?'

She wouldn't lie to him. 'Where's Daddy?'

Dermot pointed upstairs.

'I'm going to talk to Daddy. Don't go anywhere.'

'Where would I go, silly?' asked Fiach as he sat back down among his animals.

'I don't know, the moon?'

'You're silly.'

'No, you are the silly,' said Beatrice.

She climbed the stairs repeating this all the way. Hoping Conor would hear her and be ready for her.

'No, you're the silly.'

*

Shay opened the front door to Beatrice. Without a word he wrapped her in a long, tight hug. She could hear Eva in the bathroom with the girls.

'Did you talk to him?' asked Shay.

'He's so angry. He won't let me talk to Fiach.'

Shay breathed out slowly. 'That's not right. That's not like Conor.'

Eva came into the hall with the girls wrapped in towels. When she saw Beatrice, she gave them a nudge. 'Go on, get your jammies on.' Their eyes flicked from adult to adult and sensed it wise to do what they were told. 'Are you coming in?' asked Eva.

Beatrice remained on the front step. 'Why did you tell him?'

Eva avoided looking at her. You could hear the beating of her panicked heart.

'What?' Shay pivoted back and forth between the two women. 'Eva?' They ignored him.

'Come inside, please?' asked Eva.

Beatrice looked down at the doorstep and knew she would never step foot inside Eva's house again. 'No.'

Eva pushed past Shay and came out onto the front step with Beatrice.

'Fiach saw Frank kiss you in the hall and told the girls and they told me.' Eva glanced at Shay. 'This was on Monday, after Fiach bit Ella.'

'Oh my God,' said Beatrice. She had to turn away from them. This felt worse than anything she did with Frank. Fiach saw them and knew there was something so wrong he couldn't tell anyone. The weight of it. 'You should have told me first. Me. I needed to talk to Fiach. And Conor. It was for me to do. To do for my family. You should've told me.'

They were all standing too close. Eva stepped back inside. 'I'm sorry but I didn't think, I was drunk, I know that's no excuse, but I was upset too. Drunk and upset. You know how that goes.'

214

Beatrice grimaced. 'Always that excuse. I was drunk. It was the drink did it.'

'Well, there's worse things,' said Eva.

Beatrice lunged forward, her hand raised. Shay's arm shot out to protect Eva, but she'd already pulled back. She turned and walked quickly down the street.

Beatrice checked herself into a hotel on the canal, into the only available room, overlooking the hotel's beer garden. She lay on top of the covers, too exhausted to undress, and listened to other people having a good time.

38

Anne-Marie. Tuesday 4.30 p.m.

Tuesdays at 4.30 was their time with Anne-Marie. After three months of counselling sessions once a week, Conor had a full routine worked out. He had to finish in the surgery at three thirty. Five minutes to urinate, wash up, put on his jacket, find his keys. A fifteen- to twenty-minute drive to Clontarf – Anne-Marie had been highly recommended – five minutes to find a park, pay the meter, thirty minutes left for a coffee and a bun to prepare himself. Cinnamon. Warmed. Cream cheese icing melting down the sides. But leaving the surgery on time was often impossible. Anne-Marie demanded her fee whether they turned up or not. Sometimes there'd only be five minutes left of the session. Five minutes for him to explain why he was late, why it was no reflection on his commitment to the counselling, how it in no way implied that he wasn't invested in finding a way out of this nightmare. It wasn't his fault people kept getting sick. Afterwards in the car, when he'd take another seventeen minutes to calm down, he couldn't help wondering why, when he'd *never* managed to be anywhere on time if he was coming from work, would Bea *always* expect him to be on time now. Even when he had Fiach, an elderly father and a dog to manage, a house to tidy, a fridge to fill, and stomachs to feed. He imagined this talking point had another few weeks left in it. It was progress on the forty-five-minute sessions of his angry crying.

Tuesday nights he would pick up fish and chips on the way home for himself, Dermot and Fiach. Fiach pronounced Tuesday the best night of the week. Conor thought it the worst. He missed having Bea to come home to. Especially on

Tuesdays when he wanted comfort after battling the new Bea and her ally, Anne-Marie. Conor preferred Wednesdays, when Fiach went to Bea's apartment in Christchurch. They were paying a fortune for a month-to-month lease on a two-bedroom apartment. The time it would take to find anything more suitable was more time that she couldn't have Fiach stay with her, and she wasn't prepared to wait. On Wednesdays he could stop and breathe, and he could only do that because Fiach was where he needed to be. The weekends, when Fiach was with Bea from Friday to Sunday, were lonely. Dermot spent his days with Molly, though she rarely recognised him. Even Jaro had stopped asking him for a play.

Dermot regularly complained about the terrible quiet or the smell of the house being off. He'd check the fridge to see if something had gone bad, would empty the bins but couldn't work out what it was. Conor suspected it was a more complicated scent Dermot was thinking of; whatever Beatrice contributed to the bouquet of the house was gone, like a plaid rug with a colour erased. On nights when the quiet and the smell – or lack of – couldn't be expunged, they went to the corner pub for a pint. Sometimes two. Dermot liked to sit at the bar. 'Up here you can see all the comings and the goings.'

Before, in all the imaginings of what they would do when Dermot moved in, going for a weekly pint together seemed a rich, precious activity. Now, the two of them sitting at the bar, staring at the bottles on the wall, no one waiting for them to come home, seemed so sad Conor couldn't wait to finish his pint and leave. If they had a second pint, Dermot, emboldened, would fill the silences with Beatrice.

'It's no mystery, no magic, Conor,' said Dermot. 'It's a promise you make when she walks up that aisle. You have to ask yourself if you're a man who keeps his promise.'

'What about Bea's promise to me?' asked Conor. His jaw ached with tension.

'She's trying, son.'

'Did you ever ask yourself if Mam *wanted* you to keep your promise to her?'

Dermot frowned, considering.

'She'd have had fewer choices back then, if she'd left you, instead of you leaving her,' said Conor. 'It would have been much harder for her as a single mother. She would've been judged.'

Dermot tensed but kept his voice calm. 'Truth is, if she ever did want to leave, and I'm sure there were times, all I can say is I'm glad she didn't.' He gave a nod to someone at the door.

'Who's that?'

'Haven't a clue.' Dermot picked up his pint. His hand was shaking.

'This is the best I can do right now,' said Conor.

'That's all you can do.'

Conor's first impulse was to move Fiach to another school, but Eva persuaded him to wait until September. A new school was probably more than Fiach could cope with. He had been disruptive, aggressive, or tearful since Beatrice moved out. Everything eased as soon as he spent more time with his mother. Dermot drove Conor crazy with his 'told you so'. But Conor wasn't surprised Fiach was less distressed; he'd known this was a necessary compromise. What had surprised and dismayed him was how long he'd fought it. When Conor conceded sleepover days with Beatrice, Eva implied he was heroic, doubted she would've been as quick to come to the same compromise. Her constant reassurance that he was doing well, and doing right, helped restore him to the man he thought he was. A good man. A compassionate man.

It was a Saturday morning late in May when Eva dropped in on the way home from the market with fresh bagels for him. He was only up, had thrown on joggers and a t-shirt to answer the door. He didn't know where Dermot was, only that he wasn't home, because he would've answered the door. They went down to the kitchen to make coffee. Last night's plastic takeaway containers were stacked on the island. The only time the house looked as it used to was on Thursdays in the first few hours after the cleaner had been.

Conor opened the courtyard doors and found the air was gentle and warm. They sat out in the sun with coffee and bagels and jam and talked about small, easy things: the orange lupins blooming, the pigeons courting on the chimney stack, the fat white clouds so perfect they could've been in a children's book. They talked about the long summer holidays coming up and what they'd do about the kids. They agreed on sports camp and art camp, shared pick-ups and drop-offs. For a while, sitting in his garden with summer coming and Eva beside him, he felt woozy with an unfamiliar happiness. She admitted how close she was to resigning her job, how often she gave an imaginary finger to her colleagues, who suddenly seemed unable to do anything but complain and, worse, expect her to do something. She offered to take Fiach with her and the girls to her parents in Leitrim for a week of running through fields and climbing trees. Conor immediately said yes, wanting a summer like that for himself. He had to check with Bea, but she probably wouldn't agree because he had already said no to her taking Fiach to Germany for a holiday. Or to Spain, her second choice. He wouldn't let her take Fiach out of the country in case she never brought him back. This fear of impending catastrophe – irreversible and hopeless – was never far away. Eva put her arms around him and held him. She had comforted him through several crying jags. So many that he'd stopped being embarrassed. Here we go again, he'd say as he caved. This time was different. He could hear her heartbeat. Could feel how warm her skin was from the sun. Could smell apples in her shampoo. As he concentrated on her, her warmth, he felt the sun on his own back. He took a breath and looked up at her; saw the crease between her eyebrows, her uncertainty. Her mouth moved as if she was going to say something, then thought better of it, was going to smile, then thought it wasn't appropriate. He waited for her to pull away and, when she didn't, everything changed.

'I think I might be falling for you,' he said.

'I know you are,' she said. They were still so close he felt her breath on his face.

'It's a bit of a problem.'

'Is it?'

He laughed. She didn't.

'D'you know what you're doing?' he asked. 'I don't think I'm reliable in any way.'

Eva tilted her head as she thought about it. She always considered his questions seriously. Then she kissed him.

'Wait, are you sure?'

Eva pulled him even closer and kissed him until he had no idea where he was nor who he was. When they paused to take a breath, they looked in each other's eyes and laughed. And laughed. He took her hand and led her upstairs. At the top of the stairs, Conor stopped; he couldn't go any further. There were only three doors: his and Bea's bedroom, Fiach's bedroom and the family bathroom.

Eva kissed him again, gently nudging him another few steps sideways into the master bedroom. He stopped before the unmade bed and turned back to her, helpless. There was nothing of Beatrice's left in the room that she could see, no pictures, no clothes, but nevertheless she was there. Eva lowered herself down onto a thick, cream Moroccan rug beside the bed. Conor fell onto his knees before her and ran his hands up her legs, his thumbs pressing into her inner thighs. She brought his hands up to her breasts, his eyes to hers. It had been days since she'd shaved her legs; she was certain Bea was as smooth as a baby's cheek. Probably lasered. And she'd never carried twelve pounds of twins in her belly. And then Eva was on her back and all she could feel

was the ridge of his erection against her thigh, his fingers sliding inside her, his mouth on her neck. His panting breath. And
something sharp digging into her buttock. He shifted his hands
beneath her, and she tried to slide off the thing, but it rolled
further up her back, and she winced as it stuck her again. She
hoisted her hip up, reached back, and found a Lego brick. She
tossed it under the bed.

Conor raised himself onto his arms. 'Okay?'

'Fine, yes, good, I mean *great*.' She giggled.

'What's that?' He pointed to a tiny tattoo on her hip.

'A swallow.'

'Why a swallow?'

'They seek the sun. I was in Greece at the time.' She laughed.
'They also symbolise fresh starts, new life. I'd just qualified.'
She stopped. The new life she was marking at the time was the
one she was making with Shay.

'It's beautiful. You're beautiful.'

It was what she'd been longing to hear but now she couldn't
look at him. 'I'm a terrible person.'

'Eva, no. Don't do that.'

Frank had asked her, one day after school, when there was
nowhere for either of them to hide, why did she tell Conor
about the affair, did it make her feel good? Did she feel righteous? She told him she didn't know why she did it but he didn't
believe her. If I were you, he'd said, I'd ask myself – what did I
get out of the telling? And he stood and waited as she absorbed
his words. And then he laughed at her.

Conor cupped her face and turned her back. 'You're a good
person in a difficult situation.'

'D'you have any tattoos?'

'No. I've seen too many on older skin.' He laughed. 'Sorry.
I'm an idiot. I'm sure yours will be fine. It's small, solid.' He
dropped down on the rug beside her. He was looking but not
looking at her, as if he'd gone somewhere else.

'Conor?' she asked. 'What's wrong?'

'Nothing. Nothing.'

He was lying. She was lying. Everything was wrong. The Lego. Her spiky legs. The hair across his abdomen. There was a spiderweb in the light fitting above. The underside of the dressing table behind her was riddled with termite holes. Turning the lights off wasn't going to make one iota of difference.

One sandal was in the hall, the other she found halfway down the stairs.

'Coffee?' Conor was on the landing, dressed.

When she reached the second sandal the front door was in sight. 'I should go,' she said as she took the last few steps to the door. He remained on the landing looking down at her. He said something that included it wasn't her it was him.

Outside, she met Dermot coming home with Jaro. She made herself smile, exchanged a few words, and walked on. The day was still warm, but cloud had muted the sun. There was no wind. The trees drooped. The faster she walked, the angrier she became, at Conor, at herself for expecting anything. This was life in all its stumbling messiness. It didn't mean they were wrong together, despite everything. An everything she didn't dare articulate.

A text came through from Conor – *Will you give me a second chance? I'd really like a second chance. xxx*

Eva replied. *Yes.*

A person unclothed was a different species. You needed to get to know them all over again.

39

Turquoise

There were days Shay loved mowing a lawn, working his way up and down until the lawn was striped with the bright green of cut grass. He traversed the hills and valleys of Mrs Daly's lawn and carved a gentle circle around the lopsided but blossoming wedding-cake tree. In one direction he had the cosy touch of a warm sun on his back, in the other the sting of sun in his eyes.

Mrs Daly watched him from the kitchen window. Each time he looped around he'd catch sight of her, nod, continue. It was ridiculous but he didn't want to ignore her. He had things he wanted to tell her over their cup of tea and a sandwich; things he wasn't sure he should, but he had no one else to talk to. When he fretted to Eva about Conor and Bea, she said Conor and Bea needed to work out what they had to work out by themselves. And while he didn't want to judge, he absolutely blamed Frank for the mess; he was always going too far. And Conor, well. In the immediate aftermath Shay had tried to intervene on Bea's behalf, but he wasn't let past the front door. Conor didn't want to talk, didn't want a pint, didn't want, or need, anything from him. Didn't want to know Shay's opinions about what he should do. Shay lost his temper, told him there's two in a marriage crisis, and at that time he was losing badly and taking Fiach down with him. And Bea, well, Shay wanted her to fight harder, get a solicitor on side, but she remained convinced patience was all she needed. Shay pitied her.

Lizzie caught him in the schoolyard while he was up a ladder, clearing out the gutters. They agreed that Conor and Bea's separation affected everyone; the circle was broken. And Fiach.

Poor Fiach. Shay's girls would report back – poor Fiach cried again in lunch. Poor Fiach wet his pants. Lizzie complained that Eva was holding out on her and kept pushing him for anything else she might have said. She needed to understand. Shay came to a shuddering stop; he had stumbled into dangerous territory, and he wasn't smart enough to sidestep any landmines. 'Sorry Lizzie, you'll have to move on. If health and safety catch me up a ladder having a chat I'm in serious trouble.'

It was a Friday night, the twins were asleep, and himself and Eva were on the sofa as usual, sitting close, drinking wine and watching *The Late Late Show*.

'Don't you feel responsible? I do,' said Shay.

'You? What did you do?'

'Frank's birthday, that's where it started, right? And you said after, we were stupid – no, reckless. You were so right. We took everything for granted.'

Eva didn't look like she remembered.

'Do *you* feel guilty?' asked Shay. 'About letting the cat out of the bag?'

She sat up again, took another swig of wine. 'I regret how I did it, but I might've done the same sober. But with kindness. Not in a text. What would you have done?'

Shay could tell Eva was feeling spiky. 'I don't know,' he said. 'Maybe nothing.'

'Even if it was your friend, your best friend, who was being betrayed?'

'But you didn't tell Lizzie?'

Eva frowned, as if she didn't know what Lizzie had to do with anything.

'Hang on. Are you saying Conor's your best friend?' Shay couldn't keep the surprise from his voice.

'You know what I mean.'

'I don't,' said Shay.

Eva pulled away from him and stood up.

'But why tell Conor and not Lizzie?'

'It's over isn't it? The affair stopped. Lizzie's better off not knowing.' She headed into the kitchen with her empty glass, talking over her shoulder. 'You're always so literal. I was speaking hypothetically.'

'I want everything to go back to how it was,' said Shay. He wished he hadn't said it out loud, he sounded like a small boy. He hoped she hadn't heard him. She reappeared in the doorway with a full glass of wine.

'How far back do you want to go?' said Eva.

'Well—'

'Jesus Christ, Shay, you can't go back. This is how it is now.' She sat back down in a rush, spilling wine onto the sofa. 'Shit. Shit. Fuck.' She ran into the kitchen.

'Get salt,' Shay shouted after her.

Eva returned with a damp cloth, scrubbed at the stain for a while, then took the cloth back into the kitchen. 'It's fine.'

The stain had grown. 'It's not,' said Shay.

'There are stains all over. It's like a world map. Who cares? There's only going to be more. Maybe we should pour wine over the whole thing, join up the stains.'

Shay fetched salt from the kitchen. He could feel her watching him.

'Go for it,' she said and left the room. He heard her in the hall, putting on her coat.

'Where are you going?'

She was going to the shops, for milk or bread or something, he couldn't catch what before the door closed behind her. This had happened a few times in the past weeks whether they needed milk or not, and often she came back empty-handed. Shay supposed she wanted the walk, but he couldn't figure out why she had to lie about it. All Eva would offer in explanation was that the shops were closed, or she had forgotten what she went out for. When he asked her how that was possible, she accused him of interrogating her. Which only started a fight.

Once, he'd picked up her phone, wanting to check texts and calls, but couldn't do it. He wished he could tether her with an invisible thread; to let her go as far as she needed without going so far she couldn't find her way back.

When he went in to Mrs Daly for his cup of tea and a sandwich, he told her about the girls and the words they were learning to read and the paintings they made and how hard Eva was working as vice-principal and how proud he was of her and how he hoped to paint the school's playground walls when he got a chance. He was thinking turquoise. Mrs Daly smiled and said goodness, yes. Wonderful. And then Shay packed up his tools, took his cash and went home.

40

Barcelona

Frank slept with his phone plugged in beside him. He claimed it was in case any middle-of-the-night ideas needed to be noted but in truth it was a welcome distraction when he couldn't sleep. At 5.13 a.m., he was so deeply asleep that he was at first grateful when Lizzie climbed over him to answer his phone. The possibility that it could be Beatrice calling in distress woke him fully. He slung Lizzie off and was out of bed and into the hall, phone in hand, before he dared say hello. It was an unknown number. 'Hello. Hello?'

The man was irate, talking in staccato bursts. Ron Doyle. From the school. Biology. The transition-year trip. Jack and Maya were being sent home. Broke curfew. Drinking. Before he could ask what went wrong, the teacher was relaying the flight details. Aer Lingus. Arriving Terminal 2, 12.55 p.m. today. They would be responsible for the cost of changing the flight. Frank was given no opportunity to respond as Ron Doyle announced it had been a very long night and he was going to bed.

Lizzie and Frank were wide awake now and awash with adrenaline. They channelled their discomfort into fury at the school for being so punitive towards Maya and Jack, for shaming their children, for costing them money, for the unnecessary and painful call to them in the middle of the night when clearly it was the school who had been careless. Teenagers were going to take whatever chances they could get. The problem wasn't their kids, but some teacher's lack of supervision.

'They're not getting another cent out of us,' announced Frank. He would lobby to get the entire trip refunded.

'They'll probably want to pretend it never happened. The kids anyway.'

'No way, they're going to be legends.'

'Frank, you're hopeless.'

When Jack and Maya emerged into the arrivals hall, they didn't look like legends. They were pale and frightened. Frank puffed up his chest, narrowed his eyes, as if preparing to blow them away with his fury. 'What do you think—'

Maya stopped breathing before she collapsed into tears. Lizzie grabbed her and started the shushing. 'Don't worry, he was only joking, it's okay, these things happen. Don't mind him.' But the tears kept falling, so many that Lizzie's shoulder became damp. Jack kept his distance, head down, holding his backpack to his chest as if it could protect him.

'Come on, let's go,' said Frank as he led the way to the car park. In the lift, no one would look at him. He wanted to tell them to stop being so dramatic. They'll have a proper story to tell in years to come, and God knows there's few enough people have stories you'd want to hear. But Lizzie had given him the look. Keep your mouth shut. Say nothing.

As soon as Frank had the front door opened, Jack charged past and up the stairs to his bedroom. Frank objected, they should talk about what happened, but was unable to muster up a full scold. He needed more information.

Maya didn't add much to what they already knew. After curfew, a group of them had escaped via the hostel's fire escape. They went to a few bars before they were refused service because they were too drunk. The Spanish measures were plentiful and cheap, and it didn't take long to get pissed. On the way back to the hostel, Jack and Maya got lost.

'These cops,' said Maya. 'They drove up, started talking to us in Spanish. We couldn't understand a thing, they couldn't understand us, so they took us back to the station. They had these rifles and these uniforms. Like Black Ops. Mr Doyle came and picked us up.'

'That's it?' said Lizzie.

'Doyle warned us before we left, any misdemeanour would result in being sent back home. I'm sorry,' said Maya, 'I'm really tired. Can I go to bed?'

'Go on, I'll bring you up some water and tuck you in.' Frank winked. Maya gave him a funny look before leaving them.

'D'you believe her?' asked Lizzie.

'Why would she lie, she's already been punished?'

'Why would they take them to the station? If they were only lost?' asked Lizzie.

'Ask her when it's you and her.'

'I will, yeah, and you ask Jack?'

Frank cringed. 'Not promising I'll get anything out of him.'

'Could you be any more useless, Durkan?'

'I can always try.'

Schools made Lizzie nervous. Nothing good happened in them. Her foot jigged against the linoleum floor, a linoleum so worn she would struggle to name the colour. Frank was forty minutes late. His phone was off, out of battery, she presumed. Typical. She didn't believe he'd forgotten. They'd prepared a speech on how damaging the school's unforgiving response was. How if they'd talked to the kids they'd discover that most of the group had broken curfew; it was Maya and Jack's bad luck to be separated from them. How the school needed to talk to the teenagers about how important it was to look out for each other and stay together. How the children were not adequately supervised. How united she and Frank were when it came to their stepchildren's wellbeing.

Fuck Frank.

When the school's principal, a perfectly nice, middle-aged woman named Siobhan, came to find Lizzie in the hall and said it was now or never and she would prefer it to be now, Lizzie followed her into the office all fired up with a righteous fury.

*

Frank was sitting in his yellow Nissan with Beatrice, parked on the verge near the Great South Wall. Beatrice had wanted to go for a walk, but the wind was vicious, with needle-pricks of rain. They sat in the car and watched a pantomime of plastic bags dancing on the little beach below. It was a sad beach, an accidental beach, too close to the city, the sewage works and a recycling plant. The car shuddered every now and then while Beatrice cried.

He had listened for over an hour to how he was the biggest mistake of her life, of how their tryst was both meaning-less and meaningful. A perverse experiment to test her mar-riage, to punish Conor for his equanimity. That Conor was a saint. That Fiach was ruined. Sometimes it felt like he'd spent more time in this car with her crying and him listen-ing than they ever spent having sex. In the early days of the aftermath, Frank had been on high alert with her, listening closely for any sign that she might decide to seek Lizzie's forgiveness, or that Conor would decide Lizzie deserved to know. He no longer feared a rage-fuelled attack from Conor. Knocking him off his bicycle was as far as it went and that was bad enough. His shoulder wasn't right for weeks. There were times he hoped Bea might turn to him for comfort and they could take up again. His life had gone to hell without her. For those few months he'd felt vital, and immortal; that electric buzz of youth, when the whole world is yours to play with. In quieter moments, he questioned if his bringing that unfettered vital self to work, that arrogance, was behind him messing up so royally on set. Frank was far too old to be for-given anything.

He continued to listen to Bea, if only to prevent her from walking into the sea. This Bea wasn't someone he had expected. He wouldn't have imagined she would attempt to rewrite everything as she was doing now. As time went on, his anger subsided under the scale of her distress. He recognised that she was able for the infidelity; it was the getting caught that had turned her inside out and made her ask, who was she? How could she hurt the people she loved? In the end, that was why he was still here; he wanted to know why too.

'Christ!' said Frank.

Beatrice was startled out of her monologue.

'I'm supposed to be somewhere else. I have to be somewhere else.'

Frank checked his watch again. He was more than late.

Frank opened the front door, threw his coat over the banister, stopped, and listened. The house was quiet. Shoes were scattered in the hall. The aroma of last night's curry remained in the air. Everything looked so benign.

'Hello?'

He heard a sound from the kitchen. Someone was home; the fact that they weren't answering worried him.

'Lizzie?'

He came to a halt at the kitchen doorway. The floor was littered with broken plates and mugs, pots and pans, last night's unwashed washing up. Lizzie was at the kitchen table. The table was clear, her hands placed neatly in front of her, but her face was uncannily like Bea's earlier, puffy, bloodshot eyes, snail tracks of tears through her make-up and a red nose.

'Lizbet, what's happened?'

'Where were you?'

'The car broke down—'

'You should've been with me!'

'The car—'

'Get a taxi!'

'I-I couldn't. There wasn't one.'

'Siobhan said she'd spoken to you on the phone before, wanted you to come in, there were concerns—'

'Siobhan who?'

'The principal of your kids' school? She called you five times. She showed me. They have to keep a record these days. They don't want to be sued. Because some people, other people,

231

these days are properly engaged with their kids. They care, you know? Some people want their kids to be happy and healthy and sane. Some people would go to the ends of the Earth for their kids.'

Lizzie was sitting very still but talking very fast; he had the sense he was hearing something that had been running through her head on a loop, with plenty of time to refine it. He was desperately trying to remember the principal's calls. There was one a couple of months ago, about Jack, questions about his behaviour in school. Problems settling in. Some high-jinks in PE with Maya. Frank could only remember that he didn't think anything much. Schools, by their nature, tended to overreact. He didn't remember returning the other calls. He had had a lot going on.

'We could've stopped it. The social worker's going to ask where we were,' said Lizzie.

'Social worker?' Frank's mind went completely blank. 'Please. Tell me what it is I'm supposed to have done or not done. Then tell me what I have to do.' He took her hands in his; he needed to bring her back to him. She swatted him away with such violence that he reared back, probably the same way she'd swept the plates off the table.

'They were having sex.'

Frank, for some reason, thought of Conor and Eva. Hallelujah, they were even. But Lizzie, sitting in the detritus of her kitchen, had to be talking about the kids.

'Which one?'

'Maya and Jack. Together.'

Frank sank into the chair opposite, his legs unable to hold him. 'Oh Jesus. Jesus.'

'It's been going on a few months. Barcelona was the first time they went, they had full—' Lizzie couldn't say the word. 'The lack of opportunity was the only thing that slowed them down.'

'Where are they?'

'Maya's upstairs. Jack went out.'

'Okay. Okay. It's complicated but at least it's not incest.'

Lizzie stared at him. 'You moron. It's worse. She says they're in love and it's none of our business what they do.'

'That's ridiculous,' said Frank. 'They're babies.'

'Where have you been?' shouted Lizzie. 'Where have you been?'

Lizzie crawled into her bed, overwhelmed. Downstairs, Frank was making a lot of noise; he was either cleaning up the delft or smashing whatever was left. Maya was crying in the next room. Lizzie pulled the pillow over her head. She'd allow herself ten minutes to calm down, then she'd do something. It was wrong, she knew it in her bones. Despite Maya's protestations, love was irrelevant.

'I thought you'd understand, you're always going on about love being all that matters,' cried Maya.

Lizzie didn't know where Maya and Jack's *love* fitted, but it was an ugly distortion in the circle of family she'd worked so hard to create. There were too many people involved. And then what, when they were done with each other and breaking each other's hearts or, God forbid, falling pregnant? Then what?

There'd never been enough space for Jack. She tried not to care that his mother was drinking herself to death in the only home he had left. She wanted him out and she needed to pull Maya back in.

Paula didn't seem to appreciate the seriousness of the situation. As far as Frank could tell, she was sober. Frank hoped Jack could move back in with Paula for the next few months, until the end of summer. Let things die down. But Jack had rejected the idea outright. He'd rather sleep on the streets, he said.

'I need you to persuade him,' said Frank.

Paula would welcome Jack home, but she wouldn't beg him. When Frank suggested Jack needed to be reassured, Paula admitted she was no angel, but neither was Jack. He'd been stealing from her when she was out. Her jewellery, cash. When Paula asked him to return the items and promised she would say no more, he ignored her. Didn't even bother denying it.

'He stole my mother's engagement ring. Pawned it some-where.'

Frank was struggling to think of a reply.

'He doesn't care for me, Frank. That's hard to be around.'

'I'll talk to him.'

'It won't do any good. He blames me for Tommy leaving. Says it was the drinking. He might be right. But I'm trying, Frank, I haven't had a drink in three weeks. Not a drop. And it's thanks to you. You've been so good to me.' Only now did Frank see that the living room, although battered and stained, was tidy. He muttered some words of encouragement.

'He's not good for my recovery. What is it they say these days? Put your own oxygen mask on first.'

Frank agreed. It took everything not to yell at her – we put our masks on first so we can save the children.

Jack stayed at a friend's house. Someone called Harry. Frank arranged to meet Jack in Marlay Park by the kiosk at eleven on an overcast morning. From a distance, Jack seemed much older, a young man with a shadow of a moustache. He could also see how uneasy Jack was; his shoulders were hunched up around his ears, and he seemed to have no idea what to do with his arms. He crossed them, he swung them, ran his fingers through greasy hair. Frank bought Jack a hot chocolate, and a coffee for himself. They tried to walk and talk but the rain came. They huddled together under a tree, fat plops of water landing around them. Jack rifled through the plastic bag of clothes that Frank had brought him. 'I don't see any socks.'

Frank made a show of looking through the bag but knew he hadn't put them in. 'I brought your charger.'

Jack sneered.

'Don't.'

Frank felt Jack flinch. He hadn't meant to be sharp, but he was feeling the pressure.

'Lizzie's upset. Maya's upset. We're *all* upset,' said Frank.

'Is Lizzie really mad?'

Frank considered lying but what was the point. 'Yes.'

'When can I come home?' Jack chewed his bottom lip.

Frank told him Paula was doing great, but she was pissed about him stealing from her. He would have to make it up to her before she'd have him back. What did he do with her things? Jack cried. He sold everything. And it wasn't all for him, he said, he shared the money around. There were a lot of boys he mentioned, outings and things, how he was trying to keep up. Lizzie was right, Jack had been trying to buy love. Frank put his arm around him. The boy was insubstantial, like a bird. He smelled of alcohol.

'Were you drinking?'

'Maybe. I want to come home,' said Jack.

'Do Harry's parents know you're drinking?'

'They don't care.' Frank thought they probably didn't. He seemed to be the only one who cared what happened to Jack.

'Tell Paula what you told me, I'm sure she'll forgive you.'

'I don't mean Mum's. Please?'

Frank stuttered as he tried to find an answer to this. 'Lizzie *will* calm down, and we can ask her again but only if you and Maya, if you promise to stop this' – Frank had no idea what to call what Maya and Jack were doing – 'this business. We can pretend it never happened.'

Jack pleaded. 'Why?'

Frank wanted to be sensitive, but he didn't understand how the kid couldn't see how impossible the situation was. 'There's no way Lizzie'll let you back if you don't promise.'

'But I can't do that. She's. When I'm with her. I. Everything's different. Everything's possible.' Jack searched for words to explain himself. Frank knew what he was going to say. He'd felt the same about Beatrice.

'I know it feels like there will never be anyone else, but you will fall in love again. There'll be someone else. This will pass.'

'I don't want it to. Why would I?'

Frank reached out to hug him, but he bolted across the park.

Frank appealed to Lizzie. Jack needed them. He made the mistake of telling Lizzie about Paula's jewellery. Lizzie, who had been wearing the gold bracelet every day since Christmas, took it off immediately. 'You don't think this was Paula's, do you?'

'I'll ask her. But it would be really stupid of him.'

'And that would surprise you?'

'Don't be a bitch,' said Frank. Lizzie didn't blink. She had turned and he was at a loss as to how to reel her back. 'He's just a boy. A troubled boy. I'm worried about him.' Frank hadn't been aware how worried he was until he said it out loud. He wasn't used to advocating for his son. That was going to change.

'I told you something was wrong. I told you to talk to him. If he can't go home to his mother the only option left is to get him back into boarding school. They'll take better care of him than you. Don't look at me like that. I'm not saying I don't care; I just don't want him anywhere near Maya. Troubled boys are dangerous.'

'How the fuck are we supposed to pay for that?' asked Frank. She knew they had no options, same as he did.

'Ask your dad. He won't say no if you tell him what's going on. He'll want it to stop as much as we do.'

'Are you mad? I'm not telling him.' Frank knew what his father would say. These things happen in other people's houses, people without the many privileges Frank had grown up with. To avoid adding to his father's disappointment, Frank had told many lies. He suspected Robert was only waiting for him to admit to being the failure he always thought he was, that his education was wasted, that he shouldn't have had more children than he could afford. And now he had to admit this failure to stop those children having sex with each other. Frank shrivelled inside.

Lizzie watched him carefully as she suggested the only other option was to ask Conor and Beatrice. As Maya's godfather, Conor would want to help, but she speculated that the timing wasn't good. They might find it a bit of an imposition at the moment. Frank's mind buzzed with white noise as he searched her expression for a clue. Imposition. Was she referring to the financial or the emotional imposition? Lizzie's face was neutral. He couldn't read her. She had the stage, her breath controlled, waiting for her cue.

'I'll ask Dad.'

'Now,' she told him. 'Go now. Or I'll go myself. And, while you're there, get some extra for your other children to live on.'

Frank's father was in the garden building raised flower beds for Rosemary so she wouldn't strain her back. Robert was an exacting man. Everything was measured, everything was square. Frank brought him out a cup of tea and a biscuit. Robert was red in the face from his exertions; sweat dripped down his temples. He was keen to finish the beds, he said, no time to sit down; he liked to pretend he was at Rosemary's beck and call. He drank his tea in two long hot gulps. Frank tried to do the same and burned his mouth.

'How are the children?' asked Robert as he screwed another plank in place.

'Good.'

'Work?'

'Writing at the moment.'

'Not directing?'

'Writing to direct. A feature.'

'A commission?' Robert turned away to find another screw.

'Garden's looking good,' said Frank. The lawn was pristine. Shrubs were flowering, the ground around them carefully weeded.

'A tidy garden signifies a person with too much time on their hands. I'm considering topiary. Rosemary would like an elephant hedge.'

Frank had seen photos on Facebook. 'Can you get a plan for that? Is it a cut-out? Or a mould. I've always wondered.'

Robert squinted at him. 'I wasn't serious.'

Frank could feel his irritation building. That wasn't a joke. It was a trap. 'I was thinking I'd like an elephant hedge.'

'If you have that kind of time on your hands. Go for it. Why wouldn't you?'

'I wasn't serious,' said Frank. He tried to laugh. And reminded his father he was writing, Monday to Friday, nine to five, and would seek funding when the script was ready and would, in effect, be paid retrospectively. 'So not a commission then?' asked Robert. 'No.' Frank needed to change tack. The defensive blather that he'd been spouting for years, about art, voice, truth, was doing him no favours. 'But yeah you're right, I don't have enough work. The series is trying out new directors this season. They're cheaper.' Frank chuckled, wanting to convey a benign worldliness he didn't feel. 'Truth is we're smashed, Dad. I've never asked before, but I need to borrow some money to get through this.' Frank held his breath.

'Sure, how much?'

'Forty thousand.'

Robert flinched.

'Jack needs to go back to Kilbradden. But to do that we have to pay the arrears and the year ahead.'

'Why on earth are you wanting to send him back there when you plainly can't afford it?'

'Our house is too small. There's tension. It's impossible,' said Frank. He could feel sweat running down the middle of his back. He tried not to fidget.

238

'I imagine it is. But the two older ones will be gone on to college or whatnot any day now.' Robert seemed worryingly uninterested.

'They're fifteen and the way things are, they're going to be living at home when they do go to college. If they do. They may never be able to afford to leave home.'

Robert considered this. 'I guess we were lucky rents were cheap when you finished school. We couldn't wait to get rid of you.' The teenager in Frank cringed. Robert laughed. 'I feel sorry for you.'

Frank believed him. 'I'm thinking of them. The kids, what's best for them—'

'I'm sure you are.'

'We lost a lot of money,' said Robert. 'Our stocks were obliterated. Like you, and everyone else, we have had to tighten our belts.'

'You still have your pension?' asked Frank.

'We live on that.'

Frank sighed. The pension was over eighty grand; his father was loaded. Robert walked away to prepare another plank for the bed. He measured and cut. His sawbench was shiny and new; his tools were top of the range, a rich man's toys. Frank waited for his father to say something, anything, make an offer but then Robert whistled a few bars of Gershwin's 'Summertime'. Frank knew it was for him; summertime and the living is easy. Robert wanted him to go away.

'Look, there's a problem with Maya and Jack. We have to separate them. Lizzie won't let Jack back in the house.'

Robert gave him his full attention. 'What kind of problem?'

'They're a bit too keen on each other. They think they're in love.'

Robert looked at him for far too long. Frank resisted jumping into a defence of himself or the kids. He would only lose.

'Why can't he go back to his mother's?' asked Robert.

'She's fragile. In recovery,' said Frank.

'She was never very stable, was she?' said Robert.

'If you're saying I should've known we'd end up here, don't.'

'I didn't say anything of the kind, Frank.'

'I've screwed up, I get it. Will you loan me the money or not?'

'Don't be so sensitive. I'm not judging you. I see unfortu-nates every day who think they have control over their lives.'

'Unfortunates?' Frank was trying not to take it personally.

'I wasn't necessarily describing you . . . Unless of course you think it fits?' Robert packed up his tools, each to their own compartment in his toolbox, and carried them into the garage. The raised beds were finished. Frank panicked; he hadn't con-sidered his father refusing. He found himself running down the path, only to meet his father coming back out of the garage.

'Dad, please?'

'I'll have to talk to the accountant. It's not easy to release that kind of cash.'

'Yep. How long might that—'

'Can't say.' Robert walked ahead of him back into the house. 'Are you staying for dinner? It would make your mother happy.'

'I have to, ah, let me call Lizzie first.'

'Don't stay to be polite. You don't owe us anything.'

'That would be one expensive dinner,' said Frank.

Robert didn't laugh. 'We'll need to draw up a repayment plan.'

Frank made accommodating noises but knew there was little to no chance of ever paying his father back. He would need Robert to die first and leave him his estate. He was sure his father knew this too. It astonished him once more that after forty-eight years his father could still find another opportunity for 'a life lesson'. Back in the cool of the hallway, Frank told his mother he had a screening to go to, kissed her goodbye and left.

Frank arrived home feeling like he'd shot a bear and skinned it and was now bringing home the hide. Jack would go back to school. Life would go back to normal.

He heard the shouting from the street. A neighbour stood in her front yard, listening, trowel in hand. Their front door was wide open. Max was only two steps into the hall. He was shouting and gesticulating, filling the space so completely that Lizzie had shrunk into a ball and was sitting at the bottom of the stairs, her head in her hands, helplessly muttering, 'I know. I know.'

Max had been away at a conference and had returned to the full horrifying details from the school. And not one word from Lizzie. She didn't think to call him? Maya, at the top of the stairs, was peeking around the corner, holding the two young ones back.

'Hello Max.' Frank lowered his voice, and spoke with a mix of authority and warmth, same as he would when tensions arose on set. Max turned to him and smiled. It wasn't a friendly smile but that of a fighter finally meeting a worthy opponent.

'Okay, Lizzie?' asked Frank. Lizzie lifted her head briefly. All the fight gone out of her. Frank tried to steer Max into the living room, desperate to move the conversation away from the children. 'Let's take a minute to calm down?' asked Frank. He held the living room door open, but Max didn't move.

'We had no idea what was going on, trust us, but I'm sure, as a family, we can find a way forward that everyone's happy with,' said Frank. 'Coffee?'

'No,' said Max.

'For a start, we're sending Jack back to boarding school,' announced Frank.

'Thank God,' said Lizzie.

'And then?' asked Max.

Frank wasn't sure what Max was getting at. 'We can go back to how things were before.'

'Like nothing happened?'

Frank floundered. 'Well, I guess, no, but—'

'It's not good enough,' said Max. He turned his back on Frank and shouted up the stairs. 'Maya, pack your bags, you're coming with me.'

Maya flatly refused to go anywhere. Lizzie hurtled up the stairs, put herself between Max and Maya. Frank tried again to steer everyone to the living room. Max reminded them that regardless of the family circumstances, cringeworthy enough, Maya was still only fifteen, this was statutory rape. It had gone way beyond a sit-down family discussion. Maya became hysterical. 'They can't charge him, can they?' Lizzie held Maya, trying to calm her down. Frank tried to call Max's bluff, no one was going to be pressing charges, but Max refused to say one way or the other. The only way Max could be sure Maya was safe was if she was with him.

Ten minutes was all it took for Maya to pack a suitcase.

Lizzie sobbed.

'You're a fucking arsehole,' Frank told Max.

It bounced off him.

Frank took Georgia and Jimmy over to a neighbour's to be minded until things calmed down. On the way back, he called Jack to say he could come home. An hour later, when Jack let himself in, Lizzie was still sitting on the stairs crying.

When she saw Jack, silhouetted in the open doorway, carrying a plastic bag of his clothes and things, she flew at him. 'What're you doing here? After what you've done?' He towered over her; even with the miserable slump in his shoulders, he was more than a foot and a half taller.

'Dad said—'

'Frank!' she yelled.

'I came to say I'm sorry,' said Jack.

'You're sorry? That's what you want to say? I gave you a bed. I fed you. I cared for you. And you sucked it up. And then you take my daughter? My daughter!'

'No – I. Maya and me . . .' Lizzie's fury confused Jack.

'What's next, what else do you want?'

'I didn't take anything from you.' Jack wrung his hands.

Frank came hurtling down the stairs and put himself between them. 'Stop it, Lizzie. She doesn't mean it, she's upset,' he told Jack.

'Upset? I'm ballistic,' said Lizzie. 'You can't stay here.' Jack backed away. He had left the door open behind him as if he knew he might need to escape.

'It just happened,' pleaded Jack. 'I'd never hurt Maya.'

'You already did,' said Lizzie.

'Lizzie, don't do this,' said Frank. 'We can work it out. It'll be okay.'

'How do you imagine that happening? I've lost my precious girl because of your son and now you expect me to mind him just the same. That we'll be *okay*. If I can't have my girl, I am not okay. And you don't get to keep your son!' She was roaring at Frank but all he could see was Jack on the threshold, crying.

'I'm sorry,' said Jack again and again. 'I'll go to my mum's. I'm really sorry.'

'You're not going anywhere.' Frank grabbed him by the arm and pulled him back inside.

'Don't you dare,' said Lizzie. She backed up and stood on the bottom step, gripped the banister with one hand, and, with the other braced against the wall, prepared to fight.

Frank held on to Jack. 'This is his home. He lives here.'

Lizzie saw that once again Frank was choosing someone else over her. All the compromises, all the sacrifices she'd made for him had no value. All the excuses, all the resentment she buried to keep them going, keep the family safe, were a total waste of time. She owed Frank nothing.

'You think he's looking out for you?' she said to Jack. 'He's only ever looked out for himself.' She turned back to Frank. 'Like father, like son, users and abusers. You can both go to hell.'

Jack let out a sob.

'You're so out of line.'

'Yeah? You think I'm out of line?' said Lizzie. 'You think I don't know what you are? What you've done? Where you've been?' She saw his hesitation.

'Oh Lizzie, what have I done this time?' he asked. He exhaled, as if exhausted by her. The bastard was bluffing.

'You can go too.'

'What?' Frank shuffled on the spot, looking around, like an old man who'd completely lost his bearings.

She grew taller as a cold resolve formed within. 'I mean it. I've had enough of you. Go.'

She walked up the stairs, and retreated to Maya's bunk, pulling the curtains around her.

Frank and Jack moved through the house, up and down the stairs, whispering as they gathered their things. She heard the front door close behind them. The quiet settled down around her like a fog. The only sound left was her heart; that it was still beating surprised her.

When Frank and Jack turned up on Paula's doorstep, she saw the bags, one each, and opened her door. Frank feared she would repeat her refusal in front of Jack but instead she pulled him into her arms. Frank watched him soften as he rounded down to take her hug. Over his shoulder, she looked at Frank and said, 'What's for you, won't go by you.'

The phrase came back to him, days later; he wasn't entirely sure what she meant by it, or who it was about, herself, him, or Jack? A mother's love. A son's return home or Frank's eviction from his home. Whatever way she meant it he was grateful to her for taking them in.

'You're family,' was all she said.

41

Beatrycze Kozlowski

On Monday, during her lunch break, Beatrice collected her first ever pair of prescription glasses. She strolled along Nassau Street, marvelling at how the world sparkled, discovering that colours contained many other colours within. She could see people's features, read their expressions, alert, or absent or annoyed at her meandering like a tourist. There was the odd smile directed at her, and she willingly returned it. She felt part of the world in a way that she hadn't when she couldn't see properly. The optician suspected she'd been short-sighted for a long time.

The man had been walking a little way in front of her. She hadn't been aware of him until he stepped off the kerb to cross the road and then looked right. Beatrice heard the bus, felt the whoosh of it passing. The driver had no time to apply brakes.

If she hadn't been wearing the glasses, the man's expression would've been a blur. She might've assumed there was surprise, or horror, a mouth wide open in a scream. But what she saw on his face, before the bus knocked him down, was a smile. A small, gentle smile, like oh there you are, as if he'd met someone he was expecting.

Days had passed and she couldn't get her head around the smile. What did it mean?

The man was fifty-seven, from Lucan and married to a woman called Amanda. They had three grown children: Louise, Emma, Adam. He was hit, struck, or killed by the bus depending on what newspaper you read. His suit was blue, his socks striped, his shoes black. He was carrying, until it flew up in the air and landed at her feet, a bacon and egg sandwich in a triangular box from M&S. Reduced.

*

Beatrice worked in Weir & Sons on Grafton Street as a sales assistant in China and Glass. Patricia, a small woman, always busy, had been there since she'd left school forty years ago. She'd taken it on herself to teach Beatrice everything she knew. Beatrice nodded politely but Patricia soon discovered that what Beatrice didn't know about stocktaking, she made up for in customer service; she knew what customers were looking for even if they hadn't realised it yet, and she had great taste. Patricia was curious about why someone of her background and apparent means needed to work in Weir's. But the questions were never direct. 'Your shoes are divine, where can I get a pair? Beatrice didn't wear her wedding ring at work, but after fifteen years it had left an indent around her finger. When Patricia asked anything related to weddings, husbands, children, Beatrice would excuse herself. Patricia assumed her husband was dead and patted her whenever anyone talked of weddings, a regular occurrence in China and Glass. Beatrice let the misunderstanding lie.

Weir & Sons was a temporary solution. Beatrice had fixed hours and didn't have to work on weekends when she had Fiach. She was still looking for work in hospitality but her refusal to do weekends brought the interviews to an abrupt halt. Down in the basement in China and Glass it was quiet; when there was a customer, she could take her time, keep it personal. Frank thought she was in the wrong job, too much time to think; she needed to be busier, or at least have more *fun*. But Weir's was all she was able for right now. She needed the routine. On the days without Fiach she endured a high-pitched ringing in her ears that cleared as soon as she was with him.

Frank had become her only friend; there was no one else she could talk to. It was a situation she didn't want to think about too much but which didn't bother him at all. 'Why wouldn't I talk to you if you needed to talk to me? Shit, *I* need to talk to *you*.' He was vague on the details, but some trouble between Jack and Lizzie meant they were staying at Paula's for a while. She wondered if she and Frank would've ever become friends, like this, necessary and meaningful, without the unfortunate affair in between.

'Nothing lasts,' Patricia would sigh as customers came in looking to replace broken plates in their wedding china. 'But nothing wrong with starting afresh,' she'd say and point them to the latest fashion in dinner sets, with bowls for pasta or *café au lait*; sets that reflect how we live now.

One Friday, Weir's were short two staff members; a nasty flu was going around. Patricia asked if Beatrice could stay on until seven.

She didn't want to say no. *Nos* made Patricia wince. 'I can't, not Fridays. I'm sorry.'

Patricia winced.

'If I don't pick up my son when I say, my husband will keep him for the weekend.'

'Your husband?'

Beatrice fought back tears. 'My husband and I, we're not living together.'

Patricia let out a low moan. 'Ah lovey, I'm so sorry.'

'I need this job.'

'God help you, love. We'll look after you. We're family here.' Patricia scurried off to find an alternative. Beatrice hoped she wouldn't tell everyone. She could bear being an object of curiosity, the foreign woman with the expensive clothing who didn't talk much, but she couldn't bear the pity.

Friday afternoons, if the weather was dry, she'd bring Fiach to Stephen's Green to say hello to the ducks. He'd named five of them after the Ninja Turtles; he'd call, and they'd come to him; whether they answered to his names or the bread in his hands he didn't seem to care. After the ducks they'd race around the fountains to the playground, where Fiach would run from one apparatus to another, bouncing like a puppy. On the swings he'd trill – *Highahighahighahigha* – and she'd do her very best.

In these first few hours of their reunion, Beatrice could feel herself expand, like stepping back into herself. Even her laughter came from deep within. The day ended with a Happy Meal in McDonald's for him and a black coffee for her. She abhorred McDonald's but she rarely said no to Fiach these days. He had a chorus of plastic cartoon characters lined up on the windowsill of his bedroom in the apartment. It was a tacky record of how many weeks she'd been living like this. They mocked her with their oversized grins.

She thought of the blue-suited man's enigmatic smile and how she might smile in the same way he did if someone said to her, this is it, you can relax now. It's over.

A motley queue had formed outside the school gates when Beatrice arrived for Fiach. She checked her watch; she was right on time. The school was running late. The last few days had been sweltering; people were wearing shorts and dresses, stripes of sunburn on their shoulders. Some hats. They looked like a queue for a Beach and BBQ cruise in Magaluf. The weather had made everyone giddy and talkative. Beatrice hung back.

A teacher came to the gates and fiddled with a key. After a few minutes he gave up and asked the parents to enter the school through the college next door. Beatrice walked fast through the college and soon outstripped the others. But then she heard footsteps running up behind her. It was Lizzie.

'Hi,' said Lizzie.

'Hi.'

'Don't usually see you—'

'Something's wrong with the gate.'

'You're looking well,' said Lizzie. 'Eva said you're working.'

Beatrice knew she didn't look well; her hair was unwashed, she was sweating through her blouse, and she had bags under her eyes. 'Yes. How are you?'

'Grea-t,' said Lizzie. She landed hard on the 't'. Her eyes were wide, as was her grin, but she didn't look *great* either.

She was wearing a faded shift, unironed, brown sandals, and her face was free of make-up.

'How are you?'

'Grea-t,' said Beatrice. Lizzie laughed. Beatrice felt herself smile. How she missed this easy understanding.

'It's been ages.'

Beatrice tried to be right on time for school pick-up, knowing Lizzie was often late. If she did see her, she'd hang back and wait until she was gone. It had worked until today.

'You should know Frank and I—' Lizzie stopped, holding tight to herself.

'Oh no,' said Beatrice. 'Has something happened?'

'Were you talking to him?'

'No. I don't know anything.'

Lizzie stared at her. 'Jesus, you're an awful liar. Just don't. Okay? I know you talk to him.'

Beatrice thought it was possible Frank had told Lizzie they talked, but more likely Lizzie was guessing. She fought the urge to run away but she also needed to know. 'Honestly, I don't know what's happened. Tell me?'

Lizzie pulled her out of the moving queue. They were in the shade, up against the college's cold, granite walls. She whispered, 'We're done, Frank and me. That's it.' Lizzie choked on her words. 'You probably saw it coming. I think everyone did.'

'Oh Lizzie. I'm sorry.' Beatrice was acutely conscious that once she would have embraced her, but today she couldn't move.

Lizzie held her head up high. 'I'm focused on the children now. We're forging ahead, one foot in front of the other. Sometimes life asks more of you than you ever imagined, and you have to embrace it.' Beatrice presumed this was a daily affirmation. She put her hand out to comfort her, but Lizzie recoiled.

'It wasn't about you if that's what you're thinking,' Lizzie whispered.

Frank had *another* woman. Beatrice despised him.

249

'Jack was out of control,' Lizzie cried. The words squeezed out of her. 'And now I've lost my girl. My gorgeous baby girl. Max thought she'd be better off with him than at home with us.'

Beatrice pulled Lizzie to her. Lizzie laid her head on her shoulder, shuddering as she sobbed. People glanced over, some curious, some wondering if they could help. Beatrice gave them tiny shakes of the head. 'I know what it's like to miss your baby,' said Beatrice.

'It was Frank's fault,' said Lizzie. 'He was distracted. And I think you know why.' Her voice, although muffled, had changed. Beatrice pulled away; she needed to see Lizzie's face. Lizzie's blue eyes fixed on Beatrice. Cold. 'You promised me.'

Beatrice stepped back, looked around her. The gate was open now and bar a couple of dawdling children and chatting parents they were alone.

Lizzie took in a sharp little breath and stared at her.

'I'm so sorry.'

'You're sorry? Seriously? Sorry for me or for yourself? It's so hard to know with you, you're all surface. All this—' Lizzie gestured at Beatrice's appearance and snorted. 'I see you. You're greedy and grabbing. And selfish. So selfish.'

Beatrice took a moment to let the sting of the words dissipate. 'If I could change anything, you must believe me, I would.'

Lizzie studied her. 'Would you? Of course it's never good to look back, is it?'

Beatrice felt something in her crack. Even though she had been drawn in by Frank, his drive, his desire, she'd never imagined she had any claim on him. Frank was too hungry. He was a seeker and would never settle for anyone or anything. 'Sometimes there's things to learn,' said Beatrice, 'so we don't make the same mistakes.'

'Ah-huh? Off you go. Knock yourself out.' Lizzie walked away, wiping her face on her sleeve as she went. Beatrice leaned back against the cold granite wall and waited for her heart to stop racing.

*

Fiach was the last child left at the classroom door. He flew over to Beatrice, bent in two by the weight of his extra weekend backpack. As she hugged him, she saw Lizzie over at Eva's classroom door. Eva nodded at Beatrice. Lizzie glanced back over her shoulder to see who Eva was looking at. For a moment, both Eva and Lizzie were looking at her. Out of habit, Beatrice raised her hand to wave. It floated uselessly in the air for a moment before she let it fall to her side. It was over and all she felt was relief.

Fiach tugged on her. 'Hurry up Mummy, the ducks are waiting for us.'

There were two girls in St Stephen's Green playground; they looked like sisters and were close to Fiach's age. They latched on to him, wanting Fiach to elevate their game of chasings. Beatrice sat on a bench and watched them run in circles. After a moment, she closed her eyes and tilted her face to bask in the burning heat of the afternoon sun. Sweat rolled down between her breasts. She felt ill. Lizzie. Lizzie. Lizzie. Lizzie's life was upended. And the children. The children. She had judged her, and all Lizzie had done was love Frank. Beatrice knew all too well the hard edges of their situations. The heartache often manifested in her body, a sparking nerve, a dagger in the temples. She couldn't live in this space for much longer. If Lizzie was right, and it was truly over with Frank, she was in a better place than Beatrice. She was free to start again.

A breeze blew her hair over her face. As she tucked the hair behind her ear she became aware of a man sitting beside her. He was leaning back against the upright, his long legs loose and wide. There was plenty of room between them; she didn't feel imposed on. He too had his face to the sun, his eyes closed. His beard was trimmed close to his jaw and what was left of his hair was cut very short. He spoke without turning his head.

'Beautiful day.'

'Yes.'

The children's squealing abruptly stopped. One of the girls had fallen and was splayed on the ground, the other two children crouched over her. But then the girl threw an arm out and tagged Fiach. He roared in protest, but the girls were already running away, giggling. Beatrice became conscious that the man beside her was sitting as upright as she was. He wasn't wearing a wedding ring.

'Are they your daughters?'

'Ah-huh.'

'Clever girls.'

His laugh was curt. 'It's exhausting. Their favourite game is good cop, bad cop.'

She laughed. 'You must be careful with children. They are ruthless, they can make you do almost anything.'

'True.' He grinned. 'Your accent, is that German?'

'Yes but I'm Irish now. You?'

He lifted his head in surprise. 'Portugal. A long time ago. Also, Irish.' He offered her his hand to shake. 'I'm Alex Santos. I've seen you here before.'

Beatrice watched Fiach as he dipped each of his nuggets and sucked the sauce off before eating them. 'Mummy!' Fiach pulled on her hand. 'I asked you a question.'

'And you want an answer?'

'Yes! Can Daddy come with us next time?'

'But he doesn't like McDonalds.' Beatrice knew there was more to Fiach's request than he was saying.

'Yes he does. He said.' Fiach nodded his little head up and down for emphasis.

'Did he ask you to ask me?'

Fiach tipped his head to one side to think about it. 'Maybeee.'

'Well sure,' said Beatrice. 'He's welcome to come anytime.' Fiach's yelp of happiness broke her heart. She had no expectations. She couldn't trust what Fiach passed on, what was written in Conor's texts, what was not written, what was said, what was forgotten or withheld. It was like learning a foreign language. A stranger in a strange land, again.

In the playground, when Alex had asked her name, she heard herself say –

'I'm Bea... Beatrycze Kozlowski.'

'Bee-a-trich Ko-slov-ski!' Alex relished each syllable as it rolled over on his tongue. Beatrice laughed.

'Can you say it again, please?' said Alex. 'Help me get it right.'

She repeated it several times, slowly and quickly, until he did.

It had been a very long time since she'd heard her birth name said out loud. On this summer's day, with the sun on her face, the children's bright chatter, the man beside her, she could feel the ground underneath her again.

I am Beatrycze Kozlowski.

42

Auction: House and Contents

Eva hit the road as soon as she'd offloaded the last of her class. It was autumn, the leaves were on the turn and a haze was settling on the fields. She turned on the radio. It was Lady Gaga. She sang along, dancing in her seat, weaving all over the road. A horn blasted. She raised both hands in the air, taunting the driver behind. He held his horn down, one long roar of dismay. Stuttering speedbumps on the left forced her to put her hands back on the wheel and straighten up. The driver overtook her at speed. She put her foot down. The car vibrated as she chewed up road and spat it out behind her.

The twins were at their after-school swimming lessons with Shay. Eva hadn't told him what she was doing; she wasn't sure what she was doing until she was doing it. Insomnia had been at her for weeks but last night she'd fallen asleep as soon as she closed her eyes. When she woke around 2 a.m. she felt completely refreshed. She went out to the kitchen and made herself a camomile tea. There was a basket of clean washing on the table waiting to be folded and sorted. Polka-dot leggings. Odd socks. Shay's work clothes, big and heavy, the fabric rough in her hands. Eva left his clothes to one side and made a neat pile of her own. In the shed she found her cabin bag; it was musty after the winter, but when her pile of folded clothes fitted in perfectly she understood it was meant to be. She zipped the case and put it back in the shed. The night was cold, the path wet as she tiptoed back inside. Was there a word for knowing people are in a house regardless of whether you can see or hear them? She could feel her children sleeping behind closed doors, feel the rumble of Shay's snoring. She slid under the covers as carefully as she could but still Shay turned towards her. He always turned to her. She prayed he wouldn't wake; what would she say to explain the chill in her, the wet feet.

Now the cabin bag was in the boot of the Fiat on the motorway heading towards Harwood House. It was almost a year to the day since Frank's birthday. Last week Eva had come across a full-page ad in the paper. Harwood House and contents were up for auction. She looked up the death notices, to find Davina Fitzsimons had died last Christmas and, despite her stories, there was no list of family and friends who loved her and would miss her. This morning, she booked a room in the village's only B & B. She planned to buy something in the auction to mark the beginning of the rest of her life.

She was leaving Shay.

Without knowing exactly when it started, she had let go of every little thing she once loved about her life, the routines, the family jokes, the fish and chips on Fridays, the aviary-like noise of them talking over each other at the table. Even their collective mess, she had once loved. She loved each of them, but she no longer loved the sum of them. The marriage. The family.

She was leaving Shay.

The thought caused her to hyperventilate. She was perched on an edge, giddily swinging between despair and exhilaration. They had their time and it was good and now they were done. She regretted nothing. If she hadn't been with Shay then she wouldn't have had the twins, wouldn't have met Lizzie and been introduced to Conor. She loved Frank and his party games. She loved Beatrice for her lust. She loved Lizzie for her courage, for showing her how the sad, strange aftermath of Frank's absence was easier to bear than living with the fear of his leaving her.

She loved Conor. And he was coming away with her.

This love felt divine. She didn't consider the word lightly. She was expanding all the time, filling with its warmth; gold sparked around her like sundogs. When she was with Conor, her body and mind merged. Her cynicism fell away. The past, the future, fell away. She was present. Shay deserved to find such a love for himself, better than the sour milk she offered him. And she wanted her girls to know what real love was, so that they would recognise it when it came their way and would know how to grab hold of it. Only then would they understand what she was about to do; and then they might forgive her.

There was thunder booming in the back of her head. A headache brewing. Sometimes it sounded like a tiny voice, a faraway voice yelling, but she couldn't make out the words. She turned up the radio.

Conor spent his days being accosted by random thoughts of Eva, anywhere, anytime; something she'd said or done, and the urge to see her would be immense. If she could get away, she'd join him for a late-night walk with Jaro. They would lose track of time and place as they walked and talked. When the weather was bad, they'd meet in the car park at the back of Tesco and make out in his car while listening to Lyric FM. He could contact her anytime, and she'd reply within seconds if she could. It was as if she was in the room with him, as if they'd never parted. When there was a long break between contact, during work or school, she had a way of restarting the chat by offering a factoid.

Did you know –

Dolphins sleep with one eye open.

Candyfloss was invented by a dentist.

If you could, it would only take one hour to drive to space.

She blew a little bubble of sweet air around them, a charmed place he could retreat to after fighting with Bea, or his dad, or wrestling with Fiach's unhappiness over the changes in his life. With Eva, he felt like he was enough, more than enough, exactly as he was.

Conor was looking forward to the weekend in a way he hadn't for some time; to walk down a street with her without fearing being seen, to have sex without fear of being heard, to avoid his father's disappointed gaze, to leave everything behind even for a day. He would be all hers, he told Eva when she called to invite him. He could hear the soft smack of her opening and closing her mouth and had learned that meant she was holding back.

'Just say it, Eva.'

She hung up.

He knew what she was thinking. A few weeks back, when they were out for a walk, Eva left him waiting outside while she went into a newsagents to buy a birthday card, the excuse she'd given for going out in the first place. Through the shop window, Conor saw Eva stop and chat with a woman who looked familiar. When the woman came out, he spun about and headed off as if he hadn't seen her. Around a corner he found a bookshop where he could hide in the aisles. It was ten minutes before Eva found him. He laughed at his own foolishness, made fun of his cowardice. But she wasn't amused. She rocked back and forth in the aisle, almost bouncing off the bookshelves.

'I hate this. I hate the lying. I can't look at Shay. I can't be in the same room as him. And it's not his fault. None of this is his fault.'

'You want to tell him?'

Her body twisted as if in pain. 'We could let whatever happens, happen?'

'What? Are you mad?'

'It's going to hurt whatever we do. We all end up in the same place?'

Conor didn't know what that place would look like, hadn't dared imagine it. He leaned in to kiss her, but couldn't help glancing left and right first. She groaned and ducked away. He watched her walk around the displays and out of sight.

'Eva!' he shouted. It was a pathetic gesture. She wasn't coming back. When he left the shop, rain was falling and there was no sign of her. He turned onto the main road and saw Eva's umbrella bobbing along some distance away. He sprinted, zigzagging around strangers to get to her, pulled her close and kissed her. Rain ran down their faces. When they parted to take a breath, they wiped the water from their eyes, and then, almost at the same time, peered over their shoulders to find out if they'd been seen. But there were few people out; those that were had their eyes down, collars up, trying to avoid the rain. Oblivious to them.

An hour before Conor planned to hit the road, Bea rang him at the clinic. His only thought was she'd found out, they'd been seen. As he held the phone in his hand, unanswered, he told himself, it's okay, it's for the best. She wasted no time in pleasantries. Fiach had a fever. He was fine, but she thought he'd want to know. Conor promised to drop in after the clinic. He wasn't worried about Fiach. He didn't need to 'drop in'. He was debating whether Bea *deserved* to be told about the weekend away with Eva or whether it was a childish impulse, a roundabout way to hurt her. He was trying not to think about Shay. It was like they were playing some strange kind of sexual relay. Would Shay be next, would he turn to Lizzie for comfort? She was sad and lonely without Frank. He couldn't imagine her saying no and he'd actively wish happiness on them. Would the six of them then, after a suitable period, move one on again, like a square dance – himself and Lizzie, Eva and Frank, Beatrice and Shay? That made Conor laugh. It wasn't a kind laugh, it was a dry, chugging laugh that had accompanied him for some months now. Almost everything merited it. They'd run out of coffee. Ha. Ha. Ha. Molly was having rages. Ha. Ha. Ha. The toilet is blocked. Ha. Ha. Ha. That lump may not have looked cancerous but the biopsy has proved it so. Ha. Ha. Ha. Sorry. Ha. Ha. Ha. Dermot urging him to give Beatrice another chance. Ha. Ha. Ha. He needed to do better.

From Beatrice's apartment, the view of St Patrick's Cathedral and the bright, green trees was refreshing but the apartment itself was so bland, Fiach's fevered pink cheeks appeared to be the only colour in the room. He was sitting in the middle of the greige sofa watching TV, unable to manage a smile. He claimed he wasn't going to vomit but felt spinny and warm.

Beatrice clattered about in the boxy kitchen and, after some time, brought out a bowl of her baba's chicken and pierogi soup for Fiach. She made it when anyone was feeling ill or exhausted and was convinced it had magical healing properties. Fiach took one look and shook his head. Conor breathed in a lungful of the sweet, salty broth, unaware he was doing it until Beatrice spoke. 'You want some?' she asked. Conor checked his watch. He was not yet late for Eva. 'If you have enough?' Beatrice watched as he finished Fiach's bowl, then handed him a second helping. Fiach curled up on the sofa, whimpering. 'My tummy hurts.' His temperature had tipped over thirty-eight degrees. They gave him another dose of Calpol. Conor decided to wait with him until the Calpol kicked in. Beatrice didn't seem to care what he did.

When Fiach's temperature didn't come down, they stripped him and put him in the bath. His bath toys floated sadly around him. Beatrice trickled lukewarm water over his back with a jug. Every now and then Fiach would moan. Conor gave him an extra half-dose of Calpol. Now he needed to stay to keep an eye on him. Beatrice dried Fiach, dressed him in his pyjamas and put him, limp as a newborn, into his bed. Conor recognised the duvet cover; it was the same as on Fiach's bed at home. Orange foxes on a blue background. He couldn't understand how Beatrice could have taken the cover with her.

'I bought it. I wanted him to feel like he was at home,' she said.

'Yes. Good idea,' said Conor. They were both standing over Fiach's bed watching him sleep. They looked up at each other and smiled, apparently having the same thought; to sit by Fiach while he slept would be unnecessarily melodramatic. Beatrice offered Conor a glass of wine but he refused because he was driving. He could leave the car here, she suggested, and walk home. Conor had a chance to tell her he should be on the road by now, on his way to meet Eva, but he didn't take it. He urged her to have a glass herself. From the fridge she brought out a stoppered bottle. One glass a night is what she allowed herself. But only one. Was she trying to confess to nascent alcoholism? He knew the feeling; sometimes he drank at night on his own and the only thing that stopped him was if he had work in the morning. And if he didn't, well. She asked how he was and he said grand. He asked how she was. She didn't answer and he had to press her for one.

'You know. You don't need me to say.' He saw how she too was greige. At this time of year, Beatrice would turn a rose gold from the sun; even her hair would brighten. She hadn't been able to keep up her daily run; her knee was bothering her. She had lost weight, probably muscle. If, as he told himself, he wasn't responsible, why did he always feel guilty around her? Conor checked the time. If he was going home, he would've gone by now. It was only a couple of minutes away if he was needed. He announced he would stay until Fiach's temperature came down, then he'd hit the road. Her lack of reaction disappointed him.

'How's work?' he asked.

'Fine.' She appeared to be weighing up whether she had the energy to risk conversation.

'I'm sorry, did you have other plans for tonight?' Conor asked. 'I could mind him if you were going out, or was someone coming over? I don't want to be in the way.'

Beatrice gave him a strange look. 'I already cancelled.'

'You were going out?' He wanted to ask with who but knew he wasn't allowed.

'Was it a date?'

Her back straightened as she shrugged. He thought she smiled.

Fiach cried out. Conor went to him, grateful for the distraction. Fiach's head hurt and he couldn't understand why Conor couldn't make it stop. His temperature hadn't come down at all. Beatrice held Fiach in her lap and rocked him. Conor lied that he might have an otoscope in the car to check his ears. He needed to call Eva to tell her he'd be late. He went down in the lift to the car park, aware that he was going through the motions for no good reason. Beatrice wouldn't know whether he was one floor down or on the street. It was cold in the car park. The strip lighting, shiny concrete floor, made him even more anxious.

When Conor rang, Eva expected him to say he was nearly there, but no, he hadn't left. He was sorry but Fiach was sick; he was going to be a couple of hours yet. He wouldn't make the restaurant but they could get something in the pub and then they'd have all day tomorrow, maybe stay another night. She muttered soothing words, hoped Fiach would quickly improve, and told him to drive safely.

On the outskirts of the village, she pulled into a service station. There were several texts from Margaret. The first asked where was she, the second how long would she be, the third, was she coming to the meeting at all? Eva searched but couldn't access any memory of a meeting. There was a voicemail too. Eva wasn't surprised by the message. Margaret had been holding back her frustrations and today she let it all out; Eva was careless, lacked foresight, hindsight, organisational skills, timekeeping skills. Margaret wouldn't be supporting her application for the permanent position. It was the worst appraisal Eva had ever received. She stood in the forecourt by the petrol pump and laughed. At first she couldn't have worked harder, dashing from one crisis to another. But since the start of the new school year, she'd stepped back and delivered the bare minimum. Nothing changed. The roof didn't cave in. And she still continued to be paid.

Eva bought two bottles of South African wine, red, with screwcaps, peanuts and a bar of dark chocolate. After the noise and movement of the motorway, after Margaret, the fluorescent lights of the garage shop and the muzak made her feel like she'd teleported into a parallel universe. She was clumsy, almost dropped the wine, and giggled in embarrassment. The cashier didn't take her eyes off her. Once outside, she rang Shay and told him her parents were finally addressing their power of attorney, she was going up to them for the night. Shay remarked on the suddenness of her departure. Eva lied that she'd been at her mother for some time on the necessity to plan for the future and now that Eunice was doing something she wanted to make absolutely sure they followed through. As she elaborated, she realised it was a flimsy, over-complicated lie, but it didn't matter; she didn't need it to last long. She told him to kiss the girls for her. He assured her they were happy as pigs in shite watching *Frozen* again and eating fish and chips. He started to say goodbye and then asked—

'Is everything okay?'

'Yeah, why?'

'Are we okay? Because it doesn't feel like we are.'

The sky was white, hanging low, the kind of evening where the dark comes suddenly.

'Eva?'

'We'll talk when I get back.' She hung up. He rang back immediately. She put her phone on silent.

In the B & B there were flowers on the bedspread, on the wallpaper, the curtains and the carpeted floor. Eva considered asking for a different room but having walked down a hall covered in flowered wallpaper she suspected the rest of the rooms would be the same. The one window looked out the back on to a concrete farmyard. Weeds snatched ground wherever they could. An ancient tractor, machinery and car parts were lying around as if abandoned in a hurry. She pulled the curtains and then, feeling claustrophobic, opened them again.

Her phone continued to light up with Shay's texts. He'd discovered she wasn't at her mother's and wasn't expected. She texted him – *I want more*. She thought of elaborating but there was nothing left to say. She added – *I'm sorry, I love you*. Then deleted all and slid the phone under a pillow.

Eva opened the wine, put some music on and danced. She was halfway through the bottle when the thought occurred to her. Was Fiach really sick? Did Beatrice know their plans? Was she trying to stop Conor from coming to her? Beatrice had proved herself selfish and destructive. She would do anything to prevent Conor moving on. She texted Conor. *Does B know about us?* It was only after she sent the text that she considered the possibility that Beatrice might see the text on Conor's home screen. Beatrice was still hopeful of a reconciliation, desperate and single-minded about it. In the schoolyard she walked bent over, like she was carrying a cross on her back, and spoke carefully, softly, as if sworn against mirth.

The chintzy wallpaper was sickening; the scarlet roses with lime green leaves, insipid wisteria racemes among wisps of something grassy, repeated themselves over and over in a pale yellow sea. She had assumed the bedspread and the curtains were identical but, when she looked closer, she saw that the scarlet flowers on the bedspread were dahlias and on the curtains they were clumps of tiny pink climbing roses. The room was like a flower shop; it wasn't only the walls, it was in the air. Eva opened the window. She studied the tractor in the yard, red, rusted and leaning; one tyre was completely melted. In the dark doorway of the barn was a man. His white hair glowed and his blue overalls reminded her of the statue of Mary in front of her convent school in Drumshanbo. This man stood in the middle of the barn's dark entrance and stared at her. His arms rose from his sides, his hands open to her, as if inviting her to come to him. She waved. He didn't respond.

Conor and Beatrice heard a strange cry from the bedroom. Fiach was sitting up on the edge of the bed, his eyes wide open. He opened his mouth and spewed out a torrent of watery vomit. It covered his chest, filled his lap, and pooled on the floor beneath him.

'Armes Schätzchen,' exclaimed Beatrice. She lifted Fiach, her hands under his arms, to carry him into the bathroom. The lift seemed to squeeze another torrent out of him, soaking Beatrice. She put him down and ran to the bathroom. Fiach stood in a puddle of vomit, tears on his cheeks, still heaving. Conor stepped behind him and carried him to the bathroom held in his outstretched arms. He stood Fiach in the empty bath, where he continued to emit ever tinier quantities of syrupy bile, tears and snot. Behind them, Beatrice crouched over the toilet, retching. Conor stripped Fiach down and washed him clean before wrapping him in a towel. Beatrice, on her haunches, leaned her head against the wall. She remained an uncompromising shade of green.

'Not you too?' asked Conor.

Her head dropped and she retched again.

'I'm going to put Fiach in your bed. Then I'll come back and clean up the bath, so you can wash. I'll clean Fiach's bed. And the hall.' He carried Fiach into Beatrice's room and slipped him under the covers. Unlike Fiach's room, which was unmistakeably his, filled with toys and covered in his drawings Blu Tacked on the walls, there was nothing remarkable in this room. The duvet and sheets were white, the bed neatly made. Clothes hung over a chair. Her make-up was in a toiletries bag on top of a chest of drawers. You wouldn't know that Beatrice lived here. She seemed to be simply passing through.

He opened the window in Fiach's room and stripped the bed, but had no idea where anything was to remake the bed or clean the carpet. He used the sheets to wipe up as much of the vomit as he could. Then he rolled them in the duvet cover and dumped them in the corner. He turned around to find Beatrice in a dressing gown with a bowl of soapy water and a cloth. She'd washed; her hair was still dripping. He saw her sway, and grabbed her and the bowl before they both fell down. She too was burning up with fever.

*

Eva walked and walked. The night was warm and bright. A full moon. No wind. She kept her phone in her hand wanting to be sure she had coverage in case Conor called again. She hadn't been certain of the way but, when she happened across the gates to Harwood House, she whooped. A sign advertised tomorrow's auction: House and Contents. Any land had been sold years before. Knee-high weeds split the long drive into two single paths. On one side she could see the uniform rooftops of an unfinished housing development butting up against the estate's tall stone wall. On the other was the wood, where you couldn't see anything beyond the first two rows of trees.

On the walk back from the pub last year with the others, there had also been a full moon. They'd cut through the woods, skittish and blind; yelping and stumbling in the rutted path, grabbing each other to avoid falling and then not letting go. Her silk dress had felt like water against her skin.

Harwood House was bright and clear against the night sky, the windows black and shuttered. The gravel underfoot crackled and crunched. Like having company. Around the back of the house was a clear scullery window, too small for anyone but a child to crawl through. Eva dragged a garden bench across and stood on it to peer inside with the torchlight on her phone. Empty shelves lined the walls. On a table in the middle of the room various items were stacked, with cardboard tags or stickers. Numbers. There were three irons, two heavy metal flat irons, numbered 127 and 128, and one pink and white Kenwood steam iron, the electric cord spiralling to the floor, number 126. There were jugs, ceramic and chipped enamel. A silver milk urn, number 115. A collection of wooden spoons, tied with a string, to be sold together.

She walked away from the house and took a photo, but coverage was down to one bar and it wouldn't send. – *Guess where I am?*

Her phone rang, startling her. Conor. His words dropped in and out. He kept saying sorry. Beatrice was too sick. What, she said. He had told her Fiach was sick. Was he lying to her? He wouldn't be coming tonight. She sat down on the bench and went over all that had been said. She texted him back. – *Come early tomorrow. The auction is at* 10. *It's not too late?*

At midnight, Conor checked on Fiach and Beatrice. They were both asleep in her bed, stretched to the edges, legs and arms outside the covers, fighting their fevers. He sat on the floor, his back against the bed. There were texts flying in from Eva. Silent flashes of light from the screen.

'Is it your dad?' Beatrice asked. She was on her side watching him, her face lit by the light of his phone.

'No.' He didn't believe she could see who was texting.

'Are you seeing someone?' she whispered. 'Only lovers call this late.'

He turned his phone off and let the dark settle around them. This was the line he needed to cross. The only way to avoid it was to lie. 'I was supposed to be with someone tonight.' He wasn't sure it was a decision he made but a surrender.

'Is it Eva?'

He let minutes pass while he considered how to answer. The bed shook. He thought she was crying but no, she was laughing. He was completely disoriented.

'Beatrice? What? What is it?'

'I hope you know what she wants because she doesn't.'

Conor slept fitfully on Beatrice's sofa until Fiach woke him shortly after 5 a.m., complaining he was thirsty. The fever was gone and he jumped around like his old self. They watched cartoons together; the boy's little body curled under his arm. He scanned Eva's messages. They'd become increasingly frantic through the night, angry and beseeching. What was going on? Why wasn't he talking to her? Was he ignoring her? The only thing he really knew about what Eva wanted was that she wanted to be with him.

266

Beatrice called out and he went in to her, Fiach stomping along behind him. She was sitting up in bed. A pink glow from the sunrise filled the room. Fiach dived into bed beside her.

'You're better?' she asked Fiach.

His head nodded up and down against her chest.

Beatrice told Conor he could go now. She too was feeling better. Choosing her words carefully, for Fiach's sake, she hoped it wasn't too late to join his *friend*, his weekend didn't have to be ruined. He leaned in, kissed Fiach, then kissed Beatrice before he remembered they didn't do that any more. She thanked him and hoped he would enjoy his weekend. He must've looked sceptical because she added, 'I am serious. I wish you to be happy.'

The apartment door swung slowly closed behind him. As he listened to the lift creaking its way up to him, all he wanted was to climb into bed with Beatrice and Fiach and sleep for a long, long time. But Eva was waiting for him and he longed for her too. With Eva he felt himself again, a little tender and new around the edges but more sure-footed. With Eva he wouldn't make the same mistakes. With Beatrice, well, he wasn't sure what was left to salvage. Whatever blame he could and would put on Beatrice, whatever fury he felt, the fact that he was standing in the hall of this apartment block, with its magnolia walls and blue carpet tiles, and his wife and son behind the closed door of number eight, meant that he had totally and utterly failed.

The lift came and went.

Harwood House contents auction started just after 10 a.m. Everyone sat on hard metal folding chairs in rows in the library. The sofas and armchairs, all with tags, had been moved to the side. Eva kept one empty seat beside her in case Conor turned up. The auctioneer was a rotund, black-suited man, both jaded and over-excitable. Lot number 46 was introduced as if it was a rare blue diamond, instead of a battered wooden inkwell stand.

267

The library's books, lot number 21, were being sold as one item. There was likely to be some treasure in there, some rare books, first editions. It was a family's collection, several generations' worth. She had seen Maria Edgeworth, Henry Ford's autobiography, and a first edition of *The Joy of Sex* on the shelves. When they moved on to the paintings, Eva learned that a number of the family portraits were painted by significant artists of their time, not that Eva recognised the names of any of them. One was of Davina Fitzsimons as a sixteen-year-old in 1952, lounging sideways on a green over-stuffed armchair, her long legs hanging over the arm, her limbs at angles to the straight lines of the bookshelves and the nine-paned window behind her. Her head was tilted to the light that was streaming in; she looked like she wanted to be elsewhere. The portraits of her male relatives, despite having many decades between them, were of a kind: a man centred among items representing his interests or achievements, books, cricket bat, a horse. The men looked directly at you, the expressions on their faces neutral as if to say this is who I am, this is my world, as if there was no artifice involved. Davina's portrait was the newest and the last. Everything finished with her. There seemed to be no one to remember her, no one to tend her grave. All the things she chose, used, loved, cursed, were being dispersed. And even they wouldn't last for ever.

Eva kept turning back to the door where latecomers stood, looking for Conor, aware of the empty chair beside her. Everyone seemed to be looking right through her.

Lot 205 was an Ayres rocking horse, with glass eyes and real horsehair. Eva saw her girls astride it, gleeful as they rocked. She threw her hand straight up in the air, but the bidding became impossible to follow and she was quickly left behind. A terrible grief tore through her, leaving her belly as hollow as the days after their birth; that same acute sense of having stepped from one world to another, the bridge in flames behind her. There was no earthly way of squaring her happiness with her girls' happiness. Her chest heaved but found no air in the room. The parquet floor under her feet buckled and rolled. Soon she was on the ground, pinned down with thin black metal chair legs. Someone pulled her up and onto her feet. She peeled off all the helping hands and ran.

Eva reversed into a parking spot outside Conor's house. She was going too fast, and drove her back wheel up onto the kerb, scraping the hubcap on the way down. His text had come an hour ago, as she was leaving County Laois.

 — *Won't be coming. Sorry. Up all night. Shattered. Talk when you get back.*

His car was on the street, neatly parked in front of hers. Was he asleep, awake? She texted. Waited. The house gave nothing away. She couldn't go home. As soon as Shay saw her, he would know she was leaving, had already left him. He would suffer. He would struggle to understand. She would struggle to explain. He would say what about the girls. The grief that overcame her in Harwood had taken up residence. There was no going back.

Conor's basement door opened and closed. She knew the sound. It took a shoulder to release it. Fiach's blond head bobbed up as he climbed the stairs to the street. At the gate, he jigged impatiently. Dermot climbed the stairs with Jaro on the lead behind him. He took Fiach's hand, and they walked down the street.

She couldn't see anything wrong with the child. Why would Conor lie?

A figure passed by the upstairs window.

She slammed the car door behind her and ran up the front steps. The door knocker, a brass lion, sounded a pleasing boom. She knocked twice more before she heard footsteps pattering down the stairs. There was a dog barking somewhere down the street. Someone shouted.

Conor threw the door open. He looked bewildered when he saw that it was her. She reached for him, and he hugged her, but he didn't invite her in. He was in jeans and barefoot.

'I'm sorry I couldn't make it,' he said. 'Did you go to the auction?'

She could not talk about Harwood.

'Buy anything?'

'I just saw Fiach leaving with Dermot?'

Conor offered his story of Fiach's fever and Beatrice's vomit, rocking on his toes, laughing to punctuate each gross detail. He spoke fast, she couldn't follow him. He shaded his eyes against the afternoon sun as he talked. His shirt was rumpled and untucked, like he'd been sleeping in it. There was a strip of bare skin peeking above his beltless jeans. Soft and rounded. She wanted to touch it.

'Eva?'

'Is this real?' she asked. She looked up at the sky; the sun was yellow, but there was no warmth from it. The trees had changed colour in the sun's wash; they glowed, otherworldly, as if stuck onto a two-dimensional world.

'What?'

He knew what she was asking. She could tell when he was obfuscating.

'Let me in?'

'I was sleeping.'

'I'm sorry. But you see, I can't go home, not without talking to you.'

Upstairs, a toilet flushed. Eva watched his face cloud. He fidgeted with the door handle, before dropping his hands to his sides and looking at her.

'That's Bea,' he said. She's still not well, I brought her home to mind her. And Fiach. It's much easier here. I'm sorry.'

There was no reason to apologise for a kindness. Eva heard footsteps traverse the landing above.

'I'm leaving Shay. I'm going to tell him today.' She heard herself laugh; the relief of saying it out loud to someone else.

'Oh, Eva,' Conor sighed. 'Are you sure? Is that what you really want?'

'I'm sure,' she said. She stepped inside the hall and stood close to him. He smelled stale, sweat, coffee, a whiff of vomit. Conor held her by the shoulders and sighed. He kissed her softly before straightening up, his hands remaining firm on her shoulders, maintaining the space between them. 'I can't talk to you right now,' he said. 'I promise I will make time tomorrow.' There was a slight pressure from his hands, she couldn't tell if it was intentional, easing her back outside. She heard footsteps above. They stopped. Someone was standing at the upstairs banister, bare toes peeking through the spindles. Beatrice.

'I love you.' Eva raised her voice. '*I love you. I love you.*' Beatrice pulled back out of sight.

He apologised again, told her that separation would be much harder than she could imagine. Told her to think again. Take her time. And the girls, think of them.

'How dare you,' said Eva.

The dog was frantic, barking at something, a cat, or a bird. Someone yelled, *Bailey! Shut the fuck up*. Bailey barked back.

Conor reached for her cheek, as if to cup it in his hand. 'Bea and I, we're talking again. We want to work this out. For Fiach's sake. Can you understand that?'

Eva recoiled. 'You're getting back together?'

'I . . . don't know. I hope so,' said Conor.

The dog yelped.

Eva cried out, 'No. No. No.'

Shay found Eva parked outside their house, crying; the front of her shirt was soaked like a teething toddler's. She couldn't, wouldn't speak to him. He brought her inside, laid her down on the bed and held on to her.

43

When the Wallpaper Becomes You

When it became clear that Eva wasn't going to pick herself up or pull herself together, Shay moved her into the girls' room, and moved the girls in with him. Their GP juggled doses of antidepressants and anti-anxiety medications. She was either awake all night or asleep all day. Sometimes Shay shouted at her to get up, eat, move. Most days she only showered when she was made to. Encouraging her to eat or drink was a major part of their day. He washed her hair. He meted out her pills and hid the rest, as their GP instructed.

Years ago, they'd watched a documentary about a surfer who was thrown off his board onto rocks and left in a vegetative state. His gorgeous, long-haired girlfriend remained dedicated to him. They'd argued. Eva thought the girl should leave. He thought she should stay, that she clearly still loved him. Eva agreed she loved him but argued that was why she should leave. She loved someone who could never return that love. It would destroy her. The surfer wasn't the tragedy; he was completely unaware of what he'd lost. But what if he woke up, Shay asked. And she wasn't there?

Conor, the good doctor, was nowhere to be seen.

Shay had asked him for help in the early days, but Conor was adamant that he wasn't the right person. Shay was so focused on Eva that he couldn't hear what Conor was trying to tell him. Lizzie did what she could, dropped in food, took the girls after school, and spent hours behind closed doors with Eva, but would never tell him what they talked about. She said it was up to Eva. Some nights she'd bring Jimmy and Georgia with her and they'd order pizza.

A package of wooden spoons wrapped in brown paper arrived from an auctioneer. The invoice named Harwood House. It was only then that Shay went back to Conor. Conor told him he and Eva had been in a relationship over the summer but now he was back with Beatrice. Perhaps that was what led to Eva coming undone.

'You think?' said Shay. He walked in circles around Conor's living room. 'You think?'

'I'm sorry,' said Conor. 'I know how you feel.'

'Yeah, I reckon you do. So, why would you do it to me? To my little girls?' Shay was crying. 'We were friends. I thought we were friends. And Eva . . . Eva. What did you do to Eva?'

Conor began to explain he was in a state himself, he didn't know what he was doing, when Shay's right fist collided with the left side of his jaw. Conor slid to the ground, stunned. He moved his jaw from side to side, checking if it was broken. Shay did the same, extending and retracting the fingers of his right hand.

'Are you all right?' asked Shay.

Conor pulled himself up onto the sofa. 'Yes. Are you?'

'No,' said Shay and let himself out.

After a couple of months, there were more good days than bad days. He'd hear laughter when the girls were in the room with Eva. Two-way conversations. A morning shower. A question for him. Did he want her to make him a sandwich? Eva emerged from her depression, shaking and timid like a wet-winged moth.

44

Maya's Getting Married

Twelve Years Later

Maya loved her tiny apartment in Friedrichshain-Kreuzberg. She loved the rough wooden boards under her bare feet. She loved the morning light that crept across the room and woke her up. She loved the linden tree in the courtyard where she would sit and smoke a cigarette after a night shift. She loved the ancient newspaper that lined the shelves in the cupboard where she kept her jumpers. She loved the sound of the children playing in the park two streets over. She loved the old lady who lived on the ground floor and greeted her every day with such unbridled enthusiasm that Maya couldn't keep up. It took six months of German lessons before Maya understood everything she said. She loved the squeak in her bed and how, when she made love to her girlfriend, it made them both laugh. When she found something she loved, she tried to hold on.

The apartment was put up for sale and they were threatened with eviction. Maya asked if Nina wanted to buy the place with her; Nina said yes because she loved her. Maya knew people could break up, no matter what tied them together. Marriage made it a little harder and, considering the financial as well as the emotional investment, it seemed sensible. So Maya asked Nina to marry her. Nina laughed. Maya was either very Irish Catholic or very bourgeois and at twenty-eight she was also very young. Maya asked if it mattered. Nina said no. Maya asked again, and this time Nina said *ja. Vielmals, ja.*

*

Maya's father offered to pay for the wedding, and she was happy to let him. All she wanted was to dance all night under fairy lights in a field. Max persuaded them to hold the party in the grounds of a country hotel so old people like him could have somewhere to sleep if they couldn't keep up. Lizzie wanted whatever Maya wanted. Maya also wanted Frank at the wedding. Lizzie said, of course.

Maya stepped carefully around her three parents. She'd lived with Frank far longer than she'd lived with Max. Frank was as comfortable as an old jumper; Max was her DNA. She'd followed Max into the baby business but had chosen midwifery over medicine; she didn't want her life to be all about work, she wanted children of her own, and wanted to be at a table with them eating dinner like they used to do in Oscar Square. Georgia became her proxy – four years into a medical degree, she regularly sought Max's advice and he was delighted to give it. When Maya saw them head-to-head over a text, they looked like father and daughter. It was only fair. Max owed Frank.

Georgia didn't have much time for Frank; she hadn't forgiven him for moving to Galway to work in Irish-language TV. He hadn't a choice, he told them, there was no work for him in Dublin. After a few glasses of wine, Lizzie told Maya that Frank was accused of sexual harassment and that's why he couldn't get work in Dublin. Maya had fended off enough middle-aged men to know that he wasn't unusual, just a fucking dinosaur, and she told him so. Georgia also blamed Frank for the wasteland of her love life, but Maya suspected Georgia's failure to launch had more to do with her singular focus on study. Jimmy was also still at home with Lizzie, playing bass in a band, recording music in his room, and constantly yelling at Lizzie and Georgia to be quiet.

Lizzie asked if Maya was going to invite Jack? Of course, said Maya, he's family. Jack lived between Lille, where Paula had settled with her new husband, and Galway with Frank.

He had the measure of Frank, gently taking the piss at regular intervals, in between laughing madly at their shared jokes. His charm was still carrying him through life. Maya was anxious that Jack hadn't yet found the thing he loved, neither a person nor an occupation.

Although more than twelve years had passed, Maya could still remember how intensely she loved Jack. How it seemed impossible that those feelings would ever change. She only told one girlfriend the truth of what happened in Barcelona. They'd been smoking and kissing at a seventeenth birthday party. The look on the girl's face. The twist of disgust. Your brother? Stepbrother, said Maya. Your father's son? My stepfather. But he lived in your house, and you had full sex with him? I loved him. We understood each other. Living with Max turned out to be exactly what Maya needed to forget the fallout and start again. She would've gone back to live with Lizzie after everything calmed down, but Lizzie and Frank were in an on-again-off-again relationship for a couple of years and she found it too confusing to be in the middle of it. Lizzie expected her to take sides. Tell me which side when, she'd say. Living in another country had its difficulties but there was less drama that way.

She also told Lizzie and Frank she was inviting her godfather, Conor Twomey, and his wife, and warned that if there were any scenes she and Nina wouldn't come back for Christmas. They laughed: one in Dublin, one in Galway. She told them she was serious.

45

Veer Right

The day was hot and clear, perfect for a September wedding. They had been travelling on the N72 for some time; a small road with pretensions. There was an eighty-kilometre speed limit and a line down the middle, but the national road looked more like a country lane, with brambles and cow parsley tumbling onto the shoulders. They were regularly honked, travelling too slow for the speeding locals, a situation Conor was grateful for when they turned a corner and found themselves nose to tail with a tractor inching forward, and no room to pass. They travelled for some distance this way before Conor became anxious they'd be late. There was no indication of a turn-off up ahead. Only field after field, stubbled and brown. Beatrice urged patience.

'Maybe we can go around. See if there's another way around,' instructed Conor.

Beatrice expanded the map, but the warren of roads off the highway was so random that she imagined the tractor would reach home before they'd deciphered a route. A boreen appeared on the left. Conor swung the car into it.

'We should stop and check if this is going to work,' said Beatrice, waiting for the GPS to catch up with the change in direction.

Conor didn't slow; in the car, he was still inclined to choose instinct over technology. The road deteriorated; more potholes than tarmacadam. She anticipated the pleasure of being proved right very soon. They'd been here before, not physically, but emotionally – this is the way, no this is the way. The end point came when someone was right, and someone was wrong.

The rule, unspoken, was that the naysayer should never be confronted with their failure, and they would simply move on as if they'd always agreed.

'It's an adventure,' he said.

When Conor had opened the invitation to Maya's wedding, Beatrice could see how touched he was that he'd been remembered. Any distance between Conor and his goddaughter was all her fault; prior to the affair he'd been an exemplary godfather. Conor went out and spent more than he should've on a coffee machine for a wedding present. The machine, he argued, needed to cover twelve years of missed birthdays and Christmases. They went back and forth on whether they'd attend but Max rang and begged them. He needed their presence to balance out the guest list, otherwise he'd be overwhelmed by Lizzie's theatrical people, and *you know what they're like*. Beatrice and Conor did. When one had no talent for performance, Lizzie and Frank's friends could make a person feel like a piece of furniture. She knew Conor was looking forward to seeing Maya and Lizzie. And they hadn't been out out for such a long time. Their lives had shrunk of necessity during the pandemic and there'd been a gentle culling of those they hadn't missed.

Conor swung into a gravel drive to check his phone. They were in a small hamlet near a T-intersection. The road signs were bent, swiped by a bus or a truck. Impossible to tell what was the way to Knocknageeha or Knockgarron. He selected a new route. Beatrice didn't care about being late. They weren't staying; not in the hotel nor the converted stables, and the local B & Bs had left her wanting. They agreed she would drive them home because Conor thought he might need a drink or two. He was tense, but upbeat, like someone nervous about giving a speech. She hoped he had nothing in mind for when they saw Frank again.

The wedding was being celebrated in a Georgian country house on the Blackwater River; the legalities were taken care of in a registry office in Dublin. A teenage boy in a too-small suit stood at the big stone gates and directed the non-hotel guests into a small car park, out of sight of the house.

Conor carried the present, wrapped in brown paper with a blue velvet ribbon, while Beatrice progressed gingerly in her heels along the tree-lined gravel drive before slipping her heels off and walking barefoot down the grass strip in the middle. The sound of a string quartet drifted down to them. Wedding guests spilled out from the house, down the granite steps, and over the forecourt. White lights above the front door spelled out *Maya & Nina*. Fuchsia and ivy wound around the granite pillars. Waiters in black floated among them, carrying silver trays of champagne and strawberries. It had been a long time since she had been to a wedding that felt so abundant. It wasn't only the flowers and the golden afternoon sun, it was the crowd and their effusive greetings, the hugs and the kisses; the obvious pleasure everyone took in being together again. Beatrice was filled with gratitude that they'd come. A waiter waved a tray of champagne in front of them. Conor knocked his back like water, fast enough to put it back on the waiter's tray and take a second. He snuck a sideways look at her and winked. She touched her glass off his.

At the top of the stairs stood Maya and Nina, backs to each other as they talked to other people; their hands reaching behind, fingers hooked on to the other. Maya wore a bias-cut ivory dress with a simple flower crown of dark-green leaves and white flowers. Her new wife was wearing peacock-blue suit trousers, an open-necked white shirt, and a matching flower crown. Conor handed their present to a passing waiter and asked him to leave it wherever the presents were stored. He slid his spare hand around Beatrice's waist and left it there.

Beatrice heard her before she saw her. A flurry of coral satin and curly, white-blonde hair cleaved Beatrice and Conor apart. Lizzie kissed and squeezed Conor, leaving a red lipstick smear across his cheek. Whether it was nerves or the drink, Lizzie was dialled up to eleven. Had they trouble finding the place? Where were they staying? Where's Fiach? Had they seen Shay? It was only when Conor told her she looked beautiful that she slowed down and smiled.

Lizzie looked Beatrice up and down, admiring her green linen shift. 'So plain. So . . .'

Beatrice waited.

'I like it,' Lizzie said and smiled. 'It's elegant. That's all I meant. You look the same. Exactly the same. How do you do it?'

Beatrice decided it was better not to attempt an answer. 'Thank you.'

She finally caught sight of Frank. He was leaning against a column, his feet crossed at the ankles, a champagne flute in his hand. His suit was dark blue, same as his pointy shoes. Had he lost weight or was it the cut of his suit? His hair was combed back, long on the neck, grey waves by his temples, set off with a silver beard. His father's death had made the *Irish Times;* she presumed he'd cashed in his inheritance. For the first time in years, she forgave herself for choosing him. Without meaning to, she found she was smiling at him. Taking her smile as an invitation, Frank descended the stairs in two leaps and came over. Conor planted his feet firmly on the ground but Frank came to a stop a safe distance away. Beatrice discovered she'd been holding her breath.

'It's good to see you both,' said Frank. He sounded sincere.

'Happy to be here,' said Conor. 'Maya looks beautiful.'

'She is.'

'Just like her mother,' said Lizzie.

Maya didn't look anything like Lizzie, regardless of beauty or anything else, and there was an awkward silence as everyone tried to work out what side of the joke to come down on.

'Jesus,' said Lizzie. 'You people.' She waved over a waiter with a tray. 'Drink!' she ordered.

'You've always been gorgeous, inside and out, Lizzie,' said Conor.

'And you've always known what to say,' said Lizzie.

Frank glanced at Beatrice, allowing a smile to flicker, before turning back to Conor. 'You're both looking well.'

'We are well,' said Conor. 'She has me cycling now.'

Frank stifled a laugh. 'In head-to-toe Lycra?'

Conor tensed. 'It prevents chafing.'

Frank laughed. 'Me too. Might as well make the most of Connemara.'

Beatrice breathed out, allowed herself to feel the effect of the champagne. 'We're happy,' she said. It was such a simple statement, delivered plainly, but it conveyed everything. Frank gave a little nod of acknowledgement.

'How's Fiach? College?' Lizzie asked Conor.

'He's great. He's studying maths, wants to be an actuary,' said Conor. It was the perfect choice for Fiach; he had remained, despite their best efforts, a cautious, careful person.

'Good for him,' said Lizzie. He doubted she knew what an actuary was.

'And Georgia and Jimmy?'

'Medicine and music.'

'You must be very proud.'

'Don't look at me,' said Frank. 'It's mostly Lizzie's doing.' Lizzie leaned against him, grateful. Beatrice couldn't tell if they were together again or not. Lizzie turned and searched the crowd. 'Shay's somewhere.'

Frank and Conor and Beatrice juggled conversational gambits, hoping for someone to pick up and run with it.

'It's a beautiful day for it.'

'Is the house Palladian or Georgian? Or is that the same thing?'

'Those trees. Magnificent.'

It was Conor who broke away first. Maya was moving through the crowd. He had a chance of catching her. 'Maya!' She turned at his voice and came straight over and hugged him. Over his shoulder, she eyed Frank and Beatrice and Lizzie. She whispered. 'Look at you all, friends again.'

Conor made a noise; he had no idea what Maya knew.

'I wasn't sure, you know, how it is with you complicated people.'

'We're complicated?'

She nodded very deliberately. 'Mum invited Shay Brennan as her plus one and then he turns up with Justine. Oh my God. It was so cringe. Best performance of her life.'

'Who's Justine?'

'The new girlfriend.'

Nina came up to Maya and melted in against her. With their long hair and flower crowns, they could've been a Botticelli painting.

'This is Nina, my *wife*. Conor, my godfather.'

'Congratulations, Nina. And you, Maya.'

Nina tipped her head in thanks. She was a lawyer, and smart and beautiful like Maya, but what there was between them, what drew them together was impossible to discern. It didn't matter what he thought, it never did; as Eva used to say, other people's marriages were a mystery, and better left that way.

'My wife grew up in Hamburg but she's Polish German,' said Conor, filling the silence. Nina couldn't have looked less interested. 'How did you two meet then?'

Nina lit up. 'We were on holiday in Madrid.'

'Not together,' said Maya. 'I was Interrailing. On my own.'

'She lost her phone, and I let her use mine to call it.'

'So, we found it, *and* I had her number.'

'She came to Berlin and looked me up,' said Nina.

'Just passing through,' said Maya.

'Sure,' said Nina. 'Then the pandemic came and she couldn't leave. She was my hostage.'

Maya giggled.

'Glad to hear some good came out of it,' said Conor. That earned him a half-smile from Nina.

'So, Conor,' said Maya. 'Tell us what it takes to have a long and happy marriage.'

Conor cringed. 'Oh Jesus, no. Don't ask me.'

'I'm serious,' said Maya. 'You and Beatrice are the only long-term married couple we know.' Maya had the same direct gaze she'd always had. He felt the weight of her question and wanted to offer something meaningful, but the longer he took to answer the more serious their faces became. He looked around for Beatrice. She was still talking to Lizzie and Frank.

'Don't leave,' said Conor.

The women startled.

He gave an apologetic laugh, as if he was joking, but he wasn't. 'Yep. That's it. That's all there is to it.' It was a truth his father had disguised as a joke when people asked how he and Molly had stayed married for so long, fifty-five years, one hundred and sixty-three days in total, before Molly died of pneumonia. Dermot followed soon after of a broken heart, takotsubo cardiomyopathy. Conor recalled a quote of Raymond Carver's; something about all he wanted from this life was to call himself beloved, to feel himself beloved. Conor had baulked at the one-sided, self-absorbed nature of the quote. He couldn't understand why Carver hadn't had anything to say about the pleasure and grounding weight of loving someone else. When Molly died, Dermot was left helplessly adrift. Conor had expected Dermot to be more prepared, given that Molly had been ailing for so long. And then, ironically, Conor was in no way prepared for Dermot to go so soon after. How did people manage to endure so much loss without someone who loved them by their side?

Nina was openly looking past him, ready to move on. He didn't blame her; he was an old man. Irrelevant now. Maya swivelled between the two of them, in a minor panic, as if she'd made promises he hadn't delivered on.

'The other way of looking at it,' said Conor, 'is you *choose* to stay, even when it's sometimes hard. Choose to love the person you're promised to.' He hoped he'd redeemed himself.

'That makes a lot of sense,' said Maya. She smiled and kissed him on the cheek. 'Thank you.'

Nina suddenly came to life. 'There's Jack!' Maya let herself be pulled away.

Jack lounged in the shade on a wrought-iron bench. He was in a green suit, open white shirt, a flower in his button-hole. The women sat down on either side of him and the three merged like triplets. Conor knew the story of Maya and Jack; Lizzie called on him the day after she kicked Frank out. They shared their broken hearts, while never mentioning the coincidence of their mutual marriage crises. Conor assumed she knew everything but wasn't prepared to test his assump-tion. In retrospect, he came to understand they never talked about the details because they were both still holding on to ideas of reconciliation. Once Jack and Maya's love story dis-integrated under pressure, Lizzie, on her own with Georgia and Jimmy, asked herself if she'd overreacted. Conor assured her there was still no real alternative; Max was never going to let Maya stay if Jack remained in the home, and Frank wasn't going to stay if Jack wasn't. Families these days were ever-increasing Venn diagrams of connections and overlaps, shrinking and expanding like an organic being. Jack, Maya and Nina appeared to be forming a new circle.

'It's the good doctor!' Shay came out of nowhere, his arms out wide to hug Conor, but then baulked at the last moment and settled for some vigorous claps on the back. Conor was grinning but inside he felt panic. They hadn't spoken since Shay punched him in the face. 'Don't look so worried. It's all good, man,' said Shay. 'Water under the bridge.' He urged a brunette waiting behind him to come forward. 'This is Justine.' She looked remarkably like Eva, with her long straight hair tucked behind her right ear. Conor called Beatrice over to say hello.

Shay was teaching in a horticultural college. Justine was a colleague. Conor nudged Beatrice. She knew what he wanted to know. 'How are the twins? And Eva?' she asked. Eva was grand, living in Leitrim, couldn't make it to the wedding because of work. Justine talked about the twins, referring to them as *their* girls, and how great they were. How well they all got on together. Shay seconded every statement Justine made. Eva was never mentioned again.

The wedding dinner was a vegan buffet that prompted Conor to reminisce fondly on the beef or salmon wedding. 'At least you knew what you were eating.' He sounded old, even to himself. When everyone moved outside for dancing under the stars, Conor and Beatrice slipped away.

The mild night had drawn a mist in from the coast. Lights in the trees along the drive floated like a string of tiny full moons. Somewhere in the field next door, a horse snorted and shuffled. Beatrice, carrying her heels once more, complained her feet were cold and wet from the dew. Conor hoisted her onto his back. She wasn't heavy, and he was fitter than he'd been for years, but he'd underestimated the effect of the drink he'd taken. He staggered and she laughed, telling him to put her down, he was going to fall over, swearing it wouldn't be her fault if he put his back out. When he reached the car and dropped her onto her feet, he was gasping for breath but stupidly proud of himself.

'You're an idiot,' she told him.

Once Conor was no longer needed to navigate their way back to the highway, he fell asleep, his head against the window, oncoming headlights washing over him, his right hand resting lightly on Beatrice's thigh. They were on a long, straight stretch of country highway, lined with cat's eyes, a stone wall on the left, forest on the right. Some pockets of mist lingered. Beatrice saw a truck approaching, fully lit, and veered ever so slightly left.

Then, like a mirage, the two headlights split into four as a car tried to overtake the truck. She lifted her foot off the accelerator, but it was too late. There was nothing she could do to change anything. There was no time for terror, there was no time left, only this moment, with Conor deeply asleep beside her and Fiach out somewhere with his college friends, this love in her. The world turned white, and there was no holding on.

In the weeks after, the only thing Conor could remember of the accident was the warmth of her thigh under his hand.

46

McDaid's Bar and Lounge

It was a couple of weeks before Christmas, the hour when the shops closed but before the night revellers arrived. Rain fell, leaving the paving shiny and slick. Lights from the shop windows criss-crossed Grafton Street like lasers. The winter had been so dark and wet, like one endless twilight, the noisy busyness of Christmas was a welcome distraction.

Eva was annoyed at herself for buying too much, more than she could comfortably carry. She was up from the country to see the girls. Ella was in her final year of economics at Trinity and Kate was in NCAD doing a masters in fashion design. In Leitrim, she worked part-time as a learning support teacher for three local primary schools. She had chickens, a dog, and an easel. She painted whatever she saw in front of her, the view from a window, reeds around Lough Allen, a wooden chair. She had no ambition, she didn't think of herself as an artist, she didn't care what happened to the work. The pleasure was in the doing; her only goal was to please herself.

In her cottage by the lake, Eva was happier than she'd ever been. In the last years of her marriage, her unhappiness had become so familiar that she couldn't recognise it for what it was. She'd called it exhaustion, boredom, anxiety, as if all she needed to be happy was a good night's sleep, a holiday, or less stress.

She was early enough to nab a corner table in McDaid's, using her shopping bags to mark out space. The barman came by and she asked for a hot whiskey. It was pleasantly quiet until a crowd of men, in suits the colours of a dirty storm, bowled in, all shouting at once, throwing heads back, baring teeth as they roared their orders at the barman. She had taken out her phone to text the girls, thinking they should meet elsewhere, when she recognised one of the men.

Conor.

His back was to her, his head tilted towards another man as he listened. His hair was grey but still thick. Otherwise, he rolled forward and back on his feet the same, nodded as he listened. She willed him to keep his back to her. There was no way out of the pub without needing him to step aside. Her whiskey appeared in front of her, and she took a hasty swallow. The burn sucked the air out of her, and she coughed uncontrollably. When she recovered, he was looking straight at her. One eyebrow raised; an *are you okay?* look. She rummaged in her bag and when she snuck a sideways glance, his back was to her again. He hadn't recognised her. She made a quick inventory as if to excuse him. Her hair had turned silver. She'd cut it short and she was wearing glasses. Her heart remained uneasy in her chest; her body was primed to run. But there was no need to run; she had become a stranger to him and that, she told herself, was how it should be.

Ella and Kate lingered in the doorway until they saw her; their bright, smiling faces brought the panic back. As unlikely as it was, she didn't want them to recognise Conor nor he them. They dived through the crowd of men, brushing past Conor, and burst out the other side, utterly focused on her. They were as quick and agile as Shay, with his long, strong limbs that seemed to stretch everywhere. They talked over each other, excited and giddy. Kate needed more money for materials. She had wheedled what she could out of Shay. Eva could only spare a fifty, but it was more than Kate had expected. Ella had been following the news and had ideas on everything from incels to saving polar bears.

Her girls were magnificent, and she told them this all the time. They were enough as they were. There was nothing they needed to climb, no ceilings to break, no firsts to make, no one they should marry, no house they needed to build, no child they must birth. She urged them to please themselves.

'Mum. Earth to Mum.'

'You're doing it again.'

They pulled her back to the stuffy air of the pub, the hubbub of drunken voices, the cracked vinyl seat beneath her.

'You're both so beautiful I can't think straight.'

The girls moaned.

'Tell us,' said Kate. 'Did you meet the gentleman again?'

An English businessman had bought a farm nearby for his retirement. Eva had met him a year ago, wearing a wax jacket and walking his Irish wolfhound. He'd gone completely native. Eva joked about him to the girls, but they latched on to the idea that a rich and handsome man was exactly what she needed. It had nothing to do with romance and everything to do with the girls wanting her minded and not wanting to do it themselves.

They held on to strange memories of her breakdown. They called them the sad Mammy days, remembered playing on the floor beside her bed while she slept, and she slept for months. Eva had few memories of that time bar the dread she felt when she woke up and saw the sun breaking through the curtains or heard the children squabbling. Shay asked her about Conor only once. They'd moved the girls back into their own room and it was their first night sleeping in the same bed. They had slow, tentative sex, like they were strangers to each other. After, Shay held her and cried.

She didn't see what good it would do telling Shay she meant to leave him. She was here now and all she felt towards him was tenderness. It was enough to start again. Conor was back with Beatrice and the whole episode felt like a bad dream. Soon life made demands that she couldn't avoid. Her father died; her mother needed her. She spent more and more time keeping her mother company in her grief, and then, when the girls were in secondary school, she would spend weekends in Leitrim for herself, walking. When the fields rolled ahead of her, and the clouds scuttered across the silvered lakes, she wanted nothing more.

It was Shay who let go of her. He would always love her, but he wanted more from a partner, and she couldn't argue with that. Along the way, without either being able to mark when, the marriage had evaporated. They had become friends who happened to be married. They fought over what was best for the girls. If she were to stay in Leitrim, and he in Dublin, they wouldn't be able to divide the week between them. There wasn't enough work for Shay in Leitrim, and he refused to be a weekend dad. In a fury, he once suggested they should split the twins up; which child did she want? Ella or Kate? It was the only way to be fair.

In the end they asked the twins what they wanted. They chose Dublin with Shay, their school and their friends, and spent weekends and school holidays with Eva. She spoke to the girls and Shay almost every night. They remained a family while living under separate roofs. Eva walked the fields until her grief became something she could bear.

No, Eva told her girls, she hadn't seen the gentleman again and, no, she wasn't going to make up some excuse to call in. She was alone but not lonely, they needed to respect that. They managed three rounds and four cheese toasties before Eva had to leave to catch the last bus. When she stood, she was grateful for the bags in each hand; they grounded her tipsy sway. They would see each other again at Christmas. The men had left, she didn't know when.

She strode down Grafton Street like a country woman. Upright and fast, welcoming the cold, sobering air. As she neared Trinity, she heard someone call her name. It was Conor. He ran towards her, breathless and grinning.

'I knew it. I went to get something to eat, with the lads, and I kept thinking was it you in McDaid's. I didn't see it was you at the time or I would've said hello. You've cut your hair.'

'I think you're mistaken. I don't know who you are.' Eva wasn't sure where that came from or why she said it, but she let it hang.

Conor's face contorted in many tiny expressions, confusion and dismay, embarrassment, and annoyance. She imagined she was watching the cogs turning and the switches flipping. He raised his eyebrows. She couldn't help but laugh. And then he was laughing.

'You had me there,' said Conor.

'How are you?'

'Great. Did you recognise me? In McDaid's?'

'I didn't see you.'

'Sure, yeah. It's been how long? Twelve years?' asked Conor.

'Fourteen.'

Why did they both feel the need to lie? Conor seemed to have the same thought. 'Christ. I'm an idiot. You didn't *want* to say hello, and that's fine, totally understandable and I've forced myself on you, I'm an eejit. Don't mind me. I'll leave you alone.' He turned away.

She grabbed his arm. 'No. Don't.'

He smiled and waited for her to speak.

'How are you? I'd like to know,' said Eva.

'That might take some time.'

'I heard about Bea. I'm so sorry.'

'Well. Yes.'

They stood in silence for a moment as Conor appeared to be working out what to say and trying not to cry. He made a sound like a laugh. 'Here we go again. I promise you, it's okay. I'm okay.' He found an old tissue in his pocket and wiped tears from his eyes.

'I wanted to contact you when I heard. So shocking. But I hesitated, thought it might be inappropriate, and then I discovered I didn't have your number anyways. I'd deleted it.'

Conor raised his eyebrows. 'Fair enough. D'you want to get a drink and tell me what you were going to say?'

'It was only that I missed her in my life,' said Eva. 'And that I loved her.'

'Same.' He smiled again.

She felt herself mirroring his expression, love, regret, pain. There was still time to get a taxi to the bus station and catch her bus to Cavan and get a taxi home. If she stayed out, she could ring the girls, sleep on the sofa, and get the bus in the morning and be back by lunchtime. She could ring the neighbour and ask her to feed the dog and the chickens. It wasn't impossible but felt like a lot of a work for a drink and an exchange of information she'd be happy enough to get second-hand. At the end of the night no doubt there'd be a friendly hug and a promise to text or email and each would wait for the other to make contact and when they didn't, they'd forget.

What she wanted was the answer to the question she'd asked herself while lying awake in the twins' bedroom day after day with the curtains pulled, breathing the same air over and over. Was it love? Was it a precious jewel of a thing that would have justified razing everything to the ground? Or was there never a choice because she had conjured it all? It was likely none of this would be discussed, and even more likely the question wouldn't be answered. Couldn't be answered. Maybe they'd talk and find they still liked talking and he'd raise his eyebrows and they'd both agree to meet up again to talk some more.

She was about to say no, she had to run to get a bus, when he took her elbow and she found herself falling into step beside him.

Acknowledgements

This book, my first, was written in short bursts over a period of years, like a car with engine trouble. Each time it needed a running push to start, the more help the better, shoulder to shoulder until the engine kicked in and I was up and running again.

To Declan Hughes, my MA supervisor at University College, Dublin, whose answer to my ongoing anxiety about where I was going wrong was always – *just write it*. Thank you. To my extraordinary friends, Dearbhla Regan and Neasa Hardiman who read the first messy 30k and threatened violence if I didn't keep going.

To Donal Ryan, my mentor at the University of Limerick Winter School in Doolin, who pushed me to the end of the first draft by telling me to write the last chapter, then fill in the gap. To Sarah Moore Fitzgerald who created the magic in Doolin that allowed this to happen.

To the Irish Writer's Centre Novel Fair and judge Rick O'Shea who selected my book and gave it wings.

To Gráinne Fox, my marvel of an agent at Fletcher & Co., who read the book time and time again to guide me through a last, incredibly smart edit. Who is always there. Dude. And to Kelly Karczewski for the extra smart notes and helpful emails. Thank you.

To Jocasta Hamilton, my astute, funny, and supportive editor, what a delight working with you. And to Katharine Morris and the team at John Murray Press, all of you, dream weavers.

To Rob Kraitt of Casarotto Ramsay, long-time ally and champion. Thank you.

To my writing pals who have been so wise, kind, funny and necessary to my survival – the first readers, the gin drinkers and the book recommenders – Olivia, Fíona, Anne, my Stinging Fly 2019 workshop group, the Dooligans, and Annie and Estelle. To my brave, early readers of the first draft and their crucial, insightful and uplifting notes – Cat Hogan and Vicky MacKenzie.

To my WGD girlfriends whose wisdom, stories and laughter have sustained me for over twenty years. Or was it the wine?

To the hardworking Irish Literary Journals, the encouragement and validation I felt from each piece published was a gift.

To English teachers all over, and to Virginia Ryan especially, thank you.

To Varuna, the National Writers' House in Australia, where several chapters were written over a month's residency, thank you.

And to the Tyrone Guthrie Centre at Annaghmakerrig, a place of beauty and retreat, where the work matters but never as much as one's well-being and that is thanks to the directors and the staff who have fed me, embraced me and made me laugh.

To the Arts Council of Ireland, immense gratitude; without the bursaries, I couldn't have afforded the time to write.

And to my mother, a voracious reader, book sharer and artist, who built the foundations. To my father, who demonstrated nothing was out of reach. To my three brothers, love you but everything's copy.

To my three men, Brendan, Alex and Sam, know that I couldn't have done it without you.

And lastly, this book is for all the women who were slow to start because they had so much else to do and no one to give the car a push.